THE LAST MILE

THE LAST MILE

KAT MARTIN

KENSINGTON
PUBLISHING CORP.

www.kensingtonbooks.com

KENSINGTON BOOKS are published by

Kensington Publishing Corp.
119 West 40th Street
New York, NY 10018

All Kensington titles, imprints, and distributed lines are available at special quantity discounts for bulk purchases for sales promotion, premiums, fund-raising, educational, or institutional use. Special book excerpts or customized printings can also be created to fit specific needs. For details, write or phone the office of the Kensington Special Sales Manager: Attn. Special Sales Department. Kensington Publishing Corp., 119 West 40th Street, New York, NY 10018. Phone: 1-800-221-2647.

Library of Congress Card Catalogue Number: 2021953418

The K with book logo Reg. US Pat & TM Off.

ISBN: 978-1-4967-3680-2

First Kensington Hardcover Edition: June 2022

ISBN: 978-1-4967-3865-3 (trade)

ISBN: 978-1-4967-3683-3 (ebook)

10 9 8 7 6 5 4 3 2 1

Printed in the United States of America

"There is something in a treasure that fastens upon a man's mind. He will pray and blaspheme and still persevere, and will curse the day he ever heard of it, and will let his last hour come upon him unawares, still believing that he missed it only by a foot. He will see it every time he closes his eyes. He will never forget it until he is dead . . . There is no way of getting away from a treasure . . . once it fastens itself upon your mind."

—Joseph Conrad, *Nostromo*

THE LAST MILE

CHAPTER ONE

AN ODD SOUND PENETRATED THE DARKNESS OF HER BEDROOM. Abby stirred awake and opened her eyes, her gaze landing on the neon-red numbers in the digital clock on the nightstand.

Three a.m. She muttered a curse. The old Victorian house she had recently inherited creaked and groaned as if it were alive. She'd get used to it, she told herself.

Rolling onto her side, she plumped her pillow, determined to go back to sleep, but the sounds returned, and this time there was no mistaking the quiet footfalls creeping along the downstairs hallway.

Abby's breathing quickened as she eased out of bed and slipped into her terry robe. Grabbing the heavy, long-handled flashlight she kept beside the bed—partly for self-defense—she moved quietly out the door, down the hall to the stairs.

The sounds grew more distinct. There was someone in her grandfather's study. She could hear them opening drawers and cabinets, clearly searching for something.

Her pulse accelerated as she realized what the intruder was trying to find, and her grip tightened on the handle of the heavy flashlight. No way was she letting the thief get away with it.

She needed to call the police, but her phone was upstairs, and by the time she got back up there, it might be too late.

The door stood slightly open, the soft yellow rays from the brass lamp on the desk providing enough light to see. Flattening herself against the wall, she peered into the study and spotted a figure dressed completely in black, searching the shelves in the armoire against the wall.

Her first thought was her cousin. Jude wanted the map, and he would be just stupid enough to sneak into her house to get it. But as she eased the door open wider, she realized the black-clad figure had a lean, sinewy build that was far too solid to be her pudgy gaming nerd cousin.

A trickle of fear slid through her. Abby steeled herself. Whoever it was, the thief wasn't leaving with the map.

Easing closer, she raised the flashlight, holding it like a bat, and swung a blow that slammed into the intruder's shoulder, knocking him sideways into the wall.

"Get out of here!" Legs splayed, she prepared to swing the flashlight again. "Get out before I call the police!"

He straightened. She could see the movement of his eyes inside the holes of his black ski mask, but instead of leaving, he charged.

Abby swung her makeshift bat again, but the man was fast, and he was strong, ripping the weapon from her hands and tossing it away, the flashlight landing with a loud clatter against the wall. She screamed as he spun her around and dragged her back against his chest. Wrapping his gloved hands around her neck, he squeezed, cutting off her air supply.

"Where is it? Tell me where it is!" He shook her hard enough to rattle her teeth, and her vision dimmed. Dragging in a breath, she clawed at the hands locked around her throat.

"Tell me!" His hold tightened, and terror struck. There was no mistaking the attacker's intent—he wanted the map badly enough to kill her.

"It's not . . . here." She fought to suck in air. "Safe . . . deposit box." It was a lie but a credible one. She had taken it from the box just that afternoon.

Her attacker swore foully but didn't release her.

"I don't believe you. I want that map!" He started dragging her toward the curtains, grabbed the sash to tie her up.

No way was she letting that happen! Forcing down her fear, Abby made two fists with her thumbs exposed, as she'd learned in her self-defense class, jerked up her arms, and jammed her thumbs into her attacker's eyes. One thumb hit its mark, gouging into his eye socket, and a scream ripped from his throat.

"You bitch!"

Kicking backward, Abby twisted and jerked free, her bare foot slamming into his kneecap. The guy stumbled as he hit the wall and swore another foul oath. Abby ran.

Out of the study, down the hall, through the entry, bursting out into the street. The grass felt wet and cold beneath her bare feet. She stepped on a stone, and pain shot up her leg, but she kept running.

The house was located on Vine Street in an old, historic section of Denver where she had already met a few of her neighbors. She raced to Mr. Godwin's house and started banging on the heavy wooden front door.

It took a while for the lock to turn and the door to swing open. Elderly Mr. Godwin appeared in his bathrobe, his gray hair sticking straight up, his eyes groggy with sleep.

Abby darted into the house. "Close the door! Hurry! And lock it!"

Mr. Godwin swiftly closed the door, his watery blue eyes wide. "Abigail, what's happened? Are you okay? What's going on?"

Abby's hand went to the bruises forming a chain around her throat. "A man broke . . . broke into the house. He tried . . . tried to kill me." She sucked in a deep breath of air. "I need to call the police."

CHAPTER TWO

Three weeks later

ABBY WALKED BENEATH THE DARK GREEN CANVAS AWNING THAT RAN the length of the two-story, redbrick building, stopping to peer through the plate-glass windows into the office. Treasure Hunters Anonymous was located in the LoDo neighborhood of Denver, an area of historic buildings turned into trendy shops and restaurants. She pushed open the door and walked inside.

"May I help you?" An attractive woman in her mid-forties with silver-touched dark hair rose from behind her computer, one among three sitting on desks along the wall. Several large wooden tables were stacked with papers and files; others were covered by topographic maps and navigation charts.

"My name is Abigail Holland," she said. "I've got an appointment with Mr. Logan."

The woman smiled. "I'm Gage's assistant, Maggie Powell. I'm afraid Gage is on the phone. He should be finished in a few minutes. Have a seat, and I'll let him know you're here."

Abby sat down in a burgundy-leather wingback chair next to the window. Aside from the chair and the small antique oak table beside it, an area that was visitor friendly, the office was clearly a work space.

Logan's assistant headed down the hall, disappeared behind

one of two closed doors, then returned a few minutes later. "Gage is finished with his phone call. You can go on in."

"Thank you."

Abby hoisted the strap of her leather purse onto her shoulder and smoothed back the copper hair she wore in a single long braid down her back. The door to Logan's office stood open. He rose and rounded a big carved antique oak desk to greet her.

"Sorry to keep you waiting. I'm Gage Logan."

"Abigail Holland." She extended her hand.

"Pleasure to meet you, Ms. Holland." Logan's big palm wrapped around her smaller one, and she felt a little kick she hadn't expected. He was six-two, she'd read when she'd researched him online, far taller than her own five-foot-four-inch frame. Dressed in khaki pants and a yellow button-down shirt, he had wide, muscular shoulders, and what appeared to be a deep, powerful chest.

"Thank you for seeing me," Abby said. He was thirty-five years old, she knew, born and raised on a big ranch west of Denver. At nineteen, he'd left home for college and never returned.

He was incredibly handsome, with dark brown hair long enough to brush his collar and a solid jaw roughened by the faint shadow of an afternoon beard. His eyes, an amazing shade of blue against his darkly suntanned skin, carried a fierce gleam of intelligence. Though she'd seen his photo on the internet and seen his face on the cover of *National Geographic*, she hadn't been prepared for the impact of meeting him in person.

"Why don't we sit down and you can tell me why you're here?" Logan led her over to a claw-foot round oak table in the corner surrounded by four oak chairs. Like the outer office, there were stacks of papers and maps around the room, on the floor and the tops of both oak file cabinets. Manila folders sat in a haphazard pile on the corner of his desk. There was a door off to one side that appeared to open to a private bathroom.

"Can I get you something?" Logan asked. "Coffee, or maybe a soda?"

"I'm fine, thank you."

He rested an elbow on the table, his shirtsleeves rolled up over muscular forearms. "I understand you have a proposition for me."

Her mind went straight to the bedroom. The man had sex appeal and plenty of it. Add to that, she had been following his exploits ever since her grandfather had mentioned him several years back and had begun to imagine him as having almost superhuman abilities. She had a fair complexion, and she hoped the color in her cheeks wouldn't betray her thoughts.

Abby smiled. "A proposition, yes. I want you to help me find a treasure. That's what you do, right? You find all sorts of missing things, historical artifacts, sunken ships, missing airplanes."

"My partner and I tend to specialize, but basically, yes, that's what we do."

"But it was you who found the lost rubies of Amanitore, right? Gems that belonged to the Queen of Nubia?"

He nodded. "The rubies actually belonged to a daughter of the queen. I've been back in the States for a while since then, but yes, I led the expedition that found them."

"I want you to help me find my grandfather's treasure."

Logan leaned back in his chair. "That was in the message you left on my phone. Interesting, but not very informative. What sort of treasure are you looking for?"

Abby's smile widened. "Gold, Mr. Logan, at least two hundred million dollars' worth."

Logan's expression didn't change, the gigantic sum clearly not impressing him. "I assume you have some reason to believe you know where to find it, or at least have some clue as to where it's supposed to be located."

"I have a map, Mr. Logan. It was willed to me when my grandfather died. In the past few months, I've been making preparations to find it, but I need your help."

"It's just Gage, and you realize most treasure maps are fake, even the old ones."

"Not this one. My grandfather was an explorer, much like you. His name was King Farrell. I believe you may have heard of him."

Logan's intense blue eyes sharpened. "King Farrell was your grandfather?"

"That's right, my mother's father. His travels kept him away a lot, but whenever he was home, we spent as much time together as possible. I loved hearing his stories, tales of his travels. When my mother fell ill, then passed away, we grew even closer." She felt a pang just saying the words out loud. She had nursed her mother during the terrible years of her cancer. She still missed her every day.

"I'm sorry for your loss. I heard your grandfather has also passed."

"That's right. King died three months ago." Abby blocked a fresh surge of emotion. "He left the map to me in his will, along with the house he owned here in Denver."

"Go on."

"Receiving his bequest gave me a choice. I could keep the house and forget the treasure. Or sell the house and use the money to finance an expedition. I sold the house."

One of his dark brown eyebrows inched up. "You're that sure the map he left you is real?"

"I know what people say about him. That all those years of searching for the Devil's Gold drove him over the edge. They said he never produced any real evidence the treasure existed. They called it King's Folly. They said he was a fool. But my grandfather was no fool."

Gage leaned back in his chair, steepling his fingers. "So you're completely certain the map is real."

"I was fairly sure when I found out he'd left it to me in his will. Now that someone's tried to kill me for it, I'm entirely certain."

Gage straightened, his posture no longer relaxed. "Tell me what happened."

Abby filled him in on the attack three weeks ago, including the description of the man in black who had broken into her house in search of the map. Over the next few days, she'd purchased a .38 revolver and had a security system installed, but she had been more than ready to move out.

"I listed the property for sale the next day. It's a lovely old Victorian, and the Denver market is strong. I had a full-price offer by the end of the week."

Those intense blue eyes ran over her, and she felt a little curl of heat in the pit of her stomach.

"Clearly you're serious about this," he said. "Unfortunately, I only met King Farrell a couple of times. I never knew him on a personal level. I'll need a lot more information before I make a decision."

"Assuming you agree, how does it work?"

"It's all fairly straightforward. Our lawyers draw up a contract. In layman's terms, you and I share equally in the cost of the expedition. You provide the information. I provide the expertise and the crew necessary to make it work. If we find something, the expenses are deducted, including any government fees and any unexpected monies that might be required, and the balance is split fifty-fifty."

She nodded, expecting similar terms. "That sounds fair enough."

"You referred to this as the Devil's Gold. From what I've read, King never gave any indication of where the gold was supposed to be. His travels took him everywhere—from Africa to the southern US border to the tip of Tierra del Fuego in Argentina. That's a lot of ground to cover."

"I can narrow it down for you. You have a reputation for honesty, Mr. Logan. If you're willing to sign a nondisclosure agreement, I'll give you all the information you need."

"It's Gage, and I'm happy to do that—if it gets that far. In the meantime, I'll have to do some digging. Give me a couple of days. Why don't we meet here again Wednesday morning, if that works for you."

"Ten o'clock?"

"That's fine."

"All right," she agreed. "Then I look forward to talking to you on Wednesday."

"If you're interested in the Amanitore rubies, I'm giving a guest lecture tomorrow night at the Museum of Nature and Science. Begins at seven p.m."

Mostly she was interested in seeing the way Logan handled himself. She would be trusting this man to help her find her grandfather's treasure. She wanted to know as much about him as she could.

"Perhaps I'll see you there." She rose from her chair, and Logan rose as well. As she walked out of the office, she could feel him watching her, and a thread of sexual awareness slipped through her.

Abby sighed. She didn't like the attraction she felt for Gage Logan. It was a complication she didn't need. If they partnered for the search, she would be spending days, possibly weeks with him. She didn't want to feel this pull that could very well be one-sided.

And if it were mutual?

Even worse. Finding the treasure meant everything to her. King Farrell had been a great man, a man she loved and respected. For years, she had begged him to take her on one of his expeditions. In the beginning, she'd been too young. By the time she was old enough, her parents were divorced, her mother had been diagnosed with fourth-stage, terminal breast cancer, and Abby was needed at home.

King had been riding high back then, traveling the world on one grand adventure after another—until he'd become obsessed with finding what he called the Devil's Gold. He had promised to take her with him on his next trip in search of what he believed would be the greatest find of his career.

But one failed effort after another had taken him on a downward spiral. He'd left the country for parts unknown, and for months there had been no word from him. Then his attorney had phoned with the news King was dead. He had made Abby the beneficiary of all his worldly possessions, including his house and the map that would lead her to the Devil's Gold.

Aside from making her rich beyond her wildest dreams, the discovery would prove King Farrell was the great explorer people had once believed.

The gold was there. King knew it. Abby intended to find it.

CHAPTER THREE

GAGE WATCHED ABIGAIL HOLLAND WALK OUT OF HIS OFFICE. SHE was an interesting mix of naïveté and determination. She was pretty, with a high forehead beneath a fringe of bangs, her fair skin touched by a smattering of freckles. Her full pink lips lifted easily into smiles, and the most glorious red-gold hair he had ever seen hung in a single loose braid down her back.

Add to that, in dark blue stretch jeans that showed off her curves and a soft yellow sweater that revealed a hint of cleavage, she was a very sexy lady. Late twenties, he would guess, and apparently single—no wedding ring and no mention of a husband or family.

He didn't like the idea that someone wanted the map she'd inherited badly enough to break into her home and attack her. She'd moved out, she had told him, and was taking precautions. Gage hoped they would be enough.

Seating himself behind the computer on his big oak desk, he googled the name King Farrell and watched a growing list of links pop up.

King's mysterious death three months ago sat at the top of the list, though there was no information as to where he had died, just the news that he was somewhere out of the country, possibly in South America, searching for lost treasure, as he had done since he'd been a young man in his twenties.

There was a lengthy obituary Gage figured Abigail had written relating King's greatest discoveries. Lost tombs in Egypt, diamonds in Africa, Viking gold in Greenland. Most of the artifacts had wound up in museums. Like Gage, King was more interested in the quest than in the money, though he'd always managed to end up with enough to live well and fund another expedition.

No matter the failure that marred King's final years, the man was nothing short of amazing. Abby's love and admiration for him appeared in every written line. Perhaps it was part of the reason she wanted to find the treasure. Salvaging King Farrell's tarnished reputation was likely as important to her as discovering the enormous cache of hidden gold King believed was there.

Gage rubbed a hand over his jaw. The hard truth was the treasure probably didn't exist.

On the other hand, aside from finding the treasure he had dubbed the Devil's Gold, King Farrell had never failed in any quest he'd undertaken. The man did his research and didn't waste time or money on a goal he couldn't achieve.

Would he have burdened his granddaughter with the task of finding the gold if he hadn't been sure it was actually there?

Then again, perhaps his competitors in the treasure-hunting community were right and King had finally gone over the edge.

Gage scrolled down the computer screen, opening link after link, reading everything he could find on King Farrell. Looking into everything he *couldn't* find on King's Folly—the Devil's Gold.

The next night, Abby purposely arrived late to the lecture hall in the Denver museum. She wanted to hear what Gage Logan had to say about his hunt for the rubies, but first she wanted a chance to observe the man undetected.

Moving quietly toward the back of the auditorium, she took a seat in the last row, grateful for the darkness that hid her arrival. The only light in the room was the spotlight shining down on the podium, where Logan's tall, imposing figure dominated the listeners, who filled most of the rows.

Tonight he wore a navy blue suit perfectly tailored to his broad-shouldered frame. A crisp white shirt set off his suntanned features, while gold cufflinks glinted at his thick wrists.

She knew he was single, which perhaps accounted for the over-whelming ratio of female to male attendees. She'd seen photos of him at various functions accompanied by attractive women, though rarely the same woman twice.

Watching him, she understood the attraction. Besides his blue-eyed good looks, he was intelligent, interesting, and dedicated to his work, qualities she admired—though she didn't have time for any sort of dalliance, especially with a man who drew women with the ease of a film star.

Abby had read dozens of articles about him—middle brother of three, both parents now deceased. Kade, the oldest sibling, had taken over the ranch when their father died, and Edge, the young-est, was in the military, or was at the time the article was written.

After two years at the university, Gage had gotten bored and set off with one of his professors, an anthropologist named Bryan Fagan, in search of a rumored fossil skeleton of *Australopithecus* located somewhere in South Africa.

From there, his adventures continued, morphing into his own expeditions. He'd had failures in his early years, including a jour-ney to South America that had resulted in the death of a woman named Cassandra Dutton, a female member of his crew.

But his skill and knowledge had improved, along with his suc-cesses, until eventually he partnered with wealthy international playboy Jack Foxx to open their own firm, Treasure Hunters Anonymous.

Though the partners usually worked independently, their searches included anything from objects of historical value, like the miss-ing camera from Mallory and Irving's failed attempt in 1924 to summit Mount Everest, to the priceless Amanitore rubies that Gage was discussing tonight.

Though she had only just met him, aside from her grandfather, Logan was among the men she most admired, which was the rea-son she wanted to hire him.

Her focus returned to the stage.

"The first contact between the Egyptians and Nubians dates back nearly seven thousand years," Gage was saying. "That's when ancient Egyptians launched their earliest expedition to the land of Punt, which meant gold."

One of the women stood to ask a question about the Egyptians' influence on Nubia and how it pertained to his search for the rubies.

"I believe studying the history of an area is extremely important. It provides crucial insight that helps us locate whatever we're searching for."

The woman, a beautiful brunette who was clearly enthralled, remained standing. "In this case, history that goes back thousands of years."

"That's correct. Ancient Egyptians called Nubia *Ta-neter*, land of the gods, and viewed it as a mysterious and unknown place of great fortune. Their trading excursions brought back gold, incense, ebony, ivory, exotic animals, and skins. One such traveler set out for home with gifts for the Pharaoh that included several gold and ruby necklaces of unimaginable value. Unfortunately, the rubies disappeared along the way."

Gage went on to explain how, two years ago, an artifact had been uncovered that set the wheels in motion.

"An Egyptian friend came to see me. He asked me to lead an expedition in search of the rubies. I agreed, and fortunately, we managed to find them."

Gage finished the rest of his lecture, and the lights came up as the question-and-answer period began—a good time to leave, Abby figured. Staying in the back, she made her way through the crowd to an exit door that led directly outside, pushed through, and stepped into the darkness.

The moment the door swung closed behind her, shutting out the light from inside, she realized the error she had made. She turned back and tried the door, wasn't surprised to find it locked. It wasn't that far to the car, she told herself. She just needed to reach the side of the building where it was brightly lit and cross to the parking lot.

Her brown leather ankle boots clicked on the asphalt as she made her way down the alley at the back of the building. She hadn't noticed anyone around when she'd stepped outside, but now she heard the sound of the door opening and closing, followed by footfalls echoing behind her.

A quick look over her shoulder and she spotted the shadowy figure of a man in an overcoat striding along in her wake. Abby quickened her pace. He was tall and spare, his overcoat flapping around his legs as his long strides carried him toward her.

A thought stirred that there was something familiar about him. Was it possible this was the same man who had broken into her house? She snatched another quick look. Same height, same lean, wide-shouldered build. Her pulse quickened along with her footsteps.

Surely there was no way he could know where she would be tonight. Not unless . . . Not unless he knew where she was staying and had followed her to the museum. Her heart rate accelerated even more.

Another quick glance confirmed her fear as she saw him closing the distance between them. Abby started running, her lungs pumping as she raced toward the light coming from around the side of the building and the museum parking lot. Behind her, pounding footsteps matched her own, the man drawing even closer.

Abby burst around the corner and kept running. People were beginning to stream out of the building through the entrance that led to the lecture hall. She quickly altered her course to catch up with them and blend into the exiting throng.

The lecture-goers spread out as they reached the parking lot, Abby among them. She spotted her red Fiat convertible and felt a rush of gratitude that the March weather was still too chilly to put the top down.

She glanced back in search of the man who was following her. If he was there, he was just another figure in the crowd. Abby didn't slow down.

She had almost reached her car when Gage Logan seemed to appear out of nowhere, his long strides quickly catching up with her shorter ones. Her heart was still thrumming, her face flushed, her breathing a little ragged. In the overhead light, she saw his dark brows pull together in a frown.

"Abigail. Are you all right?"

She swallowed, managed to nod. "I'm . . . I'm all right."

He studied her face. "Something happened. What was it?"

She glanced back toward the building, saw that most of the crowd had dispersed. "I just got a little spooked. I'm sure it was nothing."

"Tell me what happened."

She sighed, resigned to explaining. She hoped she didn't sound like an idiot. "When the lecture ended, I went out the back door. I didn't realize how dark it was until I got outside and the door locked behind me. Someone came out a few seconds later. There was something about him that looked familiar. I was afraid it was the man who broke into my house—same height and build—but . . ."

She took a calming breath, her adrenaline still pumping. "I'm sure I was wrong. There's no way he could have known I would be here tonight."

A muscle tightened in Logan's jaw. "Not unless he followed you."

Exactly what she had been thinking. "I'm staying at a friend's apartment while she's out of town, so there's no way he could know where I am."

"Are you sure?"

A shiver ran through her. It had taken her several days to move her stuff out of the old house. He could have been watching, could have followed her to the apartment.

She looked up at Logan. "No."

Gage took her arm and began to haul her off toward a vehicle parked under a nearby overhead light, a bronze Land Rover with black trim, fully tricked out with a rack on top and a heavy-duty front bumper. It fit Logan, the explorer, perfectly.

Gage popped the locks and opened the passenger door. "Get in. I'll take you home."

"I can't leave my car. I have things to do in the morning."

"I'll pick you up and bring you back." Ignoring her look of

protest, Gage herded her into the seat and firmly closed the door. As he rounded the vehicle to the driver's side, he unbuttoned his collar, loosened his tie, and dragged it off, exposing his muscular neck.

"I'll check out the house," he said, sliding in behind the wheel, tossing the tie carelessly into the back. "We'll make sure there's no unwelcome visitor there to surprise you." Cranking the engine, he put the Rover in gear and drove out of the parking lot.

Abby just sat there. Gage Logan was clearly a force to be reckoned with. She was almost sure she didn't like it. *Almost.* It had been years since there'd been anyone around to worry about her safety.

As Logan navigated the Rover in and out of the traffic on Colorado Boulevard, he relaxed back in his seat. "Where are we going?"

Abby gave him directions to her borrowed apartment on South Dexter Street. "It belongs to a friend. Tammy's staying with her boyfriend, trying to decide if she's going to make a permanent move."

"Probably a good idea to find out first."

"Jed's a white-hat kind of guy. I hope it works out for them."

The corner of his mouth edged up. "A white-hat guy. I like that."

Abby glanced at Logan. He was definitely a larger-than-life figure. Time would tell if the good things she had read about him were true.

Winding in and out of traffic, the Rover continued down the street. "I hope you enjoyed the lecture," Gage said mildly.

"I've read several articles you wrote about the rubies, so I knew most of what you were going to say."

He flicked her a sideways glance. "Then why did you go?"

"Reading about your adventures could only tell me so much. I wanted a look at Logan, the man. If we're going to work together, I need to trust you. To do that, I need to get a sense of who you are." One that was more objective than the image she had conjured in her head.

As they passed beneath an overhead light, his gaze strayed to hers. "So you think I'll agree to your proposal."

"You have to be intrigued. And from what I've read, you're very thorough. By now, you know everything there is to know about King's Folly. Or at least as much as anyone knows. You also know that, aside from his final quest, King never failed at anything he attempted. He believed the gold was there. You're just deciding if you want to risk your own reputation trying to find it."

Gage smiled, a flash of white in the darkness that relaxed his features and made him even more handsome. Her pulse kicked up for the second time that night. It was ridiculous. The last thing she needed was a distraction like Logan.

"We need to talk," he said. "If it's safe, your place will do."

She nodded, though his gaze was fixed on the road and not her. "All right."

"I hope you've got something alcoholic to drink. I'm always a little keyed up after one of these events. Being in the spotlight isn't one of my favorite activities."

She wouldn't have guessed that. King loved being in front of an adoring audience.

"King drank scotch, and he was very particular. I put most of his personal possessions in a storage locker until I figure out what I'm going to do. But I kept a bottle of Lagavulin. It's in the kitchen. If that'll do, you're welcome to it."

The corners of his mouth edged up. "That'll do very nicely. Thanks."

CHAPTER FOUR

GAGE PARKED THE ROVER IN FRONT OF A THREE-STORY, STUCCO-and-brick building only a few miles from the museum. Reaching across the console, he opened the glove compartment and took out the Smith and Wesson .45 he kept for self-defense. In his line of work, it could come in handy.

"You carry a gun?" Abby asked.

"My job takes me to interesting places. You never know when a weapon is going to be necessary." He got out of the vehicle, shoved the gun into his waistband at the back of his slacks, and let his suit coat fall in place to cover it. By the time he rounded the Rover to the passenger door, Abby was waiting for him on the curb. They took the elevator up to the third floor, and he stood by while she opened the door to apartment 318.

Gage eased her behind him, pulled the gun, and held it two-handed as he walked into the apartment. It was a simple one-bedroom, he saw as he moved from room to room, clearing the space, with hardwood floors, a beige sofa and love seat in the living area, and a modern stainless kitchen with white-and-beige granite countertops.

He shoved the gun behind him into the waistband of his slacks. "All clear."

Abby joined him in the living room. "If Tammy moves in with her boyfriend, I'll probably take over her lease."

"Probably? Sounds like you're keeping your options open."

"For now."

Speaking over her shoulder as she walked through the apartment, Abby headed for the kitchen.

Gage followed. "So tell me a little about yourself." Though he had done a brief search on social media, he hadn't found all that much. Twenty-eight years old, father out of the picture, mother died after a lengthy bout with cancer. Abby's Facebook profile said she liked to run, hike, and snow ski.

"I was born and raised in Denver. After high school, my grandfather put me through college—University of Colorado. I studied cultural anthropology. I wanted to see the world, and studying how people lived in other countries, different societies, was the best I could do back then."

"And after you got out?"

"I worked a while, just odd jobs to save enough money to travel. Then my mother got sick. I stayed with her until she died a few years ago." Abby took a shaky breath, and he could tell she still grieved her mother's death.

"For a while, I just did whatever came up: grocery checker, cocktail server, a desk clerk at the Marriott Hotel. For the past few years, I've been working for a photographer. Weddings, portraits, that kind of thing. Some of it was video work, so I have a background in that. On my own time, I do landscape pictures, portraits of people in their natural environment."

Gage watched as she crossed the kitchen, opened a cabinet door, and stretched up on her toes to reach one of the higher shelves, where he spotted a bottle of scotch.

Her short brown wool skirt rode up as she bent over the counter, emphasizing her curvy behind and exposing nicely shaped thighs. A shot of arousal slid through him and traveled straight to his groin.

"Let me get that down for you," he said a little gruffly. Enjoying the view, he almost hated to volunteer. He eased Abby out of the way and grabbed the scotch, poured two fingers into each of the two glasses she set on the counter, and handed one to her. He inhaled the aroma and took a sip, just as Abby did.

Apparently her grandfather had also taught her to appreciate some of the finer things in life.

Gage held up his glass. "To King Farrell, one hell of an explorer."

Abby held up her glass and clinked it against his. "To King— and finding the Devil's Gold."

They carried their glasses into the living room, and Abby sat down in an overstuffed chair, while Gage took the sofa.

"Getting back to our discussion," she said. "I assume you'll want the expedition documented. My photographic skills will solve that problem and give me a way to contribute to our mission."

Our mission. Gage's insides tightened. He was afraid this was the direction they were heading, that Abby planned to join him on the trip. "I'm sorry, but that poses a problem. I don't involve amateurs in any way. It's just too dangerous."

Abby leaned toward him. "I understand you suffered a casualty during one of your earlier expeditions. But the map is mine, and the risk is mine to take."

Gage just shook his head. "It's not a policy I'm willing to change. If we're going to do this, you'll have to trust me to handle it for you."

She looked at him with a trace of pity, as if she knew how much Cassie's death still bothered him, which of course she couldn't possibly know.

"Things happen, Gage. You work in a dangerous business. People were injured, some of them died during King's searches. You can't blame yourself."

He made no reply because he was exactly the one to blame. Cassandra wouldn't be dead if he hadn't been fool enough to believe he could protect her.

"If you don't head up the expedition," she pressed, "I'll find someone else who will. I have to do this, Gage. Knowing King is my grandfather, you must understand that."

She was going to go—with or without him. He already liked her. She was smart and determined. Add to that, he felt a strange obligation to a man he'd barely known but had admired and respected.

"You know my terms, Gage. Make your decision."

Gage shifted on the sofa. "I need to look at the map. I'll sign whatever document you need, but I'm not committing to anything until I see if your map has enough detail to be credible." And if finding the gold seemed plausible, he would at least be there to offer a degree of security for a determined young woman who had no idea what was in store for her.

He mentally revised that. As King's granddaughter, at least she knew some of the perils she would be facing. He almost hoped the map would prove to be a fake; then he wouldn't have to break his own rules.

Abby left the room, returning a few minutes later with a single-page document and a brass-hinged antique wooden box, beautifully dovetailed at the corners.

She set the box on the coffee table and handed him the document, which was nothing more than a nondisclosure agreement making him liable should he relay any information about the map or other knowledge he obtained through Abigail Holland or King Farrell about the Devil's Gold.

When he'd finished reading, she handed him a ballpoint pen.

Logan looked up at her. "You realize you should have me sign this in front of a notary."

"I know. We can make it official tomorrow. The truth is, I'm banking on your sterling reputation, Mr. Logan. If you decide to screw me over, I'm sure you can find a way."

His groin stirred at her choice of words, a mental image forming of the two of them in bed. Probably not smart to mention it.

Gage took the pen and signed the paper. Abby opened the box and took out the map. It was made of cowhide or deerskin, old and stained. She set it on the coffee table in front of him, and Gage bent forward to get a closer look.

Disappointment filtered through him, along with a sweep of relief. He had seen a map like hers before.

Gage sat back on the sofa. "I really thought you'd have something interesting to show me but this—"

"I know what you're going to say. There are a number of maps like this one."

"Yes. The treasure you're looking for is infamous. The Lost Dutchman Mine in the Superstition Mountains? Every amateur treasure hunter in the country has searched for it."

"You're right. Over the last hundred and seventy years, roughly two hundred and fifty people have died trying to find it. Some were killed by exposure to the harsh desert conditions; others suffered tragic accidents; some were murdered, including several who had their heads severed from their bodies."

Every serious treasure hunter had heard the stories, many of which were extremely gruesome.

"The Apaches believe the mountains are cursed," Gage said. "Who knows, maybe they are. The truth is there's no limit to what people are willing to do to find a fortune in gold—if it actually exists. I assumed the treasure King was hunting was something very different."

She leaned toward the map, and Gage caught the faint fragrance of jasmine. Another rush of blood headed south. He took a sip of scotch, hoping to relax his body's reaction to a woman he found extremely attractive.

Abby picked up the map. "You said you'd seen a map like this before."

"I know they sell copies of it in the Lost Dutchman Museum at the base of the mountains. I've even seen them online."

"Take another look." She pointed to a spot where the map had been altered. "At one point the trail has been redrawn, veering off from the east toward the south. That's my grandfather's handwriting. He was there." She pointed to an X drawn in black ink on the map. Next to it were the initials KF.

"Let me take a closer look," Gage said. "Do you mind?"

"Be my guest." She handed him the thin, stiff piece of rawhide, and he held it up to the light. The black marks had neatly been added. He wished he had one of the reproduction maps to compare it to.

"If King was there and that's where the gold is, why didn't he find it?"

"I don't know. If it was easy, he would have discovered it years ago. I think that's where he may have been when he died, but no one seems to know. His attorney received a phone call from King a month before he passed away. Apparently, King told him that unless he received another call, at the end of thirty days, he should assume King was dead and implement the will he'd made the last time he was in Denver."

"King must have known he only had a short time to live."

Abby glanced away, but Gage caught a glimpse of pain. "I think that's what happened."

"What else do you know?"

"Over the years, he told me dozens of stories. Sometimes we talked about clues he'd discovered during a trip he'd made in search of the gold."

Gage swallowed the last of his scotch, set the glass and the map down on the coffee table, and rose from the sofa. No treasure hunter worth his salt would mount an expedition with evidence like this. He didn't have to worry. Abby would be safe.

"I'm sorry, Abby, I truly am. But I'm going to have to pass on this one." He stuck out a hand Abby ignored.

"I was afraid you'd say that." Turning back to the antique box on the table, she lifted the lid, reached inside, and brought out a chunk of gold. It glittered in the lamplight, sending his pulse up a notch.

Gage sat back down. "Where did you get that?"

"It came with the map." She handed him what looked like a chunk broken off a solid gold ingot. Beveled sides, flat on the top and bottom, a little over an inch and three quarters long and an inch and a half wide, it appeared to have been part of a longer bar, with a rough edge where it had broken off. There was a stamp in the gold, the letter P, worn but legible.

Gage studied the gold, turning it over and over in his hand. "Have you had it assayed?"

Abby nodded. "Twenty-four karat. Ninety-nine percent pure gold."

He rubbed his thumb over the stamp mark. "I recognize this

style of writing. It's Spanish, very old. It's called Italica. I ran across documents written in this style when I was digging around in some archives in Seville."

"You're right. Italica was used by the Spanish from 1550 to 1800. In this case, the P stands for Peralta. That was in the letter my grandfather left with the map."

A letter he most surely wanted to read. "According to the legend," Gage said, "it was the Peralta family who found gold in the Superstitions and started the mine in the 1700s. They worked it for years, brought out gold worth millions today. As the story goes, they were using mules to transport a number of gold bars to Mexico in 1847 when the family was attacked by a group of hostile Apaches."

Abby nodded. "Legend says the family was completely wiped out. Along with any notion of where the mine was located, a secret they'd guarded for generations. That's the basic premise, or at least one of them. I figured you'd know something about it."

"I know a little about all the most valuable lost treasures in the world. Not much about that one."

"So what do you think? Are you interested now?"

He looked down at the map, thought of King Farrell and the man's absolute conviction the treasure existed. The X on the map wouldn't be easy to find, but it might be possible. And Abby was going—with or without him.

"I have his notes," she added, those amber eyes sparkling like the gold he held in his hand.

"I'll just bet you do," he said, fighting not to smile.

"There's an overlying map King drew that has longitude and latitude points along the route."

"That's a definite plus." He set the gold down next to the map on the table, rose, and once more extended his hand. "Looks like you've got a deal—partner."

Abby grinned and shook his hand.

CHAPTER FIVE

*E*XCITED, BUT NOT REALLY SURPRISED THAT GAGE HAD SWALLOWED the tempting lure she had cast, Abby returned the gold and the map to the box.

Gage frowned. "You haven't been keeping that here? That much gold is worth a lot of money. You've already had a break-in that could have gotten you killed."

"It was in a safe deposit box at the bank until I picked it up this afternoon. I wanted another look at my grandfather's notes, and I figured I'd be needing the gold for our meeting in the morning."

"Which leaves us with a problem tonight."

"You're worried about the guy at the museum."

He nodded. "There's no way to know if it was the same man who attacked you. If it was, he must have followed you. If he followed you, he knows where you live."

A shiver crawled down her spine. She remembered the attacker's fierce, lean strength. She might not be as lucky the next time.

"I have a pistol," she said. "A .38 revolver. If he breaks in, I'm not afraid to pull the trigger."

Gage shook his head. "I still don't like it. I've got a couple of spare bedrooms. My room is way down the hall." He smiled. "You can bring your pistol. If I misbehave, you can shoot me."

Abby laughed. The man could definitely be charming. His gaze ran over her, and there was something in his eyes that could only be described as heat. Renewed sexual awareness slipped through her, which wasn't good. Their association was strictly business. Abby wanted to keep it that way.

"I'll be all right," she said. "I've been living by myself for years. If the guy breaks in, he's going to be very sorry."

One of Logan's dark eyebrows went up. "What if this time he doesn't come alone?"

Unease trickled through her. Abby didn't reply.

"I'll tell you what. If you don't want to spend the night at my place, I'll stay here. I can sleep on the sofa. Believe me, it's a lot more comfortable than some of the places I've slept. If your visitor returns, there'll be two of us to deal with him."

Just the thought of Gage sleeping only partly dressed on her sofa sent a curl of heat into her stomach. "I don't know . . ."

"It's only one night, Abby. If you're going on this expedition, we'll be spending every night together until our goal is accomplished. One more shouldn't be a problem."

He was right. She wasn't about to start off their venture by making a big deal out of his staying in her apartment.

"All right, fine, if you really think it's necessary."

"Did the assayer tell you how much a chunk of gold that size is worth?"

"It weighs a little over eighteen ounces. At today's prices, that's over thirty thousand dollars."

Logan merely raised an eyebrow, giving her what she was beginning to think of as *the look*.

"All right, I get it. I'll bring you a sheet and blanket." Abby left to fetch the bedding and within minutes had a spot made up on the sofa. "There's a bathroom at the end of the hall. Unless there's something else you need, I'll see you in the morning."

"One last thing. If I make an exception and you join the expedition, I'm the one in charge. I make the rules and you follow them—no questions asked."

Wait a minute, what? She was funding half this venture. She intended to have her say in what went on. But that could wait until they were out there.

She pasted on a smile. Everyone knew rules were made to be broken. "All right, I agree."

Gage seemed satisfied, and Abby headed for her bedroom. She had almost reached the door when the rumble of a sexy male voice washed over her.

"Good night, Abigail."

Abby paused but didn't turn to face him. "Good night, Gage."

Once inside her bedroom, she leaned back against the door, her heart beating a little too fast. *Get over it*, she told herself. *He's just a man like any other*. But he wasn't. He was Gage Logan. It was like Superman was sleeping in her living room. At least to her.

Abby sighed. She'd get used to it, get used to him. They were going to be together for days, maybe even weeks. She thought of the glance he had given her, the heat in those amazing blue eyes, like the glow at the tip of a brilliant blue flame. She couldn't afford to let down her guard with Gage Logan.

Abby vowed not to let it happen.

Gage awoke with a kink in his neck. The sofa was a little too short, but as he'd said, he had slept in far worse places. It was quiet in the apartment, Abby still asleep. Faint gray light seeped through the living-room windows. Not quite dawn, but he was used to rising before the sun came up. In the bush, it was time to rouse the camp.

Wishing he had a pair of cargo pants, Gage dragged on his suit trousers, headed into the bathroom, then wandered back down the hall to the kitchen. Searching the cupboard, he found a bag of coffee above the drip coffee maker and brewed a pot.

He almost groaned at the rich dark flavor. The first sip was always the best, clearing his head and preparing him for the day ahead.

He started back into the living room as the bedroom door swung open and Abby walked out. She was wearing a knee-length fluffy yellow robe, her glorious hair unbound, more red than gold, though when she stepped into the light, he was reminded of the ingot in the antique wooden box.

At the sight of him, Abby froze, her pretty amber eyes running over his bare chest. He couldn't miss the interest there, and arousal slid through him, soon to become obvious. Turning, he rounded the sofa, grabbed his wrinkled white shirt off the love seat, shrugged into it, and rolled up the cuffs.

"Coffee's on," he said mildly, trying to bring himself under control, cursing King Farrell and the gold discovery that made it impossible to turn down Abby's proposal.

Or her demand to accompany him. Having a woman along, no matter how competent, had a way of making things tougher. If that woman happened to be beautiful and desirable, it could be a recipe for disaster.

Gage knew that firsthand.

He managed to blot out Cassandra's image before it surfaced, and focused on the woman in front of him. Abby lifted her copper hair over her shoulders, letting it ripple down her back, making him want to grab a fistful and drag her mouth up to his.

"You're up early," she said, continuing into the kitchen. "I hope you slept all right."

"No problem."

She glanced approvingly at the pot of freshly brewed coffee on the counter. "I just need a cup. Then I'll shower and get dressed, and you can take me to get my car."

He just nodded, trying not to imagine Abby naked beneath a spray of warm water. He had rarely felt such a strong attraction to a woman he barely knew, but aside from her intelligence and feminine appeal, her zest for life was contagious, stirring an excitement he hadn't felt in years.

Gage found himself looking forward to the journey they would be taking together, even if it would be impossible for him to act on his growing desire. He was a professional, first, last, and always. Nothing was going to change that.

"Unless you have an objection, I'll call my attorney," he

said. "Ask him to do the paperwork so we can get this project underway."

Abby smiled so brightly, he felt a contraction in his chest.

"That would be great," she said.

"I assume you have photos of the gold."

She nodded. "From every angle. I have everything photographically documented."

"Good, then we'll stop by the bank and you can put the gold back in your deposit box. Not the map or King's notes. I'd like a more thorough look at those before you put them away."

"All right." She took a sip of coffee. "I won't be long." Gage watched the sway of her hips as she walked down the hall, and his lower body tightened. Damn, this wasn't good.

He sighed as she disappeared into her bedroom. Whatever happened, it was going to be a painfully long journey.

On the other hand, if King Farrell was right, two hundred million in gold would more than make up for a few weeks of sexual frustration. Gage found himself smiling.

It was worse—make that better—than Abby could have imagined. Not only did the man have the face of a movie star, he had the body of an action hero to go with it.

Standing in the shower, every time she closed her eyes, she remembered the bands of muscle on Gage Logan's broad chest, his flat belly and six-pack abs, the pair of bulging biceps. The man was in amazing physical condition—that was for sure.

A requirement for the difficult ventures he undertook.

Reminding herself that finding the treasure was worth putting up with her inconvenient attraction, Abby finished her shower and braided her hair. Dressed in stretch jeans, ankle boots, and a white V-neck sweater, she returned to the living room. Both of them were ready to leave, and they were on their way in minutes.

Gage was hungry, so after they stopped at the bank and she returned the gold to her safe deposit box, he drove to a place he knew for breakfast, a café called the Waffle Iron in an abandoned firehouse. An alarm went off every once in a while, which entertained the kids, and there was even a pole in the middle of the room that firemen had once used to reach the first floor.

Gage was clearly a regular, as evidenced by the attractive blond server who seemed to know him far too well.

"Hey, Gage, how's it going?" The blonde turned over his coffee mug and filled it without being asked.

"So far so good. Mandy, meet Abigail. We're working on a project together."

Mandy filled Abby's cup. "A treasure hunt?"

"Maybe. Depends how things shake out."

The waitress eyed Abby with suspicion. "Gage doesn't take women on his expeditions. That's a rule he never breaks."

He flicked Abby a glance. "The waffles here are fantastic," he said, ignoring the comment.

Abby folded up her menu and handed it to Mandy. "Great, that's what I'll have. Oh, and a side of bacon."

Gage looked at her with approval and handed back his unopened menu. "Eggs over easy, sausage, and dry wheat toast. Thanks, Mandy."

The blonde said nothing, just flicked him a seductive glance and left to turn in their orders.

"One of your girlfriends?" Abby took a sip of coffee.

"I don't have any girlfriends."

She arched an eyebrow. "Not even a few friends with benefits?"

He shrugged his powerful shoulders, a faint smile on his lips. He was a man. He had needs. Looking at him, Abby was beginning to have a few needs of her own.

The meals arrived, as good as he had promised. From there, Gage drove to his attorney's office to pick up the contracts for her review; then they headed for the museum to retrieve her car.

"I assume you don't have a man in your life," Gage drawled as they crossed the lot to where she was parked. "No way could a regular-sized guy fit in a car that small."

Abby laughed. "It's a convertible, which makes it worth the sacrifice. Fits me just right, and I'm too busy to have a man in my life.

I want to travel, see the world. Most men just want to stay home and make babies—or practice, at any rate."

One of his dark eyebrows arched up. "So you don't like sex?"

Abby's face went warm. "With the right man, I like it fine. As I said, I'm just too busy to look for one."

Gage cast her a heavy-lidded glance, but made no comment.

CHAPTER SIX

*A*BBY FOLLOWED GAGE'S LAND ROVER BACK TO HIS OFFICE, PARK-ing the Fiat in one of the spaces reserved for Treasure Hunters Anonymous. Gage waited for her at the front door, and they went inside.

He handed her the legal papers he had picked up from his lawyer. "I figure you'll want your attorney to review these before you sign them. Be the smart thing to do."

She looked him dead in the eye. "If I can't trust you with a few pieces of paper, I'll be in big trouble when we're somewhere deep in the mountains looking for millions of dollars in gold."

His lips curved. "Good point."

"Don't worry. Before I sign, I plan to read every word." Taking a seat at one of the computer desks, she went over the documents page by page, line by line. Everything was laid out in easy-to-understand language, which surprised and pleased her. Once she was satisfied the contracts were in order, she and Gage walked to a small local bank a block away and had their signatures nota-rized.

Back in his private office, Gage retrieved his laptop, and they sat down at the round oak table in the corner.

"So where do we go from here?" Abby asked.

Gage opened his laptop and pulled up Google Maps. "Have you ever been to the Superstition Mountains?"

"No. I started studying the area after I inherited the map, so

I know they're in the middle of the Arizona desert east of Phoenix."

"Your grandfather never mentioned going there?"

"Unfortunately, no. He was always very secretive about his expeditions. He would tell me about his adventures when he got back, but he didn't talk about them beforehand. When he talked about the Devil's Gold, he never mentioned the Superstitions. From what I've learned, I know it's a designated wilderness area. That means no motorized vehicles, not even drones."

"Unfortunate but not unexpected." Using the keyboard, Gage brought up a string of photos of the mountains and the surrounding arid desert lands.

"If the terrain is as rough as it looks, we may have to go in on foot. We'll talk to people who live there, see what they suggest, but we'll definitely need to hire an outfitter to serve as a guide, someone familiar with the landscape. We might be able to go in on horseback, but more likely we'll have to walk in, use horses or mules to pack in our gear and supplies."

"We'll need permits to enter the wilderness," Abby said.

Gage nodded. "Can you take care of that?"

"Sure. If you can give me an estimate of how many we'll have in our party."

"This is only a preliminary trip. You haven't met Mateo. He's my right-hand man, someone I can always count on. He'll be meeting us there."

"You said 'preliminary.' You don't think we'll find the spot King marked on the map?"

"It's possible, but as you said, if finding the gold was easy, King would already have brought it out."

Disappointment trickled through her, which Gage must have noticed.

"We'll know a lot more once we're on the ground in Arizona."

Abby perked up at that. "That's true."

"This is a three-pronged effort, Abby. If we find anything promising on our first trip, we'll come back with more men, enough to dig, if that's what we need to do. If we find the gold or any solid evidence it's there, we'll have to deal with the authorities, figure out a way to get the gold out legally."

"Share some of the booty, you mean."

"That would be our best-case scenario. Worst case, the bureaucrats tell us to take a hike. In which case, we tell them to take a hike. If we get nothing, neither do they." Gage grinned, and Abby laughed.

"What's the closest town big enough to provide supplies?" Gage asked.

"Apache Junction."

He nodded. "We'll set up a base camp, somewhere that provides a place to sleep and access to meals. We'll probably be there at least a couple of days before we go in."

"I'll take a look around, see what I can find."

"In the meantime, I'll start working on the project from a historical perspective. I want to read everything written on the Lost Dutchman Mine."

Since she had already done tons of research on the legends surrounding the mine, she agreed. Gage was thorough. She had learned that from the lecture he had given at the museum.

"We've been at this a while," he said. "I could use another cup of coffee." He showed her the tiny kitchen in the main part of the office, where a pot had been freshly brewed. Abby took a bathroom break, poured herself a cup, then returned to Gage's office for a meeting with his assistant, Maggie Powell.

The attractive brunette turned out to be married, with two young children, and clearly was not one of Gage's conquests. She worked part-time, either at home or in the office. She was available whenever Gage needed her or when he was preparing for an expedition.

"Maggie, you've met Abigail Holland," he said. "Abby and I are going to be working on a project together."

Maggie smiled at Abby. "That's good news. I know Gage has been hoping something interesting would turn up."

Abby returned the smile, already liking the woman. "With any luck, it'll also be profitable."

"We'll be following the usual protocols," Gage said. "I'll give you an outline of our objectives, give you a starting point and a tentative schedule. As soon as you have the information you need, you can start working on a cost breakdown."

"Sounds good. Do you need me to make travel arrangements?"

"I will—as soon as Abby figures out where we'll be setting up our base of operations."

"Just let me know." Maggie went back to her desk, and Gage turned to Abby. "If you're ready to get started, there are a couple of computers in the other room. Use whichever one you want."

"I'm more efficient when I'm working on my own machine. My laptop's in my car, but I also need my cameras. I want to start documenting our progress. When we get back to Denver, we can make a video documentary of our search for the treasure." She grinned. "You'll be great. The ladies are going to love you."

He just smiled. "Let's take this one step at a time, shall we?"

Abby rose, and Gage followed her into the front office. "About your cameras . . . ," he said.

"Yes?"

The door opened before he could reply, and a tall man with slightly curly black hair walked into the office.

Gage smiled. "Jack. I figured you'd put in an appearance sooner or later. Jack, meet Abigail Holland. Abby, my partner, Jack Foxx."

"Nice to meet you, Jack," she said.

Sexy blue eyes a shade less intense than Gage's roamed over her. "The pleasure is mine, Abby." At the way he said *pleasure*, Gage's mouth tightened.

"About your camera," Gage said to her. "It's not safe for you to go back to your place alone. We can pick it up at the end of the day."

"I'll be fine by myself. It's not that far away."

"I can take her," Jack volunteered.

Gage's blue gaze cooled as it traveled to Jack, then back to her. "If you're that determined, I'll take you myself."

Jack grinned as if he had just discovered a secret, and Gage flashed him a look of warning.

Twenty minutes later, after weaving their way through traffic, they pulled up in front of Abby's borrowed apartment.

"I won't be long," she said and cracked open her door.

Gage caught her arm. "Now that the papers are signed, I'm in charge, remember?"

"Yes, but—"

"The problem that existed last night hasn't changed. Just because you put the gold back in the bank doesn't mean you're safe. There's been at least one attempt on your life, and if the guy at the museum was the same man, he might be willing to take you by force, coerce you into giving him the map."

A thread of unease slid through her. "So what would you suggest? I have work to do, same as you."

"If you want this venture to succeed, at this point, you have two options: I can put a guard on your door twenty-four seven, or you can stay at my place."

"You can't be serious." *Superman, ha!* The man was dictatorial and overbearing. How was she going to put up with him for what could end up being weeks?

But what if he was right? Was it possible the man who'd attacked her knew where she was staying? Had he followed her to the museum last night? Would he come after her again, try to force her to give him the map?

"My apartment building's extremely secure," Gage was saying. "It's big enough that you'll have all the privacy you need, and it won't be for long. As soon as everything's ready, we'll be leaving for Arizona."

The chunk of gold was back in the bank, the map in the safe in Gage's office, but she and Gage were the only ones who knew that. Abby looked into Gage's stern features and knew he wasn't going to back down.

"So what's it going to be?" he said.

"If you hire a guard, I'll be paying for half of it. I'll stay at your place. And you'd better remember—I still have my gun."

Gage grinned, then threw back his head and laughed.

Gage wasn't laughing when Abby opened the door to the apartment and the interior looked as if a bomb had gone off.

"Oh, my God!"

Easing her behind him, he walked into the living room. The sofa was overturned, the cushions sliced open; pictures had been jerked down from the walls, the backs ripped off. Kitchen drawers had been pulled out and dumped, cabinets opened, the contents spilled on the floor.

"Stay right here." For once, Abby didn't argue. She was clearly in shock at the nightmare she had stumbled into.

Gage checked the rooms, making sure the intruder or intruders were gone, then returned to the living room. "Take a look around; see if anything's missing."

Big golden eyes flashed to his face. "You think it was him? The guy who broke in before?"

"What do you think?"

She huffed out a breath at the sarcasm in his voice. "Well, hell's bells. Tammy's going to kill me."

Amusement eased some of his tension. "Don't worry, we'll clean everything up before she comes back."

Gage followed Abby on a tour of the apartment, including the bedroom and bathroom, both of which had been very thoroughly searched.

Abby sighed as they returned to the living room. "It's hard to tell for sure, but I don't think anything's missing."

"He was looking for the map, same as before. Does he also know about the gold?"

"I don't know. They were both in the old wooden box, which

was sealed when I got it. But the map was mentioned in the will. King's attorney called everyone together for the reading, anyone who received a gift. That included several museums, who had representatives there. So there are a number of people who know about it."

"You need to make a list—anyone who was at the reading, or might know about your grandfather's bequest."

She glanced around and nodded dully. "Okay."

"In the meantime, I'm bringing in reinforcements. We need to get this place cleaned up." Taking out his cell, Gage phoned Maggie. Half an hour later, a cleaning crew arrived, and Abby put them to work alongside her.

Gage pitched in, and they made fairly quick progress. There were items that needed replacing. After an explanatory phone call to her friend and a lengthy apology, Abby left a check for repairs on the counter.

Though the afternoon was shot to hell, Gage couldn't help feeling relieved that he had insisted on coming with her. Or that Abby would be staying at his place tonight.

Whoever was after the map wasn't giving up. Gage needed to look at Abby's suspect list. He wanted to find this guy before they set off on what was already certain to be a dangerous journey.

By late afternoon, the work was finally completed, the cleaning crew gone, the apartment restored as much as possible. Abby had packed several suitcases, casual clothes as well as gear suitable for the trip into the desert. Anything else could be purchased once they got to Arizona.

"You ready?" Gage asked. The suitcases were loaded. The digital cards had been stolen from her cameras, but fortunately she had extras, and the cameras hadn't been destroyed.

"I'm ready." She looked tired for the first time since he'd met her, her expression glum. She put her hand on his arm, as if to steady herself.

Gage caught her shoulders. "Everything's going to be all right. We still have what we need to find the Devil's Gold, okay?"

Abby slowly nodded. "You're right. I just . . . I didn't expect anything like this to happen."

"It's been a long day. Let's go home."

Abby looked up at him. "I don't really have a home anymore, so I guess your place will do."

She looked so forlorn, Gage leaned down and kissed her forehead. It was a very un-Gage-like thing to do.

CHAPTER SEVEN

ABBY STUMBLED AS SHE MADE HER WAY BACK TO GAGE'S LAND Rover. She felt numb all over and tired to the bone. Realizing the lengths someone was willing to go to get the map told her the sort of danger she was facing.

And the journey had not yet begun.

As they reached the Rover and Gage pulled open her door, Abby's head shot up. "Oh, my God—the storage locker. I put King's personal possessions in a storage facility. Maybe it's been vandalized, too!"

"Get in." He half-hoisted her into the car seat and slammed the door, then rounded the hood and got in behind the wheel.

"What's the address?"

Abby gave him directions to Rod's Self-Storage, a compact cluster of units not far from Tammy's apartment. As they pulled up to the gate, she punched in her personal code, and a portion of the high chain-link fence slid open.

"Second row over. Unit 25."

Gage drove up in front of a long stucco building, and they got out of the car. Abby opened the combination padlock, her heart pounding as Gage rolled up the corrugated steel door.

A sigh of relief escaped as she saw the interior of the 5- by 10-foot unit neatly stacked with cardboard boxes.

"Looks like they haven't been here," Gage said.

"Not yet. The security's good. It's not that easy to get in and out."

"What's in the boxes?"

"I gave his clothes to the Salvation Army. These are mostly his notes. His journals are in there. I didn't have room to store the stuff at Tammy's, but I didn't want to throw the notes away. I examined the journals very carefully, and there wasn't anything about the Devil's Gold. The information we need is in the notes he left me with the map. Anything else he must have taken with him on his last expedition."

"Let's load these up, and we'll store them at the office. They'll be safe there, and we can take another look, see if there's something you might have missed."

"Sounds good."

They cleaned out the storage locker, loading the boxes into the back of the Rover. Though the journals and King's more personal possessions had been left undisturbed, Abby felt even more exhausted than before.

She closed her eyes as the vehicle rolled along. She was nodding off, almost asleep when the passenger door shot open. Abby jerked awake, disoriented, her hand automatically tightening into a fist.

Gage's big palm wrapped around her fingers. "It's okay, Abby. We're home. You're safe."

"Sorry." She slid out of the car, swaying a little as she started walking. Gage's arm went around her, drew her against his side.

"Just take a minute. It's been a long day."

She took a deep breath, trying to ignore how good it felt to be pressed against his big hard body.

Abby forced herself to move away. "I'm okay. Just a little tired is all."

"I hate to say it, but it's only going to get worse."

She straightened. Gage was right. The trip ahead of them would be grueling. "I'm fine. Thanks." She glanced at the brick walls around them. "Where are we?"

"In my garage. We'll come back and get this stuff later. Come on, I'll show you your temporary home."

*   *   *

Gage hadn't told Abby his apartment was on the second floor of his office building. It was convenient, with a private rear entrance and a two-car garage. High, flat ceilings gave it the feel of a loft, and huge paned windows kept the space open and airy; it was almost like living out of doors.

In the downstairs atrium, several leafy trees grew up through circular holes in the brick floor, filling the entry with fresh clean air.

"This is where you live?" Abby's gaze missed nothing as she crossed the floor beneath the branches of the trees.

"It's handy. The market was down when the building came up for sale. There's another apartment next to mine, so I'm a landlord as well as a tenant. I'll show you around, then come back and retrieve your suitcases. The stuff in the boxes will be safe where they are till morning."

Instead of using the elevator, he led her up a flight of metal stairs, crossed to his front door, and punched in the code to turn off the alarm.

"The building is extremely secure, my apartment even more so. When you're in the treasure business, people can get strange ideas."

She made a sound in her throat. "A lesson I just learned."

Gage thought of the break-in, didn't want to imagine what might have happened if Abby had been home. "You'll be safe here." Top-of-the-line security wasn't cheap, but it was worth it. "You don't have to worry about that."

He led her into an expansive living room with gleaming hardwood floors, Persian carpets, and comfortable overstuffed furniture splashed with exotic, patterned, bright-colored pillows. Around them, his own personal treasures, souvenirs from his travels, sat on bookcases, tables, and chests, or hung on the walls.

"Your apartment is wonderful," Abby said, admiring the partially broken head of an ancient Greek statue, moving on to a big African pot with red and black designs that sat in the middle of his dining table. "It's like taking a trip around the world."

"Each item tells its own story. Most of them I like remembering."

Abby looked up at him. "We're going to make a new story, Gage, starting when we get to Arizona."

He thought of everything that had happened since he'd met her. "I think our story has already begun." A look passed between them, and desire swept through him. He wanted to make a story with Abigail Holland. He wanted to remember her naked in his bed, her golden-red hair spread out on his pillow.

He turned away, started walking down the hall. Abby followed, her laptop slung over her shoulder as he led her into the guest room.

"India," she said, her gaze running over the intricately carved wooden headboard above the queen-sized bed and a tall chest inlaid with mother of pearl. An ornately carved elephant with a padded seat served as an ottoman in front of an overstuffed chair upholstered in the same dark red woven fabric that covered the bed.

"The Maharaja's crown—the Golden Hawk," he said, remembering his time there. "We were commissioned to return the crown to the Delhi Museum after there was a massive fire and it disappeared. We tracked it down, but the effort only paid enough to cover our expenses. Interesting trip, though."

"I'll bet." Abby set her laptop on the carved writing desk in the corner. "The room is beautiful, Gage."

Her approval pleased him. He usually didn't care what other people thought about the place he chose to live. "There's a bathroom over there." He pointed to an open door. "I'll bring up your luggage so you can get settled in."

"I'll help you," she offered.

"I'd rather you get started on that list. I'd like to get some idea who's behind these attacks before we take off for Arizona."

Abby sat across from Gage at breakfast the following morning. Like the rest of the apartment, the kitchen was flooded with sunlight. White cabinets hung above caramel granite countertops, and a leafy philodendron on an ornate plant stand stood in the corner. A round antique table and chairs sat in front of tall paned windows.

They were both sipping coffee, getting ready to go over the list she'd made last night, when the doorbell buzzed downstairs.

Gage rose and hit the intercom button.

"It's Kade. I had business in the city. I was hoping you'd spring for a cup of coffee."

Gage smiled. "Come on up." He rose from his chair. "My brother," he said to her.

"The rancher or the soldier?"

"The rancher. But you won't need your gun, I promise. He's even more harmless than I am."

Abby bit back a smile as Gage walked over and buzzed the downstairs door open. Dressed in jeans and a black T-shirt that showed off a pair of spectacular biceps, his dark hair still damp from the shower and curling at the nape of his neck, the man looked like sin personified. *Harmless* wasn't the word she would use for Gage Logan.

Nor for his equally handsome brother, when the two men walked back into the kitchen.

"Kade, this is Abby. We're partnering for an upcoming expedition."

Kade smiled at Abby. He was almost as tall as Gage, with a lean, V-shaped body beneath a white western shirt closed by a row of pearl snaps.

"Good to meet you," Kade said. "My brother's been needing something to do. That caged-animal look in his eyes has been getting worse by the day."

"I promise he'll be breathing fresh country air very soon," Abby said.

Kade smiled. Taking off his dark brown Stetson, he smoothed the creases from his golden brown hair. "Ellie sends her love," he said to Gage.

"His beautiful bride," Gage explained. "How is she?"

"Feisty as ever."

"No surprise there. What about Edge? Have you seen him lately?"

"He came out to the ranch, rode up in the hills for a couple of days. He's decided to go to work for Nighthawk Security. At least for a while. I think he's gonna be okay."

"He's always been a step ahead of us. He'll be fine."

Kade walked over and poured himself a cup of coffee. For the first time, it seemed to dawn on him that it was very early and Abby was sitting at Gage's breakfast table. At least she was dressed and not still wearing her robe.

"I hope I didn't interrupt," Kade said, sipping his coffee as he eyed his brother, clearly intrigued.

"Abby came to me with information that may turn out to be valuable. Unfortunately, someone else thinks so too. She was attacked on one occasion, her apartment ransacked on another. She's staying here until we're ready to head out."

Kade sobered. "If you two need a safe place to stay, you're welcome at the ranch."

"Thanks for the offer, but we should be all right here. And we have plenty of work to do."

"Which I'm obviously keeping you from doing." Kade finished the last of his coffee and set the empty mug down in the sink. "Let me know if there's anything I can do to help."

"Will do." Gage walked him to the door, then reset the alarm after Kade had exited the building.

"You mentioned your brother Edge," Abby said. "Are the three of you close?"

Gage refilled his mug. "As we grew older we drifted apart for a while. Kade's wife, Ellie, brought us back together. I don't think any of us will let that happen again."

"You're lucky to have a family. King was all I had, and now he's gone." Emotion rolled through her, made her eyes burn. King hadn't been around a lot, but he was always there when she needed him.

Gage set a big hand over hers where it rested on the table. "You'll always have your memories. With any luck, we'll find the Devil's Gold, and you'll have even more reasons to remember him."

Abby swallowed past the lump in her throat. Her memories

of the time she had spent with her grandfather would never leave her. And he would be with them in spirit every day of their journey.

Gage sat down across from her. Abby picked up the list she had made the night before and handed it over.

As Gage studied the list, his dark brows pulled together. "You said King was all the family you had, but the names at the top of the list are your cousins."

Abby nodded. "My cousin Jude and his sister, Stacy. Their grandfather was King's younger brother. Jude's always been a jerk. He's thirty years old and still lives with his mother. His sister, Stacy, is selfish and spoiled. She dates wealthy older men and takes whatever she can get from them. Jude wasn't the guy who attacked me, but I figure he or Stacy could have hired him."

"They were both at the reading of the will?"

She nodded. "Their mother, Olivia, was also there. King left each of the kids a small amount of money. Jude was furious King left the house to me. He thought I should sell it and split the money with him and Stacy. I figured if my grandfather wanted them to have it, he would have given it to them."

Gage's mouth inched up in amusement. "Tell me about Stacy."

"My cousin is a gold digger—if you'll pardon the pun—and she's a user. Not drugs. The kind of user who's willing to do anything to get what she wants. A fortune in gold certainly qualifies."

"I can see why you don't claim them as family." He looked down at the list. "Dave Franklin and Caroline Stanfield. I know both of them. They're curators at the Museum of Science and Nature."

"King left the museum a number of valuable artifacts he brought back from various countries. He found the items before today's more restrictive archeological policies were put in place."

"Dave and Caroline are both very well respected. I can't see them involved in the kind of treachery we're talking about, but money can do strange things to people." He looked back down at the list. "Clayton Reynolds. I've never met him, but I know he's an expert on pre-Columbian and Spanish colonial art."

"Mayan culture specifically. Clay and King were friends. My grandfather had some very nice pieces in his collection. Clay was at the reading to receive the gift for the Denver Art Museum."

Gage studied the list. "Rudolph Weyburn is the name of your grandfather's attorney?"

"That's right. Rudy knew about the map. No idea if he knew about the gold in the box."

"Or if your grandfather told anyone else." Gage tapped the list. "At least we know who to keep an eye out for. I'd like to talk to your cousins, but we're on a time clock here. It's already the eleventh of March. By April, the temperature in the desert can climb into the nineties, sometimes higher. We need to get in and out before the heat turns the trip into a suicide mission."

A shiver ran through her. A lot of people had died trying to find gold in the Superstitions. In such a hostile environment, the weather was often the cause.

"So what's our next step?" she asked.

"We need maps. Lots and lots of maps. Old maps, new maps, aerial photos, satellite imagery, soil geology, regular old topo maps. Pretty much anything we can find."

"I can help with that."

He nodded. "I'll give you a list of the places we use for digital mapping, and you can get started. You ready to go to work?"

She was more than ready. Her pulse was hammering with excitement. She couldn't wait to get started, couldn't believe her grandfather's dream, now her own, was about to come true.

Or at least there was a real possibility.

She hoped King Farrell was watching from his corner of heaven.

CHAPTER EIGHT

THEY WENT INTO THE OFFICE THROUGH A DOOR DOWNSTAIRS IN the atrium entrance to Gage's apartment, Abby with her laptop slung over one shoulder, and her digital camera, a Canon EOS Rebel T-8i, draped over the other. The camera shot excellent video and stills. It wasn't cheap, but it was worth it.

As they walked down the back hall, she noticed a room filled with workout equipment: weight rack, sit-up board, benches, squat rack, and treadmill.

Abby thought of Gage's amazing body, the well-defined pecs, rippling abs, and thick biceps, and a little zing slipped through her. Clearly, the effort he made to stay in shape was also worth it.

Continuing into the main office, Abby set up her laptop on one of the desks, and Gage brought her a list of internet sites he used to order mapping information.

"That ought to get you started," he said, then turned and disappeared into his office.

Abby took a seat in front of her computer screen and went to work. She typed in "Imagehunter" and discovered the company had a hundred million images from fifty-three satellite and aerial databases. Another site, Open Topography, had high resolution topo data. Digital elevation models came from a company called Lumina.

It took most of the day to work through the process of selecting the right areas and choosing the digital information that was needed. When she finished, she ordered wilderness area maps to pick up at the Tonto National Forest Ranger District Office not far from Apache Junction.

It was way past lunchtime, but until her stomach growled, she'd been too busy to notice. Her head came up as she caught the aroma of roast beef sandwiches and spicy dill pickles.

"It's a little late for lunch," Gage said, "but I realized I was hungry, and I figured you must be too." He set a sandwich and a Diet Coke on the desk. "I sent Maggie over to Tony's Deli. They have great food, and I thought a working lunch would be better than no lunch at all."

She smiled up at him. "Thanks. All of a sudden, I'm starving."

Gage absently nodded, his mind already back at work. The man was focused, to say the least. Since they'd walked into the office, Abby seemed to have become all but invisible.

"I meant to ask you," he said. "When was the last time you had a physical? You need to be fully checked out before we leave."

"One of your rules?"

He nodded. "An important one. If you need me to set something up—"

"My grandfather had the same rule. He didn't want anyone getting sick while they were off in the middle of nowhere. You don't have to worry. I had a complete physical before I came to see you."

Gage nodded. "I just got a checkup, so we're both good to go." As Gage walked away, she noticed the muscles moving beneath the snug black T-shirt stretched over his broad back. Her abdomen clenched. Dammit, she didn't have time for that kind of thinking, especially not with Gage.

She picked up the sandwich and took a bite, but her thoughts kept straying to the attraction she couldn't seem to stifle. Work was the cure. As soon as she finished her lunch, she grabbed her camera and started taking photos of the office, which now boasted glossy printed digital maps pinned to a giant bulletin board, as well as brightly colored 3-D maps on several computer screens.

Through Gage's open office door, she spotted him behind his desk, his head bent over a book he was reading that journaled an early expedition into the Superstitions. Approaching quietly, she started snapping photos, then did a short video sweep.

Gage looked up, and for a moment, their eyes met. Abby snapped a shot that captured his dark good looks and intense blue eyes.

"Got it. Thanks." She wandered back to her desk, brought up the photo, and sucked in a breath.

There was no mistaking the hot gleam in those fierce blue eyes. Gage might be focused on work, but for a single moment in time, he had been focused completely on her. That single moment told her exactly what Gage had been thinking.

And it meant serious trouble for Abby.

Gage leaned back in the black leather chair behind his desk, his cell phone pressed against his ear. "All right, Walt, I think we understand each other. I look forward to meeting you." He ended the call just as Abby walked into his office.

"I hope I'm not interrupting."

He tried not to notice the outline of her pretty breasts beneath her sweater, failed miserably, and ignored a surge of arousal and forced himself to concentrate.

"That was Walter Jenkins. He and his son, Kyle, own the Cedar Canyon Ranch. I spoke to some people in Phoenix who know the Superstitions, and according to them, Walt and Kyle are two of the best guides in the area."

"You hired them?"

"I think they're our best bet. I still want to meet them, check out their stock and gear. The good news is they have cabins for rent on the ranch. We can stay right there."

"I made reservations at one of the motels, but I can cancel."

"Being out there should help us get familiar with the terrain and save us some time."

"I'll take care of it. I printed all the maps I could, and the rest are being FedExed overnight. We can pick up the wilderness area maps at the Ranger District Office."

He nodded. "It's getting late. I'll go over what we have first thing in the morning. I like to look at them with fresh eyes."

Abby smiled. "I'd like another look myself." She covered her mouth to stifle a yawn. "What else do you need me to do?"

Gage glanced out the window. Darkness had begun to settle over the neighborhood, and the restaurants and bars were beginning to fill up. "That's enough for today. We'll start again tomorrow."

"Are you sure? I can stay a little longer if there's something else you need me to do."

He almost smiled. He loved her enthusiasm. He remembered his first expedition and the excitement he had felt, the driving need to get the trip underway. "You'll do better work if you're rested. Let's get something to eat and go to bed early."

The moment the words were out of his mouth, he regretted them. Taking Abby to bed wasn't going to happen, at least not anytime soon. He locked down his unwanted desire and forced his thoughts back where they belonged.

"There are a couple of things I'd like to finish," Abby said, "but I have to admit a glass of wine doesn't sound half bad."

"We'll go to Dorgan's. It's an Irish pub just down the block. Grab your jacket, and let's get out of here."

Maggie had already gone home. Gage locked the office, and they headed down the street. Dorgan's was in a historic building with exposed brick walls and molded tin ceilings. As it was Friday, a band played Irish music in the corner. On weekends, it got busy and loud, but the main crowd wouldn't arrive till later.

Gage asked for a table in the back, and they both sat down. "Everything here is good. I'm a fan of the fish and chips."

"I'll try it."

The waitress walked up just then. "Hey, Gage, how's it going?" Colleen was pretty, with black hair and big blue eyes. He'd taken her out a few times, taken her to bed, but it was never anything but sex for either one of them. By the time he'd come back from his last trip, Colleen was in a serious relationship. He was glad they could still be friends.

"Colleen, this is Abby," he said.

"Nice to meet you," Abby said.

"You, too, Abby."

"We'll both have the fish and chips," Gage said. "And I'd like a Guinness. Abby wants a glass of—"

"A Guinness sounds great."

"I'll be right back." Colleen smiled and hurried away.

Abby unfolded her napkin and settled it over her lap. "Another one of your friends with benefits?"

He flicked a glance at the brunette, felt not the least bit of interest. "Just friends. No benefits these days."

"For a guy who travels as much as you do, you certainly manage to keep yourself busy."

He smiled, couldn't resist. "Jealous?"

Her chin went up. "Of course not."

Too bad, he thought. Because far too many men were casting appreciative glances in Abby's direction, and he found himself not liking it even a little.

They finished their meal, enjoying the music in the other room. "When Irish Eyes Are Smiling" echoed off the walls as they headed back out to the street.

"I hope you're keeping track of the money we're spending," Abby said. "I'm supposed to pay half, remember?"

He almost smiled. "Maggie's keeping track of the bigger items. Dinner's on me."

"But—" Abby broke off when someone on the sidewalk jostled her, and Gage reached out to catch her before she accidentally stepped off the sidewalk into the street. He looked up to see a car racing toward them, screeching to a halt right in front of them. Behind them, two men rushed out of the alley, both dressed in black, faces covered by black balaclavas.

"Abby!" Gage lunged for the man who grabbed her, knocking her out of the way and shoving the man aside as the second attacker rushed toward her. Whirling, Gage turned and lashed out with his boot, knocking the second man back, sending him sprawling on the sidewalk.

"Run!" Gage shouted. "Get back inside!"

The first man blocked her way. Six feet, thin, wearing black jeans and sneakers, he caught her, dragged her toward the car while the second man, short and stout, with tree-trunk arms, swung a blow Gage ducked.

Gage threw a punch straight from the shoulder that knocked the guy clear off his feet. He turned to see Abby fighting with the other man, scratching and clawing, her ankle boot delivering a hard kick to the man's shin. The guy hissed through his teeth and slapped her. Gage saw red.

Grabbing the guy's shoulder, he spun him around and punched him in the face hard enough to send him crashing into the side of the building.

The short, stout man was up and running. He hurled himself into the back seat of the car, and the other man careened in after him. The door slammed shut. The vehicle roared off down the street, tires screeching as it rounded the corner.

Fighting to control the fury pumping through him, Gage strained to read the license plate, but it had been purposely obscured. It was too dark to tell the model of the car, except that it was an SUV. He headed for Abby, saw her bent over, hands on her knees, braid loose, fiery hair hanging over her face. She looked up at his approach, and Gage pulled her into his arms.

"It's okay," he said, the adrenaline beginning to wear off but not the anger. "They're gone. You're okay."

Abby clung to him. He could feel her trembling, breathing way too fast. "They were trying . . . trying to kidnap me."

His hold tightened around her. *Not on my watch.* He took a deep breath and let it out slowly. He hadn't been that frightened since—he broke off the thought. "That map of yours must be pretty special. Or at least someone believes it is."

"How did they . . . how did they know where I was?"

"They've been watching you from the start. Once they saw us together, it was easy to figure out where you were."

"Should we call the police?"

He eased his hold, took a calming breath. "There's no hurry. They're long gone by now. We can call the police when we get back upstairs."

Abby swallowed. "King said the treasure was real. He told a lot of people that."

"True, and after his attorney mentioned the map at the reading, a lot of people know you have it. Come on. Let's go home." She subtly straightened as she pulled herself together. The woman had guts, he had to give her that.

Still, Gage's arm remained around her shoulders, keeping her close. "Next time I tell you to run, you do it, okay?"

She stopped and turned to look up at him. "You expected me to run while two men were attacking you?"

"I'm twice your size, and I've got training you don't have. So yes, if I tell you to run, I expect you to run from the danger and get yourself somewhere safe."

Her spine stiffened. "You're my partner, Gage. If you're in trouble, I'm not leaving. You might as well resign yourself."

He clenched his jaw, fighting not to lose his temper. The simple truth was he hadn't wanted her to go on this trip in the first place. He liked the idea less every day. As out of vogue as it was, he didn't take women into dangerous situations.

Not anymore.

He thought of Cassandra and guilt swept over him. Beautiful, intelligent Cassandra. She'd be alive today if it hadn't been for him. But Cassie had begged him to take her on the expedition, and he had agreed. He'd been younger back then, cocky after his first few successes. He had naïvely believed he could protect her. Because of him, Cassie was dead.

"We need to talk," he said a little gruffly as they reached the office and went inside, continued through the building to the atrium and upstairs to his apartment.

Abby said nothing until he closed the apartment door and set the alarm.

"So talk," she said, crossing her arms over her chest. "I have a

feeling I already know what you're going to say, and you can forget it. I'm going after the Devil's Gold. If you want to back out of
our deal, that's fine. But I'm going. With or without you."

Gage felt his temper climbing again. Abby was going after the
gold. He could see by the determined look in her eyes that nothing he said was going to dissuade her.

Gage was torn. The no-longer naïve side of him wanted her to
stay home, where she would be safe. His selfish side wanted her to
go with him. Hell, he wanted her in his bed.

"You don't have any idea what can happen on a trip like this."

"I've read everything I can find on the Superstition Mountains. I know how many people have died, how many die every
year. Three men went missing in the summer a few years back.
The sheriff finally had to call off the search and didn't find their
bodies until two years later. Most of the fatalities are people who
go in without being prepared. That's not going to happen to
us—assuming there still is an us."

She was right about that. He wouldn't go in unprepared. He
was good at what he did. Damn good. If anyone could keep her
safe, he was the one.

His chest clamped down. Exactly what he had believed when
he'd agreed to take Cassandra along.

He felt Abby's hand on his forearm, saw his tendons straining.
Her touch gently smoothed over the muscles, easing some of his
tension.

"I know you lost someone, Gage, a woman you cared about, a
woman named Cassandra Dutton."

Gage said nothing.

"Did you love her?" She was looking at him with so much pity,
he knew he had to tell her the truth.

"No. I wasn't in love with Cassandra." But selfish bastard that
he was, he hadn't ended things when he should have.

"But she was in love with you," Abby guessed.

He glanced away, trying not to remember her sweet, trusting
face. "She thought she was." He scrubbed a hand over his jaw, felt
the bruises on his knuckles and the roughness of his evening

beard. "I didn't love her, but that doesn't make it any easier. Cassie's dead because of me."

Abby opened her mouth to ask him what had happened, but Gage just shook his head. "Subject closed. If you're determined to go, I'll take you. But you have to trust me to keep you safe. That means you do what I tell you."

He wasn't sure what he read in her face, but finally she nodded. "I'll expect to have some input, but if there's trouble, I'll do what you say."

"I want your word."

With a resigned sigh, she nodded. "I give you my word."

CHAPTER NINE

*T*HE NIGHT WAS CLEAR AND DARK. A FAINT WIND RUSTLED THE LEAVES in the street, but the sound was muted by the Friday night revelers in the bars and restaurants of LoDo.

Abby made coffee while Gage phoned the police. Officer Noland, young, with broad features and curly brown hair, and Officer Riggs, older, with a touch of silver at the temples, arrived at the apartment.

Noland took a statement from her and Gage, then asked a few additional questions.

"Aside from the men's height and build, what else can you tell us about them? Any distinguishing marks? Scars, tattoos, that kind of thing?"

"They were covered head to foot in black," Abby reminded him. "So there wasn't much to see."

"I can tell you they were damned determined," Gage said. "People were starting to notice, or I don't think they would have backed off."

Abby felt a chill. "Gage fought them. If I'd been alone, I would have been in real trouble."

"You get a plate number?" Officer Riggs asked.

"Couldn't make it out," Gage said. "I'm guessing they had it covered."

"Any idea why they went after Ms. Holland?" Officer Noland asked.

Gage cast Abby a glance, warning her not to mention the map. "What do men usually want from a beautiful woman?" he said.

Noland's gaze went to Abby, from her long russet braid to the toes of her leather ankle boots. He wrote something in his notepad, but made no reply.

Abby's mind was stuck on *Gage thinks I'm beautiful.* She tucked the words away to examine later and focused on the conversation.

"I know it isn't much," she said. "We couldn't see their faces. We know the car was an SUV, but neither of us could tell what model. It was black, dark gray, or blue. It was too dark to tell for sure."

"At least there'll be a report on file," Gage said. "In case something else happens."

"Nothing else is going to happen," Abby said firmly, wishing she could convince herself.

Officer Noland closed his notebook and handed her a card. "If you think of anything else, you can call this number."

She accepted the card. "Thank you." Gage walked the policemen downstairs to the door that led outside.

"That was kind of a waste of time," Abby said when he returned.

"It's on record. If we have to deal with whoever came after you, we've laid the groundwork."

Her head came up. There was something in his voice, the same hint of violence she had heard when he'd told her to run. She wondered how far he would have gone to stop the men from abducting her. They wanted the map. She wondered what they would have done to her in order to get it.

A shudder ran through her as she looked at Gage. "You don't think they'll follow us to Arizona, do you?"

"Once we're gone, unless they've seen the map, there's no reason for them to suspect we'll be hunting for the gold in the Superstition Mountains."

Abby mulled that over. "I don't know how much the lawyer

knew. The box was sealed when I got it, but that doesn't mean no one saw the map before it went into the box."

"Or King didn't tell someone where he'd been searching."

"There were people with him on the trips he made, people he trusted, but still . . ."

"One thing's certain: whoever wants that map isn't fooling around. We need to finish our work and get on the road. After we've left Denver, it'll be harder for them to track us."

Harder but not impossible. "Unless they already know where we're going."

"Unless they already know," Gage conceded.

"So what do we still need to do?"

"Get our gear together. There's a storage room full of equipment downstairs. In the morning, I'll go through what's there and pull out what we can use. Anything else we need we can buy in Arizona."

"How soon will we be ready to leave?"

"Ready or not, we're leaving tomorrow." He glanced down at the heavy stainless watch wrapped around his thick wrist. "It's late. You'd better get some sleep."

That was a laugh. She had almost been kidnapped, might have been tortured or even killed. "After what nearly happened, I'm not sleepy."

Those intense blue eyes locked on her face. The same heat burned there that she had seen in the photo she'd taken. *I can give you what you need to make you sleep,* those amazing eyes said.

Abby's stomach contracted. She wanted to go to bed, but not alone.

"Go . . ." Gage said softly.

Abby turned and practically ran down the hall to her bedroom.

Gage was up at first light. He hadn't slept well, had spent the night on the sofa in case the men who had gone after Abby managed to find a way to breach his security system and break into his extremely secure apartment.

It hadn't happened. His brother Edge had tested the system after Gage had it installed. Edge had been army Special Forces, a Green Beret. He had skills beyond anything Gage had developed in his years of self-defense training and boxing workouts. Edge knew security up, down, and sideways, handy for a soldier who wanted to get inside without being caught.

Though Gage could take care of himself and do a more than adequate job of defending the people he cared about, he was no Green Beret. With any luck, the problem would be left behind when they departed Denver for Arizona.

Gage locked the apartment, then headed downstairs to the office and went to work, assembling as much of the gear they would need as he could find. Expeditions required a good deal of equipment. He grabbed the satellite phone out of his desk and the solar battery charger, a must whenever he was out of cell range, a lesson he had learned when his vehicle bogged down on a muddy back road in South America.

From his office, he went to the store room, pulled out sleeping bags, backpacks, tarps, kerosene burners, flashlights, batteries, bungee cords, a pack of Bic lighters—the list went on and on.

His personal gear included a vicious-looking machete and a pair of lightweight Zeiss binoculars, a good pair of wraparound Ray-Ban sunglasses, a Leatherman multi-tool, plus his .45 caliber S&W sidearm, 30.06 Winchester rifle, and ammo for each.

Once he had what he needed, he went back through and pared it all down. The outfitter, with Mateo's help, would be in charge of meals. They were headed into very rough country. It was essential to be prepared while carrying as little as possible.

Gage and Walt Jenkins had discussed going in on horseback, leading a couple of pack mules loaded with equipment and supplies, but Walt had warned that the horses could only go in so far. Once the group headed off the trail, the terrain would be too steep and dangerous for the animals.

They would take a wrangler to take care of the stock; he would bring the horses out when the animals could no longer handle the tough terrain.

None of it was unexpected. This wasn't his first rodeo.

Gage looked up at the sound of footsteps in the hall and spotted Abby walking toward him in jeans and a pink long-sleeved T-shirt with a floppy-eared rabbit on the front. She had pulled her hair into a ponytail that swung against her back.

How anyone could look sexy in a pink rabbit T-shirt, he had no idea, but the stirring in his groin said she did.

"Good morning." She smiled, held up a red thermal mug. "I brought coffee. I figured you'd be ready for a fresh cup."

"I'll have to add mind reading to your growing list of talents." He accepted the mug and took a healthy swallow, enjoyed the heat and freshly brewed taste. "You're up early."

"You said we were leaving today. Some of my clothes are still at Tammy's—those that weren't destroyed—but I'm guessing you don't want me going back there to get them."

He shook his head. "They could be watching the place, figuring you'll be back sooner or later."

"Then I need to go shopping."

He nodded. "You can do that in Arizona."

She studied the pile of equipment he had pulled off the shelves. "Looks like you're ready to go."

"I talked to Maggie earlier, told her we were moving up the timetable, and asked her to arrange air transportation."

"We're flying?" Abby asked. "I thought we'd be driving."

"Private charter," Gage said. "We need to get down there. We'll be carrying weapons along with our gear. Dealing with the airlines would take too much time."

"So you're waiting to hear from Maggie."

"That's right. We'll have a chance for another look at the maps and with any luck, your FedEx delivery will arrive. As soon as we get the flight information, we'll load the car and head for the airport."

Abby looked up at him with those big golden eyes he was beginning to find nearly irresistible. "What if they're watching us? What if they follow us to the airport?"

"We're going to make sure that doesn't happen."

"How?"

Gage couldn't stop a grin. "My brother's on his way over. He's going to run interference." Twenty minutes later, Gage's cell phone rang, signaling Edge's number.

"Fifteen minutes out," Edge said.

"Take your time. We've still got work to do here."

"No problem. I'll just hang around, keep an eye out for the bad guys."

Gage grunted. God forbid Edge got his hands on the men who had attacked them last night. "Just don't kill anyone."

"You mean unless I have to."

His lips twitched. On the other hand, at least one problem would be solved. "I'll see you soon."

Abby went upstairs to take another look through the stuff she'd brought from Tammy's and make sure she had everything she could use. It was still cold in Denver, but in March, the weather in the Superstitions was warmer, with daytime highs in the seventies, lows in the forties at night.

Unfortunately, in the desert mountains, the weather was highly unpredictable. The days could climb into the nineties, the nights drop to near freezing. Clouds could bring an unexpected downpour and flash flooding. The wind had been known to blow up a sandstorm.

Abby had just zipped the bag when she heard Gage calling from the living room.

"Abby! Come on out; there's someone here I'd like you to meet."

She hurried down the hall and saw a tall, lean-muscled, blade-haired man standing next to Gage. Recognizing the blue eyes, hard jaw, and notched chin, she knew it had to be Gage's brother.

"Abby, this is Edge," Gage said. "He's going to make sure we get to the airport without any trouble."

She smiled up at him. "Nice to meet you, Edge. Thank you for helping."

"No problem," he said. Though she could see the family resemblance, the two looked completely different, Edge with his black hair, high cheekbones, leaner face, and blade of a nose. There was a cynical twist to his lips that was missing from Gage's features.

Edge was hard, dark, and, in a different way, every bit as handsome as Gage. Still, it was the older brother who drew her. Gage was the man to whom she felt connected, had since her grandfather had first mentioned his name and Abby had seen an internet photo of him on a trip to Africa.

"You finished packing?" he asked.

"I'm ready to go. I didn't have much that would work."

"We'll buy the rest when we get there."

Returning to her room, she made a final check, grabbed her laptop, and slung it over her shoulder, along with her camera. Her backup camera, a Canon Powershot Elph 190, which took surprisingly good photos as well as decent video, was packed in her carry-on. Abby grabbed the handle and wheeled it into the living room.

Gage was there, with a bigger wheeled bag and a black canvas satchel. Edge grabbed the satchel, hoisted it over one broad shoulder, and they headed out, taking the elevator this time instead of the stairs.

Edge loaded her carry-on into the back of the Land Rover next to Gage's big bag, tossed in the satchel, then helped load the rest of the gear.

"I'll follow you," Edge said. "Make sure no one else does."

Abby climbed into the passenger seat, and Gage backed the Rover out of the garage.

"Which airport?" she asked.

"Rocky Mountain Metro. It's less than twenty miles from here. We've got a Bonanza A36 flying us down, good little airplane for a relatively short trip like this."

Gage drove out of the alley and turned onto the street. A black

Nissan sports car pulled in behind them. Abby recognized the black-haired man behind the wheel.

"Wow, that car your brother's driving is hot."

"He just got it. Now that he's out of the army, he's living out his fantasies."

"So I guess he wanted to be a race car driver."

Gage grinned. "Or an outlaw."

Gage turned the corner and gunned the engine. The Rover tore down the block, shot through a busy intersection, and roared around a corner.

"If they're out there," Gage said, "I'm not making it easy for them." He slowed to round a curve, then jammed his foot on the gas pedal again. The black Nissan dropped back a few cars but stayed right with them.

Abby flipped down her sun visor to watch behind them in the mirror, saw another car appear three vehicles back.

"There's a car back there that seems to be staying right with us. But it's not a dark gray or black SUV. It's a sedan, and it's silver." She turned to look out the back window. "It just pulled in behind us about three cars back." Her pulse speeded along with the engine. "Maybe the men from last night changed cars so we wouldn't recognize them."

"Edge knows what happened. He'll be watching for anyone who might be following us, no matter what vehicle they're driving."

In the mirror, she saw Edge's Nissan pull up beside the silver sedan, then cut in front of the car and slow, forcing the sedan to slam on its brakes. At the same time, Gage hit the gas and the Rover leaped forward. The Rover careened around a corner, then roared into an alley, raced out the other end, continued down a parallel track for a mile or so, then finally skidded back onto the road.

Abby's heart was pounding, her fingers digging into the leather seats. They were halfway to the airport when Edge's black Nissan caught up with them again.

"Edge is back," Abby said.

"He's lost them. He knows where we're going. He'll keep watch until we get there."

"Seems like a handy guy to know."

The corners of Gage's mouth faintly curved. "You have no idea."

CHAPTER TEN

A SINGLE ENGINE BEECHCRAFT BONANZA WAITED ON THE TARMAC. Gage drove out to the plane and dumped the gear, then parked the Rover between two cars in an out-of-the-way space at the back of the parking lot.

They wouldn't be gone more than a week, less if the trip turned out to be a wild goose chase—or if by some miracle they found the spot King had marked on the map. In which case they would be making a second trip for an in-depth search of the area.

He checked in at the terminal desk, and they made their way outside to board the plane. The pilot was a guy in his forties named Christopher Conners. Good solid guy, competent pilot. Gage had flown with him before.

"Good to see you again, Mr. Logan," the pilot said, sunlight glinting off the silver in his dark hair.

"Let's skip the formalities, Chris. It's just Gage and Abby."

Chris smiled. "Great. I've got all your bags loaded. If you're ready, you can go ahead and board. I'll make my final exterior in-spection and get her ready for takeoff."

Gage helped Abby into the plane through the double cargo doors that were a nice feature of the A36. The tan leather interior was arranged club-seating style, so Gage sat down across from her, giving them both more room.

He clicked on his seat belt as the pilot strapped himself in and began his preflight check. The engines fired, and in minutes, the plane was taxiing down the runway, then lifting into the air.

It was a mild day in the Rockies, with only a few white cumulus clouds in the distance, which made for mostly smooth air. Gage folded down the table so he and Abby could work.

For the past few days, he'd been researching the history and legends surrounding the infamous gold mine in the Superstitions, as well as the Peralta family, who had originally found it, at least according to the legends.

He'd studied past efforts to find the lost mine, read searches documented in journals and books, and tales passed down over the years. No way to know exactly which stories were true, but it was important to have as much background information as possible. He knew Abby had done similar research before she'd walked into his office.

He allowed himself a moment to study her as she stared out the window. She seemed fascinated by the colors and patchwork shapes of the land below, the shadow of the plane moving over the landscape. She wanted to see things, learn things.

She was a seeker of knowledge, same as he was. She was fiery and independent, and he was drawn to her more every day.

He settled back in his seat. He couldn't have her. Not now. Not until this was over. Once he did, his constant thoughts of her would end, and she'd be just another memory, something he could file away to take out and savor through the years.

He watched the play of sunlight through the window, setting her burnished hair ablaze. Her sweater outlined her tempting breasts, and his palms itched to cup them.

Not yet, he told himself. He was a patient man, or at least he could be when there was something worth waiting for. Gage had a feeling Abby Holland was a memory worth the wait.

They'd been in the air less than three hours when the plane began its descent into the Scottsdale Airport. Maggie had a rental car, a big white Ford Explorer, waiting at the terminal to carry them to Apache Junction. Though Gage was anxious to get underway, Abby insisted on taking photos of the plane, Gage standing next to it, and pictures of the airport terminal.

"What's our first order of business?" she asked, once they were settled in the SUV, their gear stowed in back.

"Let's hit the nearest Sportsman's Warehouse. There's equipment I need, things you'll be needing as well."

"Sounds good."

Abby pulled up Siri on her iPhone, and the female voice began giving them directions.

"Where's Mateo?" Abby asked as the big SUV pulled out of the airport parking lot. "I thought he might be meeting us here."

"He's already out at the ranch."

"Tell me about him," Abby said.

Gage settled back in the driver's seat. "We met while I was in Guatemala. A family named Castro hired me to find some heirlooms that had disappeared during the colonial period. One of the locals recommended Mateo as a guide. The man knows his way around the natural world like no one I've ever seen. Desert. Jungle. Doesn't matter. It's like he seamlessly just blends in."

"Where does he live?"

"Mateo moves around, works wherever he's needed. We've become friends over the years. If I call him, he comes."

"What exactly does he do for you?"

"He runs the day-to-day operations of the expedition, works with the outfitter, helps him choose a campsite each night, then helps get the camp set up. He's the most remarkable tracker I've ever seen, and he's got an unbelievable ability to ferret out information from the locals."

"So basically he takes care of whatever needs to be done."

"That's right. Anything that comes up, Mateo handles. You might say he watches my back." Gage pulled into the parking lot of the big sporting goods store.

"You'll need a rain slicker and some good above-the-ankle hiking boots," he said. "Make sure you have a warm jacket, preferably a lightweight puffy style that takes up minimal space. The nights still get cold."

She nodded. "I live in Denver. I have the jacket I need, and I've got a good pair of hiking boots. I do need a slicker, heavy socks, a couple of other things."

Twenty minutes later, Gage smiled at the armload of purchases Abby hauled up to the counter. He helped her carry the shopping bags out to the car; then they headed for the ranch in the desert foothills near Lost Dutchman State Park.

The ranch was a little over ten miles out of town. Even in March, it was warm, the sky a pure cobalt blue above the arid desert landscape. Thorny mesquite trees and miles of greasewood pushed up through sandy soil. An array of saguaro cactus added interest to what should have been a monotonous vista but instead was strangely compelling.

Eventually, the road narrowed to a two-lane that swelled and dipped over the uneven land as it left civilization behind.

"I've only been to the desert once," Abby said. "When I was in college, I went with some friends to the Grand Canyon. This part of Arizona is lower and drier. But in a different way, it's beautiful."

Exactly what Gage had been thinking. "It is. Beautiful but deadly."

Abby flicked him a glance but made no reply.

Then, in the distance, there it was, rising like a medieval fortress from the flat, seemingly endless desert surrounding it.

"There it is!" Abby pointed excitedly, as if he didn't notice the forbidding cliffs that rose hundreds of feet into the air, a monolith that captured the eye and refused to let go. "Superstition Mountain."

Gage slowed the vehicle enough to give them each a chance to look. "Pretty amazing," he said. "The photos don't do it justice."

"No," Abby said softly.

They both fell silent as the SUV traveled farther down Apache Trail toward their destination. Gage spotted the tall wooden gate with the words CEDAR CANYON RANCH burned into the wood over the top.

As he pulled the SUV to a halt in front of a cluster of wooden buildings, cracked open the door, and got out, the older man he recognized from the Cedar Canyon website walked up to greet them.

"Walt Jenkins," the man said, extending a weathered, darkly suntanned hand. "Welcome to the Cedar Canyon Ranch." He was average height, early seventies. In a short-sleeved blue plaid western shirt, he was bone-thin, his arms long and sinewy.

"Gage Logan," he said, accepting the handshake Walt offered.

Abby rounded the hood of the car to join them. She extended her hand. "Abby Holland. Nice to meet you." She and Walt shook.

"This is my boy, Kyle," Walt said proudly as his son walked up.

Kyle gave a friendly tug on the brim of his battered straw cowboy hat. "Welcome to the Cedar Canyon Ranch." He was spare but not as thin as his dad, solidly muscled, suntanned, dressed in jeans and boots. With his dark hair and dark eyes, the guy was handsome, a few years younger than Gage, late twenties, with a wicked smile he turned on Abby that made Gage want to hit him.

Fortunately for all of them, Abby's smile held a warm greeting but no invitation for anything more.

The muscles in Gage's shoulders relaxed. *Dammit.* He wasn't the jealous type, and even if he were, he had no claim on Abby.

"Your man, Mateo, is already here," Walt said. "Cabin five, but he ain't there now. Took off walking about an hour ago. Said he'd be back in time for supper."

"I was looking forward to meeting him," Abby said.

"Mateo has a way of disappearing, then suddenly reappearing out of nowhere," Gage said. "It's kind of spooky, but you get used to it."

Walt just smiled. "Come on. I'll show you where to stow your gear." They crossed the open area in the middle of the compound to a row of small wood-frame cabins, each with a covered front porch. Beyond them was a weathered red barn and several corrals.

Walt opened the door to cabin number 1, while Kyle opened

the door to cabin 2. Abby disappeared inside with Kyle, and Gage followed Walt into the living room of cabin 1.

"There's a bigger place we rent to families," Walt said, "but these others here are all alike. Each has a bedroom and bath, a little seating area in front of the wood-burning stove. Still cold enough at night—there's some logs there if you feel like building a fire. Got a sink, and there's a coffee maker next to it on the counter, one of them little fridges underneath."

"It's nice." Gage had expected only the basics, but the cabin was surprisingly homey, with a love seat and chair in front of the stove and a patchwork quilt on the queen-sized bed. He tried not to let his thoughts stray in that direction, but for an instant, he imagined Abby lying naked in the middle of the bed in welcome, her glorious flame-colored hair spread over the pillow.

He shut down the image and turned back to his host.

"Supper's at six," Walt said. "You'll meet my wife, Mae. She's a durn good cook."

Gage smiled. "Good food's always appreciated." He left to move the car, parked it in a spot in front of the cabin, then started unloading their gear. He was back inside when he looked up to see Abby standing in the open doorway.

"Come on in," he said.

She walked inside and looked around. "Mine's the same except for my quilt is red and yours is blue. I wonder if his wife made them."

Gage tried not to glance at the bed, to keep the image he'd seen earlier from reappearing in his head. "Walt says Mae is—and I'm quoting—'a durn good cook.'"

Abby laughed. "I'm hungry, so that's great news."

Gage clamped down a shot of lust. He was hungry, but at the moment, it wasn't for food.

He glanced behind Abby toward the door. "Where's your new-found friend? Last I saw, he was carrying your suitcase, following you around like a puppy."

Her eyes shot to his. "I thought Kyle was nice."

"I'm sure he is. Long as he keeps his mind on business, we'll be fine."

"Keeps his mind on business? As opposed to what?"

"Your sweet little ass." The look on her face was priceless. He checked his watch. "It's almost time for supper. Let's go for a walk, check out the stock, then go get something to eat."

Abby said nothing, just flicked him a disapproving glance, and walked past him out the door.

CHAPTER ELEVEN

ABBY WALKED WITH GAGE AROUND THE COMPOUND. SHE WENT TO get her camera, then paused to snap a photo here and there. There was a pasture next to the corral where a long-eared mule lipped the sparse grass coming up through the sandy soil. Several other mules grazed on a pile of hay near the fence.

"The mules look healthy," Abby said.

Gage nodded. "You can tell they're well-cared for. So far, so good."

There were horses grazing in a field farther away: a paint, a palomino, a sorrel, a couple of bays with shiny red coats and black tails. As they entered the shady barn, the smell of hay and horses drifted in the air. A tall white mare poked her head out of the stall, and a sorrel nickered at their approach.

Pausing in front of the stall, Gage ran a big hand over the mare's sleek neck. There was a jagged scar on the back of his hand that Abby had noticed before. She wondered how he'd got it.

"I never asked if you could ride," Gage said.

Abby smiled. "I live in Denver. It's basically an overgrown cow town. I'm no expert, but I can ride well enough to get where we're going."

Gage nodded. "I figured."

"You did? Why is that?"

"Because you're the type of person who doesn't go after something without being prepared."

"I hope that's a compliment."

"From my point of view, it's essential."

She took his hand, the scar catching the sunlight. "What happened?"

"Python. They can be vicious."

"It must have really hurt," she said, tracing the outline with her finger.

He looked down at the scar and shrugged. "Hazard of the job."

Abby thought of the scar her grandfather carried on his forearm—from a sword, he had said, then told her the story of a Bedouin chief who was jealous of King and a woman the chief wanted to add to his harem. Finding treasure wasn't easy, but it certainly wasn't a dull way to make a living.

They made a pass through the barn, then, satisfied that the animals could make the trip into rough country, headed for the ranch house.

"It's been hours since we've eaten," Abby said. "You must be hungry."

Something hot and urgent appeared in Gage's eyes. "Oh, I'm hungry," he drawled, and Abby felt a sweep of heat that ignited her whole body.

His expression abruptly altered, and the heat disappeared, but Abby's insides were still shaking. She had never lusted for a man before, hadn't understood how fierce a demand it could be.

She took a steadying breath. She was certain Gage wouldn't act on whatever desire he was feeling. He valued his iron control as much as his reputation. Abby wished she could be as certain about herself.

In the ranch house kitchen, the meal was served family style, the guests all seated at a long wooden table covered with a bright red-checked cloth. Abby took some photos and did a video sweep of the people in the room.

A group of four had rented the larger cabin: mother, father, and two young children. A pair of college girls were staying in cabin 3; a middle-aged couple celebrating their anniversary in cabin 4; and Mateo in cabin 5, the one farthest away, fitting, from what Gage had told her about him.

Mateo Morales was waiting for them in the dining room, an attractive man in his thirties with high cheekbones and smooth dark skin. He had slightly wavy, shoulder-length black hair and a lean build, with sinews that stood out in his arms and neck. He looked tough and capable, as she had expected from Gage's description.

"Mateo, this is Abigail Holland," Gage said. "I told you about her when we spoke on the phone."

"Ms. Holland." He made a polite nod of his head, his words tinged with a Spanish accent. "It is a pleasure to meet you."

"You as well, Mateo." She smiled. "Please . . . call me Abby."

Mateo's return smile held approval. Gage explained that the man was a trusted friend, one who had saved his life on more than one occasion. Abby figured they were fortunate to have him along.

Supper was served: roast beef and gravy, carrots, potatoes, and homemade bread, with apple pie for dessert. Mae, a silver-haired, wide-hipped woman, was indeed a "durn good cook."

When the meal was over, Mateo quietly set off for his cabin. Gage walked Abby to hers, then stood patiently on the porch as she unlocked her door.

"Want to come in for a nightcap?" she asked. "I brought that bottle of scotch we were drinking."

Gage's lips edged into a smile. "Smart girl. I brought one myself, though once we're in the bush, there's a strict no-drinking policy."

"Then I guess we should indulge ourselves while we can."

The heat was back in his eyes. "One drink," he said and followed her into the cabin. "More than that could be dangerous."

As the door closed, she set her camera aside and turned to look at him, realized how close they were standing. With his thick dark brown hair, solid jaw, and piercing blue eyes, dear God, the man was handsome. She flashed back to Gage in her living room, naked to the waist, the muscled shoulders and thick biceps, the ladder of muscle down his flat belly.

She rested her palms on his chest and looked up at him. "Dangerous for me? . . . Or for you?"

Gage's blue eyes seemed to burn. The hands that locked around her waist felt like bands of steel as he dragged her against him. He was aroused, she realized, the hard heavy length of him pressing against her, the message clear.

He wanted her.

Abby's mouth went dry while dampness slid into her core. One of Gage's big hands dug into her hair, holding her in place as he tipped her head back and his mouth crushed down over hers.

Heat and ravenous need, power, and strength combined in a kiss that was more taking than tender. His tongue plunged in as he deepened the kiss, stirring hot licks of desire and making her knees feel weak. It wasn't what she had expected, and exactly what she wanted.

Rising on her toes, Abby kissed him back with the same lusty need, clinging to his powerful shoulders, her nipples hard as they pressed into his heavily muscled chest. Gage slanted his lips over hers, kissing her one way, then the other, delving deep, making her tremble.

The kiss was about to burn out of control when Gage's lips softened and the kiss turned gentle, coaxing instead of taking, teasing one side of her mouth and then the other. Abby moaned and her arms slid up around his neck.

Gage kissed her one last time, then caught her wrists and drew them away, stepped back so they were no longer touching.

"I shouldn't have done that, but I had to know. Unfortunately, I was right. You taste even better than I imagined."

"Gage . . ."

Still breathing hard, his eyes a fierce shade of blue in his suntanned face, he shook his head. "As much as I want you, this can't happen. Not now. I don't sleep with my clients."

Embarrassment trickled through her. "How very professional of you."

"That's right. It's one of the reasons I don't take women on an expedition. Too much temptation."

Irritation slid through her. "You don't need to worry. I want this trip to succeed far more than you do." She looked back at him, determined to save her pride. "I just . . . I was curious, that's all. You have a certain reputation. I wanted to know if it had any basis in fact. Now that my curiosity has been satisfied, your professionalism is safe."

Gage's jaw turned hard. He was still aroused, his broad chest rising and falling faster than normal.

He reached out and caught her shoulders. "I don't think you understand. This isn't over. Once we're safely back home, we're going to finish this. I've wanted you since the moment you walked into my office. That hasn't changed. I've dreamed of having you naked and spread open beneath me, dreamed of being inside you. Now that I know that's what you want, too, I promise you it's going to happen."

Her pulse throbbed and fresh desire curled through her.

Gage bent his head and kissed her one last time. "Until then, I have a job to do, and so do you." Turning, he walked to the door. "Lock this place up and get some sleep. I'll see you in the morning." The door clicked shut behind him.

Stunned, Abby just stood there staring at the place where he had been. Her embarrassment, she realized, was gone. Gage had been dreaming about her. He wanted her as much as she wanted him.

She took a shaky breath, recognizing for the first time the danger she had put herself in.

Abby had admired Gage Logan for years. She'd been attracted to him even before she'd met him. But Gage wasn't interested in anything but sex. He was the great explorer. He had women falling at his feet. He wanted her, yes, but as soon as he'd had his fill, he'd be gone.

Abby wasn't a no-strings kind of woman. Now that she had come to know him, the attraction had only grown stronger. If she let herself fall for Gage, he would break her heart.

A shaky breath trembled out. At least, she was safe for the time being. Gage's strict no-drinking policy also applied to sex. All she had to do was remember the consequences of letting her guard down, allowing herself to fall more deeply under his spell.

She couldn't let it happen. She refused to become just another of Gage's women. She was worth more than that.

Abby locked the door and poured a couple of inches of scotch into a glass. The first sip warmed her; the second eased some of her tension.

She could handle Gage Logan. She was a smart, independent woman. The thought occurred that she wanted Gage, but maybe someone else would do. Maybe another man could help her get her head on straight and she could forget Gage Logan. Kyle Jenkins's handsome face arose. The sexy young cowboy had made his interest clear.

But instead of excitement or desire, Abby felt oddly disloyal. It was insane. She didn't owe Gage her loyalty or anything else. She meant nothing to him, not even enough for him to break one of his ridiculous rules. The problem was she didn't want Kyle. The man she wanted was sleeping in the cabin next door.

Abby downed the scotch, undressed, and climbed in bed. If Gage wanted to play games, so could she. Abby smiled as she relaxed back on her pillow, thinking of ways to drive Gage over the edge. It could be fun, she told herself. As long as she didn't let her guard down or her heart get involved.

But first and far more important was finding the Devil's Gold, restoring King's legacy. There was still a chance the men in Denver knew she and Gage were headed to the ranch. A chance that whoever wanted the map would follow them into the mountains, make another attempt to steal the map, or lie in wait till they'd found the gold, then try to steal it from them.

Until this was over, the simple truth was, she needed Gage Logan.

King Farrell was no fool.

And neither was his granddaughter.

* * *

Though the bed was surprisingly comfortable, Gage spent most of the night tossing and turning, replaying the scene in the cabin next door. Part of him wished he had taken Abby up on her impulsive offer. The other half wished he had left her back in Denver.

A trip like this was dangerous, even without the very strong possibility that the men they'd left behind would follow them into the desert. And capable or not, Abby was still a greenhorn. After what had happened to Cassandra, he didn't want the responsibility of trying to protect a woman he cared about.

Cared about. The words spun through his head. He more than cared about Abby. His body still ached for her. Images of all that fiery hair and those sexy curves kept him awake half the night. But it was her confidence and determination that appealed to him most, her zest for life that stirred something deep inside him.

It seemed as if he'd just fallen asleep when sunlight burned through the windows, rousing him. With a groan, he rolled over to check the time, climbed out of bed and hit the tiny shower, then dressed in a pair of khaki cargo pants and an olive drab T-shirt and headed next door to check on Abby.

She was already gone, he discovered, and he turned his attention to the ranch house, hoping he hadn't missed breakfast. Grabbing a plate, he filled it from the steaming dishes on the sideboard—eggs, bacon, country potatoes, and toast—then carried his plate over and sat down beside her.

She had plaited her hair in that single loose braid she'd been wearing the day he'd met her. The urge to remove the band and run his fingers through all those silky strands had his body stirring to life.

Abby looked up from beneath her thick dark lashes and gave him a too-sweet smile. "Sleep well?"

Amusement trickled through him. "No. Believe me, I paid the price for what *didn't* happen last night."

Abby laughed softly, breaking the tension.

Gage ran a finger down her cheek. "I meant what I said. We aren't finished. Not by a long shot."

One of her eyebrows came up. "Then again, maybe we are."

He smiled. "I guess we'll have to wait and see."

Their eyes locked, and a challenge passed between them. Then both of them went back to eating.

"What's on our schedule today?" Abby asked.

"I want to go over to the Superstition Museum, take a look at some of their records. We've got an appointment with Isaac Mason, the guy in charge. I've also got the names of a couple of people who are experts on the history of the mines in the area."

She nodded. "When will we actually be going in?"

"Mateo is working out the final details. Walt's a little old for a trip this tough, so Kyle is going to guide. With luck, we'll be heading into the mountains at first light tomorrow."

He could almost see the excitement shining in Abby's golden eyes.

"You don't waste any time," she said.

His gaze remained on her face. "Maybe I have a good reason to finish and get us back to Denver."

Abby's cheeks flushed. "I guess we'll see," she said, echoing his words.

Gage just smiled. Abby wasn't the only one who could be determined. Sooner or later, Abigail Holland was going to find that out.

CHAPTER TWELVE

*T*HEY HEADED FOR THE SUPERSTITION MOUNTAIN MUSEUM, WHICH sat on a ten-acre chunk of desert back down the road toward town. There wasn't much there, Abby thought, as Gage drove up the dusty lane and parked the SUV, but as they began to wander the trails, passing a huge ore crusher that caught Gage's attention, an old barn, and a number of wooden outbuildings, there was definitely plenty to be learned.

"Lots of mines in this area at one time," Gage said. "Most of them played out by now."

"So it's logical there could have been a big discovery in the Superstitions way back when."

"Or more than one. The trouble is, hundreds of people have tried to find gold in the Superstitions, and no one ever has. At least not since Jacob Waltz."

"The Dutchman."

"That's right."

"No one until now," Abby said with a grin.

Gage's smile reminded her of his hot kiss last night, and desire curled in her abdomen. She had never been obsessed with a man before, and she didn't like it.

Focusing on the here and now, she passed a WATCH FOR SNAKES sign and ignored a shiver. As they headed into the museum, a man in his fifties with light brown hair going gray walked toward them.

"You must be Logan," he said to Gage. Abby figured the man had probably looked Gage up after he'd made the appointment and recognized him from photos and articles on the internet.

"That's right. Gage Logan."

"I'm Isaac Mason." The men shook hands. Gage introduced her, and Isaac shook her hand. "Always nice to talk to people interested in history."

Gage asked questions as Isaac gave them a tour of the museum. "We're particularly interested in anything you can tell us about the Peralta family," Gage said.

Isaac started nodding. "The connection between the Superstitions and the Peraltas dates back to the sixteen hundreds. Pedro Peralta was governor of New Mexico in 1610 when it was a province of New Spain."

Abby had read that, understood the long-standing family connection to the area.

"Not much is known about them until Miguel Peralta's name pops up in the mid seventeen hundreds," Isaac continued. "That's when the family discovered gold in the Superstitions, or so the story goes."

"As I understand it," Gage said, "the gold was carried back and forth between the mine and Mexico for the next hundred years."

Isaac nodded. "The Apaches were their greatest threat. From the start, the tribe wanted them gone. They believed the mountains belonged to them, and anyone who trespassed was fair game. A lot of Mexicans died defending the mine. Or at least that's what people believe."

"What about the massacre?" Gage asked. "That's supposed to have been the demise of the family and the last anyone heard of the Peralta mine."

"In 1848 or thereabouts, a large party of family members was taking a load of gold back to Mexico, which they did a number of times each year. One of them was leading a pack string loaded with gold bars when the Apaches attacked. All of the Peraltas were killed. The Apaches buried the bodies and hid the gold. A few years later, soldiers found the remains. Newspapers of the time reported finding the bones of the mules with saddlebags full of gold."

"What about the soldier, William Edwards?" Abby asked.

Isaac looked at her with a hint of respect. "Not many know that part of the story. A cavalry trooper named William Edwards claimed he was present when the bodies were found. Claimed he found a gold tooth in one of the skulls, the mark of the Spanish aristocracy in those days, which the wealthy Peralta family would have been part of. He may have even found some of the gold. He and his son searched for years but never found the mine. At least that's the story."

Isaac led them over to a wall filled with framed maps. "These mark the trails of some of the expeditions that went in search of the gold."

Abby instantly recognized one of the maps as similar to the old rawhide drawing in the bag currently locked in the Explorer, the safest place to store it while they were away from the ranch.

Of course, King's markings were not on the map hanging on the wall.

"Lots of people have looked for the Peralta mine," Isaac said. "But it was Jacob Waltz and his partner, Jacob Weiner, who claimed to have found it. Brought out sixty thousand in gold ore before he died. Be worth a million now."

"What happened to Weiner?" Gage asked.

"Killed by Apaches. Waltz blamed himself for leaving his friend alone while he went to Phoenix for supplies. He stayed in a bordello with his girlfriend, lingered longer than he should have, came back, and found his partner tortured and mutilated. Never was the same after that."

"I read that on his deathbed he gave clues to the location of the mine," Abby said.

Isaac nodded. "Unfortunately, he was delirious. No one could make enough sense of what he said to actually find the mine."

"The Lost Dutchman," Gage said.

"He was German. *Deutsch.* So that's what people called it. No way to know if it was the Peralta mine, though there was a rumor not all the family had died in the massacre and Waltz had crossed paths with one of the descendants. Supposedly, he had done the man a favor and been given the location of the mine, or a cache of gold from the mine as a reward, something like that."

Whatever it was, Abby thought, it was somehow connected to the Devil's Gold.

"I caution you," Isaac said. "There are a dozen different versions of the story. Just depends on who's telling the tale."

Gage smiled and stuck out his hand. "You've been a big help, Isaac. Thanks for your time."

"My pleasure."

"Thanks so much," Abby added.

They left the museum and headed back toward the ranch. Gage made a stop at a small wood-frame house on a dried-out acre of land where they talked to an old prospector named Dobbie Gill. He'd been a guide in his younger days, had spent thirty-five years as a "Dutch hunter."

Dobbie scratched the sparse patch of gray hair on his head. "Wasted half my life looking for that damned mine. Went in on my days off. Had a friend went along with me. Finally, just got too danged old."

"So you never found anything?" Abby asked.

"Found lots of different stuff. Old abandoned cabins. Some Apache ruins. Couple of unmarked graves. Closest we ever come to finding what might have been the mine was up on Bluff Spring Mountain."

Abby's senses went on alert. She glanced at Gage, saw he had also homed in on the location that matched a spot on King's map.

"Bluff Spring Mountain," Gage repeated, hoping to get Dobbie talking again.

"Story was the Mexicans kept horses and mules somewhere up there. Used 'em to transport the gold back to Mexico, but the animals had to be guarded day and night to keep the Apaches from stealing them. We found a flat spot up near the saddle that showed signs of long years' use as a camp. Would have been a good spot to defend, and there's some year-round water holes up there.

Whenever we got a chance, we'd go back and dig, see what we could find."

He grinned, showing a missing bottom tooth. "Never found the mine, but we had some mighty fine adventures."

Abby laughed. "That's what it's really about, isn't it? Learning things and seeing what's out there?"

"Yes, ma'am, that's about it." Dobbie led the way back to his front door. "I wish y'all good luck in your travels. But you best be careful. Lots of folks go in and don't never come back out."

The ominous words stayed with Abby as she climbed into the Ford Explorer.

The engine started, and Gage pulled onto the road. "You heard what the man said. Lots of people go in and never come out. It's not too late for you to change your mind."

Abby just laughed. "Not on your life. I didn't come all this way to turn around and go home."

Gage shook his head, but she caught his smile.

"It was worth a try." He increased his speed, pushing the Explorer faster down Apache Trail toward the ranch. "Mateo is also digging around today. We'll talk after supper, make our final plans. If everything falls in line, we'll head into the mountains first thing tomorrow morning."

A thrill shot through her. Her dreams of adventure and finding treasure were getting closer.

Then she thought of the ruthless men they had left in Denver. Could their attackers have followed them?

Just how far would they be willing to go to find the Devil's Gold?

There was a new car in the parking lot when they arrived at the ranch, a white Chevy Suburban with Arizona rental plates. Walt was showing the latest guests, two men in jeans and bill caps, to the cabin formerly occupied by the middle-aged couple celebrating their anniversary.

When it was time for supper, Gage walked Abby to the ranch house, but the men weren't among the group seated at the long wooden dining table.

"I don't see the new arrivals," Abby said to him as he sat down beside her, their plates overflowing with baked potatoes and rib-eye steaks cooked outside on the grill. "You don't think they could have come from Denver and followed us down here?"

Gage sliced into his meat, cooked nice and rare. "It wouldn't be easy to track us, but it's possible."

"I didn't get a good look at them when we pulled in, but even if I had, I don't think I'd be able to recognize them as the men from Denver."

"I talked to Walt. He said they came up from Phoenix. Since they're driving a rental, that probably means they flew into Sky Harbor."

"That doesn't make me feel any better."

"I know what you mean." He swallowed another tender bite of steak. "We'll keep an eye on them, at least until we leave."

They finished their meat and potatoes, and a piece of Mae's chocolate cake for dessert. Afterward, Gage walked Abby to his cabin, and Mateo joined them there.

"A couple of new guests arrived today," Gage said to his friend as they sat down in front of the old iron stove. "I don't like the timing, or the fact they didn't show up for supper, but it doesn't mean they're here because of us. We'll be gone first thing in the morning. Walt and Kyle know we're heading into the mountains from the east, but the wrangler won't know until we leave in the morning, and none of them know where we're going once we leave the main trail."

They hadn't yet met the wrangler, Kyle's helper, a guy named Smiley Wilcox. Wilcox didn't live on the ranch and only worked part-time, which suited Gage just fine. The fewer people who knew their intentions, the better.

Gage continued, filling Mateo in on what they had learned at the museum that day and from the old prospector, Dobbie Gill.

"Gill's reference to Bluff Spring Mountain matches what's written in King's notes," Gage said. "It's also on the map. We need to follow each of King's markers, which means we'll be heading up the route that leads to the flat area on the side of the mountain, just as he did."

Mateo nodded. "I spoke to some people. They gave me the name of an old Apache who lives up in the hills. He liked to talk, said the trail we'll be following was once an old road used many years ago. He said it used to be wide enough for a wagon, but after much time, the weather has made it nearly impassable. He says it is very steep and zigzags dangerously back and forth to the summit."

"That's good intel, Mateo."

"Kyle Jenkins knows the old wagon road," Mateo said, shoving his shoulder-length black hair back from his face. "He says once we reach it, the first five miles are very difficult. After that, it will be impossible to go farther on horseback."

Gage nodded. "We knew that was likely." King's notes and his map had shown the spot where he and his party had given up their horses and gone ahead on foot.

"What's our timing?" Gage asked. "We on schedule for tomorrow morning?"

"Everything is ready," Mateo said. "Kyle will have our horses saddled at first light. As soon as the mules are loaded, we will be ready to leave."

They were taking two mules, one for provisions, including water, food, and pellets to feed the livestock; the other for outdoor gear and equipment: a metal detector, maps, digging tools, a shovel, and a pick. At some point, their lightweight sleeping bags would be transferred from behind the horses' saddles to the bottom of their backpacks, along with their personal gear—not to exceed twenty-five percent of their body weight.

"Remember, this is a wilderness area. We pack it in, we pack it out. Any questions?" Gage asked.

"What about the two men who just checked in? How do we know they won't follow us?" Abby asked.

"They may try. We won't make it easy. I talked to Walt, made a slight last-minute adjustment. We're going to trailer the stock and go in from the site of an old homestead a few miles farther down the road from our original point of departure. Walt and Kyle are the only ones who know where that is. I'm paying a bonus for their silence, half now, half when we safely return. All we can do is hope we can trust them.

"Anything else?" When no one spoke, Gage rose from the table. "All right, then. We'd all better get some sleep. We'll be leaving before breakfast, so it's coffee in your cabins and power bars on the trail until we stop for lunch."

Gage pulled Abby aside as she stood up, and Mateo slipped quietly out the door.

"From now on, we need to stay focused," Gage said. "You'll have to be vigilant, constantly aware of your surroundings. I want you to stay close. No wandering off on your own. There are all sorts of hazards out there, everything from snakes and wild animals to crumbling soil, cliffs, and deep ravines. You understand?"

She nodded. "I'll be careful."

He damned well hoped so. He was responsible for her safety, whether she liked it or not. He walked her to her cabin, stood next to her on the porch. "Get some sleep." He smiled. "Before I change my mind and take up where we left off last night."

Abby flicked him a don't-be-so-sure-of-yourself glance, and Gage pulled her into his arms.

"One last thing." Tipping her chin up, he kissed her. Abby stiffened, but then her plump lips softened under his, her arms went around his neck, and she kissed him back. Firm full breasts pressed into his chest. Her nipples hardened into stiff little buds, and Gage groaned.

The kiss turned deeper, hotter, fiercer. His hand strayed down over the curve of her bottom, cupping and pulling her more firmly against him, letting her feel his erection. He was hard as a stone, aching to be inside her, and rapidly losing control. Forcing his brain to function, he clamped down on the hunger raging through him, kissed her softly one last time, and eased away.

He caught her chin, turning her face up to look at him. "That's so you'll remember what's going to happen when this is over."

Abby ran a finger over her kiss-dampened lips. Her cheeks were flushed, her eyes glazed with passion. He went harder just looking at her. Damn, he wanted this woman.

"Good night, Abby," he said gruffly as she turned away from him and walked through her door. He didn't leave till he heard the lock click into place and knew she was safe.

Back in his cabin, Gage rubbed a hand over the bristles along his jaw, turned off the lights, and went to bed. It took a while before his unspent desire faded and he was finally able to sleep. Just before dawn, he jerked awake, fighting the last remnants of a lingering dream.

Cassandra crying for help, telling him she loved him, him watching in horror as she plunged to her death. Then her beautiful face changing—no longer blond, blue-eyed Cassandra, but golden-eyed, fiery-haired Abby. His stomach knotted. He hadn't been able to save Cassandra, but nothing, he vowed, was going to keep him from protecting Abigail Holland.

CHAPTER THIRTEEN

A SPECTACULAR SUNRISE BRIGHTENED THE DESERT SKY EARLY THE following morning. Abby had never seen anything more beautiful than the pink, red, and gold painting the distant horizon, illuminating the mesquite and tall saguaro cactus strewn over the rugged landscape.

Dressed in jeans and boots, her hair plaited into a single braid, she applied sunscreen, then grabbed a wide-brimmed straw hat to protect her skin from the sun. Abby slung her camera over her shoulder, grabbed the black canvas backpack Gage had provided for the trip, and loaded her near-empty carry-on into the back of the SUV to await their return.

As she walked toward the barn, she noticed the white Chevy Suburban was gone. Maybe the men were watching the sunrise or hiking one of the desert trails. It was a credible explanation, but it bothered her to think they might be out there somewhere, watching.

Gage and Mateo were already in the barn when she arrived, Gage in faded jeans and a snug dark brown Henley, a big pair of worn cowboy boots on his feet. A trickle of awareness slid through her. How could the size of a man's boots turn her on?

Gage settled a brown, soft felt, Aussie-style cattleman's hat on his head and canted the brim low across his forehead. For an instant, her eyes met his beneath the brim of the hat, and desire clenched low in her belly. Dear God, the man could have stepped right out of a Hollywood movie.

One thing was certain, the guy in the expensively tailored suit behind the podium at the museum rocked in jeans and boots.

"Good morning." Gage strode toward her, grabbed the canvas backpack out of her hand, giving her a moment to catch her breath. "Let me help you with that."

He carried the pack over to where Kyle and the wrangler, Smiley Wilcox, a tough, stringy-looking cowboy in his sixties, with iron gray hair and a drooping mustache, were loading the mule panniers. Gage explained that the weight had to be evenly distributed on each side of the animals' backs to keep the load from shifting.

Abby unslung her camera and began shooting video, documenting the beginning of what she was sure would be an epic journey, hopefully with a spectacular ending.

Just as they were ready to set out, Kyle noticed that Abby's brown-and-white pinto had thrown a shoe.

"No worries," Kyle said, flashing her a dimpled grin. "I've got it covered." He quickly went into blacksmith mode and replaced the shoe, but the problem knocked them slightly off schedule.

As she watched the young cowboy work, she spotted Gage a few feet away. He was frowning, his jaw a hard line. Surely he wasn't jealous of Kyle? Kyle was good-looking, but compared to Gage, he was still a boy.

Finally, they were ready to go, the mules and horses loaded into Walt's big horse trailer for the drive down the road. Walt was behind the wheel of his dual-wheeled, extended-cab pickup, Kyle riding shotgun. Abby and Gage settled in the back seat, while Mateo rode with Smiley in the bed of the truck.

They headed for Lost Dutchman State Park, showed their permits, then drove up the road. Another few miles and the pickup turned off Apache Trail onto a dirt road winding up into the desert hills.

It was amazing country, with rugged vistas that stretched for miles, jagged mountains rising up from flat, endless desert, arid hills that climbed to rugged peaks.

When they reached the trailhead, Gage and Kyle unloaded the stock and checked the gear. Abby looked up to see Gage strapping on the big machete she had noticed among his gear, tying the sheath to his thigh.

Abby swung into the saddle of the pretty little paint named Sandy. Gage shoved his rifle into the scabbard on his saddle and swung up on a stout, thick-necked bay gelding named Cinnamon that everyone just called Sin. Abby thought the powerful horse was the perfect fit for Gage.

The horses began to sidestep and blow, eager to be on their way. Mateo settled into the saddle of a sorrel mare the color of a new copper penny. Abby smiled to think the animal's coat was about the same shade as her hair.

Walt wished them luck and reminded Kyle to be careful.

"Stay in touch as much as you can," he told his son. But cell service in the rugged mountains was spotty and unreliable at best. Gage had a satellite phone, but it was basically for emergencies.

They set out with Kyle in the lead, followed by Abby, Gage, then Mateo. Smiley brought up the rear, leading the pack mules.

With a final wave over her shoulder at Walt, Abby nudged the paint horse forward, following Kyle as they started up the trail. Ahead of them, drab sandy soil and rock formed high banks on both sides of the trail. Steeper mountains loomed in the distance, chunky layers that had broken into pieces and been eroded into whimsical shapes over thousands of years.

A couple of hours into the journey, what had started as a wide, well-worn trail used by hikers narrowed from several yards to a few feet in width. As they made the first major turn, following the map, the trail narrowed even more, the terrain changing from a hard-beaten footpath to a crumbling, rocky, ever-steepening track winding its way into the forbidding hills.

By noon, the excitement of the journey had dimmed a little. Two power bars and a cup of coffee weren't enough to keep Abby's stomach from growling. Unused to gripping the saddle, her thigh muscles were screaming for a break. As if Gage read her thoughts, he called a halt a few minutes later, and Abby said a silent prayer of thanks.

She groaned as she started to dismount, then felt Gage's big hands clamp around her waist, lifting her the rest of the way to the ground.

"Walk around a little," he said. "It'll help shake out the stiffness."

She just nodded.

"Stay on the trail and keep your eyes open for anything that bites."

Abby felt a chill though the day was sunny and warm. She'd seen a big, thick-bodied scorpion basking on a rock, its barbed stinger curled over its back. She would definitely keep her eyes open.

Being very careful where she walked, she made a pit stop behind a cluster of granite boulders, then backtracked to where Gage was handing out the sandwiches Mae had prepared for the first day of their journey, along with bottles of water. Once they made camp, they would be switching to refillable bottles, packing out the plastic ones.

"What about the stock?" Abby asked. "I thought Walt said there were catch basins along the way that would provide water for the horses and mules."

"Kyle says there's one up the trail a little farther. Since it rained last week, there should be plenty for the animals." For their own use, they would be boiling the water first or using a purification pen.

She glanced around. No water, nothing but desert, sandy rock layers, and gray granite boulders, but Walt and Kyle knew the area—at least as far as they would be taking the horses. After that, they would be following King's directions.

Abby finished her sandwich and drank half the bottle of water.

"Time to head out," Gage said, sliding his sunglasses back over his eyes.

Abby put hers on as well. "Where's Mateo?"

"He's scouting ahead. He'll meet us up the trail."

As Abby approached the paint, she felt Gage's big body behind her. "Need a hand?"

She smiled as she looked down at his cupped hands, stepped into them, and he hoisted her up into the saddle.

"Thanks." But her smile disappeared as the pain in her thighs radiated into her bottom. And the day was only getting started.

Gage swung aboard his big bay gelding, caught the reins of Mateo's sorrel, and set off up the trail to where his friend would be waiting.

Mateo was scouting ahead, as he always did on these trips. Gage trusted Kyle to know the area. The kid had been born in Apache Junction and had worked with his father since he was a boy. But Mateo had an uncanny ability to mesh with his surroundings, to understand the natural world in a way few men ever did.

Though Mateo had never been in the Superstitions, he had spent months in the deserts of other countries. On an archeological dig in Mexico, Gage had seen his skills. Mateo's input was invaluable, especially here. The Superstitions were known for unexpected perils that could turn deadly for the unwary.

Gage turned in the saddle to survey his surroundings, the rocky ridges and deep ravines they were heading into. It was dangerous country, and the reason he rode behind Abby, where he could keep an eye on her and make sure she stayed safe.

He almost smiled. He hadn't thought of the consequences of watching the shifting movement of her tiny waist above her sexy behind. For hours, he'd been half aroused when he needed to stay focused.

Gage sighed. Part of him regretted not sleeping with Abby when he'd had the chance. Another part worried it would only have made him want her more. Sooner or later, he intended to explore his feelings for her, but now was not the time.

As the trail grew steeper, then dropped into a low spot that dipped beneath an overhanging ledge, Gage forced his mind back where it belonged and spotted their destination, a granite depression filled with rainwater that had spilled down from the rocks above, washing the stones smooth over the years.

Kyle pulled his horse to a halt and dismounted. Gage swung down from the saddle, saw Abby do the same. Smiley led the mules a little closer to the water, swung down, and joined them as they led their thirsty animals to a place where they could drink their fill.

Mateo appeared out of the shadows and walked up beside him. "Dangerous country," Mateo said, retrieving the reins to his horse. "Lots of snakes."

"See any of the human variety?"

"No, but I saw plenty of human signs. We are not alone out here."

"You think it could be the men from Denver?"

"I do not know. The two men who showed up at the ranch last night must have left early this morning."

"Maybe they went hiking."

"Maybe," Mateo said, but a look passed between them. They would have to keep an eye out just in case.

"People come here hunting gold," Mateo said. "From what I have learned, there are many who search for the famous lost mine."

Gage nodded. "The Lost Dutchman. It's a pastime for locals, and finding it is every treasure hunter's dream."

"But you believe the old man found it, this King Farrell." He tipped his head toward Abby. "Your woman's *abuelo*."

"I told you she isn't my woman." *At least not yet.*

"We both know it will happen soon."

"I can't let it happen. Not out here."

Mateo looked at him with a touch of amusement but made no reply.

"I think the old man may have found something," Gage said. "Not sure exactly what. King Farrell was the best at what he did, and there are plenty of mines in the area. Abby has enough faith in him to stake everything she owns on this trip."

"If the gold is here, you will find it for her."

Gage smiled. "Thanks for the vote of confidence."

The horses and mules finished drinking, and the group prepared to continue up the trail. Gage wanted to reach the spot Kyle had chosen to camp well before nightfall. He wanted Mateo to scout the area, look for any sign of trouble, change locations if necessary.

Gage led the big bay up next to Abby's paint. "You doing okay?"

"I'm not used to riding." She tilted her head to look up at him from beneath the brim of her straw hat. "I'm stiff and sore, but I'll be okay in a day or two."

"We've got a ways to go before we stop for the night."

She nodded. "I'll be fine." She smiled. "I saw my first road-runner today. I couldn't believe how fast he was."

She glanced around, her gaze lingering on the walls of rock they were traveling through. "At first, this place . . . it just looks forbidding, but after a while you start to see things, like how amazingly blue the sky is, how the rocks give you a glimpse into the distant past

"I read somewhere the Superstitions are the remains of an ancient super volcano. What we're heading into is a giant caldera."

Her gaze returned to the big granite boulders ahead. "Imagine how this place would have looked back then."

"Yeah," he said, but he was having trouble taking his eyes off Abby. Instead of being frightened and repelled by the harsh desert terrain, she was enthralled by its magnificence. They were feelings Gage understood, the reason he traveled all over the world. It didn't matter where you went—there was always something new to see and learn.

Dragging his gaze away from her, he glanced around, saw Kyle, Mateo, and Smiley all waiting for them.

"We'd better go," he said a little gruffly, gripped Abby's waist and swung her up on the horse. She hissed out a breath when her bottom connected with the saddle; then she grinned.

Gage felt that grin all the way from his heart to his groin. He was in serious trouble with this woman, he thought as he shoved a boot into the stirrup and swung up on the bay.

And though this wasn't the time or place, sooner or later he was going to have her.

CHAPTER FOURTEEN

THEY MADE CAMP EIGHT MILES IN, THE LOCATION OF KING'S FIRST GPS coordinates, a spot marked on the map. Kyle chose an open, level area on the high side of the trail, not far from where water collected in a shallow rock depression, enough to take care of the horses and mules.

Abby had heard Kyle tell Gage that tomorrow by late afternoon, they should reach the point where the old wagon road cut their trail, and they would change course. About three miles down the wagon road was as far as they could travel on horseback.

Smiley would head back to the ranch with the horses, packing their trash out with him, while the rest of them continued on foot, Gage, Mateo, or Kyle leading the mules.

Abby wasn't sure if walking was good news or bad. She winced as an ache traveled up her thighs into her lower back. She still wasn't used to riding. But she was in good shape, and she had prepared herself for the trip. Maybe walking would be easier.

She thought of the spiny cactus she had so far avoided and scoffed. Nothing out here was easy.

As soon as they dismounted, the men went to work setting up camp. In the middle of the open space, Kyle built a fire, while Smiley watered the horses and mules. Mateo collected a bucket of water, which he put on to boil for cooking. Later they would boil more to fill their water bottles.

Meanwhile, Gage spread a tarp off to one side of the camp and motioned for Abby to bring her sleeping bag over and join him.

"Don't unzip it yet," he said. "You don't want any unwelcome visitors moving in. Same goes in the morning, roll up your bag as soon as you get up. And check your boots before you put them on."

She fought a shiver at the implications. She didn't want one of those scorpions she had seen joining her in bed or curling up in the toe of her hiking boot. She was grateful for all the things King had taught her, though camping in the pine forests of Colorado was far more hospitable than this hostile environment.

She wished she'd had a chance to join her grandfather on one of his adventures, but something always got in the way. College, her mother's illness, then losing her to cancer. Abby hadn't dated much over the years, had only been in one serious relationship, with a college professor named Benjamin Gallagher.

She'd given up her one chance to join King in his search for the Devil's Gold to be with Benjamin, who'd turned out to be everything she didn't want in a man. A liar and a cheat, not worth spit. He had broken her heart, though it could have been much worse. She was older now and wiser.

Abby smiled to think that at last she was actually here, part of an expedition in search of her grandfather's treasure. She only wished he could be with her.

Ignoring a sweep of sadness, Abby glanced across the clearing to where Kyle and Smiley worked to get supper ready. They had brought freeze-dried packaged meals, a choice of chicken and dumplings, biscuits and gravy, beef stroganoff, or chili mac.

"Not exactly a gourmet dinner," Gage drawled as they sat around the campfire and dug into what out here passed for food. "But it'll keep us going." He smiled. "We'll all be looking forward to Mae's cooking by the time we get back."

That's for sure, Abby thought as she took another bite and tried not to grimace at the taste. Kyle did after-supper cleanup while she and Gage walked up a game trail to the top of the hill.

This time of year, the sun set at about six-thirty, painting the sky in pink, turquoise, and red, a lovely backdrop for the giant saguaro that stood like sentinels guarding the mountains.

"It's beautiful, isn't it?" she said.

Gage's eyes followed hers to the colors saturating the distant peaks. "Every place in the world is different. If you look, you'll find each has its own special beauty." He glanced down at her. "I'm glad you're able to see it here."

Her gaze held his. "How could I not?"

Gage reached out and ran a finger down her cheek. "Some people don't. They refuse to leave their comfort zones, look at things from a different perspective."

Abby fell silent, her gaze still locked with his. She couldn't look away from the intensity in his blue eyes. He moved a fraction closer. She thought he was going to kiss her, and anticipation sizzled through her. Instead, he turned away.

"It's been a long day," he said. "We'd better get back."

Abby managed to nod. "All right." They headed down the gentle slope and returned to camp. Exhausted, she opened her bedroll, took off her boots, then slid into the lightweight bag.

Overhead, an array of stars, like crystals on black velvet, captured her attention. Her eyelids were beginning to feel heavy when a pack of coyotes began to howl, jolting her awake.

"Easy," Gage said. "It's just coyotes. Nothing to worry about."

"I know. I've heard them before, just never this close." She looked over at him and smiled. "I like hearing them. It's kind of nice knowing they're out there."

"They can be pretty tough on your house cat, but they aren't as dangerous as wolves."

Abby said nothing. Her gaze had wandered back to Gage, and it occurred to her he would be sleeping right beside her. She smiled as she closed her eyes. Like the coyotes, it was nice to know he was there.

By noon the following day, the sun was a bright silver-gold orb, heating the landscape. As Gage's horse, Sin, plodded along the trail, vultures circled overhead, big, black, and ominous. Death was out there. Gage never forgot that when he was in rough country like this.

Yesterday's ride into the mountains had been easy. *Too easy*, said the tingle at the back of his neck. It was a subliminal warning, and Gage always listened.

As Kyle had predicted, just three miles in, they crossed the old wagon road, turned their animals uphill, and followed it. As the old Apache had said, the worn ruts in the road zigzagged steeply upward, and there were obstacles—boulders that had washed down the mountain and places where the ground had shifted—making it nearly impassable.

A few miles farther, the wagon road narrowed to a single wheel rut. Along the trail, in places, the ground had fallen away on one side, leaving a drop-off of several hundred feet. The horses plodded onward, but the going was getting rougher.

Gage finally called a halt, and they stopped to rest, giving the animals a break and Gage time to look at King's notes and the map. Abby and Mateo joined him.

"We've reached the next checkpoint," Gage said, using his handheld Garmin Montana GPS to confirm the longitude and latitude written on the map. He checked King's notes.

"'When the wagon road turns south, look north over the ridge and you can see the Four Peaks lined up as one. In another direction, you can see a high, needle-pointed rock. At the base of the rock, there is a drainage we used for water.'"

Gage searched the horizon, located the points King referred to, glanced over to see Abby doing the same. Looking downhill into the rocks below, he spotted the water hole King had mentioned.

"We'll make camp somewhere close," he said. "Lead the animals down to water. In the morning, Smiley can take the string and head back to the ranch." There was cell service where they had unloaded the trailer. Smiley would be able to call Walt to come pick him up.

Everyone set to work. Kyle and Smiley had a practiced routine, Smiley caring for the livestock while Kyle readied the camp. As Gage unrolled the tarp for their sleeping bags, his gaze went in search of Abby.

He walked over to Kyle, who was scrounging wood for the fire. "Have you seen Abby?"

"She took her camera and went for a walk. Said she wanted to get some background shots before it got dark, said she wouldn't go far."

An uneasy feeling slipped through him. "Which direction?"

Kyle pointed toward a cluster of granite boulders just a few yards away. As soon as Gage rounded the boulders, he spotted her, standing stock-still not far away, every muscle rigid, the color leached out of her face.

Warning bells went off in his head. Gage heard the distinctive rattle, and his whole body tightened with dread. Kyle must have heard it, too. He dropped the armload of wood he was carrying and hurried toward them. Gage held up a hand, warning him back, and eased quietly closer.

"Don't move," he said softly, drawing the machete out of the sheath on his thigh. A diamond-back rattlesnake nearly as thick as his bicep hissed and rattled, coiled and ready to strike from its place on a rock ledge that was eye level with Abby's face.

Gage eased close beside her, slowly raising the blade. "Stay exactly where you are." For an instant, Abby's eyes sliced to his, and he read her fear. Abby didn't move, and Gage swung the blade, its deadly arc neatly severing the snake's head from its thick body, sending it flying into the brush a few feet away.

Gage sheathed the knife with a metallic ring, took a couple of steps, and swept Abby into his arms.

"I've got you. Everything's okay."

Shaking all over, she burrowed into him and just held on. Gage tightened his hold. From the corner of his eye, he saw Kyle and Smiley drifting back to camp now that Abby was safe.

Gage took a deep breath, fighting images of Abby and the snake, trying not to think about what could have happened. Another deep breath and he managed to block the memory of the icy fear that had sliced through him when he'd seen the snake's forked tongue slithering out, almost touching Abby's lovely face.

She rested her cheek on his chest. "I was watching everywhere I walked. I-I didn't think to look up at the ledge."

He smoothed a hand over her hair. "It's all right. It wasn't your fault. Things happen in places like this." Which was the reason he hadn't wanted her to come along.

Abby eased away. "When I first saw you carrying that big knife, I thought it was overkill. You know what I mean? Now I'm very glad you had it."

"Learned a long time ago, a big knife can do everything a little knife can and a whole lot more."

"So that snake found out." She glanced back at the ledge. "He was really big. King said the bigger they are, the less venom in their bite. He said they get smarter as they get older." She gave him a wobbly smile. "They learn to save enough poison to catch their dinner."

Abby had almost been bitten by the biggest, ugliest rattlesnake Gage had ever seen, and she was smiling. He desperately wanted to kiss her. He wanted to hold her and reassure himself she was okay.

"We'd better get back," he said instead.

Abby nodded, took a step, and her legs gave way beneath her. Gage caught her around the waist before she hit the ground.

"Post-adrenaline effect," he said, keeping her upright and steady. "It'll wear off in a minute." Instead of lifting her into his arms and carrying her back, as every instinct told him to do, he gave her a minute to compose herself.

"You ready?"

She nodded and started walking, her legs still a little shaky. He'd been staying close to her. From now on, he'd be staying even closer. In this rough country, there was no way to know when danger was going to strike next.

And the warning was still there, tingling at the back of his neck.

CHAPTER FIFTEEN

*T*HE WEATHER TURNED DICEY, FAT BLACK CLOUDS BILLOWING UP OVER the horizon. The warm, sunny weather predicted in the Apache Junction newspaper, the *East Valley Tribune*, had changed.

Abby waved goodbye to Smiley, who started down the trail back to the ranch at first light, the horses roped together single file behind him.

"Is he going to be all right?" Abby asked Kyle. "He'll be out there by himself tonight." The two of them were working side by side, both of them repacking the gear they had taken off their horses and would now be carrying in their backpacks.

A few feet away, Gage did the same, his knife strapped to his thigh, his sheathed rifle within easy reach on one of the mule panniers.

"Smiley won't be alone," Kyle said. "For safety's sake, my dad and I made a last-minute change before we left. Dad's riding in today, meeting Smiley at the halfway point. They'll camp for the night and ride back together in the morning."

"That's good. After what happened with the snake, I can see how easy it is to get hurt out here."

Kyle's gaze traveled to Gage, who was still loading his backpack. Now that they would be traveling on foot, Gage's jeans and cowboy boots were gone, headed back with the horses, replaced by cargo pants and hiking boots. "This is new to you, but Gage seems to know what he's doing."

"He's traveled all over the world, been in a lot of dangerous places."

"It shows." Kyle looked back at Abby. "So I guess you two are . . . involved?"

"Not exactly," Abby said.

"Exactly," Gage said as he walked up. "At the moment, we're focusing on finding what we came here for. Once we're home, our priorities won't be the same."

Kyle looked at Abby. "Good to know." Tugging his straw hat lower, he slung his pack over his shoulder, turned, and walked away.

Abby wanted to call him back, clarify the situation. She liked Kyle Jenkins. And she and Gage weren't really together.

"He's a good kid, but he isn't for you," Gage said.

Her hackles went up. "How do you know? Maybe he's exactly what I need."

"I'm what you need, and we both know it. Now let's get packed up and get going. Be best if we could make a few miles before it starts raining. We'll need to find some kind of shelter before then. From the looks of it, the tarps won't be enough."

But Abby was still stuck on *I'm what you need, and we both know it.*

As if he were some sort of mind reader. But part of her believed him. Gage was exactly right for her. Or at least he seemed to be. Of course, that was what she had thought about Benjamin.

Ben had said he wanted to travel as much as she did. They would be a perfect fit. He had family money, so he could do whatever he wanted, and he wanted her to go with him.

What he really wanted was a different woman in his bed every place they went. Their first stop was San Diego, where she told herself her suspicions about him were wrong. They made it as far as Hawaii before Abby caught him in bed with a waitress. It took half her savings to pay for her plane ticket home.

Gage attracted women with the ease of a snake charmer, but the relationships never lasted. Unlike Ben, he didn't deny it. Though she might be fun for a while, Abby wasn't sure she wanted to be just another one of Gage's women.

Mateo appeared out of nowhere and walked up beside them. "Storm is coming," he said. "Big thunderclouds. It looks bad. I will go ahead, see what kind of shelter I can find."

"All right, but don't go too far," Gage said. "This is brutal country. Be worse once it starts to rain. We need to stay together."

Mateo nodded, moving the thick black hair he'd tied back with a strip of rawhide. He took off walking, following the narrow path that showed on King's map, a steep winding trail that dropped down into a canyon.

Gage laid King's map next to a topo map and compared the two. "Rough going ahead. You ready to get started?"

"I'm ready." She picked up her backpack, but Gage took it from her hands and hefted it a couple of times. "You're overweight but not by much."

"I can carry it."

"I'm sure you can—for a while. Once we reach shelter, we can sort through it, redistribute some of it."

She bit back a disagreeable comment. She had pared her stuff down that morning, kept only the basics, and sent everything else back with Smiley and the horses. But as Gage held the canvas pack up so she could stick her arms through the straps, then settled it on her back, it did feel a little heavier than the twenty-five percent of her body weight—less than thirty pounds—it was supposed to be.

And as they headed up the narrow trail beneath an ominous sky and the pack began to weigh her down, she figured Gage, as usual, was right.

Today he walked up front. Following King's map, they had left the main trail, so this was new territory for Kyle as well as the rest of them. With Gage taking point, Abby in the middle, and Kyle leading the mules behind her, they set off under ominous skies and a strong, steady wind. Thunder rumbled in the distance, and a light mist began to fall.

They donned their rain slickers and kept walking. The wind picked up while the temperature dropped. Gage kept moving, the mules plodding along, Mort in front, Snickers behind him, their heads down and their long ears drooping.

By the time they caught up with Mateo, they were hiking into a steady, driving rain.

Mateo pointed toward a dark spot in the side of the mountain. "We go up there. It is a good climb but worth it. The cave is deep, but open. No creatures. I gathered some firewood, enough to keep us warm."

"Good work," Gage said.

"I'll tend the mules," Kyle said.

Gage turned to Abby. "I'll go up first and drop my pack, come back for yours and help you up."

She wanted to argue. If she couldn't carry her weight, she wouldn't have come. "Fine," she said, taking the easier route.

Gage frowned at the hint of irritation in her voice, turned, and started climbing, his powerful arms and legs carrying him effortlessly up through the rocks. Abby waited until he was halfway to the mouth of the cave and started up behind him.

The path was steep and rocky, but not impassible. She kept her eyes peeled for snakes and scorpions, placed one hiking boot carefully in front of the other, watching for solid footing and hand holds, and just kept climbing.

Gage was swearing when she reached the cave, ducked inside, and dropped her pack.

"I thought I told you to wait."

Abby propped a hand on her hip beneath her rain slicker. "I don't want special treatment, Gage. I'm a member of this team. I wouldn't be here if I thought I couldn't keep up."

His jaw tightened. She could tell he was holding on to his temper. Then his shoulders relaxed. "You're right. You're obviously in good physical condition. If your pack gets heavy, let me know and we'll adjust it. We can fit a little more on the mules."

Pleasure at his words slipped through her. "It *is* a little heavy," she conceded. "I'll go back through it, see what I can do without."

Their eyes met, and a moment of understanding passed between them. Then Mateo arrived, and right behind him, Kyle stepped into the cave. He slung his backpack against the wall. "Good spot. I'll have to remember where it is if I come back this way again."

The cave was really more of a windblown, scooped-out depression in the side of a rock wall, not too deep, with a wide opening in the front. Mateo built a fire, which warmed the cave without being too smoky, and the place was dry enough that they could shed their slickers.

They ate bagels, hard salami, and cheese for a late lunch. Gage went over the maps again and checked his gear, while the rest of them sat back and watched the rain beating down, so heavy at times it was difficult to see outside.

By late afternoon, when the downpour hadn't lessened, it was obvious they would be spending the night. Kyle went down to check on the mules and bring back more wood, and Mateo volunteered to cook supper. Clearly, he wasn't fond of freeze-dried beef stroganoff.

As Abby watched him work, she felt Gage's presence beside her. His Aussie soft-brimmed hat was gone, his thick brown hair still damp from the misty air. She wanted to reach up and run her fingers through it, push it back from his forehead. A little curl of heat slipped through her. She wanted to lean up and press her mouth against his.

"I've spread the tarp," he said, distracting her, thank God. "Where's your sleeping bag?"

Snared by something Mateo was doing, instead of answering, her gaze swung to the long white coil of meat he was pulling out of a plastic bag.

"Is that . . . ?" Even with the skin off, she knew. "The rattlesnake you killed? Mateo's cooking it for supper?"

A smile broke over Gage's face. "It's supposed to taste like chicken. I think it's sweeter, more like lobster."

"Lobster. Right. I don't think I can convince myself."

Gage chuckled.

"I'll get my bedroll," she said. There was plenty of room to move around in the cave without bending over. She fetched her backpack, untied her bedroll from the bottom, and spread it open next to Gage's, but didn't unzip it. Though the cave seemed uninhabited, she didn't want to take any chances.

As darkness fell, Gage turned on the lamp. The smell of roasting meat drifted across the cave, and her stomach grumbled. Though she didn't eat much, supper wasn't as bad as she had imagined. She'd seen rattlesnake served as an appetizer on gourmet menus in the city. She told herself she was eating a very expensive meal.

When they finished, Kyle and Mateo cleaned up, and Abby headed for her bedroll.

"I could get used to this," Gage said, watching as she sat down and pulled off her boots.

"What? Sleeping in a cave?"

"Sleeping next to you," he said. "Though I doubt we'd get much sleep."

Her abdomen clenched. She flicked him a sideways glance. He slept without a shirt, and her mouth watered at the sight of his heavily muscled chest. "You haven't forgotten your rules, have you?"

In the light of the lamp, his gaze ran over her. "Sadly, no."

But when the lamp went out and Kyle and Mateo drifted toward their bedrolls, she heard Gage move, felt the heat of his big body as he leaned toward her, caught her chin, and his mouth came down over hers.

Heat spread out through her limbs. She made a little sound in her throat as he gentled the kiss, then pulled away.

"Just so you don't forget what's going to happen when we get back."

Abby said nothing. Her lips were still tingling, her heart beating too fast. She could still feel the warmth of Gage's bare chest through the fabric of her T-shirt, the way his muscles bunched when he moved. His kiss was torture of the very best kind.

Abby couldn't help thinking that in the chess game she and Gage were playing, it was her turn to make the next move.

CHAPTER SIXTEEN

*D*ARKNESS SETTLED OVER THE CAVE. THE SOUND OF THE STEADILY pounding rain drew Gage into a deep, unfettered slumber. He'd been asleep most of the night when a loud rumbling shook the stone floor beneath his sleeping bag, and he jerked upright, his whole body going rigid.

"What's happening?" Abby clutched his arm in a death grip.

Gage grabbed his flashlight and flipped it on, rolled to his feet, and ran to the mouth of the cave.

Mateo was already there. "Flash flood. The water washes down the side of the mountain through the canyon below." Where they had been only hours ago.

Gage shined the light on the ravine they'd been traversing, saw uprooted trees and branches rushing past in a sea of brown, muddy water. Boulders were swept away, patches of dirt crumbling off the mountainside into the violent onslaught.

"What about the mules?" Gage asked as Kyle appeared beside him.

"Hobbled them up on the slope of the hill. Damned good thing."

"The water would have taken them if you hadn't."

Kyle nodded. "My dad knows these mountains. When he talks, I'm smart enough to listen."

Gage clamped a hand on his shoulder.

"What about the trail?" Abby asked anxiously, staring down at the dark, turbulent river dimly illuminated by the spot of light shining down from so far above. "It's going to be washed away."

"Only parts of it," Gage said. "We'll have to make adjustments. We won't know how much of a problem it is until morning. Nothing we can do until then." But dawn was close. With all the excitement, there was no way he'd be able to go back to sleep.

"I need to check the mules," Kyle said, beginning to pace the floor of the cave. "They'll be frightened to death. I don't want anything to happen to them."

Gage shook his head. "Too dangerous. One slip and you'll wind up in the water. In minutes, you could be dead." He panned the ground with the flashlight, but the mules were too far away to see.

Time passed. Minutes turned into an hour.

"The rain has stopped," Mateo said, his ear tuned to the quiet that had replaced the drumbeat against the walls outside the cave. "It won't take long for the water to slow enough for us to leave."

Gage studied the horizon, saw the faint gray light of dawn. "Let's pack up and be ready to go."

"There is still enough wood for a fire," Mateo said. "I will make coffee while we wait."

Gage nodded.

By the time it was light enough to see, the floodwaters had dropped to a muddy trickle, and all of them were packed and ready to leave. The bad news was, the water had washed out a portion of the rocks below the cave, taking out the path they had used to make the ascent.

It was tough going up. Going down could be deadly.

"We're roping up," Gage said. "The rocks are going to be like glass, the handholds unreliable. The climb's bound to be treacherous."

"I'll go first," Kyle volunteered, tugging down the brim of his damp straw cowboy hat. "I need to get to the mules."

Gage nodded. "I'll anchor you."

Grabbing the nylon rope tied to his pack, he made a loop and lifted it over Kyle's head, pulled it snug around his waist. Gage set his boot against the cave wall and fed out the line as Kyle began his descent. He picked his way down the steep rock face, slipped a couple of times, drawing a gasp from Abby, but Gage kept the rope taut. Kyle made the trip safely to the washed-out trail and disappeared in search of the mules.

"Mateo, you're next." Gage pulled up the rope and prepared for the second man to make the trip. Mateo was agile and experienced. He waved when he reached the bottom.

"Your turn, Abby."

"What about you? Who's going to anchor you?"

He grinned. "If I fall, I guess you'll just have to catch me."

"It's not funny, Gage."

His smile slipped away. "Somebody has to be the anchor, honey. I'm biggest, therefore the logical choice."

He roped her up the same way he had the others. "Mateo will be waiting at the bottom. If you get in trouble, remember, I've got you."

She nodded, adjusted the rope, and stepped out of the cave. The first half of the descent went well as Abby carefully picked her way down the muddy trail. Then the going got tougher. The ground was wet and slick with stones and debris, big chunks of the path swept away.

Gage tensed as Abby stepped on a rock, which twisted beneath her weight, and her feet went out from under her. She cried out as she slid down the mountain and swung out into thin air. The rope went taut in Gage's hands, and though he maintained control, his mouth went dry.

This was Abby. He couldn't let anything happen to her.

Gage tightened his grip on the rope and pulled her back far enough for her feet to find purchase on solid ground.

"I'm all right!" She waved and called up to him.

It didn't lessen the frantic pounding of his heart or the flash of memory that carried him back to another perilous journey. Back to a woman's terrified cries and his failed efforts to save her.

Gage shook the memory off as Abby reached the bottom and stepped out of the loop around her waist. Gage brought the rope back up, looped the coil over his shoulder, and started down the steep rock face. Where the route got dicey, he tied the rope around a boulder and hand-over-handed the rest of his way down the mountain to what was left of the washed-out trail.

Abby was waiting. She walked over and threw her arms around his neck. "I don't care if I'm breaking the rules. I'm just glad you're down safely." Gage allowed himself a moment to enjoy her embrace, burying his face in her hair.

"You scared me," he admitted.

"I'm okay." She eased back out of his arms. "But one of the mules is gone."

"Drowned?"

She shook her head. "Kyle thinks he broke loose and headed back to the ranch."

"Which mule?"

Kyle answered as he walked up, leading the second mule. "Snickers, the one we were using to carry your equipment and some of the maps. I left the panniers under a staked down tarp so everything is there, just no way to carry it."

"We'll pare everything down to basics, pack Mort with the heavy stuff, and divide the rest of the load among us."

"Whatever we leave behind," Kyle said, "my dad and I can pack out later."

"That sounds good. Let's get going." Gage dug through everything in both mules' panniers, extracting the most important items. "We'll only need enough pellets to feed one animal. We're boiling and treating our water. With the rain, the water basins should be full, but it's imperative to have at least enough on hand for emergencies."

Like the weather changing and the basin drying up, or the water holes not being where they were shown on the map.

"I hate to leave my digital camera," Abby said. "But my little Elph 190 is a lot smaller and takes great video and stills."

Gage nodded. They sorted through everything, bringing the food, pellets for the mule, emergency water, the maps, and as much of their tarps and prospecting gear as they could manage. Gage always carried the sat phone and charger in his pack, so that wasn't a problem.

It took over an hour to get organized, then the rest of the morning to navigate around the washout, using game trails to move through the hostile landscape. The rain had thrown them off schedule yesterday. After the flash flood, today's slow traveling threw them even further behind.

Mateo scouted ahead, returning to guide them along the safest route back to the trail marked on King's map. It was after noon, the sun burning down on them, hotter today than yesterday, the air steamy after all the rain.

"Let's take a break," Gage said. "We need to hydrate and power down some calories, and I need to check the GPS, see how close we are to reaching our original route."

"I need a pit stop," Abby said, heading for a granite outcropping just up the trail.

"Don't go far," Gage warned, thinking of her brush with the rattlesnake.

She waved him off and disappeared around the boulders out of sight.

A few feet below, the flash-flood washout trailed off to the right, while the game trail that Mateo had them following rounded the mountain to the left.

Gage was just finishing a power bar, chasing it with a bottle of boiled water, when he heard Abby scream. Fear hit him as the sound of his name echoed through the mountains. Gage started running.

CHAPTER SEVENTEEN

*A*BBY LEANED BACK AGAINST THE BOULDER, HER LEGS SHAKING SO badly she was afraid they wouldn't hold her up. She felt light-headed, her mouth bone dry.

The washout caused by the floodwaters snaked through the dead grass and boulders a few feet below. The violent current had carried a huge clump of debris: cottonwood branches, root balls from upended trees, spiny cactus, and medium-sized boulders, a deadly knot that swept down the ravine, wiping out everything in its path.

Including the man with his eyes open, staring sightlessly at the silver orb burning down from the sky. The deadly knot had jammed into a tight spot between two towering rock walls, holding its prey captive.

"Abby!" Gage shouted her name as she spotted him racing toward her. He caught her shoulders. "What is it? What's wrong?" He must have noticed the pallor of her face or felt her trembling because a big arm slid around her waist, and he drew her closer. "Tell me what happened."

She swallowed, pointed toward the grisly corpse—the broken body, the bones angled into impossible positions.

"Jesus." Gage let out a slow breath and turned her into his shoulder to block the scene. "Poor bastard must have got swept up in the floodwaters."

Abby hung on for a moment, then took a calming breath and

eased away. She thought about the man who had died, couldn't help wondering about his family. Her heart squeezed. Another victim of the notorious Superstitions.

She flicked a glance at the dead man, then quickly looked away. "Surely he wasn't out here by himself." She swallowed. "If he was with friends, why haven't they come looking for him?"

"Maybe they've been looking but haven't been able to find him."

Mateo and Kyle ran up just then. Gage pointed and Kyle cursed.

"One thing my dad taught me," Kyle said. "You don't mess around with the weather out here. It rains, you get your ass somewhere safe." He looked over at Gage. "You've got a sat phone, right? We need to call 911."

Gage nodded. "I'll take care of it." The hand at Abby's waist firmly urged her away from the disturbing scene. She let him guide her back to where the mule was tethered. Their packs rested on the ground nearby.

Gage took off his wraparound Ray-Bans and rubbed his eyes, then shoved the sunglasses back in place. He dug out his sat phone, activated it, and made the call, explaining what had happened and giving the 911 dispatcher the GPS coordinates of the victim's body. The sheriff's department would be responding. Gage promised to wait at the scene until law enforcement arrived.

"They're bringing in a chopper," Gage said. "We'll need to make a statement once they get here."

"I wonder who he is," Abby said. "Or was." She looked up to see Mateo quietly walking toward them, the dark skin over cheekbones stretched taut.

"I think he is one of the men who have been following us," Mateo said.

"What the hell?" Gage frowned. "Why didn't you tell me?"

"Yesterday I spotted their tracks, three men, maybe more. Then it started raining."

"And?"

"I wanted to be sure, but the rain destroyed any sign."

"But you think a group of men have been following us and the dead guy was one of them."

"Yes."

Gage swore. "Let's find out if you're right." He started walking, and Abby hurried to catch up with him.

"What are you doing?" Kyle asked as he joined them.

"The dead man's fully dressed. Good chance he's got ID somewhere on him."

"What about the police?" Abby asked.

"Sheriff's department," he corrected. "We'll tell them the truth—we searched the body trying to find some identification." They reached the spot above the washout.

"Stay here," Gage said. As if she had any desire to go near a dead man.

Kyle stood next to her, watching Gage and Mateo make the descent, picking their way carefully down the slope, then over the debris in the washout. The body appeared to be wedged in tight.

"Dad and I ran across an old skeleton once. Bones were scattered. Never found out who it was." His gaze fixed on the body. "Not the same as this."

"No . . ." Abby whispered.

Gage reached into one of the front pockets of the man's jeans, then searched the other. Pulling out a black leather wallet, he stuck it into a deep pocket of his cargo pants. Both men climbed up from the washout.

"You found it," Abby said when he returned.

Gage took out the wallet and flipped it open, read the guy's driver's license. "Boyd McGrath. Address on Lawrence Street in Denver."

Adrenaline jolted through her. "Denver. It's got to be them."

"One of them, for sure. I took a good look at the body. Tall. Lean, broad-shouldered build. Could be the guy who attacked you."

"Attacked you?" Kyle repeated. "What's going on here?"

"It's a long story," Gage said. "You know we're hunting gold.

We didn't tell you other people are also on the hunt. They believe we've got the information they need to find it. We hoped we'd left them in Denver." He held up the wallet. "Doesn't look that way."

"Boyd McGrath . . ." Abby repeated. "Why does that name sound familiar?" Her head jerked up. "Oh, my God, I know who he is. I remember my cousin Jude talking about him. Boyd was in the military. Jude idolized him. I had a feeling my cousin had something to do with this."

"Looks like you were right."

Abby made a little sound in her throat. "I didn't want the man dead. I just wanted him to leave me alone."

"If he's the guy who attacked you, his greed made him dead. You didn't have a damned thing to do with it."

"How did they find you?" Kyle asked.

"Don't know for sure," Gage said.

"My cousin, Jude, is a gamer. He can get just about anything off the internet. He could have tracked my credit card. Or Gage's."

"Those two guys who checked in at the ranch the night before we left," Gage said. "We never saw their faces. Could be Boyd McGrath was one of them."

"His body's too mangled for me to recognize him," Kyle said. "Let me see the picture on his driver's license."

Gage flipped open the wallet. Kyle studied the photo and shook his head. "I don't know. I wasn't paying much attention. I was busy making sure we were ready to leave the next morning. If he was one of them, could be they were watching us when we left."

Gage nodded. "We lost valuable time yesterday. Without all the gear, they'd be able to travel a whole lot faster. Could have been right behind us by the time the rain started."

Mateo looked at Kyle. "If they ran into Smiley on his way out, he could have given them the location of our last campsite."

Abby's gaze jerked to Gage. "You don't think they would have hurt him?"

"I need to call my dad," Kyle said. "He and Smiley are due back at the ranch today. They may be in cell range by now."

Abby's heart pounded as she waited for Kyle's call to go through. His body relaxed a little when Walt picked up the phone.

"Dad. I was hoping you'd have çell service by now. We've run into some trouble. Are you and Smiley okay?"

She could only hear part of the conversation, but from the grim look that settled over Kyle's features, it wasn't good news. He told his father what had happened. Walt said something she couldn't hear. Kyle ended the call and handed the phone back to Gage.

"Dad's okay. They're about a mile from the horse trailer. Smiley's in pretty rough shape. Just got three bars or they would have called."

Worry darkened Gage's features. "What happened?"

"Dad says three men waylaid Smiley on his way to the rendezvous point. They beat him up, threatened to shoot him if he didn't tell them which way we went. Smiley gave them our last location, figured you and Mateo were savvy enough to handle them if they managed to find you. Figured they probably wouldn't— even though they'd talked to old Spitting Crow about which way you were going."

Mateo spoke up. "He is the Apache who told me about the wagon road."

"They must have someone with them who knows the mountains," Gage said. "Any idea who it could be?"

Kyle nodded. "Guy named Ray Peters would be my guess. Ray's in his forties, lived here all his life. He's the kind of guy who's always got an angle. You don't want to turn your back on him, but he knows the Superstitions almost as well as my dad."

"Wouldn't Smiley have recognized him?"

"Maybe he stayed out of sight. If it's Ray, he'd have at least one of his cronies with him. Doesn't go anywhere without backup."

Gage stared off toward the stark, cactus-covered mountains in the distance. "Smiley needs to call the police."

Kyle shook his head. "Not his way. My dad, either. Dad wants me to bring you out. I told him there was no way you'd quit when we were so close."

Gage's blue eyes zeroed in on Abby. "Walt's right. Be smarter to head back to the ranch."

Abby felt the words like a punch in the stomach. "You can't be serious. You said yourself greed killed Boyd. He got greedy and paid the price."

"Abby—"

She turned to Kyle. "There's a hundred percent bonus if you'll keep going. We should be there by late tomorrow, the next morning at the latest. What do you say?"

Kyle lifted his battered straw hat and resettled it low on his forehead. "You really think you're gonna find something?"

"My grandfather thought so. So do the men following us. So yes, I think there's something there, and I think finding it's worth the risk."

"All right, I'm in." Kyle looked at Gage. "What do you say, Gage?"

Abby's gaze locked on Gage. "You've been in worse situations— I know you have. We can't give up. Not yet."

Gage started shaking his head. "If I were by myself—"

"Well, you aren't. You're with me, and we had a deal. If we go back, I'll just start over with someone who won't quit on me when the going gets tough."

Gage's jaw hardened. A knot bunched in his cheek. "Damn you, Abby. That's not the reason, and you know it."

She lifted her chin. "Kyle's willing to go. If you want to head back, maybe we'll just go on without you."

"Whoa, wait a minute." Kyle held up a hand. "I'm not getting in the middle of this."

Gage's blue eyes could have burned through steel. A muscle jerked in his cheek. "All right, Abby, you win." He turned to Kyle. "Looks like the hunt is still on. Soon as the police are finished, we're on our way." Gage cast her a last furious glance and stalked off down the trail.

Abby felt a pinch in her heart. She had goaded him unfairly, and she knew it. Gage wasn't a quitter. He was only trying to protect her. But she hadn't come this far to fail.

She noticed the tight muscles across his back and his stiff shoulders as he retreated. She'd been bluffing about Kyle. As much as she wanted to find the treasure, the two of them going in without backup, without Gage and Mateo, would be stupid.

She ached to tell him the truth. And find a way to convince him to forgive her.

CHAPTER EIGHTEEN

FOLLOWING GAGE'S GPS COORDINATES, THE HELICOPTER ARRIVED within the hour, landing on a flat spot on the slope of a mountain a hundred yards away. Four people got out: two uniformed sheriff's deputies and two CSIs, one of them a woman.

The female CSI, with a camera slung over her shoulder, headed directly for the body, accompanied by her partner. While the deputies surveyed the storm damage and prepared to interview Gage and the others, the CSIs worked the death scene, which included photographing the surroundings and extracting the body from the debris.

Deputy Christopher Mayes, a muscular African American man in his forties, began asking questions, starting with Gage. His partner, Deputy Salazar, younger, with coarse black hair and dark eyes, led Kyle aside and interviewed him.

Since McGrath's death was almost certainly an accident, the questions were straightforward and didn't take long. Gage had talked to Abby, and they had agreed not to mention the possible connection between Boyd McGrath and the attack on Abby in Denver. There was no proof, and they had enough trouble already.

The deputies completed their questions before the CSIs were finished removing the body and dealing with the death scene, but the afternoon was beginning to wane, so the cops released them to continue their journey.

Gage had spoken only a few words to Abby since their earlier argument. Every time he thought of her defiance, her willingness to ignore his dictates and put herself at risk, he got angry all over again. Though he admitted to a grudging hint of respect.

Abby's determination was one of the things that had attracted him to her in the first place. Along with her willingness to go head-to-head with him, which few men and even fewer women had the nerve to do.

It took several hours of hiking through unexplored territory, much of it uphill, to find the original trail marked on King's map. Gage and Kyle were now both openly carrying weapons, Gage's .45 caliber Smith and Wesson holstered on his belt, Kyle armed with a Glock 19. Now that they knew they were being followed, it was better to be prepared.

The route forward was even more difficult than what they had endured so far, with sections of the trail crumbled away, leaving only a ledge barely wide enough for the sure-footed mule to pass.

They stopped to rest, power snack, and hydrate. With only an hour of daylight left, Mateo set off ahead to find a place to camp. After they'd left the death scene, they headed into more unfamiliar terrain, and Mateo had taken the lead.

"Keep your eyes open," Gage warned him. "There's no way to know if we've still got men dogging our trail."

Mateo nodded and quietly disappeared around the first bend.

They continued up the trail, so steep in places Gage wasn't sure the mule could make it. But old Mort was as stubborn as Abby, and Kyle seemed to take the harsh conditions as a personal challenge.

The days had been steadily growing hotter, the afternoon sun throbbing down mercilessly. Gage figured Abby was exhausted, but she didn't complain. She was in the hunt all the way, and he couldn't help admiring her for it.

They kept pushing onward. By the time Mateo returned, everyone was more than ready to end the day.

"Good place to camp ahead," Mateo said. "Not far. Trail gets better after that."

"That's good news," Gage said.

With their upended schedule, they wouldn't be spending the night at the GPS coordinates that indicated where King's campsite had been. But tomorrow, unless something went wrong, they would reach the last X marked on King's map.

Abby would either find her grandfather's gold, or she wouldn't.

Gage tried to quell his mounting excitement, but he was a treasure hunter. Abby wanted to find the Devil's Gold—and so did he.

It was dark, a campfire burning, their packaged dinners consumed. Gage still hadn't talked to Abby. Needing some space to clear his head, he set off for a spot he'd noticed at the edge of the clearing. In the distance, moonlight outlined barren peaks.

His mind went to Abby and the fight they'd had. As if his thoughts had called her, light footfalls came up behind him, and small hands settled on his shoulders. Gage tensed.

"I'm sorry," she said. "I know you aren't a quitter. I know you aren't afraid of those men."

Gage turned to face her.

"Please don't be angry," she said.

He studied her face in the silvery light, the smooth curve of her cheek, the full pinkness of her lips. "If I hadn't agreed to continue, would you have left with Kyle?" The words came out of nowhere. He hadn't realized that aside from his concern for Abby, he was jealous.

"Finding the treasure means everything to me—you've known that from the start. But I know going without you and Mateo would have been a stupid thing to do."

"Knowing something is stupid and not doing it are two different things. Would you have gone without me?"

She reached up and cupped his cheek. "I want you with me when we find it. I want to share that moment with you. Would I have gone with Kyle? The truth is I don't know." Abby went up on her toes and softly kissed him. "I'm just grateful you're here."

A little of his anger faded. Not enough.

Abby kissed him again, just a sweet brush of her mouth over his, but the gentle press of her lips turned his thoughts from anger to lust. He was already hard, the zipper at the front of his cargo pants stretched taut. He had wanted this woman since the first time he'd seen her.

His arm went around her waist, and he pulled her close, his arousal like steel where it pressed against her.

"If we were somewhere else, I'd have you. I'd make you want me as much as I want you."

"I already want you, Gage. I think I've wanted you since that first day in your office."

Heat roared through him. Desire wrapped around him like a fist. His hands slid beneath her T-shirt. He unsnapped her bra and filled his palms with her breasts. The tips were pebbled rock hard. He wanted to lower his head and taste them, nip the tight little berries with his teeth, suck the fullness into his mouth.

He wanted to strip her naked, drag her down on the soft earth, and take her until neither of them could move, then start all over again. Gage kissed her long and deep, wrapped her thick braid around his hand and tilted her head back, kissed her until she was clinging to his shoulders and making little sounds in her throat.

Abby was a fire in his blood. He wasn't sure how much longer he could withstand the flames.

It took every ounce of his will to pull away. "Tomorrow we'll find your treasure," he said gruffly. "Then we'll finish this."

Abby trembled. "What about your precious rules?"

Gage made no reply, just took her hand and led her back toward camp. Abby didn't protest, not with Kyle and Mateo out of sight only a few yards away.

Her fingers felt small and warm nestled in his big hand. Just the touch of her skin made his heart beat faster.

Gage clenched his jaw. Abby was a dangerous distraction. One man was already dead. He didn't want anyone else falling victim to the Devil's Gold.

The final leg of their journey was a grueling trek beneath a hot desert sun. Abby was determined to reach their destination. Gage was pressing hard to make it happen. Mateo disappeared off and on, scouting ahead and checking their back trail, while Kyle plodded along with Mort at a steady, unwavering pace that ensured they would reach their goal.

By mid-afternoon, they were ahead of schedule. When Mateo reported a series of water holes linked together by an ancient chain of falls that dropped down the side of the mountain, Gage called for a badly needed break.

Though the falls were dry, worn smooth over eons, the recent rain had completely filled the rock basins at the bottom of each one, creating pools on three different levels.

While Gage studied the maps, Kyle watered the mule and tethered him to graze, took a quick swim, then stretched out with his hat over his eyes for a nap. Mateo, happier when he was off on his own, had enjoyed the pools earlier and headed back up the trail.

Abby was busily snapping photos and shooting video as Gage grabbed a towel out of one of the panniers and disappeared down the game trail toward the middle water hole. Ignoring a little voice that warned her to head for a different pool, she tucked the camera away, grabbed a towel, and silently fell in behind him.

By the time she caught up, Gage's clothes and his weapon were neatly stacked on a rock near the edge of the basin, and he was already in the water, which was only waist deep. Bare-chested, his muscles bunching with every move, he was an amazing sight.

Backing into a shadowy alcove, Abby unlaced her hiking boots and toed them off, unzipped her jeans and shoved them down her legs, then pulled her T-shirt off over her head, leaving her in her bra and panties.

Her gaze returned to Gage as she unbraided her hair. She could hardly wait to go into the water, but instead, she remained in the shadows, entranced by the beauty of the man in front of her.

He had a thick chest dusted with fine dark brown hair, wide, heavily muscled shoulders, six-pack abs, and a pair of incredible biceps. A sliver of warmth slid into the pit of her stomach as Gage scrubbed his hair and body with a handful of sand, then ducked under to rinse.

Abby remained in the shadows as he rose like an ancient god out of the sea. His legs were long and muscled. His thighs and calves flexed and tightened as he walked out of the pool.

Gage took a couple of steps and reached down to pick up his towel. Water sluiced down his back and over his tight buttocks. Even with his back to her, he must have caught some sign of movement because his head came up and for several seconds he stood frozen.

Slowly he turned, seeking, then finding her in the shadows. She could have sworn his nostrils flared. Her eyes widened as she realized he was fully aroused, his shaft high and hard against his flat belly.

Their eyes locked, their gazes held. Completely unembarrassed, Gage wrapped the towel around his waist and stalked toward her like a lion who had scented his prey.

Abby's stomach quivered. She stood transfixed as Gage stopped in front of her and hauled her the length of his big, wet body.

"Fuck the rules," he said, and his mouth crushed down over hers.

Heat and overwhelming need swept through her, desire unlike anything she had ever felt before. Gage deepened the kiss, and her fingers dug into his muscled shoulders. Her insides melted like butter, and a little moan slipped from her lips.

She barely noticed as he walked her backward to a place of safety out of sight behind a tall sandstone wall. Abby didn't protest when he unhooked her bra and dragged it off, then bent his head and fastened his mouth over her breast.

Oh, dear God! Nothing had ever felt so good as the touch of his tongue swirling around her nipple, his teeth biting the end just hard enough to send a little shot of pleasure/pain racing over her skin.

He captured her other breast, suckled and tasted until she felt dizzy. "Gage . . ." Her legs trembled with the effort to stay on her feet.

Gage kissed her again, a deep, hot, open-mouthed kiss that sent damp heat into her core. Kneeling in front of her, he stripped off her panties, then pressed his mouth to the inside of her thigh.

"Something to look forward to when we have more time," he promised, sending warm color into her cheeks.

Rising, he kissed her again, his big hand sliding down to stroke her, finding her slick and ready, eliciting a soft moan of pleasure. He cupped her bottom and lifted her against him, wrapped her legs around his waist, and kissed her. The feel of his mouth moving hotly over hers, his tongue sweeping in, taking what he wanted, had her melting against him.

His arousal felt hot and hard where it nestled at her core. Then he was sliding inside, filling her completely. *Oh, dear God.* He was big, and he knew exactly how to use what he had been blessed with, drawing out, then thrusting back in. Out and then in, easy at first, giving her time to get accustomed to his size, then moving faster, taking her deeper and harder.

Her hands slid around his neck, and she closed her eyes, absorbing the incredible feel of his solid body invading her smaller, softer form. With each of his determined strokes, pleasure swirled and tightened inside her, carrying her higher and higher, closer to the edge.

The pinnacle loomed ahead.

"Come for me, baby," he coaxed, and the command in that deep, sexy voice spun Abby into the void. Stars burst in the blackness behind her eyes, and sweetness enveloped her. A moan es-

caped as she rested her head on his shoulder and hung on through
one sensation after another. The French called it the *little death*—
like dying and going to heaven—and truly it was.

Gage's muscles tightened as he neared release. She could feel
him preparing to withdraw, but the idea was simply unbearable.

"Don't leave me. I-I'm on the pill." Gage's whole body vibrated
with his effort at control. His strokes slowed, then deepened,
grew even more intense, driving her to a second amazing climax,
both of them cresting together.

For several long moments, he just held her, Abby curled against
his chest. It felt like exactly the right place to be. Gage kissed her
softly. With her body still wrapped around him, he turned and
walked back into the clear warm water, washing away any evidence
of what they had done.

Gage let her go, steadying her until her feet settled in the sand
at the bottom of the pool.

"I didn't mean for that to happen," he said. "But I'm not sorry
it did."

Abby looked up at him, her body still limp with pleasure. "Neither am I."

"This changes things," he said.

She frowned. "How do you mean?"

"It means you're mine now. Whatever this is between us isn't
finished, and I don't share what's mine."

Abby stiffened. "I'm not interested in anyone but you, Gage.
But since we're clearing the air, I don't share either."

The corner of his mouth edged up. She had the odd thought
that somehow she had pleased him.

"Understood," he said. "When the time is right, we'll take up
where we left off."

Renewed desire slipped through her.

Gage looked down at her as they stood together naked in the
pool. "You make one helluva tempting sight, Ms. Holland. I need
to get back while I still have the willpower to leave. I'll give you a
moment to yourself."

Abby just nodded. She definitely needed a moment.

"Don't take too long," Gage cautioned. "We need to get moving if we're going to reach our destination." He sloshed toward shore, giving her a view of his spectacular backside. Grabbing the towel, he wrapped it around his waist, turned, and flashed her a smile. "Time to find out if your grandfather was right."

Abby smiled back. It was time to find the Devil's Gold.

CHAPTER NINETEEN

WITH MATEO SCOUTING AHEAD, GAGE SET OFF UP THE TRAIL, FOL-
lowed by Abby, then Kyle leading the mule. For a while, the trail
smoothed out and became less hazardous. Gage stopped several
times so Abby could shoot photos and video of the journey, pan-
ning over various chollas, prickly pears, and tall yellow stalks of
yucca.

Following the game trail marked on King's map, Gage kept a
close eye on their surroundings, on constant guard for anyone up
in the hills above them. More often than he liked, his mind
drifted to Abby and what had happened at the pool.

Jesus, he had never been more aroused in his life. The moment
he'd spotted Abby watching him from the shadows, he'd felt like
a stallion scenting its mate. He had never experienced such a
strong attraction to a woman, and he wasn't sure he liked it. He'd
wanted her again even before he'd climbed out of the water.

But taking her the first time had been a mistake. It was his job
to keep Abby and the others safe. To do that, he needed to keep
his wits about him and his mind sharply focused.

If he hadn't believed Abby wanted him as badly as he wanted
her, he might not have weakened. Abby probably hadn't realized
it yet, but Gage believed her desires ran as deep and hot as his
own. It was going to be nearly impossible to stay away from her
until they got back to Denver.

Glancing ahead, he climbed to a flat spot in the trail and
looked back to be sure Abby, Kyle, and Mort came up safely be-

hind him. The courageous long-eared mule had earned a place in his affections. Gage was determined to get the animal safely back home.

As Abby and Kyle caught up with him, Gage surveyed the peaks and ravines around them, looking for any sign of a threat. He never forgot the constant danger these mountains posed—or that there were men out there stalking them.

Even after the death of one of their own, Gage didn't believe they'd given up, not after coming this far. Not with two hundred million in gold at stake.

So far there'd been no direct assault. At this point, that could only mean one thing. Their adversaries no longer wanted the map.

They wanted the gold.

As Gage's small band neared their destination, the threat became even greater.

It was late afternoon when Gage spotted Mateo coming back down the trail. He was smiling broadly, his steps lighter than they'd been since the journey began.

"That saddle near the top of the mountain?" The flat spot on King's map. "It is just over the ridge." Mateo was clearly eager to get there, and so was Gage.

"All right, let's go."

Mateo led them farther up a steep trail running along the east side of Bluff Spring Mountain to a wide flat that matched the description in King's notes. As Gage paused to look at the map, Abby came up beside him.

"You think this is it?" she asked.

"Longitude and latitude are right." He read from King's notes. "Cross the ridge, go down past a large, pointed, isolated hill on the left-hand side, then up the first right-hand canyon, out onto a flat. Don't mistake the canyon for the trail. The trail leads up the first long draw, then down into a canyon filled with sycamore trees."

"I spotted a line of sycamores as we came up this last leg," Kyle said.

"So we're here." Abby's gaze ran over the barren landscape. "This is the place King found the Devil's Gold."

"I guess we'll see." The flat was near the top of the mountain, yet protected by jagged bluffs on one side and vertical canyon walls on the other.

"I saw human signs," Mateo said, his black eyes following Gage's. "Very old. I think this place was used by people many years ago."

Gage nodded. "There's evidence the Mexicans kept horses and mules somewhere in the mountains to transport the gold they took out of the mine. The animals needed to be guarded, so there were men stationed here."

According to King's notes, there was a spring near the cottonwoods that could be used to water the animals in times of drought, and if the weather turned bad, the animals could be sheltered in the steep surrounding canyons.

Abby glanced around. "The mountains here form a natural stronghold."

Gage followed her gaze. "With guards posted on the top, it would be the perfect place to defend against the Apaches."

"*Sí*," Mateo agreed. "I found old charcoal beds nearby."

Abby turned to Gage. "They could have had a smelter up here," she said, excitement in her voice.

"If this is where the Peralta mine was located," Gage said, "they could have melted the gold into ingots before they were transported out of the mountains."

"We need to go over King's notes again," Abby said.

Gage nodded. "Let's get camp set up, study the maps, and go over the notes. We can take a quick look around before it gets dark, then start searching first thing in the morning."

Abby grinned. "It's here. I know it."

Gage smiled, her enthusiasm contagious. And the way she looked at him, as if he were some kind of hero for bringing her here . . . Gage felt a tightness in his chest.

He thought about what had happened at the pool. The next time they were together, he'd make sure it wasn't some hurried affair. Abby deserved better, and he wanted to give it to her.

Even more, he wanted to give her the Devil's Gold.

* * *

As the hours passed, all Abby could think about was her grandfather and finding the treasure—proving King Farrell right,
restoring his reputation as one of the world's great explorers.

As soon as Kyle and Mateo had the camp set up, she and Gage
walked the area. Gage wanted to get a feel for the terrain before
they began to unravel the specific clues King had written in his
notes. But dark came early in these mountains. They barely had
time to complete the circle, to assess what they would be facing in
the morning.

Lying in her sleeping bag, Abby stared up at the diamond spray
of stars overhead. It was well after midnight, and she was still wide
awake. Though neither she nor Gage had mentioned what had
happened at the pool, her thoughts had returned there a dozen
different times.

She was still surprised she'd had the courage to pursue him,
though having spectacular sex with Gage was no surprise at all.
He was everything she'd imagined and more.

Passionate, virile, and a skillful lover with an incredible body.
Though Abby didn't like to think of the women Gage had slept
with, or would in the future, for now he was hers, and she believed he would keep his side of the bargain, unlike Ben.

Since their arrival that afternoon, she had done her best to
keep him out of her thoughts. They were there to find the treasure. She needed to be completely focused on that goal.

But as she lay on her bedroll, she felt his presence less than a
foot away, sleeping lightly, seemingly alert for any sign of trouble.
His Winchester rifle lay on the other side of his bedroll within
easy reach, his semiautomatic pistol on the ground above his
head.

With a sigh, Abby finally gave up on sleep and quietly eased out
of her bag. The dying embers of the campfire glowed red in the
night, beckoning her in that direction. Seating herself on the
rock she had sat on during supper—a meal of freeze-dried
chicken and dumplings that tasted more like feathers—she found
herself smiling.

Tomorrow, Mateo promised, they would be eating roast rabbit. Apparently, he had spotted a few of them and set a box trap made of branches to catch them. Mateo was an interesting man, extremely intelligent and insightful. An old soul, some would say. Abby had come to appreciate his unusual skills.

She was staring into the glowing coals when she spotted him in the darkness, moving toward her as quietly as a shadow. He crouched beside her, able to sit comfortably that way for surprising lengths of time.

"You do not sleep," he said.

"I'm nervous about tomorrow—and excited at the same time." She looked up at him, drawn by something that encouraged her trust. "It isn't just the money."

He nodded, loosening strands of black hair from the leather strip at the nape of his neck. "Gage told me about your grandfather. He said King Farrell was a very great man."

"He was a great explorer. I want this for him as much as for me."

"And Gage? Do you also want it for him?"

The words hit on something inside her. "I hadn't thought of it that way, but yes. I do. Gage is a man like my grandfather. He's brave and determined. And trustworthy, I think. My grandfather talked about him once. He said Gage Logan was someone who could contribute great things to the world."

They sat in silence for a while, watching the red glow of the fire slowly fading. A coyote howled in the distance, followed by two more. She liked the way they called out to each other, as if they were part of a family.

She thought of her grandfather and how much she missed him. She thought of Gage and how much she had come to care for him. Abby could no longer convince herself that what she felt for Gage was purely sexual attraction. In her heart, she knew it was far more than that.

She picked up a stick and stirred the coals. "Were you there when . . . umm . . . Cassandra was killed?"

Mateo's head came up. His eyes found hers in the darkness. "Yes."

"I don't think Gage has ever really gotten over it. Will you tell me what happened?"

"It is his story to tell."

"If you tell me, I might be able to help him."

Mateo fell silent. Abby waited, sure he wouldn't say more.

"It happened in Honduras. Gage was escorting a pair of archeologists to newly discovered ruins near Pacavita. Cassandra's father worked for an American company in San Salvador. That is where they met. Cassandra was beautiful and smart. She was in love with him."

"Gage said she loved him, but he wasn't in love with her."

"I think that made it worse for him. He enjoyed her in bed, so when she begged to go with him, he agreed. It was not supposed to be a difficult trip."

"What went wrong?"

"Cassandra could not handle the jungle. She was miserable, and she let everyone know. We had only been gone a few days when the accident happened. We were crossing a rope bridge over a gorge. Gage went first to make sure it was safe. Two men went next with no problem. I waited with Cassandra. When it was her turn, Gage encouraged her to go slow and not look down."

"What happened?"

"Halfway across, she panicked. One of her feet slipped off the rope, then she fell partway through. For several seconds she just hung there, but instead of waiting for Gage to reach her, to help her back to her feet, something went wrong. Gage nearly died himself trying to save her, but it was too late. She plunged to her death at the bottom of the gorge."

"Oh, my God."

"Gage brought her body home. The expedition failed, and Gage never went back."

Abby's eyes burned. Her heart ached for the woman who had died so young. And for Gage. "Thank you for telling me, Mateo."

"You are not like Cassandra. Gage knows this. I believe he cares for you, but it may not be enough."

Abby said nothing. She could only imagine the guilt and pain Gage had suffered. He wouldn't risk that kind of pain again.

She told herself it didn't matter, that her heart wasn't involved, and she would make certain it never would be.

"You must sleep," Mateo said, rising to his feet. "Tomorrow you hunt your *abuelo*'s gold."

"Yes . . ." Abby stood up from the rock. "Tomorrow we search for it. Good night, Mateo, and thank you."

He made a faint movement of his head. "Good night, Abby."

She climbed back into her sleeping bag and closed her eyes, but her mind raced with thoughts of Gage and the woman who had loved him.

It was nearly dawn when she finally fell asleep. The echo of a woman's cries as she plunged to her death crept into her dreams.

CHAPTER TWENTY

S HE SHOULD HAVE BEEN GROGGY AS SHE ROLLED OUT OF BED AFTER a mostly sleepless night. Instead, Abby felt invigorated, excited clear to her bones.

Kyle made coffee, then went to tend the mule while Abby took photos and video of the camp. They powered up on protein bars, drank boiled water for hydration, then refilled their bottles. Kyle and Mateo both headed off to stand watch on different sides of the camp as she and Gage searched. Mateo would be scouting their back trail, looking for any sign of the men, but Gage was clearly worried.

"Keep your eyes open," he'd said to them. "Watch for sunlight reflections, anything that might signal their location." He glanced at the peaks and ridges that could provide a hiding place. "If they're out there, they'll be somewhere above us. Keep your weapons handy."

Kyle's hand went to the Glock holstered at his waist. Mateo was armed only with a knife, but Abby figured he knew how to use it a dozen different ways, including self-defense.

Gage headed for a flat rock at the edge of their campsite and spread open the various maps they had brought with them. Abby took out King's notes and joined him.

They reviewed the first few paragraphs. Gage paused and looked around.

"This is the harshest country we've encountered so far." His gaze ran over the barren landscape, just boulders and cactus and dirt. "On the surface, there isn't much to distinguish this place from a hundred others. Read the next passage."

Abby looked back at King's notes. "'Find the low stone wall at the base of the arroyo. If you study it closely, you'll see it's not part of the natural landscape. It's man-made.'"

It took thirty minutes of intense searching to locate a stone wall that was only a foot high and so worn it simply looked like a pile of rocks. Abby's excitement swelled the moment she recognized it as the place in King's notes. Though she had read the notes a dozen times, it was different now that they were actually there.

"I found it!" she called out to Gage, who turned and strode along the narrow path at the base of the arroyo until he reached her side.

"There!" She pointed. "That's the wall."

Gage crouched next to the pile of rocks, surveying the fit of the stones, which was too perfect to be an accident of nature. "Once you see the pattern, you can tell this was part of a larger structure."

Abby looked down at King's notes. "'Looking east from the stone wall, dig down two feet to an old wooden ammunition box. Inside the box is what you'll need to find the treasure.'"

"I'll get the shovel," Gage said and returned a few minutes later with the handle gripped in his hand. Placing a big boot on the head of the blade, he drove the shovel into the ground and started digging.

Abby's heart raced faster with each load of dirt he scooped out and tossed aside. Her mouth felt dry but her palms were damp.

"Please . . ." she whispered softly.

The low stone wall was about six feet long. The first hole yielded nothing. Gage moved the blade, dug down a couple of feet, and found nothing. With the ground so dry and hard, it wasn't easy work. A third dry hole. Gage moved the shovel and started digging again.

Abby's tension built. Maybe there was another group of stones that formed a wall. Maybe she should re-read the notes, check for something she'd missed.

She looked at Gage, who had stripped off his shirt. A fine sheen of perspiration covered his heavily muscled body. Even with her mind fixed on the treasure, desire slipped through her.

It wasn't fair. Not when she had so little effect on his iron control.

The shovel dug in, and Abby's thoughts returned to the treasure. With a soft thunk, the blade hit something solid. Gage dropped to his knees, and Abby dropped down beside him. As they scooped out the dry, powdery earth, she caught a glimpse of what appeared to be a piece of wood.

They scooped out more dirt, and the top of an old wooden box appeared.

Gage dug around it, then reached down to lift it out. His muscles strained. The box was heavy. Gage took a more solid grip on the box, hefted it out of the hole, and set it on the ground. In faded red letters, SHUR SHOT REMINGTON ARMS appeared on the side of the dovetailed box.

"Looks like this is it," Gage said. "You ready?"

She swallowed and nodded, her long braid moving against her back. "I'm ready."

Gage slid out his big knife and pried open the lid, set it aside. The box was filled with sand.

Gage growled something she couldn't quite hear, but Abby was already digging through the sand, scooping handfuls out of the box.

Abby sucked in a breath at the quick glint of gold. Her heart thumped so hard a pain throbbed beneath her breastbone.

Reaching into the box, she sifted down and pulled out a shiny chunk of ingot much like the one she'd left in Denver. Next to it was a folded sheet of paper, clearly a letter. Abby handed the gold to Gage and opened the letter with trembling hands.

"What's it say?" Gage asked.

She took a breath and started to read. "*'If the person who found this note is my granddaughter, then I am no longer on this earth.'*" Her eyes suddenly welled. She glanced up at Gage, blinked to clear her vision, then went back to reading.

"*'Do not grieve for me, Abby. I was blessed with a long life filled with ex-*

citement and glory. I do not regret a single day. I have left you my few worldly possessions, but in leaving you the map, I gave you the gift you wanted most in the world—a grand adventure.'"

Her heart sank. Sending her out on a wild trek through the desert—fulfilling her lifelong dream of adventure—was something King would do.

"Keep reading," Gage said darkly.

"*'Do not despair, sweet girl. The Devil's Gold is real.'*" She couldn't resist a quick look at Gage. He was frowning. Abby kept reading. "*'If you are here, you know about the Peraltas. You've learned everything you need to know and have proven yourself strong enough to go after the treasure.'*"

Gage swore softly. "The old bastard couldn't find it, so he wants you to keep searching."

Abby ignored him, fresh excitement pouring through her. "*'According to legend, the Peralta family was wiped out by Apaches. But not all of them died. Those who survived returned to Mexico—taking a final load of gold bullion with them. It was the last trip they made.'*"

She paused, her heart speeding up again.

"Go on," Gage commanded.

"*'For years they had transported gold ingots to their plantation in the Yucatán. I found a few pieces here in the mountains, but most of the gold is still in Mexico. I'm going back for it. I asked an old friend, a man named Silas Cummings, to bring the box here in case something happened to me and I didn't return. Good luck, my sweet girl. Your loving grandfather, King.'*"

She dashed away the tears she hadn't felt on her cheeks and took a shaky breath. "I remember King mentioning his friend Silas a couple of times, but he never said the two of them were together in the Superstitions. Maybe we should try to find him."

"Maybe we should go home and forget this whole damn thing."

Abby looked down at the letter. "At the bottom it says that everything I need to find the treasure in Mexico is in a safe deposit box in the Wells Fargo Bank on Broadway Street in Denver." She reached back into the box, sifted through a little more of the sandy soil, and pulled out a deposit box key. Emotion clogged her throat.

"Looks like they were right," Gage said. "King Farrell went over the edge."

Abby looked up at him, saw that his jaw was clenched iron hard. "I know you're disappointed. I don't know what to say."

"There's nothing left to say. Time to pack up and go home. At least he left you enough gold to pay for your trip." Gage handed her the gleaming chunk of ingot. She turned it over to see the old-style P stamped into the gold.

Peralta.

Gage stalked away, but Abby's mind was already back in Denver. What was in the safe deposit box? How difficult would it be to find the gold?

Mexico was a whole lot different from Arizona. She needed help. She needed Gage. Judging from the stiff set of his shoulders, he wouldn't be easy to convince.

She folded the letter and tucked it and the key into the pocket of her jeans. She reached down and touched the ammunition box, the last link she had with her grandfather, carefully replaced the lid. It was ridiculously sentimental, but maybe they could find a way to carry it out in one of the mule panniers.

Gage was already packing when Abby walked up beside him.

"At least we don't have to follow King's trail on the way back," he said. "We can take the shorter route, be out of here in two days."

Abby said nothing, just started collecting her gear and loading her backpack. She was as anxious to get back to Denver as Gage, but for a far different reason.

Abby glanced up to see Mateo walking back down the mountain toward camp.

"You are leaving," he said to Gage. "Did you find what you were seeking?"

"No," Gage said.

"Not exactly," Abby corrected.

"I found something near the charcoal beds I thought you should see."

Gage paused as he tied his bedroll into place at the bottom of his backpack. "What is it?"

"Broken pieces of clay. Black marks show very high heat." He handed a jagged piece to Gage, who turned it over in his hand.

Abby took the broken shard and examined it. "Fire clay crucibles. I read about them." She looked up at Gage. "Vessels that could withstand the heat it would have taken to melt the gold."

Gage's eyes made a quick search of their surroundings, spotted Kyle at the top of the hill, standing guard, then returned his attention to Mateo. "Show me."

The pile of broken clay vessels lay within yards of the charcoal beds. Gage picked up one of the shards, and Abby did the same.

"This proves King was right," she said. "They smelted the gold into ingots and transported them to Mexico."

Gage shook his head. "There's no way to know that. Not without more proof."

"The proof is in the safe deposit box in Denver."

Gage said nothing, just pocketed the broken piece of clay, turned, and started walking back to camp.

Abby looked up to see Kyle coming down off the hill. He glanced behind him, set a hand on his battered straw cowboy hat, and started running.

That's when the first shots rang out.

CHAPTER TWENTY-ONE

GAGE GRABBED ABBY AND DRAGGED HER DOWN BEHIND A BIG GRAN-
ite boulder, drawing his .45 and firing several rounds in the direction the shots had come from. Mateo dove for cover in a shallow
ravine. Kyle took several leaping strides and jumped in beside
him, drew his weapon, and also started firing.

With limited ammunition, they didn't waste rounds, just pulled
off enough shots to let their attackers know they were armed and
wouldn't hesitate to defend themselves.

More shots rang out, pinging off the rocks around them. "We
can't move as long as they've got us pinned down," Abby said.
"What are we going to do?"

"What we aren't going to do is sit here like ducks in a shooting
gallery. Stay here." Keeping low, he eased backward and dropped
into the shallow ravine, then started making his way around to
where Kyle and Mateo had taken cover.

"They're in those rocks at the top of the ridge," Kyle said when
he reached them.

"How many?"

"Not sure," Kyle said. "Two, maybe three."

Gage clenched his jaw. He'd been sure they were out there.
He'd been hoping to stay ahead of them. "I'm going to circle
around to the right, come up on them from behind. First, I need
my rifle."

"You're going to be pretty exposed," Kyle said, spotting the
30.06 Winchester on the ground near Gage's backpack.

"That's why you're going to cover me."

Kyle glanced around. "Where's Mateo?"

Gage caught a glimpse of him moving among the shadows of a granite outcropping on the left. "He'll be wherever we need him most." Gage clamped Kyle on the shoulder. "Stay low and keep an eye on Abby."

"Will do." Kyle settled in, his Glock aimed toward the boulders at the top of the mountain. Taking aim, he started firing, drawing attention away from Gage, who ran a zigzag pattern back to his gun.

Several shots rang out, hitting the dirt near Gage's boots, kicking up dust as he grabbed the rifle and darted for cover. From the directions the shots were fired, he figured three gunmen. More shots rang out, echoing into the surrounding hills.

Moving from one rock to another, Gage managed to reach a jagged mound of boulders on the right side of the flat and disappear out of sight.

Kyle pulled off a round, and several shots blasted the air in his direction.

"Hold your fire!" one of the shooters called down. "We just want to talk!"

They were moving in, Gage figured, shifting to a closer position. There was no way these men had come to talk.

Careful to stay out of sight, he continued climbing from rock to rock, circling to the right, traveling upward until he was above his target. Two men crouched in the rocks below, one with a rifle, the other with a semiautomatic handgun, both weapons aimed toward camp. The one with the rifle had a shaved head and cannon-sized arms; the other was younger, blond, blue-eyed in a sweat-stained Izod and dirty designer jeans, clearly a city boy—the Denver connection.

Where the hell was the third?

Sighting down the barrel of his Winchester, Gage panned the mountains around him. By the time he had spotted his quarry, it was too late.

"Hold your fire!" the third man shouted, a thin, hard-faced guy with stringy brown hair and long, sinewy arms, one of which was locked around Abby's waist as he dragged her out of the ravine into the center of the camp. The barrel of a pistol pressed against the side of her head.

Gage's stomach knotted. He swore a soft oath.

"You want the woman to stay alive, toss out your weapons!"

None of them moved.

"I'm not playing games! We know you found the gold. Give it to us, and we'll let the woman go!"

Gage leveled the rifle at the man holding Abby. From his position in the rocks above and to the right, he could make the head shot and take the guy out. His finger tightened on the trigger. Nerves skittered through him. What if he hit Abby? Or he missed, and the bastard killed her? The knot in Gage's stomach tightened, and his steady aim wavered. He was already responsible for one woman's death.

The thought was a knife in his gut.

"Put down your weapons!" the third man repeated. "Come out and walk toward me very slowly."

Seconds passed.

"Been a while, Ray," Kyle called into the lengthening silence. "I figured it was you and some of your good-for-nothing scumball cronies. I know you've done some shit, but I didn't think you were a killer."

"We just want the gold!" Ray Peters called back. "Hand it over and you can leave!"

Abby struggled against the sinewy arm pinning her in place. "There wasn't any gold," she said calmly, though Gage picked up the faint tremor in her voice. "The box was empty."

"Bullshit." But Peters's expression changed from confident to uneasy. He moved the gun from Abby's head and pressed it into her ribs. "We all saw you digging. Now you're packing to leave."

"The box we found was empty," Abby repeated. "Take a look. You can see for yourself." She pointed toward the ammunition box in front of the crumbling stone wall.

Peters started dragging Abby in that direction, and her gaze flew up the mountain as if she knew exactly where Gage stood in the shadows. As Ray leaned down to remove the lid, Abby sank her teeth into his arm. Peters screamed, jerked, and Abby tore free, using her elbow to knock his gun arm up and sending his pistol flying into the air.

Gage fired, aiming for Peters's shoulder instead of his head, now that he was unarmed, spinning him into the dirt. As Kyle moved toward Ray, Gage swung the rifle toward the two men below him, levering in a round and firing into the ground right in front of them.

"Don't move a muscle! Stay right where you are!"

Kyle held Ray at gunpoint, while Gage descended through the rocks toward the men. Just as he reached them, the bald guy jerked up his rifle and swung the barrel toward Gage. Mateo's knife glinted as he appeared like a specter and pressed the blade against the side of the man's thick neck.

"I would not do that if I were you," Mateo said.

"Toss your weapons." Gage strode toward them. "Do it now!"

The bald guy with the big arms tossed his rifle, and the greedy, stupid city boy tossed his pistol, both weapons landing with a clatter in the rocks a few yards away.

"On your feet!"

As the two men rose from their positions, Mateo slid his knife back into the sheath at his waist and dropped back into a position behind them.

Gage marched them down a game trail leading back to camp, flicking a sideways glance at Peters, who sat cross-legged in the dirt, blood seeping through the fingers gripping his wounded shoulder.

Glock pointed at Peters's head, Kyle grinned. "Nice shot, Gage."

"You got him talking, and Abby disarmed him. Good job all around."

Hoping Gage wouldn't notice she was trembling, Abby helped Kyle secure the three men, binding their wrists behind their backs with a piece of rope and tying their ankles. She helped Kyle bandage Peters's wound, but it continued to seep a thin line of blood.

While they worked, Gage walked over to his sat phone to call 911. Abby figured dispatch would be informing the local sheriff's office as well as the Tonto National Forest Ranger District Office. The use of motorized vehicles in a designated wilderness was forbidden, but the violent assault that had resulted in a man being shot changed the equation.

"Help's on the way," Gage said. "Shouldn't take them long to get here." Heading straight for the younger man, he searched the guy's pockets and pulled out his wallet, read his driver's license. "Sean Younger. Address in Denver." Gage nudged the guy's leg with his boot. "You working for Jude Farrell?"

Abby's chest tightened, though she was fairly sure it was true. When Sean made no reply, Gage reached down and cuffed the back of his dark blond head.

"I asked you a question."

Abby stared into his face, which was sunburned and beginning to peel. "I know my cousin is involved in this. You might as well admit it."

"Good idea," Gage agreed. "Unless you plan to go to jail with these two and let your buddy Jude off the hook."

Sean looked horrified, his pale eyebrows climbing to the top of his sunburned forehead. "Wait a minute! I didn't do anything. We were just supposed to follow you, see if there was really any gold. If it was real, Jude figured he'd contest the will and get the money. It was Ray's idea to use Abby to get the treasure."

"What about your dead friend, Boyd McGrath?" Gage asked. "I guess you don't consider that a problem."

"I-it was an accident. Boyd was scouting ahead when it started to rain. When he didn't come back, we figured he'd holed up somewhere till the storm was over. We didn't realize what had happened until we saw the chopper. We followed it, and there he was, dead, pinned in the rocks below."

"Who hired Peters to follow us?" Gage asked.

"Boyd did. I wanted to go back when I realized Boyd was dead, but Ray refused to quit, and I couldn't get back on my own."

Gage nodded sagely. "I get it. Rock and a hard place, right? Next time, consider the consequences before you do something stupid." Gage looked over at the big bald guy. "Your buddy over there . . . what's his name?"

"He's not my buddy. He's a friend of Ray's. His name is Mack Ringo. He's from Phoenix. I helped you, okay? So will you put in a good word for me with the cops?"

"That's up to Abby." He turned toward her. "We need to talk."

"I got this," Kyle said, his grip relaxed on the pistol he kept pointed at the men.

Gage walked Abby to a place at the edge of camp where they were out of sight behind a formidable stack of boulders.

"You okay?" he asked.

A trembly breath whispered out. "I'm okay." It was only half true; her legs still felt shaky.

"When I saw you with that gun pointed at your head . . ." Gage swallowed. He glanced away, then back. "Peters could have killed you, Abby. One second you're alive, the next you're dead, and there's no going back, no way to change things."

She thought that he was talking about the past as well as the present, and her heart went out to him.

He shook his head. "Just thinking about it makes my stomach crawl. I don't want anything to happen to you, honey. I couldn't handle it. Not again."

She brought his big hand to her lips and pressed a kiss into his palm. "I'm okay. With all of us working together, we took care of the situation. We make a good team, Gage. Surely you can see that."

Gage made no reply, but his fingers wrapped around the hand holding his, and he drew her against him, leaned down, and kissed her, a soft press of his lips over hers, gently coaxing yet unbelievably compelling. Abby melted into him, pressing her body the length of his, absorbing his heat and solid strength.

Gage was a man she could depend on. He had proven it again today.

Some of her tension drained away. Gage had a way of making her feel safe and protected. Though she knew the consequences of her increasing need for him, Abby rested her hands on his shoulders, leaned up, and deepened the kiss, stirring a hot lash of hunger that burned right through her. She wanted to touch him—all of him—wanted to be back at the pool, naked with Gage inside her.

The kiss lingered a moment more, then gentled. He kissed her one last time and eased away, but the heat in his blue eyes didn't lessen. Abby finally came back to herself enough to hear the whop-whop-whop of the approaching helicopter.

Gage's mouth curved up. "If we don't stop now, love, the sheriff is liable to arrest us instead of them."

Abby managed to smile, which wasn't easy with her body still on fire.

Gage reached out and ran a finger down her cheek. "We'll have time together once we get back. You can stay at my place till you decide your next move."

Abby let the comment pass. She didn't want to tell him she already knew her next move. She was going to Mexico to finish what she had started. She hoped he would go with her—she needed him now more than ever—but either way, she wasn't quitting.

She was King Farrell's granddaughter. She wasn't going to let him down. Or herself. Not after coming this far.

She took a deep breath and walked with Gage back to camp.

They still had to face the sheriff. Then a hard, two-day journey out of the mountains to the second rendezvous point, where Walt would pick them up.

Denver was still days away. Abby couldn't wait to get there.

CHAPTER TWENTY-TWO

AFTER SHERIFF'S DEPUTIES FINISHED WHAT SEEMED HOURS OF END-less questions, they took the three men into custody, the charges ranging from assault with a deadly weapon to attempted armed robbery. Gage and their small band finally set out for home but made little progress before nightfall.

Everyone was edgy after their run-in with Peters and his men, and exhausted from the letdown of not finding the Devil's Gold. Anxious to get out of the mountains, they rose early the next morning and headed out beneath a brutal sun.

The two-day trek was uneventful, or maybe Abby was just getting used to the harsh terrain and living on packaged dried food. At least no one was shooting at them.

They arrived back at the Cedar Canyon Ranch that afternoon, checked on Smiley, who was recovering nicely, and were happy to learn the other mule had made its way back safely. Mort's braying, joyful homecoming with his four-legged friend seemed to especially please Gage, who had grown fond of the hardworking animal.

Mae fed them sandwiches and potato salad, and Walt gave them the use of an empty cabin so they could shower and put on clean clothes before they left for the airport.

With an extra few minutes to spare, Abby pulled out her laptop and Googled her grandfather's friend, Silas Cummings, the guy who had left the treasure box. There was scant information about him, nothing at all on social media. Then his obituary popped up. Silas had died two months ago at the age of eighty-one. He had spent his life as an outfitter and guide in the Superstitions. No mention of any living relatives. But in leaving the box for her, giving her the adventure she had always wanted, he had been a good friend to King.

Abby closed her laptop and hurried out to join Gage for a final farewell to the friends they had made on the ranch. She said a teary goodbye to Kyle and hugged him, holding on long enough for Gage's dark eyebrows to narrow. But a journey like theirs made for lifelong friends, and she hoped Kyle would be one of them.

Mateo got another long hug, which he warmly returned. The man was every bit as amazing as Gage had promised. "I hope we'll meet again soon," Abby said to him, a subtle hint that she hoped Mateo would be joining her and Gage on their continued hunt for the Devil's Gold.

Gage eyed her with a hint of suspicion but made no comment.

The flight home was easy, and it felt good to be back in a city surrounded by forested, snow-topped mountains instead of desert, cactus, and rattlesnakes.

The first thing Gage did after their charter flight landed at Rocky Mountain Metro was check out Trip Advisor and head for the closest place to get a steak, a restaurant called Hickory and Ash. They both ate until their ribs hurt, then Gage drove the rest of the way back to the city.

"We've got unfinished business with your cousin," he said as the vehicle rolled along. "We'll pay him a visit first thing in the morning."

Nerves tingled through her at the hard edge in his voice. She didn't blame him. Someone could have been killed—most likely her. Completely exhausted, she leaned back in the seat of the Rover and closed her eyes for the balance of the ride into the city. It was dark by the time they arrived in the LoDo district.

As the elevator door opened on the second floor of Gage's building and they made their way into his apartment, Abby released a quiet breath. Though the place looked the same—

hardwood floors, Persian carpets, comfortable furniture, and an intriguing mix of objects from around the world—much had changed.

Starting with Gage taking the handle of her carry-on and wheeling it into his own roomy, masculine bedroom instead of the guest room. She had never been in the room before.

She took a look around, appreciating the polished wood floors and the open arrangement of the furniture. A king-sized four-poster draped with soft white netting dominated the room.

There were several wood-paneled walls, one behind a tufted brown leather sofa. A grouping of three tall red patterned jars sat in the corner, and an oil painting of a stalking lion took up most of another wall.

A lion, she thought, for a lion of a man.

"It suits you," she said.

"You like it?"

She smiled. "I do."

Gage tugged the carry-on farther into the room. "We're sleeping together. Might as well make it official."

The action surprised her. Gage wasn't a one-woman man. She hadn't expected him to want this kind of closeness. She hadn't even been certain he'd want the relationship to continue.

"Are you sure? I thought—"

"I want you. If you think what happened between us in the mountains was anywhere near enough, you're sorely mistaken." To prove it, Gage pulled her into his arms and very thoroughly kissed her.

Surely we're both too tired to make love, Abby thought in some distant part of her brain, but her body seemed to disagree. As Gage deepened the kiss and his big hands took control, heat burned through her, and the last of her weariness slipped away.

In minutes, she was naked and so was he. She wished she had more time to admire his amazing body, but the hungry need inside her demanded to be sated, and Gage seemed as ravenous as the lion on his wall.

They made love for hours, first in a frenzy of passion that

ended in an earth-shattering climax, then more slowly, a lazy journey of exploration that spiraled into a second satisfying release. Exhaustion finally caught up with them, and she fell asleep in Gage's arms.

It was almost dawn, gray light filtering through the curtains, when his restless movements awakened her. Abby found herself sprawled over his thick chest, her head on a muscled shoulder, one of his arms draped possessively across her middle. Sleeping on the ground inches apart wasn't anywhere near the same as being held by him, loved by him.

Not loved, she reminded herself. Aroused by him, satisfied by him. Gage wasn't the kind of man a woman dared to love. Still, it was a moment she wanted to remember. Abby closed her eyes, determined to absorb every sweet detail, but Gage's restless movements ended any hope of more sleep.

Suddenly his big body jerked upright and his eyes flew open. "Cassie, no!" Gage blinked himself awake, leaned back against the headboard, and raked his hands through his thick dark hair. He looked at Abby, his blue eyes filled with regret and pain.

"It was only a nightmare," Abby said, stroking a hand gently down his arm. "It's over. Everything's okay."

Gage released a slow breath. "Sorry. I didn't mean to scare you. I should have thought about the nightmares before I suggested you sleep in here."

A muscle tightened in his jaw as he swung his long legs to the side of the bed. "Not a subject I like to discuss."

"Gage . . ." Abby reached for him, but he moved away. She watched him stride naked toward the bathroom, and desire swept through her, entirely unexpected after the incredible night they had shared.

Gage paused at the bathroom door and turned back to her. "On second thought, it's probably better if you sleep in the guest room. That way, I won't keep you awake."

Hurt slithered through her. She had known their affair wouldn't last long, but she hadn't expected it to end so soon. Apparently last night had been enough for him. Or maybe she had somehow disappointed him.

She bit her lip. Or perhaps there was a woman in Denver he hadn't mentioned before.

She lifted her chin, determined not to let him see the pain that tightened her chest. "If that's the way you want it."

Gage closed the bathroom door, and she heard the rush of water as he turned on the shower. Abby buried the hurt and longing, pulled on her jeans and T-shirt, grabbed her carry-on, and headed for the bathroom off the guest room down the hall.

She would call Tammy, find out if her friend was still staying with Jed. With luck, Tammy would let her use the apartment while it was still empty. Hopefully, the vandalism had been repaired to Tammy's satisfaction, earning her friend's forgiveness.

After a quick shower, she changed into a pair of stretch jeans that showed off her curves and a lightweight blue V-neck sweater that showed some cleavage.

She wasn't above a little revenge. Let him see what he was missing.

Her carry-on repacked, Abby called Tammy.

"Jed and I are doing great," Tammy said. "I'm crazy about him, Abby. Staying at my place isn't a problem. You're still interested in taking over the lease, right?"

She thought of Gage and swallowed. "That's right. I've got some things to do this morning. Then we can talk about it."

"Great. Jed's working. I'll be home all day. Come over whenever you're ready."

Abby ended the call and towed her bag into the kitchen in search of Gage, only to discover he wasn't there. She thought about leaving him a note and simply calling an Uber, but after everything they'd been through together, it didn't seem right.

The key to the safe deposit box seemed to burn in her pocket. She was anxious to find out what King had left her at the bank. She'd been hoping Gage would go with her, the first step in getting him to agree to continue the search. But after his abrupt departure this morning, their partnership was likely at an end.

Her heart squeezed. She was already half in love with him.

Since he didn't return her feelings, maybe it was better this way, better to put Gage behind her and head for Mexico with someone else. Or hire someone once she got down there.

Abby steeled herself. She had known this could happen. She had no one to blame but herself.

Figuring he was in his office, she gathered her courage and went downstairs to confront him. Instead, as she headed down the hall toward his office door, she ran into Jack Foxx.

Tall, black-haired, and ridiculously good-looking, Foxx ran his startling blue eyes over her in a lingering perusal that would have had most women's hearts pounding. Unfortunately, at the moment, hers was mostly in shreds.

Foxx smiled. "Welcome home, pretty lady."

Abby blushed at the compliment. The man certainly lived up to his rakish reputation. "Thanks, it's good to be back."

"So I guess your treasure hunt was a bust. Plenty of excitement though, as Gage tells it. I'm glad you didn't get hurt."

"The trip was tough, but the truth is, I loved it. At least most of it. The desert was amazingly beautiful, just in a different way from the mountains here."

Foxx started nodding. "I spent some time in the Ennedi in Africa. The desert's definitely got its own special appeal."

"It does. As for the treasure . . . I wouldn't call it a bust. We just completed the first phase, is all. I'm heading to the bank as soon as it opens. My grandfather left the information I need to continue."

Foxx frowned, his sleek black brows pulling together. "Gage mentioned something about Mexico, but he said the search was over. You aren't still planning to go down there?"

"It's no secret. I told Gage from the start I was going after the treasure. That hasn't changed."

She didn't have to turn to know he stood behind her. She could feel his powerful presence across a room full of people.

"We need to talk," Gage said.

Jack Foxx flashed her a grin. "Good luck," he said.

Abby turned to Gage, who tipped his head toward his office.

Shoulders straight, she walked past him into the room, and Gage closed the door.

"I can't believe you're thinking of going to Mexico," he said, cutting straight to the point. "After what happened in the Superstitions, I thought you'd come to your senses. Dammit, you almost got killed!"

"We knew the risk before we started."

"You need to face the truth. Your grandfather wants you to keep searching for the Devil's Gold because he couldn't find it. That's the way it is with people like us. Once we sink our teeth into a treasure, nothing can stop us until we've either found it or we know for sure it isn't there."

"The gold is there—the ingot we brought home proves it exists. At least come with me to the bank. We'll see what's in the box. If there's nothing there to convince you, I'll . . . I'll stop searching."

Gage fell silent.

"One more thing," she said, working up her courage, forcing back the emotion hovering far too near the surface.

She managed to spit out the words. "I realize . . . after last night, things are . . . umm . . . different between us. I knew from the start you'd get bored with me and be ready to move on. It doesn't mean we can't work together like we did before."

Gage's blue eyes widened. He looked truly astonished, a hard feat to accomplish. "What are you talking about? Why in the world would you think I'm bored with you?"

"You don't want to sleep with me anymore. I thought that meant—"

"For God's sake, Abby. Last night was incredible." Gage caught her face between his big hands and kissed her, long and deep. "I'm hard right now just looking at you. I can imagine a hundred different ways I want to have you." He glanced toward the desk with a hot gleam in his eyes, and Abby flushed.

"I was an idiot this morning," he said. "The nightmares . . . I don't like thinking about the past. It isn't fair you should have to deal with it too." He ran a finger down her cheek, and she felt a warm shiver. "There's no way to know how long this thing between us will last, but if you're willing to put up with my . . . baggage, my bed is exactly where I want you to be."

The pinch in her chest said how much she wanted the same thing. Her heart squeezed. She was in so much trouble with this man. "What about the treasure?"

Tension settled in his thick shoulders. "Let's go see what's in the box. The bank's not open yet. While we're waiting, we'll pay a little visit to your cousin Jude."

CHAPTER TWENTY-THREE

ABBY CLICKED HER SEAT BELT IN PLACE AS GAGE BACKED THE ROVER out of the garage.

"What's the address?" he asked.

"I don't know the exact address offhand. It's on North Williams, right across the street from Little Cheesman Park."

Gage headed in that direction, turned onto the street in front of the park, and drove slowly so she could find the house.

"Right there." She pointed toward a stately old two-story, red-brick-and-stucco home that sat among a row of well-cared-for older residences.

"Nice neighborhood, and not cheap by the looks of the homes around it."

"The houses here are worth over a million."

Gage flicked her a sideways glance. "You said your cousin lived with his parents, so this is their place?"

"His mother's house. Aunt Olivia is a widow. The house belonged to my uncle Joseph, King's nephew. The home has been in the family for several generations."

"Plenty of room for Jude," Gage drawled. "Though I couldn't imagine living with my mama when I was thirty years old."

Abby smiled. "That's because you're a man, and Jude has never grown up."

"He's obviously a greedy little prick without much of a conscience or he wouldn't have sent his thugs after you in the first place." Gage cracked open his door and stepped out on the pavement in front of the house. Abby climbed out and joined him.

They walked up a concrete path that crossed a wide expanse of neatly trimmed lawn, up the steps to a covered front porch. Ignoring the bell, Gage hammered on the door.

When no one answered, he hit the doorbell a couple of times, tension rolling off him almost thick enough to see. When no one came to the door, his anger seemed to swell, which Abby understood. The longer they waited, the clearer her memory of Ray Peters holding a gun to her head became. And her cousin Jude had put him up to it.

Gage was about to knock again when the front door swung open. Though she was fifty, Olivia Farrell was still a beautiful woman, with heavy dark brown hair and blue eyes.

"What in the world! I was coming as fast as I could." Always conscious of her appearance in front of a handsome man, Olivia pulled the sash of her green velvet robe a little snugger around her waist, showing off her trim figure. "What could possibly be so important at this time of the morning?"

Gage's eyes narrowed and not with appreciation. Abby stepped in front of him before he could lash out. "Aunt Olivia, this is Gage Logan. We need to speak to Jude."

Olivia raised her chin. "Jude isn't up yet. He was out late last night."

"I'll be happy to wake him up." Gage pushed past her into an entry lit by a crystal chandelier. The floors were polished hardwood. White molded ceilings soared above the two-story entry. "Which room is he in?"

Olivia's mouth tightened. "Good grief, Abigail, please tell your rude friend I'll have Jude call him later, after he's had breakfast."

Gage ignored her. Taking the stairs two at a time, he paused at the top to peer down at them over the mahogany railing. "Which room?"

"You'd better tell him, Aunt Liv. Gage won't leave until he talks to Jude." *And neither will I*, she thought.

"Fine. His room is the third door on the left, but I told you, he's still asleep."

"Then it's time he woke up," Gage growled, storming on down the hall. Abby hurried up the stairs and raced down the hall, catching up with him just as he turned the doorknob and burst into the bedroom.

In a pair of rumpled flannel Avenger pajamas, Jude jerked upright, blinking against the morning light shining through the windows. His head swiveled toward the door, and he stared at Gage with wild, disbelieving eyes. "Who the hell are you?"

"Your worst nightmare." Gage grabbed the collar of Jude's pajama top at the back of his neck, hauled him out of bed and across the room, and shoved him into a chair.

"Mother! Mom!" Jude started to rise, but Gage shoved him back down.

"Sit down, and shut the hell up!"

Jude clamped his lips together but couldn't keep them from trembling. Abby cast a worried glance at Jude's round, terrified face, which seemed to heat Gage's temper even more.

He focused on Jude. "How old are you, anyway? Thirteen or thirty? You little worm. You weren't man enough to go after Abby yourself. You had to hire your buddies to do your dirty work."

"I-I don't know what y-you're talking about."

Abby felt her own temper climbing. She marched up in front of her cousin. "So I guess you haven't heard about your good friend Boyd McGrath."

"What about him?"

"Boyd is dead," Gage said coldly. "Your friend Sean is in jail, along with the two guys McGrath hired to follow us into the mountains."

The color drained from Jude's face. "I-I don't know what you're talking about."

"That so?" Gage drawled. "That's not what Sean said. He was singing like a bird as the sheriff hauled his sorry ass away."

Jude swallowed, his glance straying to the open door. Olivia

Farrell appeared out in the hallway, as haughty as a queen, though she still wore her robe.

"Don't worry, son. I called the police. It won't take them long to get here."

A sharp knock sounded at the front door. "Police! Open the door!"

Olivia smiled smugly. "My, they are certainly efficient. I just hung up the phone."

Gage didn't move. Abby looked at him, but he just shook his head. Abby had a feeling this wasn't going down the way her aunt thought. Olivia went downstairs to open the front door, and a few seconds later, the thunder of heavy footfalls pounded up the stairs.

Uniformed officers swarmed into the bedroom. "Jude Preston Farrell?"

"That's right. These people are trespassing in our home. Please arrest them."

One of the officers, tall and silver-haired—Jennings, his badge read—cracked a smile. "Sorry, buddy, you're the one under arrest."

Jude's eyes bulged. "What? What for? I-I didn't do anything."

"Tell that to the judge."

Two of the officers grabbed Jude's arms and hauled him up from the chair. "Put your hands behind your back."

Olivia returned to the doorway. She gripped the wood to steady herself, then marched into the room. "What are you doing?"

"Making an arrest, ma'am," Officer Jennings said.

"You're arresting my son?" Her chin went up. "On what charges?"

"Conspiracy to commit armed robbery and assault. Though I'm fairly sure there'll be more."

The cuffs locked into place with a click. Jude swallowed. "Mom . . . ?"

Olivia stared at the policemen down the length of her nose. "At least give him time to put on some decent clothes."

Officer Jennings glanced from mother to son and nodded. One of the other officers leaned down and unlocked the cuffs.

"We'll be right out in the hall," Jennings warned.

Olivia's gaze swung to Jude. "Don't worry, dear. Our attorney will have you out of there in a couple of hours." Leaving Jude to dress, Olivia walked out of the room, with Gage and Abby behind her. As soon as the door closed, she whirled on Abby.

"You! You're responsible for all of this. You had King wrapped around your little finger. You blinded him to his duty to the rest of his family."

"King has nothing to do with this. Jude wanted something that didn't belong to him, and he was willing to break the law to get it. Ask him about his friend Boyd McGrath. McGrath's dead because of Jude. Whatever happens to your son is exactly what he deserves."

Gage set a hand at her waist. "Time to go," he said, urging her firmly out the door and down the stairs before the argument could escalate. Neither of them spoke until they were out of the house and Abby was settled in the Rover.

Gage slid in behind the wheel. "That's one problem solved."

"What will they do to him?"

Gage cranked the engine. "I don't know, and I don't care."

Abby looked back at the house. "When we were kids, I used to feel sorry for him. He never had many friends. The ones who did hang out with him just used him for his car and the fat allowance his parents gave him."

"Put it behind you, Abby. Family or not, you don't need people like that in your life."

Gage was right. She had learned to take care of herself long ago. She didn't need any of them.

She glanced at the man behind the wheel. As long as they were together, she could count on Gage to be there for her. Her heart squeezed. For now, she could depend on Gage, but sooner or later, their affair would end, and Gage would go on with his life.

Her throat tightened. Sooner or later, Abby would be left alone.

She took a deep breath. She would survive as she always had. The time would come, but not now. Now she was in the middle of a grand adventure. She intended to see it through.

As the car rolled along, she relaxed back in her seat. "You're right, Gage. Jude's troubles are no one's fault but his own. We have our own set of problems to deal with." She checked the time on her phone. "The bank's open."

Gage's jaw tightened, but he stepped on the gas, heading the Rover toward the nearby Wells Fargo branch. Time to tackle the next hurdle—persuading Gage to keep searching for the Devil's Gold.

CHAPTER TWENTY-FOUR

*I*T WAS LESS THAN A TEN-MINUTE DRIVE TO THE WELLS FARGO ON Broadway. Gage pulled up in front of the impressive glass-domed structure, parallel parked, and fed the meter; then he set a hand at Abby's waist and they went inside.

Though he knew the morning had upset her, she'd handled the arrest of her no-good cousin with her usual courage and strength. She was moving forward. Gage was proud of her.

He thought about what had happened in his office earlier that morning. He still couldn't believe it. After the incredible night they'd shared, how could she possibly believe he'd grown tired of her? Abby thought he'd had enough of her luscious body and passionate responses?

What a joke. He was more than a little afraid he would never grow tired of Abby.

Since he had no idea what to do with the thought, Gage shoved it back where it belonged and escorted her across the granite floor to the counter, the echo of their footsteps rattling around them. A few minutes later, a woman in her forties with buzz-cut blond hair walked up.

"May I help you?"

"I'd like to get into my safe deposit box," Abby said, holding up the key.

"Certainly. Right this way."

Gage followed Abby through a swinging gate into a small private room. For the first time that morning, she seemed nervous, clenching her hand around the key hard enough for it to make an imprint in her palm.

True, King had left another chunk of gold in the desert, one he claimed was part of the treasure. But if the Peralta mine existed, it had vanished over a hundred and seventy years ago. The gold—if any real quantity had survived through the ages—could be anywhere.

The woman returned with the box, and she and Abby used their keys together to unlock it. The woman left, closing the door behind her to give them privacy.

Abby held his gaze for several seconds, then looked back down at the box. Her fingers stroked the metal surface, then she took a deep breath and lifted the lid. Two gold bars glittered at the bottom of the metal box.

"I knew it," Abby said softly. "King found it. I remember the last time I heard from him. We spoke on the phone. Just a brief conversation, then he was gone. He must have made the arrangements with Silas to take the box into the Superstitions, spoken to his attorney, then headed back to Mexico to bring out the rest of the treasure."

And never returned, Gage thought but made no comment. His gaze remained on the ingots. There was something hypnotic about the gleam of pure gold, something even a hardened treasure hunter couldn't resist.

"There's a letter," he said, torn between hoping King had actually found the Devil's Gold and revealed its location, and the knowledge that, in searching for it, Abby would once more be putting herself in danger.

She scanned the letter, carefully read every line, then looked up at Gage. "King says most of the gold was moved out of the Superstitions years before the last Apache attack. He says the Peraltas smelted the ore and transported the ingots to the family's sisal plantation in the Yucatán Peninsula. They did it for years, stashing it in Mexico for future generations."

She stared down at the letter, re-read a few lines, then looked back up at him. "King says the old family estate, Hacienda del Oro Verde, fell into ruins over the centuries, but the treasure is still there. The gold he left in the safe deposit box was part of the booty, but he wasn't able to bring the rest out. He gives specific instructions on where to find it beneath the ruined hacienda, which is located deep in the tropical forest."

She tapped the letter. "He says we'll need to cut a deal with the government, offer them a percentage of what we find before we go in. That's the only way we'll be able to bring out the gold."

She gazed down at the letter. "King wishes me luck. He warns me not to go in alone. He says to find someone I can trust to go with me." Tears welled in her eyes, and a single drop spilled onto her cheek. "He says I should take the information to you, Gage. He says Gage Logan is a man I can trust, one of the best treasure hunters in the world."

"Well, fuck."

Abby looked up at him and wiped the tear from her cheek. "I told you he talked about you. He admired you, Gage." Her voice trembled. "So do I."

Gage shook his head. "Don't ask this of me, Abby. It's too much. If something happened to you—"

"I'm going, Gage. There's nothing you can do to stop me. I need your help. Say you'll go with me."

His chest clamped down so hard he could barely drag in a breath of air. He'd stupidly believed if he took Abby into the Superstitions, she would get her fill of treasure hunting. Instead, the lure of gold had her firmly in its grip. She would go to Mexico. Nothing he could do or say would stop her.

He thought of his nightmares. They'd returned after Ray Peters held a gun to Abby's head. She could have been killed. It would have been another death on his conscience.

"We're partners," Abby pressed. "I need you, Gage."

She did need him. Hunting treasure was what he did, and he was one of the very best.

And the hard truth was he wanted to go. He wanted to be there when she found the gold, be there when her face lit up with the rush of excitement and satisfaction that only a true treasure hunter knew. He wanted to be there because he finally believed the Devil's Gold was real.

"King was right," he said. "I'm the man for the job." *The only man,* he thought. The man who cared enough about her to protect her at any cost, even his life—because no way would he let another woman die because of him. "We started this together. We'll finish it together—beginning to end."

Abby threw her arms around his neck, and he pulled her close, buried his face in her shiny copper hair.

"You won't be sorry," she said. "We're going to find it this time. I know we are."

His hold tightened around her. If the gold was still there, they would find it. But sooner or later, word of a venture like this would get out. Mexico was a dangerous place, even without the lure of gold.

The real question was could they stay alive long enough to bring it home?

CHAPTER TWENTY-FIVE

ABBY CALLED TAMMY, AND SHE AGREED TO SUBLEASE ABBY THE apartment. With a trip to Mexico in the offing, she wouldn't be moving in for a while, but she would take over the rent. Gage needed her close by, he'd said. There were details to discuss, preparations to make.

He'd kissed her again and told her how much he wanted her, shown her as soon as they were back upstairs in his apartment.

The man was insatiable. Abby smiled. Recently, she had discovered she was too.

She was working downstairs, her laptop on one of the desks in the main part of the office, when Maggie Powell walked in.

"Good morning," Maggie said.

Abby smiled. "Gage said you were coming in sometime today."

"I prefer working here instead of at home when Gage is planning an expedition. I thought . . . after he returned from Arizona . . . I thought he'd be starting something new, but apparently his plans have changed."

Abby could hear the censure in Maggie's voice. "We're going to Mexico, following a new lead."

"That's what Gage said."

"You don't sound pleased."

"I'm surprised, is all."

"Because of what happened to Cassandra." It wasn't a question. They were both women. They shared a certain intuition, particularly about situations involving a man.

"I was working for Gage when it happened. He was devastated. Cassie's death nearly destroyed him. Unless I'm wrong, the two of you are involved in more than just a business relationship. Taking you to Mexico puts him in a risky situation. If something happened to you down there, I don't think Gage could survive it."

Abby's chin went up. "Then I had better do my best to stay alive." She thought of the woman who had loved Gage and died for it. She tried not to imagine the horrific sight of Cassandra plunging to her death, or think of Gage and the incredible pain it must have caused him.

"Gage is a professional," she said. "We both know the risks. Gage wants to find the Devil's Gold as much as I do."

"This isn't the same as a trip to Arizona. Are you sure about this, Abby? Because if Gage had his way, there's no question he would leave you at home."

"This is my quest, Maggie, not his. It's something I have to do."

Maggie said nothing.

"It isn't just the money," she added. "It's my legacy. Something I need to do for my grandfather. Gage understands that. That's why he's coming with me."

Abby read the worry in Maggie's face, and her voice softened. "I care about him, Maggie. I don't want Gage to be hurt any more than you do. But I believe we can do this if we work together. I'm not like Cassandra. And I won't let him down."

Maggie watched her a moment more, then seemed to relax. "Thank you for being so frank. Gage has never really gotten over what happened to Cassandra. Maybe you'll be able to help him put it behind him."

Abby felt a bond forming between them. They both cared about Gage—in different ways, more than cared. "I know he's still suffering. I'll help him any way I can."

Maggie smiled. "Then we had better get to work. It takes a world of preparation to put a trip like this together."

Abby returned the smile. "That's for sure." Turning, she went back to work on her computer.

Aside from finding, printing, and otherwise securing maps of the area, and helping Gage with miscellaneous research, over the next weeks Abby purchased personal items she would need, checked with her doctor, and took care of a tetanus booster. She'd already had her hep A and B shots. She and Gage were prescribed malaria drugs to begin a few days before they left.

She was only taking her small camera, the Canon Powershot Elph, this time. The danger element had grown tenfold. Everyone needed to concentrate on staying safe and finding the treasure. If she got a few good photos to document their efforts, she would be happy.

As the research unfolded, Abby discovered this was going to be a far different trip from the first. Though surrounded by tropical forest, the ruins of the hacienda were less than twenty miles from the nearest small village. And the forest itself was very different from what she expected.

A tropical dry forest consisted of thick scrubby trees and bushes, dense plant life, tenacious vines, and sticky leaves. The weather was hot and dry, not moist and wet like a rain forest, with its drenching daily showers.

But even the inhospitable terrain of the forest wouldn't be their primary obstacle, the way the desert had been in the Superstitions.

Here, man was their greatest danger.

A little tremor went through her as she remembered the feel of the gun barrel pressed against the side of her head. As Gage had said, she could have died that day.

Abby shook the memory away. She was committed. At this stage, nothing could sway her.

Abby went back to work. Gage would also be working, doing everything in his power to acquire the permits necessary for a journey into the tropical forests of the Yucatán.

The work was exhausting, and it was thrilling. Abby couldn't wait to get on the plane.

Gage did what he always did when he was heading up a new expedition. He immersed himself in the work that needed to be done, focusing entirely on collecting the necessary information, organizing, and pulling everything together.

It could take up to several months to prepare for a search as extensive as this. With Abby's help, he figured they could cut it to the bone and be ready in a couple of weeks.

As she had done before, Abby worked on the various maps of the area around the ruins and the abandoned plantation itself—ironically named Hacienda del Oro Verde, House of the Green Gold, a reference to the value of the sisal plants grown there, also known as henequen.

In its heyday, henequen was an extremely valuable fiber used for making twine and rope. Or perhaps the hacienda's name had a double meaning that hinted at the gold buried underneath.

Gage was involved in planning every aspect of the journey, which included researching the historical aspects of the area, once part of the vast Mayan civilization.

He knew a little about the Yucatán Peninsula, knew it was composed of miles of dense, nearly impenetrable tropical dry forest. There were also miles of shoreline, and the capital, Mérida, the place they would arrive after a stop in Mexico City, was one of the country's largest cities.

Gage had worked in Mexico before. He knew some of the power players in the Mexican government. A man named Juan Guerra Ortega was an undersecretary at the Instituto Nacional de Antropología e Historia, the department that oversaw the protection of the prehistoric, archeological, and anthropological heritage of Mexico.

Ortega, along with several of his colleagues, was interested in what Gage might find during his search of a remote area of the Yucatán—Gage's description of the expedition.

Ortega arranged a meeting with Victor Luego Alamán, an assistant to the Secretariat of Finance and Public Credit, the department that handled taxes, spending, debt, and income, anything to do with sustained economic growth.

Alamán was a powerful man in the government. He was also, according to Ortega, a greedy, slightly amoral bastard who managed to line his pockets with federal funds and not get caught.

If Gage could make a deal with Alamán for the government to receive a percentage of whatever treasure they might find, he would gain access to the vast forests and lands that included the ruins of the eighteenth-century Hacienda del Oro Verde.

Of course, the deal would include *mordida*—cash on the side— for Alamán.

The meet was set for a week from tomorrow at a small café across the street from the Palacio Nacional, the location of the executive branch of government.

Shoving up from his chair, Gage left his office and went in search of Maggie, seated at her desk in the main part of the building.

"We've got a start date, Mag. I need you to arrange a flight to Mexico City, arriving a week from today. Get us a suite at the Gran Hotel. I've got a meeting close by the next morning. If it's successful, we'll head for Mérida the following day. Book us an open-ended flight in case we have to stay longer in Mexico City." *In case we have to do a little more convincing.*

"I'll take care of it." Maggie didn't ask who the *we* included. Abby had been staying in his apartment since their return from Arizona, spending every night in his bed.

Unfortunately, both of them had been working round the clock, their energy entirely focused on the trip, which put a big dent in his sex life. Still, it felt good just to have her there, curling up with him when they finally fell exhausted into bed.

Inwardly, he grinned to think of the way she had awakened him this morning. Enjoying a dream about Abby pressing soft kisses over his chest, he awoke to find it wasn't a dream at all, that his body was responding to the pretty mouth doing erotic things to him he had only imagined.

Gage reminded himself that eventually the affair would take its natural course and come to an end, just as it had the times he'd been involved with a woman before. His job was not conducive to a long-term relationship.

Gage felt an unexpected pang at the thought, a reminder not to let down his guard and get in too deep. He needed to keep things simple. Good sex, friendship, and a profitable business relationship. That was all.

"One more thing," he said to Maggie, forcing his mind back where it belonged. "There's a place outside Mérida, the Hacienda San José. We'll need rooms for at least three nights." Mateo would be meeting them there. He was already in Mexico, talking to locals, working up information on the area around the old hacienda, arranging for a base of operations somewhere nearby.

"I'll make it happen," Maggie said.

Gage returned to his office and went back to work, going over the list of things he needed to do before they left Denver. Since the business of finding treasure was part discovery and an equal part danger, they needed competent security.

His next call went to his brother.

Abby was working on the computer in the main office when a familiar voice reached her.

"Looks like you're hard at it." Clayton Reynolds stood in the doorway, blond hair gleaming like the gold her grandfather had left her. Abby hadn't seen him since the reading of her grandfather's will.

Dressed in beige slacks and a pale blue Izod knit that matched his eyes, Clay smiled and started toward her. At thirty-eight, he had the lean build of the tennis athlete he had been in college, where he'd earned a PhD in pre-Columbian history, specifically the Mayan civilization.

He and King had worked with UNESCO on a World Heritage project, which had led to their friendship. Clay had asked her out once, but Abby's mother had been dying, and dating was the last thing on her mind.

She rose from her chair and went to greet him. "It's good to see you, Clay. How did you know where to find me?"

He took her hands, leaned over, and brushed a kiss on her cheek. "The day they read King's will, it was clear you meant to go after the treasure. King and I had discussed the map on several occasions. When word leaked out that Gage Logan was heading up a new expedition, I put two and two together."

He gently squeezed her hands. "I didn't get a chance to offer my condolences on King's passing or acknowledge the wonderful gift he left the museum. I thought I'd see if I could find you and tell you in person."

Abby smiled. "I appreciate your thoughtfulness, Clay. I miss my grandfather very much."

"We all miss him, Abby." He glanced around the office at the tables stacked with maps and files. "So how are things going? I spoke to King before he left Denver on his last trip. He mentioned he might be traveling across the border into Mexico. I assume you're headed in that direction."

Before she could respond, Gage's heavy footfalls sounded as he crossed the room.

"Dangerous to make assumptions about other people's business," he said. "And you would be . . . ?"

Abby's eyes widened at his tone. "Gage, this is Clayton Reynolds. He was a friend of King's."

"Reynolds, yes. Mayan culture, isn't it?"

"That's right." Clay stuck out a hand, and the men shook.

"So what can we do for you?" Gage asked, clearly not happy to have an uninvited guest.

"I just came by to speak to Abby. I thought perhaps she might have time for lunch or at least a cup of coffee."

"We're on a tight schedule," Gage said. "Maybe when we get back."

Abby felt a trickle of irritation. She and Clay were friends. If Gage didn't approve, that was just too bad.

Abby smiled. "I appreciate the offer, Clay, but as Gage says, we're really swamped. I'll give you a call if I get a spare moment."

As tall as Gage, Clay was more than just attractive, though Abby had never had any real interest in him.

"I'll look forward to it." He smiled. "Well, then, good luck wherever you're headed." Abby thought that he would have pursued his invitation if Gage wasn't making it more than clear that it was time for him to leave.

"I'll walk you out," Abby said, flicking Gage a disapproving glance. By the time she returned, she figured he would be back at work. Instead, she found him sitting in the chair at her desk.

"There's something we need to discuss," he said, rising. Setting a hand at her waist, he steered her into his office and firmly closed the door.

The next thing she knew, she was pinned between the door and a solid wall of muscle, Gage's mouth coming down over hers. Warm, firm lips took control, softened, and sent a flood of heat out through her limbs. She gripped his shoulders to stay on her feet and gave in to the hot sensations.

Gage's kisses gentled, turned coaxing. Moist lips traveled along her throat, nipping and tasting.

"I've been neglecting you lately," Gage said softly, pushing the lock on the door as he used his teeth to nibble an earlobe. "Time to put work aside and remedy that."

She could feel his heavy erection pulsing against her, tempting her with its fierce demands.

Gage's big hand slid beneath the T-shirt she was wearing with a pair of yoga pants and sandals, unhooked her bra, and cupped a breast. Abby moaned as he teased her nipple into a rigid peak, arousing her until she was trembling.

Gage kissed her again, and she found herself clinging to his neck as he moved her backward, farther into the office. It barely registered that he had pulled the blinds on his windows.

Kissing her all the while, he backed her up till she bumped into his desk. Gage shoved a stack of files off to one side and kissed her—a long, thorough, hot, wet kiss that had her moaning. Then he turned her around and bent her over the desk. Her sandals fell off as he dragged down her stretch pants and tossed them aside, then positioned himself behind her.

"Just so you don't forget how good we are together." Gage freed himself, and then he was inside her, setting up a rhythm that had her arching her back to take him deeper. Increasing the rhythm, he moved faster, took her harder, the friction setting her body on fire.

Abby moaned as his grip tightened on her hips and he drove into her. The first sweet shivers of climax struck, the ripples expanding into waves of bliss that had her clenching her teeth to keep from crying out his name.

Gage didn't stop. Not until she reached a second shattering release, timing his own to match so they came together. Long seconds passed. A low moan slipped from her throat as the world slowly righted itself.

Gage smoothed a hand over her hips, eased her back against him, and his arm tightened around her. He kissed the nape of her neck.

"You okay?" he asked gruffly.

"I don't know. I can't move. I think I'm paralyzed."

Gage chuckled. Turning her into his arms, he kissed her one last time. "Much as I'd like to carry you upstairs and start all over again, you know we have to go back to work."

"I know." She blew out a breath that fluttered her bangs and grinned impishly. "Maybe we can take a few more breaks like this one."

Gage laughed.

Abby grabbed her clothes and headed into his bathroom to freshen up. When she came out, Gage was waiting.

"So you and Reynolds . . . You never mentioned the two of you were involved."

"Because we never were." She cocked an eyebrow, flicked a glance at the desk and back to Gage. "That's what this was about? You were jealous of Clay?"

"No. Well, not exactly. The way Reynolds was looking at you reminded me I haven't been very attentive lately."

"I don't have any interest in Clay, and after the last trip, I know how you get when you're focused on a hunt."

He frowned. "I'm not sure I like how well you're coming to know me."

Abby said nothing. The words were a reminder that Gage wouldn't allow himself to get involved too deeply. Sooner or later, he would move on. She had already accepted that, knew their relationship had a time limit. Still, she couldn't help a soft pang in her heart.

"As you said, I've got plenty of work to do. I'll see you later." Abby headed for the door. They would be leaving soon for Mexico. Nothing was more important. Especially not her unwanted feelings for Gage.

CHAPTER TWENTY-SIX

AFTER A STOP IN HOUSTON, UNITED AIRLINES FLIGHT 3216 ARRIVED at Mexico City International Airport at 2:15 in the afternoon.

A white Lincoln stretch limo waited to take them to the Gran Hotel Ciudad de Mexico in the Zócalo district downtown, the area that housed the national palace, the seat of the Mexican government.

As Gage leaned back in the deep red leather seat, he couldn't resist a glance at Abby, who stared out the window as if she were in a trance.

Gage smiled. The city was in every way amazing. With its wide, tree-lined boulevards and beautiful colonial buildings, it reminded him of Madrid. Not surprising since the Spanish had conquered the Aztecs in the sixteenth century and built the first cathedral in Mexico City on top of an Aztec temple.

"It's beautiful," Abby said, clearly in awe. "There's so much color. It's everywhere."

Color splashed everything from murals and street art to food vendors and musicians playing guitars, drums, and horns with a distinctive Latin beat. Though the buildings in the center of the city were hundreds of years old, in the distance, towering, sophisticated, ultra-modern structures dominated the skyline.

"I wish we had more time," Abby said wistfully.

Gage understood. He had wanted to see the world, and so far he hadn't been disappointed. There was a dark side to every city,

cruelty and injustice in every country, but the good mostly out-
weighed the bad. Everyplace he went held a certain unique appeal.

"We'll finish our business, and as soon as we get the chance,
we'll come back."

The minute the words were out of his mouth, he realized his
mistake. Once the expedition was over, so was his time with Abby.

For a moment, her gaze met his, and he saw his thoughts mir-
rored there. She made no reply, just turned to look out the back
window as if she might have missed something. Then he felt her
hand on his arm.

Worried golden eyes met his. "Gage—I think someone's following us."

He turned toward the window. "Which car?"

"Older silver Mercedes. I noticed it as we left the airport, but I
didn't think anything about it. It's been behind us all the way into
the city."

"Could just be he's headed in the same direction."

"Could be, I guess."

But now that Abby had pointed it out, Gage kept an eye on the
vehicle, which stayed at a steady distance about six cars back.
More and more people knew he was heading up an expedition.
Arrangements had been made, discussions with people who were
experts on the history of the area, people in the government like
Juan Ortega.

Abby's greedy cousin, now out on bail, knew the two of them
were going after the treasure. Reynolds had guessed; anyone
who'd known King Farrell might have their suspicions. Even a
local Denver TV station had phoned, asking to interview him
about his next project, a request he had denied.

By tomorrow, Victor Alamán would know.

None of them were aware of the details, or the exact location
in Mexico of the treasure he was hunting, but their interest had
surely been piqued.

Gage moved away from his seat toward the front of the limo
and spoke to the driver in Spanish. He wasn't completely fluent,

but he'd been raised on a ranch where the foreman and several
of the hands were Latino. When he was a boy, they'd had fun
teaching him their language.

"*Toma el siguiente derecho,*" he said. Take the next right. "Go
down a few blocks," he continued in Spanish, "then circle back to
the street we're on."

Gage moved back to his seat next to Abby. The driver made the
turn, and Gage watched through the rear window. The silver Mercedes appeared behind them a few seconds later.

"You were right," Gage said, tension settling in his shoulders.
"Someone's definitely on our tail."

Abby quickly turned to look. "What should we do?"

"Hope to hell they're just tracking our movements. We're
meeting Edge in Mérida. From then on, we'll be armed."

Gage didn't miss the slight hitch in Abby's breathing. "Edge is
taking care of it?"

Gage nodded, his glance returning to the window. "He was deployed in South America for a while. After he got out of the army,
he did personal protection for a corporate exec who worked for
PepsiCo in Mexico City before he came back to Denver. He knows
his way around down here." He also spoke Spanish far better than
Gage.

As the limo made another turn, the silver Mercedes appeared a
few cars back. "They don't seem to be worried about being spotted," Abby said.

Which could be good or bad. Harmless government interest or
men with serious intentions. Either way, Gage didn't like it.

"Should we try to lose them?"

"There's a good chance they already know where we're headed.
If our meeting in the morning goes as planned, we'll change our
airline reservations and leave for Mérida as soon as we can get a
flight. We'll do our best to keep them guessing."

The beautiful old historic hotel, with its ornate colonial design,
lion's head columns, and stained-glass front doors, appeared up
ahead. The driver pulled over to the curb, then came around and
opened the rear passenger door.

As they climbed out onto the sidewalk, the silver Mercedes drove past. The windows were tinted too dark to see inside, but the vehicle was an unsettling reminder of just how dangerous their search could get.

With its stained-glass dome above an open lobby surrounded by ornate wrought-iron balconies, the five-star luxury Gran Hotel was beautiful. A crystal chandelier hung over the entry as they made their way inside and were checked into the roomy master suite Maggie had reserved for them.

The spectacular view of the Zócalo, with its magnificent Metropolitan Cathedral and the Palacio de Hiero Centro, distracted Abby for a while, but by nightfall their encounter with whoever was following them kept her on edge, and even Gage's skillful lovemaking in a spectacular four-poster bed couldn't put Abby to sleep.

Sometime near dawn, she dozed for a couple of hours, then opened her eyes when she heard the shower running and realized Gage was already awake and preparing for the day ahead.

She passed him on his way out of the bathroom, went in to shower, then dressed in the apricot skirt suit and cream silk blouse she had brought for their meeting with Victor Luego Alamán.

Grabbing her small leather clutch, she walked into the living room to see Gage dressed in an expensively tailored dark blue suit, white shirt, and red and yellow tie. With his height and broad shoulders, he exuded power and authority, exactly his intention, and Abby felt an embarrassing shot of lust.

The corner of Gage's mouth tipped up. "I wish I had time for what you're thinking. I'll make up for it when we get to Mérida."

Warm color flooded her cheeks. Pride demanded she ignore him. "I have no idea what you're talking about, but I'm ready whenever you are."

He grinned. When he noticed her business attire, his dark brown eyebrows drew together. "I'm sorry, Abby, this is something I have to do alone. If Alamán agrees to our terms and gets us the permissions we need, we'll be paying him a substantial fee for his efforts. Taking a bribe isn't something he's going to want to do in front of a witness."

Inwardly, she sighed, surprised she hadn't thought of that herself. "It makes sense, but surely there's something I can do to help."

"If the deal goes down, we can head for Mérida. I'm already packed. I'll text you as soon as I know what's going on. If it's good news, you can call the airlines and change our flight."

"All right, I'll take care of it."

"And stay in the room. If you're hungry, order room service. If they know about the treasure, whoever was following us might come after you for information. I don't want to take any chances."

Her stomach did a roll. Kidnapping was a constant problem in third-world countries, even a developing country like Mexico.

She walked over and pressed a soft kiss on his lips. "Good luck with Alamán."

Gage hauled her into his arms and kissed her the way she'd been wanting him to do since she'd seen him standing in the living room.

"Be careful," he said a little gruffly. "I'll be back as soon as I can."

Gage headed off to his meeting, while Abby changed into a pair of jeans and a white scoop-neck top for traveling, hopeful they would be heading to Mérida that afternoon. Better to stay one step ahead of your enemies. She had learned that in the Superstitions.

While she waited for Gage's text, she went in and packed her carry-on and set it beside the door next to his. The rest of their luggage had been sent directly to Mérida to be picked up by Edge or Mateo.

By the time she finished, her stomach was growling. She checked her phone. No text from Gage. Figuring on a long day, Abby ordered huevos rancheros and chorizo, though as her nervousness grew, she wasn't sure how much she could eat.

She checked her messages while she waited for the food. Still no text from Gage.

"So we have a deal," Gage said from his seat across the table from Victor Luego Alamán. "Your department will provide the necessary permits, and in return, the Mexican government will receive sixty percent of anything we might find of value during our expedition." There was no question of a fifty-fifty split. The government held all the aces.

He and Alamán were dining on the roof terrace of the Balcón del Zócalo on Avenida Cinco de Mayo, just a few blocks from the hotel. The open-air restaurant overlooking the city was the perfect spot for a clandestine meeting. Like hiding in plain sight.

A small man with sallow skin and longer-on-top, short-on-the-sides, coal-black hair, Alamán wiped his mouth with a white linen napkin. "And . . . ?" he prompted.

"And in gratitude for your assistance, you will personally receive a gift in the amount of ten thousand US dollars, as well as three percent of our share of the bounty, should our endeavor be successful."

Alamán's thin lips curved into a wolfish smile as Gage reached into his pocket and pulled out a plain white envelope stuffed with hundred-dollar bills. A second envelope held more cash, but the greedy, eager look in Alamán's black eyes said it wouldn't be needed.

Gage passed the envelope across the table.

Alamán's slender hand reached for the cash. He slid the envelope into his inside coat pocket without counting the bills and rose from the table. "The permits will arrive at your hotel within the hour." His thin smile returned. "*Gracias para la comida.*" Thanks for lunch.

"*De nada,*" Gage said.

As soon as Alamán disappeared out the door, Gage texted Abby.

MEETING SUCCESSFUL. PERMITS ARRIVE WITHIN THE HOUR. ON MY WAY BACK NOW.

* * *

Abby checked her phone and saw Gage's text just as the door-bell rang. Her room service order had taken longer than she expected, but with Gage's success, at least her appetite had returned.

Sliding the chain off the lock, she pulled open the door and stepped back to allow the white-coated waiter to wheel in a linen-draped food trolley. He lifted off a tray loaded with silver domes, and the room filled with delicious aromas.

"Where would you like this, señorita?" He was in his thirties, with smooth dark skin, a neatly trimmed mustache, and side-burns.

"Over on the coffee table is fine." The waiter set the tray down and started back the way he had come, but instead of leaving, he opened the door, and a second waiter, bigger, more solidly built, with stick-straight black hair, walked into the room.

Abby's heart began to pound. "What are you doing? I don't need anything else. Please leave."

The two men rapidly closed the distance, and Abby bolted, dodging, trying to get past them to the door. She managed to dart past the first waiter, but the bigger man with the straight black hair grabbed her around the waist, jerked her back into the room, and slammed the door.

Abby tried to scream, but the mustached waiter shoved a white rag in her face. The first breath she took left her woozy. She managed to turn her head away and start fighting the waiter who held her, kicking and scratching, raking her short nails down the side of his face, drawing blood.

"*Puta!*" Doubling up his fist, he punched her in the jaw so hard her head spun and her knees buckled. Abby grabbed onto a side table and managed to pull herself up, but a long-fingered hand pressed the cloth over her mouth again.

Abby swayed, her muscles going limp as she was lifted off the floor and carried toward the food trolley, which was actually a laundry cart, and dumped inside.

Her head was still spinning. Vaguely, she heard the rattle of the lock turning, the door opening, then Gage's foul curse.

The sound of breaking glass followed, and the solid thud of fists pounding into flesh. She shook her head to rouse herself, managed to shove up from the bottom of the cart in time to see Gage's muscled shoulder barrel into the midsection of the mustached waiter, carrying him across the room and slamming him into a wall.

As the man staggered to his feet, Gage spun toward the bigger, straight-haired man and threw a hard punch that knocked him several feet back before the guy swung a blow that Gage managed to duck.

Still dizzy, Abby climbed out of the cart. A painted vase sat on the side table. Grabbing the vase, she crashed it over the mustached waiter's head.

"*Mierda!*" he swore, stumbling backward into the wall again. He looked over at his friend, who was still going fist to fist with Gage. "*Vamos, hombre! Ahora!*"

He opened the door and raced out, quickly followed by the bigger man, whose nose was bleeding, leaving a trail of red down the front of his short white waiter's jacket.

Shaking all over, Abby leaned against the table for support. Then Gage was there, pulling her into his arms, holding her tight against him.

"Are you okay?" he asked, his muscles still vibrating with tension. "Did they hurt you?"

Abby swallowed. "I-I'm okay. You got here just in time."

Gage nodded with relief, but a muscle knotted in his jaw.

The warmth of his body erased the last of her fear. Her eyes were still a little glassy, and her jaw ached, a dark bruise forming where the man had hit her.

She looked up at Gage. "You know, this treasure hunting business can be a real pain."

Gage's worried blue eyes shot to her battered face. Abby blew out a breath that fluttered the fringe of bangs on her forehead. She grinned.

Gage laughed and finally let her go. His humor slowly faded. When he looked at her again, a slow-burning anger darkened his features. "This is exactly the reason I didn't want you coming down here. God knows what would have happened if I'd gotten here a few minutes later."

Abby's own temper surfaced. "Well, you didn't, and I'm okay. We knew something like this could happen. We'll just have to be more careful."

Gage's jaw tightened. "You can count on that," he said.

CHAPTER TWENTY-SEVEN

THE TWO-HOUR FLIGHT TO MÉRIDA GOT THEM THERE AT FIVE P.M. Mateo was waiting for them in front of the terminal in an olive drab Humvee that looked like something out of a war zone.

Gage walked over and shook his friend's hand, then gripped his shoulder. "Good to see you, my friend."

"You, too, *amigo.*" Strands of Mateo's black hair, loose from the rawhide thong at the back of his neck, blew across his face. He smiled warmly at Abby. "Welcome to Meh-he-co," he said, using the soft Spanish pronunciation as he reached over to grab the handle of her carry-on.

Abby went up on her toes and kissed his lean cheek. "It's good to see you again, Mateo. Thank you so much for coming."

He just smiled and returned his attention to Gage. "Everything is set. Your brother waits at the hacienda."

Gage nodded. "Good. We've already had some trouble." He tried not to think what might have happened to Abby if he hadn't gone straight back to the hotel. Clearly, their pursuers knew about the treasure and believed she had the information they needed to find it.

Truth was, she did. Which put her in grave danger. Abby and everyone else involved in the search. Until the gold was found and brought out—or they gave up and left Mexico—they needed to be on constant alert.

"Two men posing as waiters came into the room while I was

away from the hotel," Gage explained as he and Mateo loaded the luggage into the back of the Hummer. "They were after Abby." Turning, he caught her chin and moved her face to display the dark bruise on her jaw.

Mateo frowned.

"I got back in time, or they would have succeeded," Gage said. "I'm damned glad Edge is here."

"*Sí*, your brother arrived well-prepared."

After his years in Special Forces, Edge never did anything without being prepared. There was no way to tell just how much opposition they would be facing before this was over. Or how far their pursuers would be willing to go.

They climbed into the Hummer. With Mateo at the wheel, they left the airport and took Mexico/261 to Mexico/180E for the hour-long drive out of Mérida, a city with one of Mexico's largest populations, half of which was of Mayan descent.

Gage had chosen to stay at the historic Hacienda San José, an upscale boutique hotel, because it had been one of the oldest sisal plantations in the Yucatán and was located not far from the ruins. There were hundreds of haciendas in Mexico, some still beautifully maintained, others falling into disrepair or almost totally gone.

Though the Hacienda San José had been completely remodeled, its historical aspects hadn't been altered. Gage figured it would give them some sense of what the original Peralta plantation might have looked like before it descended into ruins.

At the last minute, he'd had Maggie extend the reservation, giving any interested party the illusion that the hacienda was their headquarters for the search.

Instead, they would be taking rooms in what barely passed for lodgings about an hour's drive away, in the tiny town of Alux'ob, the Mayan name for the spirits the locals believed inhabited the area—small invisible creatures who supposedly whistled to scare off predators or thieves.

Fitting, Gage thought, considering what they had come to retrieve.

The Hummer turned off the main highway onto a narrow road lined with lush green tropical vegetation. Vines covered stone archways, and palm trees sprouted alongside the road.

The vehicle continued to the hotel, and Mateo pulled to a stop in front. Gage helped Abby down from the Hummer, his insides tightening as his gaze snagged on the spreading dark spot on her jaw.

As much as he'd wanted to call the police, there was no way he could. Too many people knew about the expedition as it was.

Abby's attackers were still on the loose, but at least he'd managed to land a few solid punches, one that had broken the bigger man's nose. He felt a sweep of satisfaction at the memory of Abby crashing a vase over the mustached waiter's head, dispensing some small measure of justice.

Mateo took Abby's carry-on, and they walked into a spacious open-air lobby with lofty wooden ceilings and bright-painted walls: red, blue, and yellow against crisp white. A polished red-tile floor stretched down the halls.

Unfortunately, they had traded the comfortable 80-degree weather of Mexico City for the moist 95-degree heat of the Yucatán. Inside the hotel, air conditioning cooled much of the interior, and ceiling fans whirred overhead.

With only fifteen rooms and most of the occupants out sightseeing in the area, there weren't many people about, which suited Gage just fine. A dark-skinned desk clerk with the large curved beak depicted in many Mayan drawings handed over two keys to the suite Maggie had reserved.

"Your room has a beautiful view of the garden, Señor Logan. I hope you and your lady enjoy it."

"I'm sure we will." Gage handed a key to Abby, who was taking in the hand-carved furniture, open archways, and lush greenery that freshened the interior.

Gage declined the clerk's guidance to the room, set a hand at Abby's waist, and urged her down the hall in the direction the man pointed. Halfway there, he spotted his brother approaching.

"Glad you got here safely." Edge gripped his shoulder and leaned in, then bent and kissed Abby's cheek. He frowned at the bruise on her jaw. "I got your text. You weren't kidding when you said you had some trouble at the hotel. You okay, Abby?"

"I'm all right. Glad Gage showed up when he did." She flicked him a glance that reminded him she was here to stay and not going home until this was over. Gage almost smiled. He had to admit she was as determined as he was.

"I hope you got in a few good punches," his brother said.

Gage grunted, his mind returning to the clash at the hotel. "Not enough. Abby cracked one of the bastards over the head with a ceramic vase. He'll have a headache for a while." She was feisty, all right, he thought. Especially in bed. Gage's groin tightened.

Edge smiled at Abby and winked, and Gage felt a shot of irritation. With his glossy, slightly curly black hair, longer since his departure from the military, blue eyes, and high cheekbones, Edge had always attracted women. Fortunately for him, he had never pursued a female who belonged to Gage.

"When did you check in?" Gage asked him.

"Been in the area a while. Checked in here this afternoon." Edge had been doing preliminary reconnaissance, per their plan. Gage had no idea how long Mateo had been in the Yucatán— long enough, undoubtedly, to know his way around. His ability to mix with the locals was one of the things that made him so valuable.

Gage grabbed the handle of his carry-on. "Why don't we head down to my suite? We can order some food and talk things over while Abby and I settle in."

"Good idea," Edge said easily. If his brother was surprised he had brought Abby on the expedition, that she would be sleeping in his bed, it didn't show.

Gage led the way to their suite and opened the door into an airy, high-ceilinged room painted in white and the same tropical green as the lush potted palms on the red tile floors. An open-ceilinged thatched roof rose overhead, and the king-sized bed was draped with netting.

Gage flicked a glance at Abby. Tonight he would take her in this luxurious bed, but as soon as they were installed in their crowded, threadbare accommodations in Alux'ob, he would have to keep his hands off her. Not an easy task, he had discovered.

By the time they collected the luggage that had been shipped directly to the hotel and Mateo had ordered supper for all of them, it was after seven and already dark outside.

"Your text said you got the permits," Edge said as they sat in wooden chairs around a rustic table in the corner of the suite.

"It cost us a pretty penny," Gage said. "But if we find what we're looking for, it'll be worth it."

"You think the trouble at the hotel will follow you down here?"

"I think there's a very good chance, though once we leave for Alux'ob, it may take them a while to find us."

"I took a look at the town," Edge said. "The place is about as low-key as it gets, not much more than a clearing on the side of a dirt road leading into the tropical forest. There's a cantina, the hotel—if you can call it that, the Posada Utsil—and a single-pump gas station."

"Sounds perfect," Gage drawled. "We won't have to worry about tourists."

"That's for sure," Edge said. He sprawled back in his chair, making the wood screech, and stretched his long legs out in front of him. "Unfortunately, we've got a little problem we didn't plan on."

"What's that?" Gage asked.

"From what I've learned, there are three cartels working this area: Los Zetas, the Pacific Cartel, and the Gulf Cartel. Unfortunately for us, Los Zetas and the Gulf Cartel are having territorial issues. They're a time bomb ready to explode."

Gage's jaw tightened. "Just what we need."

"I have heard this, also," Mateo said. "The people in the villages are worried."

Gage shook his head. "Nothing we can do but charge forward."

"Actually, I've made a few plans in that regard," Edge said. "I've got a couple of people flying in, vets I know we can trust. They'll act as part of my team while you're working."

"Great. When do they get here?"

"Couple of days. They'll be meeting us in Alux'ob."

"We'll need more rooms."

"Already took care of it."

Gage nodded. "I plan to spend tonight and tomorrow night here, so that should work just right. I want to take a look around, get a feel for the area. We can move some of our gear into the rooms in Alux'ob, check it out, and get our base of operations set up. As soon as that's happened, we can pinpoint the location of the old hacienda and take our first look."

Neither Edge nor Mateo had actually been to the ruins. There was no way to know who was watching, and they needed to be prepared before showing their hand.

"We need to figure different routes in and out in case we have to move in a hurry," Edge said. "If the treasure's there, we need the extraction to be as fast and efficient as possible. We get in, get what we came for, and get the hell out—the sooner the better."

A knock at the door interrupted their conversation. The waiter arrived with a rattling cart. He walked over and opened tall wooden doors that led out to a private patio surrounded by tropical forest. Though the dry forest itself posed a hostile environment, it was also beautiful.

Bright red flowers covered the ground, white orchids nestled in the roots of a massive banyan, and more flowers hung from a nearby tree in thick yellow clusters.

A soft floral scent hung in the air as the waiter laid a supper of traditional Mayan food on a linen-draped table. The evening temperature was cooler, but still warm.

Gage seated Abby next to him at the table. As soon as Edge and Mateo sat down, the waiter quietly disappeared.

"What are we eating, Mateo?" Abby asked, studying the colorful meal on her plate.

Mateo smiled. "It is called *chocinita pibil*, a slow-cooked pork dish. It is served with corn tortillas, pickled red onion, habanero salsa, and cilantro." He pointed to another dish. "Yucatecan tamales filled with chicken. They are covered with *achiote*, an earthy, mildly tangy paste made from the annatto seed."

"Looks delicious," Abby said.

"*Sí*, and we have *marquesitas* for dessert. Like a French crêpe," he explained. "Only thinner and crunchier. These are filled with chocolate, but it could be anything from cheese to Nutella."

"Let's dig in," Gage said. "A day or two of luxury is the most we're going to get."

"They are here." Paulo Escobar stood in the doorway of the study.

"Here? In Sacniete?" The town's name was a Mayan word that meant White Flower. Hardly fitting, Arturo thought, considering the criminal element that did business in the small, inconsequential village.

"They arrived in Mérida two days ago," Paulo explained. He was dark-haired and thin-faced, nothing but lean, sinewy muscle. He had been working for Arturo since the glory days when Arturo had money to burn, an inheritance from his wealthy father. Those days were past, but Paulo and some of Arturo's most trusted men had stayed with him, certain the good times would come again.

Maybe they finally had.

"The girl and the others are staying at the Hacienda San José." It was a well-known hotel in the Yucatán.

"So the old man was right." Arturo rose from the chair behind the ornate desk in his study, one of the last few pieces of original furniture he hadn't been forced to sell. "It wasn't just more of his lunatic ranting and raving."

"It is true he was feverish, nearly out of his mind, but Zuma believed him from the start. The old man talked about the gold. He said the girl would come. Now she is here."

"She has come to retrieve the gold," Arturo said. Just as the old man had believed she would.

"Perhaps all we need to do is follow where she leads," Paulo suggested.

"And if she and Logan are smart enough to elude our watchdogs and manage to find the gold?"

Paulo was wise enough not to reply.

"Send a man to watch the hotel. Have him report their movements back to me."

Paulo left the study, and Arturo leaned back in his chair. Through the arched windows, he could see what used to be a magnificent garden with a rectangular pool off to one side. Now the garden was overgrown, long stringy weeds poking up through the ancient carved stones taken from the ruins of a Mayan temple, stones that were used to build the floors and terraces of the house.

The pool was now empty, its interior walls crumbling, just like the rest of the Velásquez family's once-beautiful estate.

As the oldest son, he had inherited Hacienda Cieba through his father, who expected him to be its guardian, to pass it down to future generations. Instead, he had invested his inheritance unwisely in one scheme after another, until his father's fortune had dwindled to almost nothing.

The hacienda and the property around it were all he had left. He had sold off the furnishings in the once-magnificent bedrooms, library, and gallery, even several hectares of land. He had kept the main salon and his study as they were, a façade for the few visitors that still came to the house.

The rest of the hacienda had fallen into disrepair, and he didn't have the money to return it to its once-glorious state.

Worse yet, he was dependent on his younger brother's charity just to maintain what he had left. Ramón was a powerful cartel leader and even more ruthless than Arturo. Ramón wielded the sword of money and authority, and Arturo had no choice but to bow to his commands.

The muscles in Arturo's neck tightened. He had failed his father, failed his grandfather and his ancestors before them.

Unless . . .

Unless the sick old man that Zuma had brought to him had been telling the truth. In his delirium, he had spoken of a great fortune, a treasure he had been hunting for years.

He had found it, he'd said in his barely lucid ramblings. Gold worth millions of dollars.

Arturo needed to speak to Zuma, confirm what they knew so far. Then he could move forward with his plan.

CHAPTER TWENTY-EIGHT

*A*BBY RODE NEXT TO GAGE IN THE SECOND HUMMER, WHICH bumped and swayed over the dirt road leading to their destination, Alux'ob, the tiny town closest to the ruins of the Hacienda del Oro Verde, fifteen miles away.

Mateo drove the Hummer in front of them, Edge riding shotgun. *Shotgun*, she mentally repeated, smiling since the men in both vehicles were armed to the teeth.

Edge and Gage each carried a pair of semiautomatic pistols; Edge was also armed with a Mossberg Thunder Ranch shotgun, or so she'd been told, and Gage had his big knife strapped to his thigh. No one ever seemed to know what weapons Mateo carried, but she was sure he had something.

All of them were strong men, and tough enough to take on cartel members—or anyone else—if it came to that. With the scruff of beard along Gage's square jaw and an olive drab T-shirt stretched over his massive chest, he looked capable and determined, and sexy as hell.

As the vehicle hit a pothole in the road, Abby flicked him a sideways glance. Gage gripped the steering wheel, causing his thick biceps to bulge beneath his short-sleeved T-shirt, and her mouth actually watered. She knew exactly what all those delicious muscles looked like, exactly how they felt beneath her hands, remembered how good his big body felt pressing her down in the mattress.

She thought about what had happened between them in the net-draped king-sized bed last night and wished it would happen again.

Not likely with their shabby new lodgings being a less-than-one-star accommodation in the middle of the tropical forest. She'd be lucky if their room had a toilet.

She cast Gage a glance. Though his weapons were out of sight, stuffed into the pockets of his cargo pants, they were within easy reach should they run into trouble.

A definite possibility. Where millions of dollars in gold were concerned, anything could happen.

Abby thought back to the kidnap attempt in Mexico City and wondered if the men had followed. Their secret was no longer well-guarded. Too many people knew they had come to Mexico in search of gold.

The taillights of Mateo's Hummer flashed on as the vehicle slowed. Edge had devised a means of leaving the Hacienda San José unseen; then he had made certain they weren't followed.

They were approaching what looked like a wide spot in the narrow dirt road. A couple of square buildings with flat metal roofs sat on each side, one with a lone gas pump out in front. A red-painted building at the far end of what passed for a town had a sign out front that read, POSADA UTSIL, a combination of Mayan and Spanish that translated as Best Hotel.

Abby sighed. *Home sweet home*, she thought.

Gage checked them in, parked in a space in front of the room, and unloaded some of their gear into one of the extra rooms he had rented. With the rooms Edge had added, they took up the entire hotel.

"Not much, is it?" Gage said, surveying the tight quarters that had a double bed, a single nightstand holding a lamp with a partially broken shade, and a three-drawer dresser that had seen better days. There was a wobbly ceiling fan above a trio of naked bulbs that lit the room with harsh, unforgiving light.

Abby breathed a sigh of relief when she spotted a rusty toilet through the open bathroom door. At least she wouldn't have to share with the other men.

"I bet you've stayed in a lot worse places," she said to Gage, smiling.

He chuckled. "That's an understatement."

"So what do the locals think we're doing here?"

Gage set his carry-on on the bed, unzipped it, and flipped open the lid to unpack. "We're tourists exploring the area. I'm your husband. I'm keeping you company while you're taking photos and writing an article on the flora and fauna of the tropical dry forest."

Her husband. Her heart stuttered at the thought of what it might be like if they were truly married. If the man were anyone but Gage Logan, it might be something she could imagine. But Gage wasn't the type to settle down, and as she thought of it, neither was she. She was too independent, too used to taking care of herself.

Abby buried the thought, surprised at the pang of yearning she felt.

Her eyes ran over Gage's unshaven jaw and the knife strapped to his thigh. "You look more like a mercenary than a tourist," she said. "What are Mateo, Edge, and his security people supposed to be doing here?"

Gage just shrugged. "Doesn't really matter. We're paying our hosts well. We've rented the entire hotel at triple the rate for the next two weeks, maybe longer. No one's going to push it."

Abby finished unpacking her meager supply of clothes and looked up at a soft rap on the door.

Mateo stood in the outside corridor, his arm around the shoulders of a young, dark-haired, dark-eyed boy. "This is Carlos. We met when I was here before. Carlos is going to be our helper."

Gage looked the boy over and frowned. "Are you sure about this?" Carlos was far too thin, scrawny to the point of emaciation, with straight black hair that hung halfway to his shoulders, blunt cut on the ends. His narrow feet were bare. Abby felt a tug in her heart.

"Carlos can sleep in one of the extra rooms," Mateo said.

"What about his parents?" Gage asked.

"He is an orphan. Carlos knows the area for miles around. He needs the work, and we can use his help."

Gage studied the boy a moment more and finally nodded. "All right, then." He walked over and crouched in front of Carlos. "*Cuantos años tienes?*" How old are you?

"I am ten," Carlos replied in fairly good English.

One of Gage's dark eyebrows went up. "Where did you learn to speak English?"

"My mother taught me. She was a teacher in Utsil for a while. Then we moved to Alux'ob, and she died."

Gage's blue eyes darkened. "What about your father?"

Carlos just shrugged his bony shoulders. "I do not know."

Gage rose to his feet and stuck out a big hand, which completely engulfed the boy's small one as they shook. "It's nice to meet you, Carlos." He turned. "This is Abby."

Abby smiled. "I'm sure you'll be a great help, Carlos."

The boy puffed out his narrow chest. "Whatever you need—you will tell Carlos and he will get it for you."

Abby's smile widened. "That sounds great." She looked up at Gage. "You know, I'm getting hungry. I bet Carlos knows a good place for us to eat."

The boy's black eyes lit up. "*Sí*, Señora Abby, I know a very good place."

Abby reached down and took hold of his small brown hand, felt it curl trustingly around her own, and her heart slowly melted. He was just a boy, and he was completely alone. She knew what that felt like, and it was far worse for a child. "Anyone else want to come?"

Gage shot her a look. "You aren't going anywhere by yourself, sweetheart. So yes, I'm coming along."

The endearment had her gaze shooting to his, though it was simply part of the game they were playing. After what had happened in Mexico City, Gage was determined to keep her safe.

She looked down at the boy. "All right, Carlos, let's go."

They headed along the dirt street to the Cantina Imperial, in one of the flat-roofed square buildings on the opposite side of the road, this one painted bright blue. Gage pushed open the swinging door and held it so she, Carlos, and Mateo could enter. Edge was out doing whatever he did to ensure their security and wouldn't be back before nightfall.

The dimly lit interior of the cantina was a cool respite from the outside heat, but the tile-floored room wasn't empty. Clusters of men sat at rough wooden tables off to one side, disreputable-looking with their shaggy hair, mustaches, dirty clothes, and rubber-soled leather sandals.

They sat up straighter as Abby and their small group walked past, and she could feel their eyes on her. Her pulse quickened. She was suddenly glad Gage was there and that he was armed.

They ordered the dishes Carlos suggested, and the meal was brought out: *poc chuc*, slices of pork marinated in sour orange and achiote sauce, and *sopes*, tortillas stuffed with beans, topped with shredded chicken and lettuce.

The boy wolfed down the food as if he were starving, which his appearance said he was. At least he would have decent meals for the next two weeks.

Unless they were able to find and retrieve the gold before then.

Tonight they were going to the spot pinpointed on King's map, the ruins of the original Peralta plantation, about fifteen miles from the town. They would scout the area and plot their course. If everything looked as it should, they would go back tomorrow and search for the treasure in the light of day.

The Devil's Gold was in reach. Abby could feel it.

Tonight, she thought, their search would truly begin.

Gage could sense danger a mile away. In this case, it was lurking in the corners of the Cantina Imperial, nothing more than a painted stucco structure with an open tin ceiling, shutters that closed over windows without glass, and a red tile floor.

He didn't miss the weapons some of the men openly carried, semiautomatic pistols, stout wooden bats, and knives, the blades occasionally flashing in a ray of sunlight that managed to force its way inside. Cartel members, he figured, though he had no idea which group.

Los Zetas, or one of the others—either way, it wasn't good news.

And the way the men were looking at Abby made the hackles rise on the back of his neck. She was a beautiful woman. He caught a few lewd remarks in Spanish, and his jaw tightened, his protective instincts kicking in. Gage forced himself to ignore them.

There were at least twelve men in the bar, possibly more in the back room. If a fight broke out, the odds weren't good. An incident could be deadly.

The boy didn't seem to notice, engrossed in his meal as he was. Next to him, Mateo had schooled his features into a mask that showed no concern, though Gage knew he wasn't happy to see the men in town. Mateo cast him an occasional warning glance, aware of his protective feelings for Abby, reminding him of the high stakes they were playing for.

They finished the meal, and Gage paid the bill. He set a hand possessively at Abby's waist as they walked out of the cantina, letting the men know exactly whom she belonged to.

There was lust in the men's dark eyes. Watching the unconsciously sexy way she walked toward the door, Gage found his own blood pounding. He remembered making love to her last night, thought how good they were together, and wanted her all over again. Abby was his. At least until this was over.

Her gaze ran over him as they walked back to the hotel, and he could feel the heat that sparked between them. A sagging bed in a primitive hotel room with paper-thin walls was the last place he wanted to take her.

And yet when Mateo and the boy headed to their respective quarters for a brief nap in the brutal afternoon heat, Gage closed the door to their room, turned her into his arms, and kissed her. He cupped her face and kissed the corners of her mouth, then sank into her soft lips again.

"I want you," he said on another slow kiss. "I know it's not the time or place, but my body doesn't seem to care." He took her hand and moved it down to cover his heavy erection.

Abby's fingers closed around him. "I want you, too. I always seem to want you."

Gage groaned.

"It's a bad idea," he said, kissing the side of her neck. "These walls are like paper."

Abby's arms slid around his neck. "Edge's room is next door, and he's not in."

Gage nipped her earlobe. "You think you can be quiet?"

The corners of her mouth tipped up. "Depends on what you do to me."

He chuckled. "I'm going to make you come. That much I can promise." Gage kissed her again, forcing himself to be gentle, coaxing her lips apart, then deepening the kiss and taking what he wanted. Abby's response was immediate, her mouth softening under his, her nipples tightening as her breasts flattened against him.

Even with the ceiling fan stirring up a breeze, it was hot in the room. Gage stripped off his T-shirt and tossed it away, thought of the men in the cantina, and left on his cargo pants in case there was trouble.

Abby peeled her T-shirt off over her head, unfastened her bra and tossed it away.

"Take off the rest," Gage commanded. She liked it when he took control, and after the way the men in the cantina had looked at her, he needed to mark her, brand her as his, bind her to him in some way.

"Unbraid your hair."

Standing naked in front of him, she pulled off the band holding her long golden-red braid and combed her fingers through it, separating the fiery strands, spreading them around her shoulders. His groin tightened painfully, urging him to take her.

Gage ignored the demands of his body, refusing to be hurried. Not today.

"Come here," he said softly, waiting patiently as she approached, her eyes never leaving his face. The moments dragged out, making him harder still.

"I've never told you how beautiful you are," he said, trailing a finger down her cheek. "I've never said that I think about being inside you even when you're not around."

She reached out and flattened her palms on his chest. "I think about you, too, Gage. I remember the way you touch me, and I want more."

His heartbeat quickened. He reached out and cupped a pale, ripe breast, ran his thumb back and forth across her nipple. Abby trembled as he bent his head and took the fullness into his mouth. She combed her fingers through his hair, silently begging for more.

Unzipping his cargo pants, Gage freed himself, kissed her deeply as he lifted her up and wrapped her legs around his waist. Her arms slid around his neck. He carried her across the room and sat down on the edge of the bed, adjusting her so she straddled him, a knee on each side, spreading her open for his touch.

Abby's head fell back as he began to stroke her, knowing what she liked and exactly the way she liked it. She was ready for him, as she always was, her body hot and slick as he positioned his hard length and slid himself inside.

Abby moaned, and her hold tightened around his neck.

"Easy . . ." Refusing to be rushed, he gripped her hips to hold her in place and began to move, slowly at first, then driving deep, taking what he wanted, giving her what she wanted too.

Abby clung to him, her long, fiery hair shifting across her back, her body moving in perfect rhythm with his.

He wanted to tell her how good she felt, how she matched him better than any woman he had ever known. He might have, if it weren't for the power it would give her, a power he couldn't afford to concede.

"Hold on, baby," he said, slamming into her faster, deeper, harder. "Stay with me." The breeze from the ceiling fan washed over him, but it did nothing to cool his blood.

Abby arched her back, taking even more of him, and he felt her tighten around him. Fierce pleasure washed through him, hot and intense, drawing every muscle taut. His release came hard and fast, matching hers as they reached the peak together.

Long seconds passed, yet his heart still hammered wildly. Abby pressed her lips against his sweat-slick skin right over his heart, and something shifted inside him, expanded into an emotion he had never felt before. Something he couldn't afford to feel.

Something he refused to allow.

What was it about this woman that touched him in a way no other woman had? Whatever it was, he couldn't permit his feelings to grow any deeper. There was no place for a woman in the life he led. He had learned that lesson before.

Whatever his feelings, he needed to end them now, before it was too late.

Unwrapping her arms from around his neck, he lifted her away and settled her naked on the bed. He went into the bathroom to clean up, came out and pulled on a fresh T-shirt, then headed for the door.

"You're going out?" Abby asked. "Where are you going?" She looked beautiful, with the faint sheen of moisture on her skin, her shiny hair a tangle around her shoulders. He wanted to turn back, go over to the bed, and take her again.

"I need some air," he said. "Why don't you nap for a while? I won't be gone long." And he wouldn't go far. He didn't trust the men in the cantina.

Worse yet, now he knew he couldn't trust himself. Not when it came to his feelings for Abby. He needed to put things back the way they were before, keep the physical part of their relationship, but separate everything else.

It wouldn't be easy, but Gage was determined.

With a last glance at Abby, he stepped out into the heat and closed the door.

The heavy metal click felt like a lock closing off his heart.

CHAPTER TWENTY-NINE

*P*ITCH DARKNESS CLOAKED THE DENSE FOREST AS THE HUMMER drove along the narrow, overgrown lane leading to the ruins of the old hacienda, once the Peralta plantation. Twin yellow circles shining from the headlights were all that illuminated their way.

As before, Mateo and Edge rode in the vehicle in front of them. They'd been in the area to get a feel for what they would be facing, though not to the ruins themselves. Secrets had a way of getting out.

Abby turned on her cell phone and pulled up the satellite map she had downloaded before they'd left Denver. Until now, they hadn't used their phones since the incident in Mexico City. They didn't want to be tracked. There was no service this far out of Alux'ob. Even there, communication was spotty. But the map was already downloaded to the phone.

"We're almost there," Abby said, following the lines on the screen. The vehicle ahead made a turn to the right, and Gage followed. A few seconds later, a stone arch appeared in front of them, overgrown with vines and weeds. As they passed beneath the arch, she could see the road ahead curving off toward their destination.

An animal darted out in the road, panicked, turned, and scuttled away.

"Anteater," Gage said. "Big one." It was about five feet long, with a pointed snout and yellowish-white and black fur. "They're nocturnal," he added.

Abby's heart was still racing from the near miss and seeing such an incredible animal in the wild. "So I just learned."

"They're actually very shy."

"With the size of those claws, I'd rather not run into one in the forest."

In the colored lights on the dash, she caught Gage's smile.

They drove another quarter mile and came to a long slab of stone topped by arched columns, all that was left of the front entrance to what had once been a grand hacienda.

Ahead of them, Mateo slowed, then continued along the road, circling around the house to the back. Off to one side, outbuildings were now piles of stone covered by vines and bushes that had grown up through the cracks.

They reached what had been the rear entrance, and both vehicles pulled to a stop. They left the headlights on so they could see what remained of the hacienda. From what Abby could tell, there was nothing but stone walls two to four feet high, part of the foundation.

They climbed out of the vehicles, and Abby unrolled the drawing Gage had made from satellite views of the grounds, combined with the information King had left in the safe deposit box.

Edge walked up, and so did Mateo. "Not much left," Edge said, his gaze tracking the shapes outlined by the headlights.

Abby spread the drawing open on the hood of the car, and Gage clicked on his long-handled flashlight to study it. His gaze went back to the remnants of the house. "Mostly, it's just the original foundation, the perimeter stones King described."

The old plantations were built in a similar design, much like the Hacienda San José, with a long, gallery-style front entrance, a rambling single-story residence, and gardens in the rear. According to the brochure Abby had read, there were fifteen bedrooms and suites in the Hacienda San José, probably at least an equal number here.

"How big do you think it was?" Abby asked.

"I'd say twelve to fifteen thousand square feet on the main level."

"Plus the rooms below the house," Abby said. "The wine cellar, food-storage chambers, and probably some servants' quarters."

"A lot of these old plantations had their own jail cells under the house," Gage said. "The plantations were located far away from any town, and each estate was its own small village. According to King, in a room under the ruins is where we'll find the gold."

Edge studied the drawing. "I didn't think you were planning to use heavy equipment to dig the place up."

"I'm not," Gage said. "King's already found the gold—or at least that's the premise we're working on. So there's an entrance somewhere we can get to without having to dig very deep."

Abby shined her own smaller flashlight around. "The property is so overgrown, it's going to be hard to find our way into the lower level, even with King's instructions."

"King said he covered the entrance back up when he left so it looked exactly as it had before."

"In daylight, it will be easier," Mateo said. "You have come this far. You will find it."

Gage glanced over at his friend. "Let's hope you're right."

Abby followed the track of Gage's flashlight as the beam traveled over the low rock walls that outlined the long rectangular shape of the house.

Somewhere—among the dense shrubs, plants, bushes, leafy trees, and undergrowth within the foundation—was a passage that would lead to untold wealth. Abby felt a little kick of excitement just thinking about it.

"Let's go get some sleep," Gage said. "It's going to be a long day tomorrow." He took her hand to help her navigate the rough ground back to the passenger side of the Hummer.

Glancing over her shoulder, Abby took a last look at the ruins of the old hacienda. *We'll find it, King*, she promised. And prayed she could keep her word.

After spending the night in Mérida, Edge's security team showed up in Alux'ob at eight o'clock the next morning. Finished with a breakfast of *huevos motuleños* that Carlos had fetched for them from the cantina, Gage walked Abby out to meet them.

Edge made the introductions to his crew. "Guys, this is my brother, Gage. The lady is Abigail Holland. You've already met Mateo." Edge turned to the additional two team members, a man and a woman, both veterans who had served in Afghanistan. "Gage and Abby, meet Trace Elliott and Skye Delaney. Gage, you met Trace at Kade's wedding. He worked security on the ranch for a while when Kade was having trouble."

"I remember," Gage said, reaching out to shake Elliott's hand. He remembered the man, dark-haired and good-looking, with intense blue eyes.

The woman, Skye Delaney, was average height, her skin suntanned to a smooth bronze. She had softly curling, sun-streaked brown hair, about shoulder-length, pulled back in a low ponytail. Even without makeup, she was strikingly attractive.

Her handshake was firm and strong. Edge had told him Skye had been injured in Afghanistan. Apparently, she had taken shrapnel in one leg, which had also been badly burned, in an attack on her Humvee. From what he had seen so far, it didn't slow her down.

Abby shook each of their hands. "Nice to meet you both," she said.

"Trace and I served together," Edge explained. "I've been working with him and Skye at Nighthawk for a while." Nighthawk Security, where Kade had met his wife, Ellie, a private investigator at the time.

"They're both former army," Edge said. "They're good at what they do, and they're people we can trust."

"Welcome aboard," Gage said. Bringing on more security posed a certain risk, but now, with cartel members in the area, there wasn't any choice. If the search dragged out, he would have to hire day laborers to help with the work, but he would address that problem when the time came.

Gage turned to Mateo. "Let's load the gear and head out."

Shovels, picks, rakes, hoes, metal detectors, a Leica distance measurer, two wheelbarrows, miscellaneous other equipment and gear, along with a drone, were loaded into the Hummers.

Mateo had stocked up on food before his arrival: protein bars, trail mix, peanut butter, crackers, tortillas, cheese, jerky, canned tuna, hard meats, and assorted other snacks and sweets. Coolers held bottled water, even some Gatorade. Handling the details was part of Mateo's job, and he did it well.

Gage had no idea how long it would take to locate the entrance to the lower level. With temperatures in the high 90s, they'd have to take frequent breaks and be sure to stay hydrated.

He and Abby set off with the boy in one vehicle, Mateo and Edge in the other. Trace and Skye were staying behind to make sure they weren't followed, then joining them at the site in a third vehicle, an older Jeep that Gage hoped wouldn't break down on the way.

The narrow, overgrown road deteriorated the farther they drove from town. Noise from the engine startled an occasional white-tailed deer and a couple of colorful parrots. As he rounded a turn, Abby gripped his arm, excited to spot a cinnamon-colored coati, a raccoon-like mammal with a pointed nose and a long, ringed tail.

It took less than an hour on the narrow, bumpy road to reach the old hacienda. Gage pulled through the arched stone gate, and both vehicles drove around to the back. They parked in the shade of overhanging trees, and the engines were turned off.

Working together, they unloaded the gear, while Gage mapped out a search grid covering the area inside the foundation. When the third vehicle arrived, Trace and Skye took off walking, making a perimeter check of the location. They would also be doing vehicle security sweeps while the rest of the team worked.

King's notes marked the approximate location of the underground rooms, but at the time, he had only discovered the first of what he believed were several different caches of gold.

He'd left Denver for Mexico to recover the first cache and search for the rest, but he'd never made it home. The notes he had left behind were all the information they had.

Mateo grabbed a shovel, buried the blade in the dirt, then leaned on the handle as he spoke. "You must all remember there are poisonous snakes in the area. They are not that common, but some are deadly."

"Coral snakes," Gage said. "Rattlesnakes, black cantils, and pit vipers. Abby, you know what to look for, right?"

"Believe me, I know what a rattlesnake looks like. I studied photos of the rest."

"Good girl." He thought of her near-deadly snake encounter in the Superstitions, and unease slid down his spine.

"Trace has worked down here, and so have I," Edge said. "Skye is no stranger to the hostile creatures in this kind of environment."

Carlos's skinny legs pounded the earth as he hurried over. "I will keep watch for snakes. I do not like them."

Abby laughed. "Neither do I, Carlos. You let me know if you see one."

"*Sí*, Señora Abby." Carlos assumed Abby was Gage's wife, which was the story he had told the innkeeper. *Abby Logan. Mrs. Gage Logan.* Just thinking about it sent a wave of panic through him.

Gage remembered Cassandra and the tragic end to her life. Maybe there was a time it could have happened for him and Abby. Not anymore.

"Let's get to work," he said.

CHAPTER THIRTY

T HOUGH THE DAY WAS STILL EARLY, IT WAS ALREADY HOT BY THE TIME they began to search. The weather was changing; a big tropical storm was predicted in the coming days, but it wasn't here yet.

They started with a drone flyover of the main structure, outbuildings, and surrounding hectares of land. The information the drone gathered was interesting but, aside from the discovery of an ancient cenote, only confirmed what they already knew.

Gage couldn't resist taking a look at the circular sinkhole in the limestone bedrock. There were thousands of cenotes in Mexico, most filled with groundwater. They were deep, and a beautiful shade of blue, but they could be deadly. Years ago, they had supplied water to the Mayans, who had also used them for sacrificial offerings.

The thought gave Gage a chill.

They returned to the ruins of the hacienda and went to work. Raking up vines and flowering plants, and digging up shrubs and small trees was a start. Piles of rubble covered the ground underneath, places where the walls and roof had collapsed. Timbers remained that had once held up the floors, and scores of broken pasta tiles, famous in the Yucatán, in intricate, colorful patterns.

As soon as a portion of the ground was cleared, Mateo went to work with the metal detector. The Garrett Ace 400 was a highquality sensor specifically geared to finding gold, but it also picked up other metal objects.

So far they'd found barrel staves, the handle of a water bucket, the head of an iron ax, and miscellaneous bits and pieces. No metal door hinges or anything that might indicate an entrance to the lower floor. Definitely no trace of gold.

They took an afternoon break, sat down in the shade beneath the trees, and chowed down on peanut butter and crackers, cans of tuna, and handfuls of beef jerky, all washed down with bottles of water. They rested as the sun passed directly overhead, then went back to work, starting the same routine all over again.

Gage kept an eye on Abby. She had used plenty of sunscreen, but her skin was very fair, and he didn't want her to get burned. He was responsible for her, and the sun could be vicious, even deadly.

He sank his shovel in, lifted away a blade full of dirt and debris, and tossed it into a wheelbarrow. From the corner of his eye, he watched Abby pulling her rake across a thick patch of vines. A loud shriek broke the silence as a small rodent leapt into the air in her direction.

Gage chuckled. Probably a kangaroo rat, a nocturnal rodent that lived in burrows under the ground. At the mortified look on her face, his smile widened, and he started toward her an instant before the ground opened up and swallowed her whole. Abby shrieked as she was sucked under, and Gage started running.

Mateo and Edge both charged toward her, but all of them slid to a halt a few feet from the hole, the ground around it clearly unstable.

"Abby!" From where he stood, Gage could see a portion of the rotten wooden floor had collapsed. Sprawled on the ground far below, Abby lay stunned, her body covered with debris, her face covered with dirt. Above her, a huge chunk of flooring that had been hidden by shrubs and vines hung precariously over her. The slightest movement could dislodge it.

Gage's chest clamped down. "Don't move, Abby!" Gage didn't dare go any closer. "You hear me, Abby? You'll bring the rest of it down on top of you!"

Abby's voice echoed from below. "Looks like we found a way

into the lower floor." She shifted a little, making the floor over her head bob up and down.

Gage's pulse leaped. "Dammit, I told you not to move!" He surveyed the heavy, rotting chunks of timber, the wooden planks dotted with rusty iron nails, and his mouth dried up.

Edge was already on his way to one of the Hummers to bring back a coil of rope.

"We need two," Mateo said, his dark eyes worried as he and Carlos reached the spot next to Gage. "One for Abby, and one to secure the floor."

But Edge, always a step ahead, was already returning with a coil over each shoulder.

Gage wanted to ask Abby if she was injured, but just the vibration of her voice might be enough to bring the whole rubble pile down on top of her.

"That stubby tree on the right looks solid," Gage said.

"That'll work." Edge and Mateo went to work securing the floor, checking to find the best place to tie the rope, while Gage worked out the safest way to get a line to Abby.

"I am small," Carlos said, looking up at Gage with dark worried eyes. "I could go in through the hole and help her."

Gage rested a hand on the little boy's head, his dark hair now clean and shiny. "That's very brave of you, Carlos. Let's try it this way first."

But it didn't take long to see that the boy was right. The loop Gage made and tossed toward the hole only managed to send more debris raining down on her. He studied the situation from several different angles, but there was no way he could get any closer without the rest of the floor caving in.

Edge and Mateo managed to tie the rope around a big enough chunk of floor to keep it stable, but nothing they did was going to be completely foolproof.

"Hang on, baby," Gage said. "We've got to get the floor secured before we can pull you out."

"I'm okay," she called back to him. "I can see another room down here."

He didn't answer. All he could think of was the floor collapsing, heavy beams crushing her, iron nails sinking into her soft pale flesh.

"Please stay still," he said and hoped she couldn't hear the tremor in his voice.

"We've got it tied as tight as we can get it," Edge called out.

Gage took the loop of rope and tossed it toward the hole, but the debris around the edge continued to prevent it from dropping through.

"I can do it," Carlos said.

Gage turned to him. The kid couldn't weigh more than forty pounds. Gage moved to get a better look at the opening. If Carlos inched out on his belly on the far side of the hole, he could get close enough to hand the rope to Abby.

It was dangerous. But the entire situation was dangerous. He looked at Edge, who stood a few feet away.

"We'll cut off a piece of line and tie it around him," Edge said. "Haul him up if something goes wrong."

Gage didn't want to do it. He thought of Cassandra, could still hear her piercing screams as she plunged to her death. He didn't want to put Carlos at risk as well as Abby.

He felt his brother's hand on his shoulder. "Make the call, bro. You know it's the right one."

Gage glanced back at the hole. With a deep, calming breath, he nodded.

Carlos stood still as Mateo tied a length of rope around his skinny waist and pulled the knot snug.

"You ready for this?" Gage asked.

"I can do it," the kid repeated, thumping his narrow chest.

"All right, we'll give it a try." Gage returned his gaze to the opening. "Carlos is bringing you the rope. Just stay still!"

They walked around to the other side of the hole. Carlos got down on his hands and knees, dropped to his belly, and crawled very slowly out toward the opening. The floor was more stable here, but it dipped and swayed beneath his weight. A couple of false starts, a couple of direction changes, and Carlos reached the opening.

"It will not work!" the boy called out. "I need to take it down to her."

Gage softly cursed, his body vibrating with tension.

Edge was already feeding out the line, giving the boy enough slack to drop through the opening.

"We'll haul him out as soon as you have the loop tightened around you!" Gage shouted to Abby.

"Okay!" Abby called back, trusting him as she always did.

His chest felt tight. His heart was thundering like a freight train. Time dragged. He wanted to say something, make sure she was okay, but he didn't want to distract her. He had to trust Abby as she trusted him.

Gage saw the tug on Carlos's rope, signaling Abby had the line around her, and it was time to haul the boy up. Edge and Mateo made a quick and efficient extraction, pulling Carlos out of the hole and back across the floor to solid ground.

"I did it!" The boy jumped up and down as he ran toward Edge.

"Good job." Edge smiled and ruffled the kid's dark hair.

"Hang on, Abby! We're bringing you up." Gage took a turn with the rope around the trunk of a tree, then got a firm grip on the line and braced his legs apart. Edge and Mateo joined him, and they slowly hauled Abby out of the hole. Timbers creaked, debris rained down through the opening, but the dangerous portion of the floor remained anchored in place.

Abby's head emerged, then the rest of her body. As they pulled her onto solid ground, Gage dropped the rope and ran toward her. "Are you hurt? How do you feel? Is anything broken?"

"I'm okay. I hit the ground pretty hard, but nothing's broken."

Gage pulled her into his arms. "You're okay," he repeated. "You're all right."

Abby hugged him. "I'm okay, I promise." She eased back and grinned. "I found the way in!" She punched a fist into the air. "Yes!" Abby was grinning while his insides were still quaking.

"All we have to do is clear the floor out of the way," she said with a triumphant smile.

Gage brushed the dirt off her forehead and cheeks. "You're insane, you know that?" He captured her face between his hands, bent, and very thoroughly kissed her.

Abby kissed him back, making a little sound of pleasure in her throat. She broke away and flashed another grin. "It's down there, and now we have a way to go in and get it."

Gage drew in a steadying breath. "All right, fine." His gaze scanned the three people around him: Mateo, Edge, and Carlos. "The lady says we're going to find what we're looking for down in that hole. Let's take a break, hydrate, and get to work."

Everybody smiled and nodded. They were ready for this and so was he. He just hoped like hell there wouldn't be any more accidents.

CHAPTER THIRTY-ONE

A HOT SUN SPILLED THROUGH THE WINDOWS. OVERHEAD, THE CEILing fan whipped the air. Arturo leaned back in the chair behind his ornately carved desk as the door opened and Paulo led Zuma into the room.

His gaze swept over the woman's familiar face. Even with the fine silver strands in her heavy black hair and the few extra pounds she carried, Zuma Delgado was a beautiful woman.

Years ago, for a time, they had been together, but Arturo's tastes had always run to younger women. A pretty serving maid had caught his eye, and Zuma had found them together. Their parting had been amiable. She had always known he would stray.

Zuma had taken a job as a server in the Cantina el Gato Rojo, which included rooms upstairs, where she still lived. It was there, in the Red Cat Cantina, she had met King Farrell, older, but still a handsome man, and apparently quite virile.

He stayed with Zuma whenever he came to the Yucatán, and Farrell had gone to her when he had fallen ill.

"You look exhausted," Arturo said, rising. "Why don't you sit down?"

Zuma walked toward him, head held high, loathing clear in a beautiful face now lined with age. Her bright, full skirts swirled around her ankles as she took the seat across from him, adjusting the white peasant blouse that covered her voluptuous breasts.

Arturo sat back down. "Tell me again what the old man said when he came to you," he demanded.

"He was delirious, barely clinging to life. There is no way to know if what he said is true."

"Tell me!" he demanded.

"He said he had found it—the Devil's Gold. He said he had come back to retrieve it. Then he fell ill and came to me for help."

"Anything else?"

"He mentioned his granddaughter. He said she would be coming for the gold. After that, his ramblings made no sense."

"But you believe what he told you is true."

"He was feverish, but still lucid at the time. He grew worse after suffering your ill treatment."

True, he silently admitted. Deprivation, even torture had not penetrated the mind of the man he'd imprisoned in the old prison cells beneath the Velásquez family's deteriorating hacienda.

Arturo thought of the day Zuma had come to him. A friend had fallen deathly ill, she'd said. She needed a doctor, but had no money.

The doctor Arturo had so generously provided had immediately reported the old man's ramblings, snaring Arturo's interest. A little research confirmed that King Farrell was an explorer, a famous treasure hunter. Could his delirious claims of finding millions in long-buried gold actually be true?

Whispers of treasure had been circulating in the Yucatán for more than a century. If Farrell had discovered the location of the gold, Arturo was determined to claim it.

He turned to Paulo, who stood alertly next to the door. "Did you deliver the letter?"

"*Sí.* Neither Logan nor the girl were at the hotel at the time. Rico left it at the front desk, as you instructed."

It had taken weeks to track down the granddaughter Farrell had mentioned in one of his rants. Abigail, he'd said, would be coming for the gold.

In a last desperate gamble, Arturo had hired an investigator to find her, succeeding just days before she left Denver for Mexico with a man named Gage Logan. She was after the gold, Arturo was sure, on her way to somewhere in the Yucatán, where the old man had come to recover his treasure.

As head of the Velásquez family—which included Ramón, his powerful younger brother—Arturo had put out the word that he was searching for her. Just a day after her arrival, news came that she was staying with Logan at the Hacienda San José.

Arturo glanced at the gilded clock above the mantel over the fireplace. The afternoon was slipping away, and still no word. The letter he had sent was sure to get a response from the girl.

"Call the hotel," he said. "Find out if the message has been picked up." Logan and Abigail were sharing a room in the luxurious hotel. Perhaps Logan was merely taking a few days to sample the lady's charms before venturing out in the heat of the Yucatán to retrieve the gold.

Paulo pulled out his cell phone and made the call. He inquired, then ended the call. "They have not yet returned to their room."

Arturo's eyes narrowed. "But they *are* still there."

Paulo swallowed nervously. "Rico was watching the hotel as you wished, but Logan and the girl managed to slip off without being seen. They still have a room, but they have not yet returned."

Arturo could feel the fury burning into his face. "You are telling me you don't know where they are?"

"They haven't checked out. Rico thought they would be back by now."

Arturo shot up from his chair. "This is exactly what I was afraid of!"

Paulo's hand shot out as if to protect himself. Arturo noticed with satisfaction that it trembled.

"The drive is little more than an hour," Paulo said. "I will go to the hotel myself. I will find out where they've gone, and I will personally deliver the letter."

Arturo sat back down, his mind running over the possibilities. There was no way to know for sure that the girl knew where to find the treasure. At least not until he talked to her. His lips thinned. If she knew, sooner or later she would tell him.

"You have twenty-four hours," he said. "Not a minute more. If you have not found them, you and Rico will take up residence in one of the cells beneath the house." He allowed his lips to curve in a smile that showed his teeth. "And your fate will be far worse than that of the old man."

Paulo gave a single brief nod and strode for the door. It closed soundlessly behind him.

Zuma rose from her chair. "If he finds them, can you not just follow them to the gold?"

"They may not know where it is. They may just be searching, following in the old man's footsteps. Or they may know exactly where it is and find a way to elude us—as they have already managed to do. I will find them—and I won't let it happen again."

"What if Abigail doesn't know the location of the gold?"

Arturo shrugged. "Then she will become expendable." He gave Zuma the same fake smile he had given Paulo. "Just like your old friend, King Farrell."

At Gage's insistence, Abby sat in the shade for half an hour before returning to work. Mateo had armed her with a six-inch knife so she could cut through vines or deal with another vicious rodent.

Abby smiled.

By the end of the afternoon, they had managed to secure a safe way into the chamber below the hacienda. Gage stripped off his shirt to work in the heat, and Abby found herself mesmerized by the sexy display of hard male muscle.

Soon Edge and Mateo were also working shirtless, and since she was a woman and not yet dead, she allowed herself to enjoy the view. Eventually, they were able to clear enough of the floor of debris to get into the chamber.

Unfortunately, the room was empty, as was the other room Abby had spotted. Storerooms, perhaps, or servants' quarters, without a smattering of gold or much of anything else.

They took a break to eat and hydrate in the shade of the trees where the coolers were sitting, and Abby spotted Skye walking toward them.

"Where's Trace?" Gage asked, glancing behind Skye as she reached the trees. "I thought you were both coming in." They were using handheld wireless radios to communicate out here where there was no cell service.

"We thought it would be safer for one of us to come in while the other keeps watch."

"What's going on?"

"You've got company," Skye said.

"How many?"

"Two men."

"Cartel?" Gage asked.

"I don't think so. We sent them packing, but they seemed to just be watching." She grabbed a bottle of water out of the chest, twisted off the lid, and took a long swallow. "They looked more like farmers than cartel soldiers. But it's better to keep an eye out just in case."

Abby hadn't really had a chance to get acquainted with Skye, but she liked the woman's confidence and her fierce work ethic. Like Edge, Skye and Trace both took their jobs very seriously.

Abby felt safer having them around.

A couple of times she'd noticed Edge watching Skye when she wasn't looking. With her wavy dark hair and sculpted features, she was a beautiful woman, no matter her tough exterior, but whatever Edge was thinking, he didn't let it show.

Skye ate a packet of tuna and some crackers, grabbed a candy bar, and left to change places with Trace. He arrived a few minutes later and relayed the same story, but he seemed a little more tense.

"Could be just a couple of farm workers from down the road, or they could be cartel scouts from town who figured out where we are and are keeping us under surveillance."

"Let's hope it's farm workers."

Trace ate and hydrated, grabbed a snack to take with him, and headed for the Jeep. While he and Skye resumed their patrols, Abby and the rest of the crew made a last search of the rooms beneath the house.

Even when dusk settled in and the tired group headed back without success, Abby's hopes remained high. Tomorrow they would open the walls of other empty chambers and continue the search. The underground area could be as large as the house, so they had only gotten started.

Gage would be coordinating their efforts with the information King had given them. Sooner or later, they would find the treasure—or so she hoped.

They arrived back in Alux'ob, but instead of eating at the cantina, which could be asking for trouble, Mateo had made a deal early that morning with a village woman to bring breakfast and supper to the hotel each day.

Blanca, a round woman with a long gray braid, arrived with *queso rellenos*—balls of edam cheese stuffed with minced pork, raisins, almonds, and olives—topped with *k'ool blanco* sauce and accompanied by tortillas and beans. The meal was served in the spare hotel room they used as an office and a place for Carlos to sleep.

Though the food was delicious, Abby was too tired to eat more than a few bites. Even sleeping on the sagging mattress didn't sound all that bad, not when Gage would be stretched out beside her.

She glanced in his direction. His face was freshly sun-bronzed, making his blue eyes even bluer. His dark hair was streaked with golden highlights. Instead of looking tired, he looked invigorated.

Abby caught the hot gleam in his eyes, and her exhaustion faded, shifting to anticipation.

Unfortunately, when Gage opened the door and she flipped on the overhead bulbs, illuminating the bedroom, an envelope lay in the middle of the bed. Abby walked over and picked it up. Pulling out a folded sheet of paper, she read the words.

Her heart jerked as her eyes flashed to Gage's. She could feel the color leaching out of her face, and her knees went weak. Clutching the letter, she sank down on the edge of the bed.

Gage strode toward her. "What is it?"

"I-it's a letter addressed to me. It says . . . it says King is alive."

Gage grabbed the sheet of paper out of her hand and scanned the contents. "What the hell?"

"They want me to meet them in Mérida. The letter says they'll take me to him."

Gage thumped the sheet of paper. "This could have come from anyone, Abby. There's no way your grandfather is alive after all this time. He would have sent word."

She swallowed and looked up at him. "According to the letter, he's been sick for months." She felt a tear on her cheek, reached up, and wiped away the wetness. "I have to go to him, Gage. I don't have any choice."

Gage tossed the letter back on the bed. Gripping her shoulders, he hauled her to her feet. "You remember what happened in Mexico City? I have no idea how they found us here, but I know these people are ruthless. They want the gold at any price. They'll say and do whatever it takes to get it."

Another tear rolled down her cheek. "What if it's true? What if King's alive?"

His hold on her shoulders tightened, and then he pulled her into his arms. "I'm sorry. I know how you must feel. I just don't want you getting hurt."

Abby eased away. "I have to go, Gage. You know I do."

He glanced out the window into the darkness. A muscle worked in his jaw. He sighed. "You're right. You have to go." He turned away from her and started for the door. "I'll be right back. I need to find out how this envelope got into the room."

Gage stormed outside, heading for the office. The manager lived in quarters behind it.

Abby read the letter two more times. The paper was a crisp linen texture and looked expensive, and the handwriting was elegant, yet strong.

Gage walked back into the room. "The manager put the letter in the room. I'm sure he was paid well to do it. The man who delivered it said it was urgent."

"If it's true, it *is* urgent."

"If it's true."

"I have to go, Gage. I couldn't live with myself if King were still alive and I did nothing to help him."

Gage scrubbed a hand over his face. Seconds passed before he nodded. "All right, we comply with the letter, go to the address in Mérida—but we do it prepared. We set things up our way, go in and find out what's going on, but we're armed. And we're ready to get out of there if we need to."

Abby started nodding. "Okay, that sounds good."

"And we take backup. Edge, Trace, and Skye. They're good at what they do, and we need their help." Gage reached out and tipped up her chin, bent his head, and gently kissed her.

"You scared the hell out of me when you fell in that hole today," he said. "Now it looks like things could get worse. I never should have brought you down here."

"I would have come without you."

He made no reply.

"I'm glad it's you," she said. "I'm glad you're with me." She managed to smile. "We'll do this together, just like everything else."

Something moved across his features, something warm and oddly tender. Then it was gone. "You can't get your hopes up, Abby."

"I won't," she said.

But it was a lie, and both of them knew it.

CHAPTER THIRTY-TWO

*T*HERE WAS A NUMBER ON THE LETTER. GAGE MADE THE CALL ON his satellite phone instead of his cell. The people on the other end already knew their location, but there was no way to know how many others were out there tracking them.

The line picked up, but there was only silence.

"This is Gage Logan. I assume you've been expecting our call."

"Señor Logan," a male voice said. "I look forward to meeting you. However, the message was left for Abigail. Please put her on the phone." The words were spoken in English, the Spanish accent mild. The voice sounded educated, cultured, but rang with authority.

Gage clenched his jaw and handed the phone to Abby. Her fingers brushed his as they wrapped around the receiver, and a knot of worry tightened in his stomach. More trouble. More danger for Abby.

"I want to see my grandfather." She held the phone so Gage could hear. "The note says he is alive."

"Your grandfather has been quite ill, but he is still breathing. If you wish to keep him that way, you will do exactly what I say."

Her fingers tightened around the phone. "I'll do whatever you ask."

"You will come to the address on the letter. You will arrive there no later than midnight."

It was almost ten. Mérida was over an hour away. They didn't have enough time to get things set up. Gage pointed to his watch, mouthed the words *more time.*

"We can't get there by then. It's late and dark on the roads. We need more time."

"One o'clock. No later. Be at the address I gave you, or the old man will suffer. And be sure to come alone."

Gage grabbed the phone out of her hand. "That isn't happening. I go with her or she doesn't go at all. And before we do anything, we're going to need proof King's alive. Put him on the line."

Silence fell.

"You may come, Señor Logan, if that is your wish. I have no intention of harming Ms. Holland. The proof you seek lies in a sick bed in a cell beneath my hacienda. If you do not come, his life will end tonight."

Abby's face paled.

"We'll be there by one," Gage said, and the line went dead. He walked out of the room and banged on Edge's door, which immediately swung open.

"What is it?" Edge wore clean jeans, but no shirt. Beads of water clung to the dark hair on his chest from the shower he had just taken.

"Abby got a letter from someone in Mérida. They claim her grandfather is alive but very ill. Basically, they're using King as a lure to get to Abby. They're after the gold."

Edge ran his fingers through his wavy black hair. "Jesus, Gage. I didn't realize hunting for treasure was like going to war."

"These are unusual circumstances."

"Yeah, right. So what do they want?"

"They want Abby to come to Mérida, to the address on the letter. They've given us three hours, and it's going to take more than half that long to get there."

"We'll need to work fast, get everything set up before you go in. What's your plan?"

"My plan is to leave it to you."

Edge straightened. "Good choice. What's the address?"

Gage handed him the letter.

"Trace is on watch. I can reach him on the radio. You talk to Skye. Tell her to grab her gear, including firearms, and bring it here." He ducked back into his room, and Gage caught a glimpse of him opening his laptop, typing in the property address.

Gage strode down the corridor, banged on Skye's door, and relayed Edge's message.

"We've got a problem in Mérida," he added. "I think you're about to earn some hazard pay."

Returning to his room, he found Abby, dressed in a clean pair of dark blue jeans and a black T-shirt, her face freshly washed. Gage stripped and also put on clean, dark-colored clothes.

"What's the plan?" Abby asked.

"Edge is the plan. I'm trusting my brother to figure the best way in and out of this mess."

"When do we leave?"

"As soon as Edge gets things set up. He doesn't have much time, so he'll have to improvise." Gage walked over and grabbed his gear bag, pulled out the Beretta semiautomatic Mateo had provided when they'd first arrived.

"So Trace and Skye will be going along," Abby said. "What about Mateo?"

Gage had pondered that. "Mateo is with the boy. I don't want Carlos involved. Mateo can stay here and keep an eye on him and our equipment. I'd like our stuff to be here when we get back." And Edge, Trace, and Skye were all former military. They understood the language, knew how to move as one.

"You're right," Abby said. "All three of them were soldiers. They've worked together before. Mateo might be more of a liability than an asset."

His thoughts exactly. "I'll bring Mateo up to speed and tell him what we've decided."

When he returned, he found Edge, Skye, and Trace loading their gear into the back of one of the Hummers.

"We're leaving ahead of you," Edge said. "We need to check out the location, find the best way to handle the situation. Give us a twenty-minute head start. That'll still get you there before the deadline. When you arrive, you won't see us, but we'll be there."

Gage just nodded.

"Good luck," Abby said, as Edge started walking.

He stopped and turned back. "Don't either of you try to be heroes out there. Just do what they say, and let us handle the rest."

"We'll do our best," Gage agreed, but if things went sideways, he'd do whatever was necessary to keep Abby safe.

Edge's blue eyes locked with his, and the truth passed between them. His brother was no fool. By now, he knew Abby meant more to him than just a woman to share his bed. He would protect her at any cost.

"I'll see you there," Edge said and climbed into the Hummer.

Gage turned to Abby, who stood in the doorway. Her chin was firm, her mouth set. Beneath her T-shirt, he could see the faint outline of the holstered revolver clipped to her waist.

The engine fired, and Trace pulled the Hummer out into the street. Gage checked his watch. "It'll be close," he said.

"We'll make it."

Gage just nodded. With any luck, they would be on time in Mérida. With better luck, they would live through the night.

CHAPTER THIRTY-THREE

*A*BBY TURNED ON HER PHONE AND USED SIRI TO GUIDE THEM TO the address in Mérida, a small stucco house painted blue with a flat roof and a single-car garage. This late at night, the area was dark and quiet. The grass in front of the house was stringy and needed mowing. There was a car in the driveway, an older-model black SUV.

Abby prayed Edge, Trace, and Skye were somewhere nearby, but as Edge had warned, Abby couldn't see them.

Gage pulled the second Hummer up in front of the house and turned off the engine. The front door opened, and four men walked out. The one in front was tall and lean, with thick black hair cut short and a solid, broad-shouldered build. The others were shorter, darker, one with a mustache, one with a goatee, one with a gruesome scar that ran from the corner of his mouth to his jaw.

The tall man stepped away from the others. He was in his late thirties and handsome. "Abigail Holland?"

"That's right."

His black eyes shifted to Gage. "And you are Logan."

"That's right, and you are?"

"Paulo." He turned back to Abby. "Your grandfather is not here. If you wish to see him, you will come with me." He spoke English with a thick Spanish accent. He motioned to the other three men, who formed a circle around them. "Hand over your weapons."

Gage flicked Abby a glance filled with resignation. Reaching behind his back, he pulled out the pistol he was carrying and set it on the ground.

Abby set her revolver down beside it.

"Santos, you search the woman." The guy with the scar came forward to pat her down, but he was so intent on feeling her breasts, he didn't notice the knife she had strapped to her calf beneath the leg of her jeans, the knife Mateo had given her to cut away leaves and vines at the old hacienda. Abby felt a shot of satisfaction.

"Hector, you search the big one," Paulo instructed, speaking this time in Spanish. The man with the mustache did a pat-down on Gage but found nothing more. Paulo walked over to the SUV and opened the rear passenger door. "Get in."

Abby started walking, but Gage caught her arm. "Where are we going?" he asked Paulo.

"You will find out when you get there. Get in the car."

"We'll follow you in our own car."

"I said get in the car." He pulled a pistol from a shoulder holster beneath his flowered short-sleeved shirt. "Now."

Gage's jaw hardened. He urged Abby forward, and they climbed into the back seat of the SUV.

"You drive, Tomás."

The guy with the goatee, Tomás, got in behind the wheel, and Paulo got into the front passenger seat. The guy with the mustache and the guy with the scar walked halfway down the block and got into an old blue beater.

Paulo turned and tossed them a pair of black canvas bags. "Put these over your heads." He kept the gun fixed on Abby.

As she pulled on the hood, she didn't look at Gage. She knew how hard it was for him to give up control. She heard the bag rustle as he pulled it over his head.

"Drive, Tomás," Paulo instructed, all of them now speaking Spanish.

The engine rumbled to life, and the SUV backed out of the driveway. Gage reached over and took Abby's hand, and his warmth and strength seeped into her. She held on tightly as the car made a series of turns, pulled onto what she thought must be a freeway, and speeded up. She prayed Edge and the others would be able to follow.

They rode for what she figured was probably half an hour, though it seemed far longer. The SUV drove off the main highway, made a series of turns, and finally pulled to a stop. She could hear the other car pull in behind them.

The rear door opened. "Get out," Paulo commanded, and they climbed out of the car. They were guided up some stairs and across a wide porch. As they walked through a doorway, her footsteps echoed on the surface of the floor. *Tile*, Abby thought.

Paulo removed their hoods.

Abby turned to survey her surroundings and was struck by the opulence, a crystal chandelier above the entry, a gilt mirror on the wall. The ceilings were twenty feet high, and marble columns lined a single long corridor with arched doorways off each side.

As Paulo led them forward, she could see into a large salon, elegantly furnished with carved rosewood tables and a sideboard, and a lovely pair of settees, though the green velvet upholstery was fading.

The house was at least a hundred years old, probably a lot older, one of the many haciendas in the Yucatán.

Paulo knocked at the first door down the hall, then pulled it open and led them into a room lined with tall mahogany bookcases. This room was elegantly done, with gilt-framed paintings on the walls and a graceful antique mahogany writing desk with a silk-shaded lamp on top.

A man rose behind it. He was trim and perfectly groomed in a tailored black suit and white shirt. He had a narrow, pointed face and shiny black hair that gleamed in the lamplight.

"Señorita Holland. Señor Logan. It is good of you to come."

Gage stiffened. "This is hardly a social call. I don't like your tactics, Señor . . . ?"

"You may call me Don Arturo. Until we have come to some sort of an arrangement, the rest of my name is none of your concern."

"Where's my grandfather?" Abby asked. "I want to see him."

Don Arturo made a slight inclination of his head. "As you wish. I see no point in wasting time." He turned to Paulo. "Take them downstairs."

Abby's heart was racing as she fell in behind Paulo, Gage beside her. As Paulo led them farther into the house, she could see that the rooms along the corridor were nearly empty; whatever furniture had once been there was gone.

Paulo opened a door and started down a narrow staircase that was clearly meant for the use of servants. Abby followed him down, Gage close behind her.

"We know what they want," he said softly. "And that they'll do anything to get it. Don't get your hopes up."

Electric light illuminated the stairwell and the space below. There was nothing elegant in these rooms. As they passed along the lower corridor, there was no furniture. The plaster walls were cracked, and the paint was peeling. It reminded her of the storerooms below the Hacienda del Oro Verde.

Paulo opened a door near the end of the hall. "Zuma," he called out. "They are here."

Paulo stepped back to let them pass, and Abby and Gage walked into the room to see a row of iron bars across one end. It was a prison cell. Inside, a woman sat next to a man lying on a narrow cot.

Abby rushed forward and grabbed hold of the bars. Dear God, surely the emaciated form under the thin blanket could not be King Farrell. But the recognition in the golden eyes that lifted to meet her own said that it was.

Her heart jerked, and tears blurred her vision. "What have you done to him!" She jerked on the iron bars that formed the cell door, and the door swung open. Abby rushed into the cell, her heart hammering wildly. "What have they done to you . . . ?" she whispered, wiping a tear from her cheek.

The woman rose from her place beside King. She looked about fifty, with thick silver-streaked black hair pulled into a severe bun at the nape of her neck.

Abby took the woman's place on the cot, reached down, and

gently picked up her grandfather's thin blue-veined hand. It felt icy cold. She swallowed past the lump in her throat. "King, it's . . . it's Abby. We're going to get you out of here."

King moistened his dry, cracked lips. "Abby . . ."

She swallowed back tears. "Save your strength. Don't try to talk. We're getting you out of here."

A voice came from behind her. "That, my dear, is a subject we have yet to discuss."

She whirled toward the sound, saw that the man in the study, Don Arturo, stood a few feet away and that Gage had moved closer to the door of the cell.

"He needs to be in a hospital," Abby said, rising. "I want him out of here—now."

One of Don Arturo's black eyebrows lifted. "And in return?"

"What do you want?"

"You know what I want. The location of the gold you came to recover."

She knew what they wanted. It was the reason they'd sent the note. "We haven't found it yet. We're still looking. It might not even exist."

"But you believe it does, or you would not have come all this way."

Gage shifted a little closer, his posture still relaxed. But Abby could see the tension coiling in his heavily muscled shoulders.

"How did you find us?" he asked.

A smug expression settled over Don Arturo's face. "A man of my stature has many friends in the Yucatán. I had been searching for you. Word came to me that you were staying at the Hacienda San José. Lovely hotel," he added. "Unfortunately for you, one of the servers overheard you talking about Alux'ob, and one of the gardeners saw you drive off in that direction." He smiled thinly. "And so here you are."

"You've managed to get us here," Gage conceded. "Unfortunately for you, Abby is telling the truth. We haven't found the gold. We haven't found anything but half a dozen lizards and a handful of kangaroo rats."

"Then why do you still search?"

Gage shrugged his powerful shoulders. "You never know. We might get lucky."

"You will take my people to the place you search, and I will let the old man go."

"We can take you, but you're not equipped to find the gold, even if you look. It takes training, knowing what to look for, the right kind of equipment."

As Don Arturo pondered the words, Abby smoothed damp gray hair away from King's forehead. "We're getting you out," she whispered. "You're going to be all right." She looked at the woman, saw something in her expression, fear or sadness or regret. Perhaps some of each.

"What you say makes sense," Don Arturo said. "I think you will continue to search for the gold, but until you find it, the girl stays here."

Gage's whole body tightened. "That isn't going to happen. Abby goes with me. You do anything to stop us, you'll never find the gold. You must have had King locked in here for weeks. He's clearly too sick to tell you anything. We're your last chance."

Arturo's features hardened, one of his long-fingered hands balling into a fist. "I can see she means a great deal to you. I will let you take the girl, but the old man stays here and my men go with you. The gold is the price you will pay for King Farrell's freedom."

Abby shot up from the cot. "King comes with us. He needs medical attention. You can send your men, but King leaves with us." Her gaze shot to Gage. He knew her, knew she wouldn't back down on this.

His piercing blue eyes shifted away from her and fixed on Don Arturo. "You heard the lady. King goes with us. Your men can join us on the hunt. Maybe we'll even find the gold. But if we do, you get half of it, not all. That's the deal. King's freedom for half the gold."

Abby clamped down on the words fighting to escape her throat. She didn't care what it cost. She just wanted her grandfather safe and well again. Gage cast her a look, warning her to keep silent.

She remembered her grandfather telling her it was always better to hold something back, keep a bargaining chip, keep the upper hand.

Long seconds passed.

Don Arturo's mouth slowly curved in a smile that looked more feral than friendly. "You drive a hard bargain, Señor Logan. Take the girl and the old man. My men will drive you back to your vehicle and follow you to Alux'ob. If you go to the police or try to escape, they have orders to kill you."

His wolfish smile broadened. "If you wish to leave Mexico alive, you will find the gold—for both our sakes."

CHAPTER THIRTY-FOUR

*E*DGE STOOD IN THE SHADOWS JUST INSIDE THE WALL SURROUNDING the hacienda. Trace stood watch near the rear entrance, while Skye had moved into a position in the garden near the empty swimming pool.

There was an armed guard near the front door and one out back. The tall man—Edge had heard him called Paulo—and three other men were still in the house with Gage and Abby.

Edge's radio vibrated.

"They've been in there too long," Trace said. "What do you want to do?"

Edge didn't blame him for getting antsy. Edge was worried too. But patience was something he had learned in special forces.

He thumbed the mic. "Hold your position. We let this play out."

At least for now. He hadn't heard any gunshots or any sign of a scuffle, though with the thick walls of the hacienda, sounds had trouble bleeding through.

"Roger that," Trace said.

"Copy," said Skye, who was on the same channel.

But as Trace knew, the longer Gage and Abby stayed inside, the greater the danger. Edge changed position, moving toward the window, where the light of a low-burning lamp illuminated the room.

The man had returned to his desk. No sign of Gage or Abby. *Not good.*

Edge changed position again, hoping to pick up his brother's location somewhere in the house. But the rest of the hacienda was dark, and no sounds came through the glass panes. Where were they?

Suddenly he knew. Gage had said the old haciendas—like the one they were searching—had prison cells under the house.

He checked his watch, then thumbed his mic. "Five minutes. If they aren't out by then, we go in."

"Roger that," Trace said.

"Copy," said Skye.

And they all settled in to wait.

Don Arturo had returned upstairs, leaving Paulo in charge.

"We're leaving," Abby said to King, squeezing his hand. "We're taking you to the hospital."

King's faraway gaze shifted, and his eyes sharpened on her face. "No . . . hospital," he said, the words surprisingly clear.

"You've been ill for months. You need medical attention. The doctors will take care of you, help you get well. You have to go, King."

His head lolled from one side to the other in a negative movement. "No . . . hospital," he repeated.

The woman appeared in the open cell doorway. "I am Zuma, King's friend. Please . . . we need to speak."

Abby didn't want to leave him. She needed to get her grandfather out of there as fast as possible.

"I'll stay with him," Gage said. "But we need to go."

Zuma led Abby into the hallway. She was a handsome woman, with a voluptuous figure. Abby wondered at the relationship between her and King.

"There is nothing a hospital can do for your grandfather," Zuma said. "He is dying of cancer."

"What?"

"He talked about the gold when he was delirious with pain. He said that you would be coming. He has suffered greatly because of those words."

"I won't just let him die. There has to be something we can do!"

"There is nothing to be done. In the beginning, Arturo paid

for the best doctors. He wanted to keep King alive so he could find the gold. When the doctors failed to cure him, Arturo used torture. It made your grandfather weaker and sicker, until he was in no state to talk at all."

Abby bit back a sob.

"King believed you would come," Zuma said. "He worried himself nearly to death for fear they would hurt you, but the hope it gave him also kept him alive. If you love him, you will take him out of this evil place. You will make sure his last days are comfortable."

"No . . ." Abby said, shaking her head. "There has to be another way."

Gage approached. "We need to go, Abby. I'll carry your grandfather."

Her eyes met his. There was strength there she could count on. Gage was right. As long as they stayed in this place, they were in danger. And Edge might decide they needed rescuing—which they might if they didn't leave.

"All right, let's go," she said.

Gage went into the cell and lifted King into his arms, carrying him like a baby. Once a vigorous hundred-and-seventy-pound man six feet tall, her grandfather couldn't weigh more than a hundred and forty now.

Tears blurred her vision. He couldn't die. She had only just found him again. She took a shuddering breath and wiped away the wetness on her cheeks. As she followed Gage down the hall, she felt the other woman's presence beside her.

"I am going with you," Zuma said. "King needs me. I will not fail him now."

The words brought a lump to Abby's throat. She had suspected there was something between Zuma and King. She could see it now in the woman's dark eyes. "Come on, then. Let's go."

They reached the top of the stairs, and Gage carried King along the wide central corridor toward the front door. Paulo stood waiting. He followed them outside to the SUV they had arrived in.

They settled King on a blanket in the far back. Abby climbed in beside him and took hold of his hand. Zuma slid in next to Gage in the rear seat, while Tomás got in behind the wheel and Paulo sat in the front passenger seat.

They didn't bother with hoods this time. A deal had been struck, the warning delivered. They had a partner in the hunt—and like the venomous snakes in the dry forest, that partner was deadly.

From a spot in the dense foliage outside the Posada Utsil, Edge watched half a dozen men sitting around a campfire, laughing and joking, drunk on henequen liquor, a potent brew similar to mescal. Two men slept on the ground nearby, and another two stood guard in different places around the building.

The men who had followed Gage and Abby back to the hotel had added to their cadre, hiring locals from the cantina, cartel members willing to earn a little side money. His brother and Abby were back in their room, a buxom Mexican woman and Abby's grandfather, King Farrell, in another.

Edge heard a faint sound and turned to see Trace moving out of the shadows to join him. The two men eased back into the forest where they couldn't be heard.

"Looks like our cushy security job has finally gotten serious," Trace said, his eyes on the men surrounding the hotel.

"Serious as a heart attack," Edge said. "We'll take turns keeping watch. I'll take the first shift, then you, then Skye. Gage and Abby will be heading out to the dig site in the morning."

Trace looked up at the menacing pitch-black darkness overhead, the stars covered by a thick layer of clouds. A storm was moving in, and it was predicted to be powerful.

"What happens if Gage finds the gold?" Trace asked.

"Good question. We'll need to be ready for anything."

"Roger that," Trace said and blended back into the scrubby forest.

All of them were used to sleeping wherever they could. Edge moved into a position where he could watch the guards as well as the drunks. His gaze went in search of Skye, but he couldn't see her.

She doesn't need your protection, he told himself. She was as capable at taking care of herself as any woman he had ever known. And yet he couldn't rest until he made sure she was all right.

So far, the men didn't seem to have the least suspicion they were being watched. Maybe they hadn't expected Gage to bring in security. Whatever the reason, the fact they were unaware helped even the odds.

Wishing he had a strong cup of coffee, Edge settled in to wait.

They put King in one of the extra hotel rooms. Zuma sat in a chair near the door, while Abby perched next to her grandfather on the bed. She glanced over at Gage, who lounged against the wall, watching her protectively, like a lion guarding his mate.

She liked that about him, how protective he was. It was probably because of Cassandra, but Abby liked to think it was because she meant something to Gage, that she was someone special.

Her gaze returned to her grandfather. As much as she'd tried to persuade King to go to the hospital, he had refused. He was dying. He wanted these few precious hours of freedom before he passed. Abby noticed his color was even paler, though there was a tranquility about him that hadn't been there before.

She cracked open a plastic bottle and poured water into a cup, lifted his head, and held it against his dry lips. He relaxed back on the pillow.

"I knew . . . you would . . . come," he said, his voice raspy, little more than a whisper, yet stronger than before. "I was . . . ill when I called my . . . lawyer. I knew by then I was . . . going to die. I wanted you to . . . find the treasure." He weakly squeezed her hand. "I was . . . selfish. I wanted you to prove I was right about . . . the Devil's Gold."

Her throat ached. "I'm going to prove it, King. We're going to find it. We're close. We're almost there."

He kept talking—as if he had very little time to get everything said. "I was . . . in Mérida when I . . . fell ill. I went to Zuma. We have been . . . closer than friends for many years."

Abby's attention went to the woman in the chair. Zuma was still attractive. Once, she must have been as beautiful as King was handsome.

He moistened his lips. "She found a . . . doctor for me . . . but he . . . betrayed us to Arturo Velásquez. I was . . . out of my mind, ranting about the gold . . . telling Zuma you would be coming. The doctor . . . told Velásquez, and his men . . . came for me."

"Don't talk. You need to conserve your strength."

"He tried to . . . force me to tell him . . . about the gold, but there was . . . nothing he could do to a . . . dying man determined to keep his secrets."

"King, please. You'll make yourself worse."

"I need to . . . tell you. I need you to know . . . how proud I am of you."

Her eyes burned. She brought his thin hand to her lips and kissed the bony knuckles, her throat aching, along with her heart.

"You and Logan . . . he's a good . . . man. I hoped you would choose him to be the one."

Gage straightened, his eyes watchful.

"We're . . . umm . . . very good friends."

King's mouth edged up at the corners. "More than . . . friends. I . . . see the way he . . . looks at you . . . the way you look at him."

"Please . . . you need to rest."

His thin hand squeezed hers. "You must go . . . with them tomorrow, Abby. Go with them . . . to find the treasure. Give it to Velásquez . . . if you must. The money . . . doesn't matter. It never does." His gaze shifted across the room to Gage. "Ask . . . him." He gave her hand a final squeeze as his eyes slowly closed. Seconds later, he was asleep.

Zuma rose from her chair. "I will tend him, as I have done from the start. I will come for you if he worsens."

Abby looked at King. His breathing was shallow, his chest barely moving up and down. "I'll stay," she said.

"You will need your rest if you are to find the treasure." Zuma's intense black eyes pinned her. "This you must do for King."

Gage came forward. "It's almost morning. We'll get a few hours' sleep, then head for the hacienda. It's what your grandfather wants."

"Staying will not keep him from dying," Zuma added. "Give him his dream, his greatest desire."

Abby swallowed past the tears in her throat. She nodded. She knew the way King thought, what he would want her to do. He wanted her to find the treasure, to prove he was the man people had once believed.

Gage reached out and took her arm, led her back to the room they shared. He took off his clothes and helped her take off hers. When they climbed into bed, he didn't make love to her, just kissed her forehead and settled her against his side, her head on his shoulder.

"I'll wake you when it's time," he said.

Abby nodded. She was sure she wouldn't be able to sleep, but in minutes, exhaustion claimed her.

She dreamed of King and the Devil's Gold.

CHAPTER THIRTY-FIVE

GAGE BROUGHT ABBY *PADZULES* FOR BREAKFAST—TORTILLAS FILLED with hard-boiled eggs and a tomato and pumpkin-seed sauce.

She just shook her head. "Thanks, but I'm not hungry."

"You need to eat, honey. We have no idea what we're going to be facing out there today. If you won't do it for you, do it for King."

Abby reluctantly accepted the tortilla and managed to get the food down. She dressed in her work clothes, and Gage followed her to her grandfather's room, then stood watch outside the door. Velásquez's man Hector stood a few feet away, his hand on the pistol strapped to his waist.

The wind was blowing, rattling the trees and driving dirt and leaves across the ground. Thick black clouds darkened the sky overhead, and the smell of rain hung in the air. A big tropical storm was coming, and it wasn't far away.

Gage spotted the guy with the ugly scar, Santos, lounging against the wall, a band of bullets draped across his chest, and carrying an assault rifle. Gage didn't see Edge, Trace, or Skye, but he knew they were out there.

No one seemed aware of his security team. Whoever had brought the letter must have dropped it off and just left. They'd caught a break there.

As Gage waited for Abby, he felt a rush of sympathy for what she was facing with her grandfather. He knew how it felt to lose someone you cared about. He'd lost both his parents a year apart when he'd been in his teens, and then Cassandra had died. Gage knew how badly it would hurt if Abby lost King.

Another door down the corridor opened, and Mateo walked out. Carlos was staying behind with Zuma and King. The boy had been living on his own for years, and Zuma would look out for him. He'd heard Paulo saying that Hector would be staying behind to guard them.

"How is the old man?" Mateo asked as he walked up. Gage had told Velásquez's men that Mateo was essential to the search. They had found his knife and taken it, but allowed him to accompany them this morning.

"Not good. I don't think he has much time. He wants Abby to find the treasure, so that's what we're going to do."

Mateo glanced around. By Gage's count, ten men plus Hector, who would stay behind, were being paid to ensure Velásquez wound up with the gold.

All of it, Gage was sure. No way did the man intend to settle for half.

"I talked to Victor Alamán last night," Gage said, having called on the sat phone Velásquez's men didn't know he had. "I told him what was going on down here and that if he wanted his share of the gold, he had better figure something out and fast."

"So . . . what? He is sending in the Mexican army?"

"Something like that. Mexico gets the lion's share of the treasure. They've got a big stake in this, but it takes time to set things up, and Alamán won't step in unless we find the gold."

"So we are on our own."

"At least for now," Gage said.

Abby came out of the room, wiping tears, and they headed for the Hummer. Gage glanced around and spotted one of the men he had seen in the cantina the day they had arrived; he was thick-necked, with short muscular arms and stout thighs. More of them prowled the area around the hotel. Paulo's reinforcements. Local cartel soldiers.

Mateo got into one of the Hummers, accompanied by Velás-quez's men, while Gage drove Abby in the other, with Santos in the back seat.

"*Vamos!*" The scar lifted threateningly, and Santos's hand rested on the butt of his automatic rifle.

Gage cranked the engine and pulled out onto the road, fol-lowed by Mateo in the other SUV. The cartel crew piled into the cab and truck bed of a dirty old white Toyota pickup, and all of them trailed off down the road.

Nobody talked along the way, not until they pulled onto the grounds of the old hacienda and parked in back. Gage figured Edge and his crew were either already there or had followed and would soon be in place.

A heavy mist started to fall, and the wind picked up. They put on rain slickers and unloaded the gear, including headlamps for working in the underground chambers, ignoring Velásquez's men and the gun-toting locals who relaxed under cover in the trees.

All but Santos, who planned to follow them into the tunnels under the house. Gage went down first, hand-over-hand along a thick rope. He tensed as he watched Abby descend behind him, but she made quick work of it and jumped the last few feet to the ground. Mateo joined them, and Santos followed.

The three of them went to work with picks and shovels, while Santos propped his shoulders against a crumbling wall, fingering his assault rifle in warning.

It didn't take long to break through into another chamber. Gage adjusted his headlamp and took a look inside, but the room was as empty as the last two.

"Over here!" Abby called out excitedly. "I think I've found the main corridor!"

Gage shined the beam of his headlamp through the opening, illuminating the darkness beyond. "You're right. Same floor plan as Velásquez's hacienda. All the rooms down here open off a cen-tral hallway."

Mateo swung his pick, and they knocked the hole open wider. Gage ducked through into the passage, and Abby joined him. Dim light seeped through the rotting floors overhead, but it wasn't enough to see without their lamps. Ten yards down the corridor, the floor had caved in, as it had in most of the rooms along the passage.

The rain was falling steadily now, dripping through the floor over their heads. The wind made an eerie sound as it raced over the land and whistled through the trees.

Gage heard a rumble of thunder, and heavy drops began to fall, rattling like pebbles on the old wooden floor overhead, running through cracks and rotten places in the wood. More rain poured into the opening above the original chamber, splattering on the broken tile floors.

"I don't like this," Gage said. "We're basically working in a basement that could fill up with water."

Through a gap in the timbers overhead, Abby looked up at a slice of the turbulent sky. Gage tracked her gaze, but it was impossible to see anything but a tiny patch of dark gray. Even that glimpse was blurred by the downpour of water.

"Doesn't look good," Gage said.

"Keep working!" Santos commanded, nudging him with the barrel of his rifle and ending the discussion.

They went back to work with their picks and shovels, tearing open the walls of the next chamber, but finding no sign of the gold. Mateo climbed out of the pit, and he and Paulo rigged a pulley system to haul buckets of mud and debris out of the hole, giving them more room to work.

Gage glanced over at Abby. They had removed their rain gear, which was too bulky for the strenuous work. The rain had plastered Abby's blouse and jeans to her body, outlining her full breasts and curvy behind. She was the only woman for miles around, and he had seen the men watching her.

Especially Santos, who viewed her every move with undisguised lust.

Gage's jaw went tight. Santos and the others would stay away from her as long as she kept digging. They wanted the gold even more than they wanted her.

They worked into the afternoon without pause, digging and clearing, Gage occasionally returning to King's charts, checking them against what they had found so far. The rain steadily increased, and the wind went from a fierce keening to an eerie howling.

Then the clouds opened up in a violent deluge, and sheets of rain poured out of the sky. In minutes, the water was knee deep, mud and leaves from above sliding into the hole on top of them. Santos climbed the rope ladder and took a safe position where he could watch them working below.

Abby swung her pick, loosening a portion of the wall at the back of one of the chambers, the water in the pit well up to her thighs.

Gage gripped her arm. "We've got to get out of here."

Abby nodded, her relief clear. They sloshed through the brackish water back to the rope. "Get a good grip and coil the rope around your leg to brace yourself as you climb up."

Abby started up the rope.

"Keep working!" Santos called down, his rifle aimed at Abby.

"We'll drown down here, and you'll never get your gold!" Gage shouted into the wind. "You want to explain that to Velásquez?"

Paulo appeared at the edge of the pit. "Let them come up," he said, shoving Santos aside. "They won't do us any good if they are dead."

Santos backed away, and Abby continued to the top of the rope and out of the pit. The rain was relentless, flooding into the chamber in a river of water, mud, and rotting wood, leaves, and debris.

Gage grabbed the rope and started up, hand over hand. Halfway to the top, he heard a grinding sound and looked up to see a wall of mud sliding toward him, pushing rocks and heavy beams in front of it.

He tightened his hold on the rope, but one of the timbers hit him square in the chest, knocking him back into the pit. Gage heard Abby scream, and everything went black.

"Gage!" The force of the wind tore the words from her lips as Abby ran toward the open pit in the ground. Gage's head disappeared beneath the muddy water, the heavy beam forcing him under.

"Abby, no!" Mateo raced toward her as Abby dropped feet first into the thick, swirling black water below.

The muddy torrent closed over her head, and there was no way to see. Using her hands and scissoring her legs, she reached out in search of Gage's big body, but she couldn't find him.

Her heart thundered, and fear gripped her as she came up for air, then went down again. Chunks of wood, sharp-edged fragments of tile, then her hand closed over what felt like a piece of cloth. Abby's fingers wrapped around Gage's arm, and she started pulling, but he was unconscious, unable to help, the heavy timber weighing him down. As hard as she tugged, she wasn't strong enough to haul him to the surface.

Abby shot up for air, grabbed another breath, and saw Mateo working frantically to set up a line to pull them both out. She drew in a deep breath and ducked down again, adrenaline pumping through her, giving her extra strength.

No way was she letting Gage drown! She pulled and shoved, trying to get him free of the heavy beam, but it wouldn't budge. A silent scream filled her throat. Tears burned behind her eyes, and her heart squeezed hard.

Dear God, please don't let him die!

More rain washed in, a dense stream that pooled and flooded into the hole, and suddenly the timber shifted. Abby shoved with all her strength, kicked and pushed until her lungs burned from lack of air. She couldn't hold out much longer. With the last of her strength, she pushed, and suddenly the beam slid away.

Grabbing Gage under the arms, she hauled him slowly to the

surface. Her head shot out of the water, and she gasped in a huge breath of air.

The rope hit the water in front of her, and she managed to slip it over Gage's head, around his shoulders, and under his arms. Working together, Mateo, Paulo, and Tomás pulled Gage out of the hole. Paulo tossed the rope back down to her while Mateo worked over Gage.

By the time she was out of the water and scrambling frantically to where Gage lay on the ground, he was spitting up muddy water and gasping for air.

Fresh tears burned her eyes. "Gage . . ." He rolled onto his back, and she threw her arms around him. "Gage . . ."

Gage drew her closer. "I'm . . . okay," he said, coughing. "I'm all right."

Abby started crying. She was losing King. She had almost lost Gage. She tried to stop the tears, but they just kept rolling down her cheeks.

"It's all right, baby." Gage stroked a hand over the wet hair plastered to her head. "Everything's okay." His forehead was bleeding, his shirt torn open and hanging off his muscled shoulders. A tropical storm raged around them, the rain so thick it was impossible to see. Men with guns and rifles surrounded them.

But Gage was alive, and so was she.

Abby wiped away her tears and kissed him full on the mouth. "You're right, honey. Everything is just fine."

Edge shook off Trace's restraining arms, turned and stalked deeper into the forest. He was breathing hard, his hands balled into shaking fists.

His brother had almost died. If it hadn't been for Abby, he'd have drowned in that muddy hole. What good would security be if his brother was dead?

But Trace was right. They needed to wait until the last possible moment, let the situation come to the razor's edge between life and death, before he gave up their position and rushed in to help.

Gage was surrounded by hostile forces. These men wanted the gold.

And the woman.

The situation could erupt into gunfire at any moment. They needed to hold their positions, be ready to go in. They were trained for situations like this. Ten men against the three of them?

A hard smile touched his lips. The odds were definitely in their favor.

He heard the faint movement of a shrub, then Skye appeared beside him. They stood hidden inside the edge of the forest, all of them in camo, including their slickers.

"You okay?" she asked, her voice soft and throaty, a sexy tone that always sent a jolt of heat straight to his groin. She'd kill him if she knew.

"I'm okay," he said. "It was rough there at the end."

She looked up at him with the prettiest green eyes he had ever seen. "I'm glad your brother is okay." With the rain thundering against the leaves and shrubs in a deluge, there was no way anyone could hear them.

The cartel men huddled in the trees around the ruins. They'd been drinking for the last hour.

The odds were getting even better.

"Abby's tough," Skye said. "I didn't see it at first."

Neither had he, not until today. She had saved his brother's life.

"She fits him," Skye said.

"Gage won't see it that way."

"Why not? He's obviously crazy about her."

"Long story." He thought of the woman, Cassandra, who had died. Gage still blamed himself. He wouldn't let another woman in, no matter how much he cared.

Skye handed Edge a protein bar and a bottle of water. "You think they'll stop for the day?"

"Who knows. They want the gold. To them, the risk is worth taking."

Skye nodded, turned, and slipped back into the forest out of sight.

Edge pulled the hood of his slicker forward so the rain stayed out of his face, opened the plastic water bottle and took a long swallow, then sat down in the foliage at the base of a tree and settled in to wait.

CHAPTER THIRTY-SIX

WHEN THE STORM DIDN'T LET UP, PAULO CALLED A HALT TO THE digging, and they drove back to the hotel. The men who lived in the village either went home or took refuge in the cantina, all but Paulo and his cohorts, who took turns standing guard under the eaves in the corridors around the hotel.

Edge and his team were nowhere to be seen. Gage could reach Edge on the sat phone, but communication of any sort was risky. He wouldn't call unless he had to. The Jeep was gone, parked somewhere out of sight, providing temporary shelter.

Santos stood outside the room Abby had gone into, the room where her grandfather lay dying. Gage could read the lustful anticipation in the man's cold black eyes. Santos's desire for Abby was growing. The instant they found the gold, Santos would kill him and rape her.

Gage was counting on his brother not to let that happen.

In typical tropical fashion, the storm blew over as fast as it had appeared. By morning, a hot sun burned across the land, turning puddles to steam and the air dense with humidity.

They returned to the dig site to find the level of the water in the chamber had receded, but it would be at least another day before they could take up the search where they had left off.

While Santos watched, Gage pulled out the charts and King's notes and spread them open for Abby and Mateo on the fender of the Hummer.

"There may be another location worth checking out while we're waiting," Gage said, pointing to a rough floor plan of the hacienda King had drawn. "None of these old houses had indoor kitchens. Too much chance of setting the place on fire." He pointed to a square drawn out behind the main structure.

"King didn't mention this building in his notes, but it's here on the plans he drew. I think it was the kitchen."

"We should clear the ground and use the metal detectors," Mateo suggested.

"Good idea," Gage said. As they set to work, the rest of the men from the village arrived, all of them carrying firearms. They spread out around the ruins under the trees, out of the sun.

Gage wondered if Paulo had made a mistake in hiring them. If the gold was discovered, whatever money Velásquez was paying them might not be enough.

They worked all morning, Gage and Mateo stripping off their shirts in the unbearable heat. Abby wore a sleeveless blouse and a pair of khaki cargo pants that shouldn't have made Santos's eyes gleam or the ugly scar pull down the edge of his mouth, but did.

Gage softly cursed.

He glanced up to see Mateo setting down his metal detector and walking toward him. Abby set her rake aside and joined them.

"I found something," Mateo said. Gage glanced around, but the men, as usual, were either napping in the shade or drinking. All but Santos, who watched Abby, and Paulo, who took his job seriously.

With his back to the men, Mateo opened his hand to reveal an ancient clay figurine, the miniature image of a running man.

"Pre-Columbian," Gage said, picking up the piece to examine it. He handed it to Abby, who ran her fingers carefully over the object.

"It's beautiful," she said.

"Definitely Mayan," Gage said.

Paulo appeared just then. "What is it? What have you found?"

Gage handed him the figurine. "A piece of Mayan art."

Paulo shrugged and handed it back. "You can find these all over Mexico." He turned and went back to where he'd been standing in the shade with Tomás.

Mateo quickly set something else in his palm. A tiny golden frog with emerald eyes glinted in the sunlight. It was magnificent.

Abby sucked in a breath.

"Nice. Put it away, and we'll take a closer look tonight."

Mateo stuffed the golden frog back in the pocket of his jeans, and they returned to work.

Another hour passed before Gage's shovel hit something solid. Abby came over to see what it was, and they cleared away the vegetation to expose what looked like an old cellar door.

Anticipation coursed through him. He and Mateo lifted the heavy wooden door, which was still intact, possibly added at a later date. They gathered their backpacks and put on their headlamps. The light shined down a set of rock stairs leading underground to storage rooms beneath the kitchen.

The floor above the chamber was still in good enough condition to keep out the rain. Except for a puddle here and there, the room was dry and empty, though a couple of rotting wooden crates and a stack of broken tiles stood in one corner.

"What's that?" Abby started toward what looked like something carved into the wall.

"Get back!" Gage gripped her arm and hauled her back against him.

"Oh, my God!"

His arm tightened around her. "Boa constrictors, a whole nest of them."

"They're . . . they're huge." Six to nine feet long, with thick, muscular bodies, at least five of them wound around each other in a massive ball of patterned skin and flicking tongues.

Mateo shined his light past the snakes to the panel behind them.

"It's a stone relief," Gage said. "Let's get rid of the snakes and take a look."

"Get rid of them," Abby repeated. "How?"

Just then Paulo appeared at the top of the stairs, shining his flashlight into the darkness.

"Over to your right," Gage said to him.

The flashlight moved in that direction. "*Dios mio!*"

"Want to give us a hand?"

"I do not like snakes." He made the sign of the cross. "I think I leave this problem to you." He ducked out of the chamber.

Gage grinned at Mateo. "I don't see anyone but you and me. They aren't venomous, but they can be deadly if they manage to wrap themselves around you." He looked at Mateo. "You game?"

Mateo shrugged. "I guess we must do this."

Gage eased Abby out of the way. It took a while, but working together, one of them holding the heads, trying to avoid a vicious bite, the other holding the thick, thrashing tails, they managed to clear the chamber.

Moving the snakes, which were pure muscle, some of them weighing over thirty pounds, was not an easy task. They carried them, writhing and squirming, into the forest and released them, scattering cartel men, who gave them a very wide berth.

Gage and Mateo returned to the chamber, where Abby was already at work on the stone relief.

She pointed to the center of the panel. "I recognize this figure from a picture Clay Reynolds once showed me. It's the Snake King. Kaanul Dynasty. Their power extended all the way down to Honduras."

He thought of the nest of constrictors. "Definitely fitting."

"That's about all I know. We were just making conversation."

The thought of Abby with Reynolds sent a jolt of heat to the back of his neck. He remembered the day Reynolds had come to see her, remembered his own jealousy, how he'd taken Abby bent over his desk. He wished they were somewhere he could claim her again.

Abby went back to work on the stone relief. "I noticed this while you two were dealing with the snakes."

"What is it?" Gage moved closer.

"I don't think this panel is carved into the wall. I think it's been put here to block whatever's behind it. I think we might be able to move it aside."

He examined the thick stone panel. A close look showed Abby was right. "So let's get it out of the way."

"What about Paulo?"

Gage smiled. "I don't think he'll be coming down here anytime soon."

Mateo came forward to help. It was tough going, but Gage could feel the stone begin to move. They pushed and shoved. With a last great heave, the heavy panel slid off to one side to reveal another room.

Abby shined her light through the opening. "Oh, my God. Gage! Oh my God, oh my God, oh my God!"

In the beam of the headlamp, gold glittered everywhere. Mayan gold. Stacks of it. Trinkets and coins, calendars and figurines, jade masks, inlaid skulls, gold-and-silver medallions. There were tiny golden statues and jeweled rings and long, thin golden earrings.

"Plunder," he said. "Whoever did this must have been raiding tombs for years to collect so much." He glanced around. "From the way it's piled up, I'd say it was stored here after the house fell into ruins."

"I can't believe we found it!" Abby's gaze traveled around the room. "King was right," she said softly, her words tinged with reverence. "There must be millions of dollars' worth of gold in this room."

"You know we can't keep it," Gage said. "This is national historical treasure. It's protected."

Her eyes ran over the mounds of gold. "I know."

"I need to call Victor Alamán—and pray he can get his men here before the others find out what we've got."

Grabbing his gear bag, Gage pulled out his sat phone and made the call, then waited impatiently for Victor's assistant to put him through.

"It's Logan," he said. "We've found it. Unfortunately, there are a dozen men here who believe it's theirs. As soon as they find out what we've got, they'll come after it. If you want your share, you'd better get your men down here ASAP."

"I will take care of it," Victor said.

Gage ended the call and stuffed the phone out of sight in his pack. "They're on their way. We need to move the stone back in place."

They ran to the panel and started shoving, trying to slide the carved relief back to cover the opening. The panel was almost halfway there when Paulo's light hit Gage in the face. The beam slid past him, shined over the panel, into the half-exposed room beyond. Gold glittered in the beam of light.

"Stop right where you are!" Paulo jerked his pistol. "Move over there! *Vamos!* Get out of the way!"

Gage silently cursed.

He eased Abby behind him, and the three of them moved away from the treasure room. He could feel Abby trembling. Santos appeared at the top of the stairs, then Tomás. All of them had pulled their weapons.

As the men descended the stairs into the chamber, Paulo shined his light into the treasure room. Gold glinted, piles of it.

"*Dios mio!*" Santos exclaimed. "We are rich!"

"The gold belongs to Don Arturo," Paulo reminded him. "It is not yours, but you will be well paid for helping him find it."

Santos swung his assault rifle toward Paulo. "We take the gold. We are the ones who found it. We take the gold and disappear. You go with us, or we leave your body here to rot in the bowels of these ruins. You choose."

"What about the men from the village?" Paulo said. "If we bring out the gold, they will kill us to get it."

"Then we get rid of them first." He panned the gun toward Gage, Abby, and Mateo. "We get rid of all of them."

"You shoot us, and they'll hear the shots," Gage said. "They'll know you found the treasure."

Santos's lips thinned, tugging the ugly scar at one corner. "Upstairs." He motioned with the rifle. "And keep your mouth shut about the gold."

They moved up the stairs ahead of the men, Gage's hand at Abby's waist, keeping her close, Mateo behind him. Alamán's soldiers were on their way, but Gage had to keep them alive long enough for the soldiers to get there. Edge was out there, but interfering too soon could get them killed.

As Paulo and Santos marched them across the ground at gunpoint, the cartel men sensed the change in the atmosphere. All of them began moving forward, fanning out from under the trees, drawing their weapons and aiming them toward Velásquez's men.

"Hey, *gringos,*" one of them called out. "What did you find down there?"

Gage didn't answer. One wrong word could get them killed.

"They found nothing," Santos said. "There was nothing to find. Paulo will give you your money, and you can go home."

The men held their positions. The stout man with the thick arms and legs came forward, an AK-47 gripped in his blunt-fingered hands. "We do not believe you. You found the gold, and we want our share."

"Don't be a fool, Felipe," Paulo said. "The gold belongs to Arturo Velásquez. Ramón Velásquez is his brother. You know the power he wields. Go against Ramón and you will die. You and every member of your family. You know what I say is true."

The men glanced back and forth between them, but didn't move, their guns held steady.

Felipe strode up to Paulo. "We will see what you have found. Then we will talk." Grabbing Paulo's flashlight, he continued over to the stairs and disappeared below.

Seconds passed. No one moved or said a word. The guns in the men's hands never wavered.

Felipe reappeared with a thin round medallion the size of a dinner plate. Brilliant sunlight glinted off the golden circle in blinding rays.

"There is treasure unlike any you have ever seen!" He held up the gold medallion with one hand, the other on his automatic rifle. "What do you say, men? We take the gold. We take our families, and we leave this place forever. We can live like kings!"

A cheer went up from the men, and a chill ran down Gage's spine. Each side was armed and pointing their weapons at the other—and he, Abby, and Mateo stood between them.

Then everything happened at once. Santos fired at Felipe, dropping him like a stone. Edge whistled a loud shrill signal they had used as kids, and Gage shoved Abby to the ground. He covered her with his body, and Mateo hit the ground beside him.

A barrage of gunfire echoed through the air above their heads, and bullets slammed into the dirt around them. Santos was firing his rifle in automatic bursts, his targets screaming as lead slashed them down like sheaves of wheat.

Paulo grunted and fell. Tomás took off running, made it a few feet before a bullet caught him between the shoulder blades and he went down.

"We need to move!" Gage shot to his feet, grabbed Abby's arm, and pulled her up with him. The cartel men began closing in, firing as the three of them raced toward the stone foundation of the house in search of cover.

Abby jumped over the wall, and Gage followed, Mateo at his side, all three of them ducking down behind the stones. A handful of cartel men continued toward them, running flat out. A bullet slanted down from somewhere above, taking one of them out. More bullets, and another man fell, then another, bullets raining down from three different locations.

Edge, Trace, and Skye.

A bullet slammed into a cartel man, knocking him backward into the dirt, a trail of blood bubbling out of his chest. Edge and his team were taking down the cartel men, one after another.

Santos's face appeared above him, the barrel of his assault rifle pointing into Gage's face an instant before a soldier in camo rose behind him. A blade flashed, slicing across Santos's throat. Blood erupted. He sank to the ground on his knees, then pitched forward.

Gage grabbed Abby and pulled her close, turning her head into his shoulder, running a soothing hand up and down her back.

The sound of gunfire had ceased. Nothing but the sigh of the wind through the trees.

"It's over." Gage released a long, slow breath of relief. "We're safe."

Edge wiped the blade of his knife on his camo pants and slid the weapon back into the sheath strapped to his thigh.

"Thanks, little brother," Gage said, rising, bringing Abby up with him.

"No problem." But Edge's face looked grim, and there was a darkness in his eyes that Gage had never seen. Trace appeared from one direction, and Skye walked toward them from another, their faces equally grim. Killing a man was never easy.

"I gather you found the gold," Edge said.

"Some of it. Not all."

Abby looked up at him. "What?"

"Unless I missed them," Gage said, "I didn't see any gold bars."

"No, but—"

The sound of a helicopter overhead interrupted their conversation. It settled in a field behind the house. The helicopter bay doors slid open, and a dozen uniformed soldiers wearing flak vests and carrying weapons leaped to the ground.

Victor Alamán, in a perfectly tailored black suit, climbed out of the chopper and strode toward them.

He glanced at the blood and death, the bodies scattered around the field. "Looks like you didn't need my help after all."

"We managed," Gage said. "Mostly they killed each other." He pointed. "You'll find the treasure at the bottom of those stairs. Mayan plunder," he said.

Alamán frowned. "Mayan? I thought you were looking for gold ingots."

Gage shrugged his shoulders. "Maybe next time."

Victor scrubbed a hand over his face. He sighed. "We'll have to turn it over to the antiquities department at the Instituto Nacional de Antropología e Historia. There are laws restricting the sale or removal of any national treasure."

"I know. I'm sorry. We'll be leaving soon. If we find anything else before we go, I assume our deal still stands."

Alamán nodded absently, his gaze sliding toward the top of the stairs. He motioned to a younger man also wearing a suit, apparently his assistant, who came forward. The two men briefly conversed, then disappeared down the stairs.

Around them, soldiers checked on the men lying on the ground. Those still breathing were transported aboard the chopper. Gage watched Paulo limping toward the helicopter at gunpoint. Santos was dead, along with most of the cartel crew. Tomás was being carried to the helo. Gage still didn't know which cartel group the village men belonged to.

"Hector is back at the hotel," Abby reminded him.

Gage nodded as they headed for their vehicles. "We'll send him back to Velásquez with the bad news."

"What? There's no gold?"

Gage's mouth edged into a weary smile. "Not for him."

CHAPTER THIRTY-SEVEN

ABBY SAT AT KING'S BEDSIDE, HOLDING ONTO HIS HAND. GAGE stood a few feet away. Zuma had left to give them time alone.

Abby kissed King's liver-spotted hand.

"Tell me . . ." he wheezed. "Say it. It's written . . . all over . . . your face."

She took a deep breath. "We found the treasure, Grandfather. Mayan gold. It was underneath the hacienda's outside kitchen."

King's eyes narrowed. He looked paler, thinner than he had just that morning. Her throat tightened. He was fading fast, and there was nothing she could do.

"You found Mayan treasure? Mayan gold . . . under the kitchen?"

She nodded. "A room full of ancient gold artifacts. It was incredible. I've never seen anything so beautiful. But . . . you know the antiquities laws. We had to give it to the Mexican government."

A slow smile curved King's lips. "You found your own . . . treasure, sweet girl. Not mine. You have the blood of a true . . . treasure hunter."

Abby felt a tug in her heart. She smiled. "Gage thinks whoever plundered the Mayan treasure must have started collecting it years after the Peraltas were gone and the hacienda was in ruins. The underground room was just a convenient place to hide it. Maybe the thieves were caught and never gave up the location, or maybe they were killed. Gage still thinks there's more gold out there."

King's smile broadened into a grin. "I know . . . there is." His amber eyes slid toward Gage.

"The Peralta gold," Gage said, coming away from the wall. "There were no gold ingots in that room, but I think we're close to finding them."

They told King everything that had happened since that morning and that they were free of Velásquez's hold.

"Why didn't you bring the gold out when you first found it?" Abby asked King.

"I'd only come down here . . . to search. I followed the clues . . . I had put together over . . . the years, but I still wasn't . . . sure I would find it. Afterward . . . I went back to . . . make arrangements. I needed men . . . equipment . . . needed to deal with the . . . government."

King squeezed Abby's hand. "I don't have much . . . time. But enough, I think . . . to finish what I . . . started. Get me out of this . . . bed, and I'll show you . . . where to find . . . the Devil's Gold."

Abby started shaking her head. The long conversation was taking its toll. "You need to rest. You need to—"

Gage's big hands settled on her shoulders. "It's King's treasure. He deserves to be the one to find it."

Tears burned behind her eyes. Her chest ached. She turned back to her grandfather, a thick lump swelling in her throat. He had so little time. They had so little time left together.

"Gage is right. You deserve to be there. You deserve to be the one to find the gold."

King's head relaxed against the pillow, and a smile spread over his face.

They started making plans. Hector had left to tell Velásquez that the treasure had been claimed by the government. By now, Don Arturo understood the gold was gone and there was no reason for him to pursue them.

By the end of the day, the treasure would have been retrieved by government officials. The room below the kitchen wasn't an archeological site, merely a place where Mayan plunder had been stored. The artifacts would be taken someplace safe where they could be studied.

Which meant tomorrow King could return to the hacienda. But a lot had changed since he had been there. There was a chance he wouldn't be able to find the gold again or that someone else had been there after he'd left and now it was gone.

Still, Abby couldn't tamp down her excitement. No way would she be able to sleep.

Pumped full of adrenaline, she returned to the room, went to Gage, slid her arms around his neck, and pulled his head down to hers for a kiss. She pressed soft kisses to the corners of his mouth, the base of his throat, then kissed his lips again. Arousal pressed against the fly of his cargo pants.

Abby smiled and nipped his bottom lip. "Help me get some sleep?"

Gage kissed her long and deep. "My pleasure." It was warm in the room, but the storm had cooled the outside temperature a little, and the ceiling fan did the rest.

Abby stripped off her clothes and took down her hair, then helped Gage undress, kissing him all the while. The tiny shower wasn't big enough for both of them, so they took turns. It felt good to be clean again as she led him over to the bed. Gage liked to be in charge, but when he tried to take control, she shook her head.

"Not tonight. Tonight you're mine."

His nostrils flared as she nudged him onto the mattress and followed him down. They kissed for a while. No one could kiss like Gage, his lips soft, melding with hers, sinking in, coaxing and teasing, then taking command. She gave herself up to the heady male taste of him as the kiss went deeper, hotter, wetter.

She was on fire by the time she began to move down his beautiful body, her lips skimming over his muscular pecs, his six-pack abs, and flat belly, ringing his navel with her tongue.

Gage groaned as she went lower, wrapping her hands around

him, testing the hardness, the feel of smooth skin over steel. Her
mouth followed, giving him pleasure, loving the masculine feel of
him, the power it gave her.

His fingers slid into her hair, enjoying her ministrations, then
pulling her away, dragging her mouth back to his for a kiss.

"I want to be inside you," he said thickly, lifting her easily and
setting her astride him. "You still want to be in charge?" The
husky timbre of his voice sent fresh need sliding through her.

"Yes . . ." she breathed, finding it hard to force out the word.
She was hot, alive with wanting. Lifting herself, she eased down
on him, took more of him, then moved to take even more.

Gage hissed out a breath.

Abby leaned over and braced her hands on his shoulders, her
long hair sweeping down, cocooning them in their own private
world. Her body pulsed as she started to move, rising and sinking,
building the heat. The muscles across Gage's flat stomach tightened as he fought for control, and Abby slowed, determined to
draw out the pleasure.

Gage just shook his head. "My turn," he said. Big hands gripped
her hips to hold her in place, and he thrust upward. Out and
then in, driving her up until she arched her back, taking him
deeper, aching for release.

"Gage . . ." she pleaded.

"You want more?"

"Yes . . . please, Gage . . ."

His hold tightened, and he gave her what she wanted, took her
faster, deeper, harder. Sounds came from her throat she didn't
recognize, pleas for more along with his name. Then her body
tightened, and she exploded in pleasure, the heat burning through
her, the flood of sweetness, the black infinity of bliss.

Gage drove her up again, then followed, his own climax fierce.

Abby slumped onto his muscled chest, her body and mind still
filled with him. "I love you," she thought. "I love you so much."

Beneath her, she felt Gage stiffen. Dear God, she hadn't said
the words aloud, had she? But the remote way his hand smoothed
over her hair said that she had.

Gage set her aside and moved off the bed, went into the bathroom, and returned, handed her a warm damp cloth. He settled
himself on the bed beside her and nestled her against his side,
but he didn't say a word.

"I didn't mean to say it. It just . . . it just popped out."

"Go to sleep. We've got a big day tomorrow."

Abby swallowed past the lump in her throat. Her grandfather
was dying. Soon her adventure with Gage would be over and he
would leave. Abby would be alone again—the way she always was.

Her heart felt shredded, but there was nothing she could do.
Tears burned, but no way was she letting him see. She prayed tomorrow they would find the gold and then they could go home.

Once she got back, she would find a way to get over Gage.

She thought of Clay Reynolds. Clay was interested in her as a
woman, not just a partner who shared his bed.

Her throat ached along with her heart. She had no interest in
Clay. She was in love with Gage Logan. He was the right man for
her. She was the right woman for him. But there was no way to
make him see.

Abby closed her eyes. Tears leaked from beneath her lashes.
No matter how hard she tried, she couldn't fall asleep.

Gage couldn't sleep. His mind was too full of Abby. He'd
known she cared about him. More than cared. But love? The
word wasn't in his vocabulary.

His mind went to Cassandra. She'd thought she was in love
with him. He'd told her it would never work. They were just too
different.

But what about Abby?

They fit together. He couldn't deny it. For chrissake, the woman
had saved his life! She was brave and strong and determined.

And he was crazy about her.

It didn't matter. After what had happened to Cassie, he couldn't
risk that kind of involvement again. What if it didn't work out between them? He couldn't bear the thought of hurting her the way

he'd hurt Cassandra. In the end, Cassie's feelings for him had killed her.

He was responsible for one woman's death. Abby had already come close to dying. Just the thought made his stomach burn.

Exhausted, he finally drifted into a restless slumber, only to awaken a few hours later. He rolled out of bed before dawn, showered, dressed, and left the room. He was tired, his mind sluggish, but thoughts of finding the Peralta gold—the Devil's Gold—began to fire his adrenaline, and anticipation filled him.

The woman from the village, Blanca, showed up with breakfast. Gage, Mateo, and Carlos ate first. Edge and his team, once more staying in the hotel, showed up and ate too. Finally, Abby arrived.

Gage felt a tug in his heart. He thought of the words she had said to him last night, words he couldn't return. "You okay?"

She looked up at him, her expression purposely bland. "Today we're going to find the Devil's Gold. Why wouldn't I be?"

He thought of last night, and guilt assailed him.

Zuma came in and began putting a meal together for her and King.

"You think he's up to this?" Gage asked as she filled a tray.

"He lives by a thin thread of sheer will," Zuma said. "King wants to find the gold for Abby."

"And for himself," Gage said.

"*Sí*, it is his dream."

"Then we had better make sure it happens." He turned to Mateo. "What's the atmosphere like in the village? They lost a number of men yesterday. The ones who didn't die were arrested and hauled away, probably never to be seen again."

"They went against Ramón Velásquez. The villagers just pray the families will not be murdered."

"You think they will be?"

"I hope not."

"So do I, though Arturo deserves to pay a hard price for what he did to King."

"Probably it will not happen," Mateo said.

Gage made no reply. Arturo's failure to retrieve the gold and

the loss of his men weren't nearly punishment enough. The deteriorated state of his hacienda showed how close he was to complete financial ruin, and there was no gold to save him. That was
something at least.

They packed up their gear and headed back to the dig site,
Gage and Trace loading King on a pallet in the back of the Hum-
mer. Abby climbed in beside him while Zuma sat up front with
Gage. Carlos rode in the second vehicle with Mateo.

When the Jeep carrying Edge, Trace, and Skye arrived at the
hacienda, they set up perimeter surveillance, but everything
seemed quiet. There was nothing left to remind them of the car-
nage yesterday except an occasional dark spot in the soil where
blood had soaked into the ground.

Fortunately, the area King pointed them toward was away from
the field where the shooting had taken place. Using a litter that
Edge and Trace had fashioned from stripped tree branches, they
carried the old man to the chamber where Gage had originally
been digging.

Abby walked up to him. "King says we were right in the first
place. What we found under the house was a room off the main
corridor. The gold's stored in another room off to one side."

Gage nodded, feeling a sense of satisfaction at the work they
had already done. "We'd have found it sooner or later."

"Unless Velásquez's men had killed us first," Abby said.

Gage looked down at her, fighting an overwhelming urge to
pull her into his arms. "A definite possibility," he agreed. She was
different today, already backing away from him, distancing herself. He didn't like it.

From his litter beside the chamber, King could look into the
hole where they'd been digging, the place where Abby had saved
his life. A chill crawled over Gage's skin. The place where she
could have drowned.

It was exactly the reason they couldn't be together. He couldn't
survive a loss like that again.

He studied the muddy hole in the ground. The bad news was it
no longer looked the same. The storm waters had caved in one

side, and though the water had receded, mounds of dirt, timbers, and flooring had been left behind.

King raised himself up on the litter. "Bring me my . . . notes."

Gage retrieved the information, carried it over, and spread the pages open on the ground next to the litter. King studied the charts and his notes, looking back at the pit, then beyond.

"There," he said, pointing. "The lower floor is full of mud . . . but the dirt washed in from . . . over there." He struggled, wheezing and coughing, finally managed to catch his breath. "Get me up."

With Gage's help, King managed to gain his feet. Gage lifted one of King's arms over his shoulder and Abby did the same on the other side. Together they helped him make it to the spot he indicated, a concave depression that hadn't been there before the storm. Mud and debris, timbers and broken tiles littered the area, but . . .

"There!" King pointed a shaking hand, a huge grin on his face.

The glint of gold was unmistakable. "Jesus . . ." Gage climbed into the hole and sank ankle deep in the mud. So did Mateo, both of them pulling wood and debris out of the way, exposing a pile of gleaming gold bars. Abby joined them, and more gold ingots came into view.

There were stacks of them in the depression, others scattered all around. The more debris they cleared away, the more gold bars appeared.

"The Devil's Gold," King said with reverence from his place on the ground above the hole.

It took a lot of hard work, but when they were finished and all of the gold had been uncovered, Abby sat down beside her grandfather.

"You were right all along," she said, taking hold of his hand.

King looked up at her, his smile wan. "You'll tell them? You'll show them . . . the gold?"

She leaned over and kissed his hollow, beard-roughened cheek. "I'll tell them. Gage will tell them. We'll make them eat their words."

King nodded, pleased. He lay back on the ground and closed his eyes. Abby held on to his hand.

Long seconds passed. The sun came out from behind the clouds, and even the mud that clung to the gold couldn't dull the glitter.

Gage watched as Zuma approached and knelt on the ground beside them. She checked King's pulse, leaned over his face to see if he was still breathing. She looked at Gage and shook her head.

Zuma turned to Abby. "Go to your man," she said. "He will look after you now. Your grandfather is gone."

"No." Abby's eyes filled. She shook her head. "Not yet." She bent over King, still holding his hand, trying to feel his breath on her face. "You can't go yet. Do you hear me? We just found the gold." She started crying, a rush of tears that broke Gage's heart.

He went to her, eased her to her feet, and turned her into his arms. "You made him happy, honey. You gave him the most precious gift he's ever received. You gave him his dream."

Abby started crying, and Gage pressed her face into his shoulder. "We'll take care of him. We'll take him home."

Her tears turned to sobs, and Gage just held her. He ached for her, ached for her terrible loss. He wanted to absorb her pain, protect her from the heartache, make everything right for her again.

Was that love?

Gage prayed it wasn't.

But as he led her away, his chest tight and his heart beating dully, he was very much afraid it was.

CHAPTER THIRTY-EIGHT

*I*T TOOK TWO TRIPS TO MÉRIDA TO TRANSPORT PEOPLE, EQUIPMENT, and 6,052 solid gold bars, each weighing approximately 32 troy ounces. Two pounds. Market value $59,649 dollars per bar.

A little over $363,000,000 in total, according to Abby's calculations.

"How can there be so many?" Abby asked. "It would have taken hundreds of trips from the mine."

"Unless there was more than one mine," Gage said.

"That's right! There were rumors about a Peralta mine in the Sierra Nevada mountains of California."

"Could be, I guess. We'll probably never know."

Not that it really mattered. Wherever the gold had come from, they were rich. Sixty percent would go to the Mexican government, of course, but forty percent would be theirs.

They were depositing the government's portion into a private vault in Mérida, 3,632 bars worth $217,860,000. Two thousand, four hundred and twenty bars were going home with them, $145,000,000 in gold.

Less the *mordida* they would be sending Victor Alamán, $4,356,000 in cash, the bribe they'd promised to pay.

Abby thought of her grandfather with a bittersweet pang. King had been right about the gold from the start.

But then she had never really doubted him.

She couldn't wait to get back to the States with the news—King Farrell had found the Devil's Gold!

King's good name would be restored, and all of them would be rich. It was a huge achievement, a once-in-a-lifetime thrill.

Her buoyant mood slowly faded. Once she was back in Denver, her time with Gage would be over.

Her throat ached. She could no longer stay in Gage's apartment. By his silence, he had made his feelings clear. Abby loved Gage, the forever kind of love that only came once in a lifetime. She would never truly get over him, but she didn't want a man who didn't—couldn't—love her in return.

"You ready?" Gage asked, clean-shaven again, so handsome in his yellow knit pullover and tan slacks her heart hurt just to look at him. His beautiful blue eyes touched her face, and she thought he seemed oddly troubled.

He still had a lot to worry about. They were shipping millions of dollars in gold. Until it was safely stored in Denver, neither of them could relax.

"I'm all packed," she said, a fake smile on her lips. They were staying in a suite at the Fiesta Americana in Mérida, about a twenty-minute drive to the airport.

They had sent their gear ahead, all but a carry-on each. She flicked a last painful glance at the big king-sized bed. They had slept together last night, made frantic, almost desperate love, probably for the last time.

Gage seemed to know it, accept it. She ached to think of it, but so did she.

Gage grabbed the handle of her carry-on and wheeled it out of the bedroom. Mateo joined them in the lobby. Zuma and Carlos were also there, looking nervous and excited. Incredibly, Gage had arranged for both of them to return to the States.

Zuma had been instrumental in rescuing a kidnap victim, but her assistance had caused the death of a number of cartel members. Ramón Velásquez, a notorious cartel leader, and his brother, Arturo, posed a credible threat to her life.

And since Carlos was staying with Zuma, the boy could get caught in the crossfire. Or at least that was the case Gage had made.

Zuma had fallen in love with the little boy. They were going to

Denver together, where she planned to raise Carlos as her son. Abby would be helping them find a place to live, and Gage planned to set up a trust fund for them.

Money was no longer an object for any of them. After expenses, Mateo, Edge, Trace, and Skye would be receiving a ten percent share. Over ten million apiece. The rest went to the partners, Gage Logan and Abigail Holland.

She was ludicrously rich.

And utterly miserable.

"I got an interesting phone call a couple of days ago." Gage leaned back in the seat of the black SUV limo carrying them to the airport. Edge, Trace, and Skye had left ahead of them and were already there. Mateo, Zuma, and Carlos rode in another limo a few minutes behind.

"What's going on?" Abby asked.

"Turns out, transporting five thousand pounds of gold bullion can be a little tricky. There's no duty on bringing the gold into the country, but physically getting it there is another matter entirely."

"I have no idea what that entails, but I assumed you'd be shipping it through regular channels."

"Not exactly."

The limo pulled up in front of the private jet terminal instead of going around to the International Departure Gate. The driver opened the door, and they got out of the car.

Setting a hand at Abby's waist, Gage led her over to the glass front door, and they pushed through into the terminal; the limo driver wheeled the carry-ons into the building behind them.

Abby looked up to see a tall, lean, extremely handsome dark-haired man striding toward them, a big smile on his face.

Gage's partner, Jack Foxx.

Gage stuck out a hand, and Foxx grabbed it, pulled him in for a bro-hug. "So I guess we don't have to worry about paying the rent anymore." Not that the man had any money problems. The international playboy was worth nearly a billion dollars.

Gage grinned. "Not for quite a while, at least."

Foxx laughed. He turned to Abby. "I hear you saved this big

bastard's life. I liked you the first time I met you. I'm a little in love with you now."

A flush crept into Abby's cheeks. Gage frowned.

"I couldn't very well let him drown," she said, smiling. "We hadn't found the treasure yet."

Foxx grinned, digging dimples into his cheeks. "Speaking of treasure," he said.

"One of his favorite subjects," Gage drawled.

"Everything's loaded on the plane and ready to go," Jack said. "Edge and his security people are already aboard." His attention shifted to Abby, and his expression turned serious. "Your grandfather's casket has been loaded, Abby. I'm sorry for your loss."

She swallowed. "Thank you."

Foxx returned his attention to Gage. "Soon as the rest of your people arrive, the plane's ready to leave."

Gage took her arm and led her across the terminal to the plate-glass windows. A big jet airplane sat on the tarmac, its engines running.

"Boeing BBJ Max 7," Jack said, walking up beside them. "Belongs to a friend of mine. My G-6 couldn't carry the load." He looked out the window, and his grin returned. "Costs about a hundred million, these days. I think you're gonna like it."

Abby couldn't imagine knowing a friend who would loan you a hundred-million-dollar airplane. But the Gulfstream Foxx owned hadn't come cheap.

Mateo showed up with Zuma and Carlos. Foxx had worked with Mateo, who seemed pleased to see him.

"Nice work, Mateo," Foxx said, smiling.

"Good to see you, my friend." The men shook hands.

"Jack, meet Zuma Delgado," Gage said. "And this little guy is Carlos." Gage set a hand on Carlos's dark-haired head. The boy wore clean clothes and new shoes, which he was extremely proud of.

Carlos stuck his hand out to Jack. "It is nice to meet you, Señor Jack."

Foxx grinned and shook the boy's hand. "Good to meet you, too, Carlos."

They crossed the tarmac to the big jet that waited, engines humming. It looked more like an airliner than a private jet.

"You two go on ahead," Jack said to Carlos. The little boy excitedly grabbed Zuma's hand, and they hurried toward the metal steps leading up to the door of the cabin. The rest of them followed across the tarmac.

Mateo reached the top of the stairs. Abby and Gage still stood at the bottom with Jack when a group of soldiers raced across the tarmac in a pair of camouflage Jeeps. Abby's pulse leaped as the Jeeps slid to a halt, the soldiers jumped down and spread out around them.

"What the hell?" Gage said.

"Stay right where you are!" The man in charge gave the command in broken English. "Raise your hands!"

Abby trembled as she lifted her arms into the air. She flicked a glance at Gage, whose jaw looked iron hard. Foxx's expression betrayed nothing.

A small man in a tailored gray suit, thick black hair cut short on the sides and long on top, walked toward them across the tarmac. Abby's eyes widened. *Victor Alamán*, the man Gage had phoned for help during their firefight with Velásquez's men and the local cartel crew.

Gage eased her a little behind him. "What's going on, Victor? You didn't get the . . . gift . . . I had messengered over?"

A cashier's check for over four million dollars—the bribe they had paid him.

"*Sí*, I did. Sadly, I realized three percent of the enormous fortune you found was no longer a fair amount, not after the help I gave you."

Abby's gaze took in the half dozen armed men who pointed weapons in their direction.

"So you want to renegotiate," Gage said flatly.

"That is correct. You give me the gold and get to leave Mexico with your friends, instead of facing years in prison for trying to cheat the government out of its fair share of the bounty."

"Your government was paid exactly what we agreed on."

A gust of wind ruffled the longer hair on top of Alamán's head. "Unfortunately, there is no way for you to prove that. I assume the gold is in the cargo bay of the plane. It shouldn't take too long to unload it and get you on your way."

Gage turned to Abby, his brilliant blue eyes fixed on her face. "Get on the plane, Abby. Jack, you go with her."

"I'm staying here," she said. No way was she leaving Gage behind to face the consequences alone.

Jack didn't move. His equally blue eyes locked with Gage's in some sort of silent communication.

Jack turned toward her. "We need to get on the plane, Abby." There was steel in those blue eyes now. For the first time she realized there was a lot more to Jack Foxx than just a carefree playboy.

"Now," he repeated. Gripping her arm, he urged her past Gage toward the metal stairs. "Go . . ." he said, squeezing her arm. It was a signal, she realized. Gage was helpless to do anything as long as he was worried about her safety.

Abby hurriedly climbed the stairs to tell Edge, Trace, and Skye what was going on, but they were already standing just out of sight inside the door, two kneeling, one standing, weapons drawn. Skye pulled her inside and motioned for her to get down. Jack ran into the plane behind her.

Abby raced to the window, terrified for Gage, petrified he was about to get shot.

CHAPTER THIRTY-NINE

*N*o WAY ARE THESE GUYS MILITARY, GAGE THOUGHT. THEY WERE dressed in camo, wearing slouch hats, but they weren't the soldiers who had helicoptered in to the hacienda ruins. These men had on leather shoes, not boots, and their bodies betrayed their lack of conditioning.

Jack had noticed it. Gage figured Edge knew, too.

"I need to speak to the captain," Gage told Victor. "He won't open the cargo bay doors unless I tell him in person." Alamán had no idea Foxx was actually in charge of the airplane. Plus, the guy never was very smart.

Victor looked around for someone else to send with the message, but everyone was already on the plane.

"Do not do anything you will regret," Victor warned.

Gage turned and started up the stairs. He was a few feet away from the door when Edge, Trace, and Skye surged into the opening and started firing, scattering fake soldiers across the tarmac, raining down hellfire, and providing cover.

Gage dove through the doorway, barely inside when the plane started rolling. The portable metal stairs slid away, slamming into the wing as the engines accelerated, tipping over as the jet rushed past, moving down the runway as fast as the big turbines could push.

Edge knelt in the open doorway and kept firing while Trace and Skye blasted away over his head. Bullets slammed into the tarmac, then began taking out some of the men shooting at them. Return fire pinged off the metal around the door frame, but the engines were whining, speeding them along the concrete at breakneck speed.

Shots pinged off the landing gear as the plane roared toward the end of the runway. Edge slammed the door and secured it.

"Everybody get strapped in!" Gage shouted, sitting down next to Abby and fastening his seat belt. Everyone but Edge and his crew were already seated. Foxx sat down and buckled up. Edge, Trace, and Skye strapped in as the heavy jet lifted off the tarmac like a big graceful bird.

The roar of the engines filled the cabin, and the g-force pushed Gage back in his seat. No one said a word until the jet began to stabilize and level off at somewhere around thirty-five thousand feet.

Gage turned to Abby, whose face looked pale. "You okay?"

"No, I'm not okay. You could have been killed! You should have given them the damned gold!"

Gage looked over her head to where Jack sat grinning. "No way, sweetheart," Foxx said.

Gage chuckled. "You won't be grinning when your friend hands you the bill for the damages to his plane."

Foxx's grin widened. "Worth every dime."

Gage just shook his head. For the first time, he looked around at the opulent interior of the jet. Long white leather divans curved along one side of the living area. There was a dining table with matching wide white leather seats, and a lounge with a bar. Beyond it, an office with a conference table and six wide seats upholstered in shiny black leather.

"Carries eighteen passengers the way it's configured," Jack said. "There's a nice bedroom suite in the back."

"It's spectacular. Now if it just gets us home."

Foxx popped his belt and stood up. He looked at the group strapped into their seats, all of them still wide-eyed and uneasy. Jack walked over to Carlos and crouched down to the boy's level.

"You okay?"

"I have never been on a plane," Carlos said as if that explained all the gunfire and the race to the end of the runway.

"Yeah, well, it's usually not quite so exciting," Jack said, rising to his feet.

"Or this fancy," Abby added, joining them. "I can't believe this." She glanced around the luxurious interior. "I'm spoiled forever."

Jack glanced at the passengers seated in the opulent cabin. "Anyone here besides me feel like a drink?"

"I could certainly use one," Gage drawled.

"I'm in," Abby agreed.

"We're roughing it this trip," Foxx said. "No cabin crew to wait on us."

Gage smiled. "I think we'll survive."

The three of them went over to the bar, and Jack poured two scotches and a glass of white wine for Abby. The security team declined. The rest of the group, including Mateo, drank sodas.

It was just under sixteen hundred miles from Mérida to Denver, roughly a three-and-a-half-hour flight. They would go through customs there. No duty on the gold, but a FinCEN 105 form had to be filled out.

Gage had arranged for an armored vehicle to be waiting to take the gold to a depository. Some of it would be going into bank safe deposit boxes for easy access; some would be sold for cash.

Gage glanced over at Abby, who sat next to Zuma, the two of them laughing at something Carlos had said. Once all the legal work was finished and Abby had received her share, their partnership would officially be over.

His chest clamped down. In the brilliant sunlight streaming through the cabin windows, her thick braid gleamed like a trail of fire down her back. Her face glowed with excitement, and now he knew that courage and brains went along with that beautiful face and sexy body.

His stomach knotted. He didn't want Abby to leave. It was as simple and as complicated as that.

He was brooding about it, sipping his second scotch, when the silver-haired co-pilot came out of the cockpit and went over to talk to Jack, who stood a few feet away talking to Mateo.

As the co-pilot walked away, Gage joined them. "What's going on?"

"It appears we've got a little mechanical problem," Jack said, taking a swallow of his drink.

Gage thought of the bullets that had pinged off the landing gear. "What kind of problem?"

"When the metal stairs hit the wing, they damaged the leading edge slats. Those are the lift flaps that allow the wings to operate at a higher angle of attack on landing."

"Which means?"

"Which means they maximize lift and drag so the plane can slow down and come to a stop before it reaches the end of the runway."

"I think I'm beginning to get the picture. If the plane can't slow down fast enough, it goes off the end of the pavement."

Jack lifted his scotch in salute. "Buy the man another drink."

Gage scoffed. "As appealing as that sounds right now, I don't think getting drunk when we're looking at a possible plane crash is a good idea."

"Probably not," Jack said and upended his scotch.

"Is there anything we can do?"

"The captain will radio the tower and fill them in, make arrangements to land on the longest runway possible. On approach, he'll lower the plane's pitch and power. Meanwhile, the rest of us will hope and pray like hell we stop before we reach the end of the concrete."

Gage looked around the luxurious cabin. Everyone had finally relaxed. "Don't tell the others. No use worrying them before it's time."

Jack nodded.

Gage returned to his seat, and so did Jack. The rest of the trip was uneventful. As they neared their destination, the captain's voice came over the loudspeaker.

"Please return to your seats and fasten your seat belts. We're starting our approach to Denver."

Abby returned and sat down beside him, buckled herself into the seat. "Boy, the trip went by fast."

Gage nodded.

But it was the longest flight he could ever recall.

Abby listened to the captain's voice with growing trepidation. He was explaining the problem with the flaps and telling them to prepare for a very rough landing. She turned to Gage, who sat beside her on the divan.

"We're . . . we're having mechanical trouble?"

"The stairs hit the wing when we accelerated, damaging the flaps on one side. It makes landing a lot more difficult, but not impossible. Let's make sure everyone is as secure as they can be, get them off the divan into more stable seats—the ones at the dining or conference table look the best."

Abby and Gage made a sweep of the cabin, making sure everyone was secure and solidly belted in, then strapped themselves into two of the big dining chairs.

Jack Foxx came over to speak to Gage. "Captain's got everything set. We'll be landing fast and hard, so you need to be ready." Foxx went around to the others and delivered the same message, told them to be prepared to put their heads down in the crash position.

Crash position. The words sent a tremor down Abby's spine.

"We've been lucky so far," she said, thinking of the gold they had found and that they'd survived several close calls. "I hope our luck holds out."

"So do I." Gage reached over and took her hand, held it snugly in his bigger one.

The plane began to circle as it descended. She heard the clank of the landing gear locking into place; then the nose tipped downward to the runway as the plane angled toward the ground.

Abby looked up at Gage, whose face was set in hard, grim lines. Every emotion she felt for him rushed into her heart. If they died, she would never see him again. Or maybe just Gage would die, or she would. Anything could happen.

She leaned over and kissed his cheek. "I love you," she said. "I know you don't want to hear it, but it's true, and I wanted you to know . . . in case . . . in case something happens."

"Dammit, Abby, nothing is going to—" The wheels slammed down on the tarmac, jarring the entire cabin. The plane bounced up, swooped down and hit again, shimmied, and kept rolling. The ground rushed past, turned into a blur of colors flying by outside the windows. The tower rushed past, but the plane kept going.

Through the porthole, she saw fire engines lined up near the end of the runway, their red lights flashing. Her stomach tightened as the brakes clamped down. She smelled burning rubber. The wheels locked, then released, locked and released. The plane slowed, but not enough. They were rapidly reaching the end of the runway, nothing but dirt and sagebrush beyond.

The brakes gripped and released, gripped and released. The plane shuddered and continued to slow.

"Put your heads down, everyone!" Gage called out as they hit the end of the tarmac and bounced across the field, rolled and bounced, rolled and bounced, finally slowed and slid to a stop.

Abby's heart thundered, and her mouth felt bone dry. Foxx popped his belt, hurried over to the emergency escape hatch, pulled a lever, and a rubber slide deployed and filled with a rush of air.

Fire engines raced toward them.

"Let's go!" Gage commanded, rounding up the others and herding them toward the slide. "Zuma, you first, then Carlos."

The buxom woman sat down and shoved off, slid to the bottom and stood up, ready to catch Carlos. The boy grinned up at Abby as he slid down the chute, raising his arms over his head on his way to the ground.

"You're next," Gage said, manhandling Abby into position as if he didn't trust her to actually leave. Mateo followed. Skye, Trace, then Edge, Gage, and Foxx, then the captain and co-captain.

When they were all safely off the plane, Abby breathed a sigh of relief.

Gage strode up to her and pulled her into his arms. "Dammit, Abby, I love you too." He cupped her face in his hands. "I wish things could be different." And then he kissed her, long and deep. When the kiss finally ended, he turned and walked away.

It was the sweetest, saddest moment of her life.

CHAPTER FORTY

THE NEXT FEW DAYS WERE HECTIC. ABBY SPOKE TO TAMMY, MADE arrangements to take over her best friend's lease, and moved out of Gage's apartment. She hadn't seen much of him since their return to Denver. Several meetings with bankers and lawyers had forced them together, but aside from that, Gage was determined to keep his distance.

Abby felt the same. Every time she saw him, the pain of losing him surfaced all over again.

The day of King's funeral was the worst. What Abby had envisioned as a small group of friends in the Ivy Chapel at the Fairmount Cemetery turned into a media circus. King Farrell had proven all of them wrong. He was hailed as a world-class explorer, the man who'd finally found the long-lost Devil's Gold.

Everyone who had ever crossed King's path showed up for the memorial service. When she hadn't heard from Gage, Abby accepted Clay Reynolds's offer to escort her. Clay made no secret of his interest in her, taking her to lunch on several occasions, then supper at the elegant Ocean Prime Restaurant.

Clay had been entertaining and solicitous, and having him with her at the funeral seemed better than facing the ordeal alone.

Clay took her arm and guided her down the steps as they left the chapel, both dressed in black, the crowd following them across the grass to the graveside, where the minister gave another, shorter account of the long and spectacular life King had lived.

Mateo was there, Edge, Skye Delaney, and Trace Elliott. Skye had picked up Zuma and Carlos and brought them with her. All of them had come forward to express their sympathy and give her a badly needed hug. Afterward, Zuma had remained a few minutes longer to say a personal good-bye to King.

Finally, everyone but Abby and Clay were gone. Standing in front of the grave, she clutched the map King had left her all those weeks ago, the worn piece of parchment showing the trail through the Superstition Mountains that had begun her amazing adventure.

Abby kissed the map, leaned over, and tucked it under the blanket of white roses that draped her grandfather's coffin.

"Thank you for giving me the best time of my life," she said. *With the best man I've ever known*, she thought, and wiped tears from her cheeks.

"You ready?" Clay asked. He looked handsome today, his blond hair lightly tousled by the breeze, his blue eyes filled with concern.

Abby nodded. She took the arm he offered and started walking. For a moment, she thought the man in the black suit, white shirt, and gleaming gold French cuffs standing at the back of the canopy was an illusion.

Gage. Her already battered heart clenched, the ache surfacing all over again.

Gage came toward her, reached down, and took both her hands in his. He bent and kissed her cheek. "I'm really sorry, honey."

"I-I didn't think you were here," she said, her gaze running over his beloved face. He looked tired as he rarely did, and she wondered if he had missed her. "I didn't see you in the chapel."

"I was in the back of the room. Nothing could have kept me away."

Fresh tears welled. "Gage . . ."

"Leave her alone," Clay said, stepping protectively in front of her. "Haven't you hurt her enough?"

"Clay!"

"From what I heard, you nearly got her killed in Mexico," Clay continued. "Get out of her life, Logan, and leave her alone."

Gage's expression turned murderous. Then something moved across his features, and his attention shifted to Abby. "So I guess there's more going on here than I thought. Didn't take you long to find a replacement."

Hurt slipped through her. How could he think for a moment that she could have already found someone new? The hurt had her snapping back at him. "At least Clay isn't afraid to go after what he wants."

Gage said nothing, just held her gaze a moment more, turned, and strode away. Abby's heart went with him.

For the next two weeks, Clay called repeatedly, but she ignored his phone calls. She wasn't interested in Clay Reynolds, no matter what Gage thought.

Since the funeral, she'd been helping Zuma get settled and Carlos get enrolled in school. It was almost like having a family again. She was wealthy now. She should be happy. She was, she told herself.

Except that she missed Gage.

And she was bored. She wasn't the type to sit around her apartment and watch TV, or spend a fortune shopping, or indulge herself at the spa.

She needed to find something useful to do.

Clay Reynolds was head of New World Collections at the Denver Art Museum. The Mayer Center promoted scholarship in the field of pre-Columbian and Spanish colonial art. Sitting on the sofa in her living room, Abby hit Clay's contact number.

After several rings, he picked up. "Abby."

"Hello, Clay."

"I didn't expect to hear from you. You didn't return any of my phone calls." There was something in his voice—anger, she thought, a little surprised. Or resentment. Something.

"Actually, I was hoping you'd have a suggestion for me. I'm looking for something to keep me busy. I thought there might be some kind of work for me at the museum."

His voice softened. "So you and Logan . . . you're not together anymore? After what happened at the funeral, I thought maybe . . ."

"We aren't together. Not anymore."

"So you're interested in working with the museum. That's a great idea. The Devil's Gold is still a hot topic. Perhaps you could do a series of lectures on the subject, incorporate your experiences, the work you did in Mexico to find the treasure—what it felt like when you finally succeeded."

"Yes, I think I could do that. I've done a lot of research on the history of the men and women who searched for the treasure over the years. I think people might find their stories interesting."

"Why don't we talk about it over dinner at my house?"

Apprehension slid through her. With every date, Clay had become more aggressive. It was one of the reasons she hadn't returned his calls.

"Better yet, why don't I cook you supper here?" Where she could have a little more control. "I could finally get some use out of my kitchen. Are you free day after tomorrow?"

"I can make that work," Clay said.

Abby gave him her address. "Seven p.m.?"

"I'll see you then."

Abby hung up the phone. She hoped Clay wouldn't get the wrong idea. She still wasn't interested in him as anything more than a friend, but working with the museum might be a good way to spend her time, and there was a chance Clay could help her.

It wasn't what she'd dreamed of doing after coming home with millions of dollars in gold. She'd imagined doing something far more exciting.

Abby thought of Gage but blocked his image from her mind and heart.

Gage sat at the kitchen table, staring at the wall. He'd always loved coming home from a journey, being back in his own space, surrounded by his own personal treasures.

Now that Abby was gone, he hated being in the apartment by himself.

All morning, he'd wandered the empty rooms, trying not to think of her, but she always seemed to be lurking in the corners of his mind. Her laughter, her smile, her kisses.

He needed something to do, something that would capture his interest. Something that would take him out of the country, where he wouldn't dwell on the things they'd done together, remember making love to her. Ache to make love to her again.

He tried not to think of the last time he'd seen her, the terrible sadness in her face as she'd said goodbye to King, a man who meant so much to her.

The thought of her with Clay Reynolds made his stomach burn. Reynolds didn't deserve her. She belonged to Gage. In his heart, she always would.

The intercom sounded, signaling a visitor in the entry downstairs. "It's me, bro," Edge said. "Buzz me in."

His brother didn't drop by that often. Gage was glad he had come. Edge pounded up the stairs, crossed to the front door, and Gage pulled it open.

"It's been a while," he said, stepping back to invite his brother in. "It's good to see you. How about a beer or something?"

"Beer sounds good."

They walked into the kitchen, and Gage pulled two bottles of ice-cold Corona out of the fridge. "Sorry, no lime." Popping off the caps, he set a bottle on the kitchen table in front of Edge, sat down across from him, and took a drink of his beer. "So what's going on?"

"That's what I came to ask *you*." His brother's gaze sharpened on his face. "You look like crap, bro. You haven't shaved in days, and I swear you're losing weight." Edge glanced around the kitchen. "Jesus, man. You haven't even put the dishes in the dishwasher."

Gage sprawled back in his chair. "So what? I'm taking a break. Even after the government sucks up half the money, I'll still have millions in the bank."

Edge gave him a knowing stare. "It's Abby, isn't it? She was with some guy at the funeral, and it's been biting your ass ever since."

Gage grunted. "Clay frigging Reynolds. There's something off about that guy. I could feel it the first time I met him."

"The *something off* is he's set his sights on Abby. Why don't you just admit you're in love with her and go over there and get her?"

Gage tipped back his beer and took a long swallow. "All right, I love her. So what? It doesn't make any difference. I'm not cut out for married life. I'm out of the country half the time."

"So take her with you."

Gage just shook his head.

"Why not?"

"You've got a short memory, little brother. I almost got her killed in Mexico. What if she had died? I've already killed one woman. If something happened to Abby—" He broke off and shook his head.

"That's bullshit," Edge said. "And deep down, you know it. Abby's different. She lives and breathes adventure, just like you. She's made for you, bro, a perfect fit. Finding a woman like that . . . it's a gift, man. God doesn't give you that kind of gift every day."

Gage said nothing. There was nothing he could say.

Even his brother didn't know the truth.

And Gage wasn't about to tell him.

CHAPTER FORTY-ONE

ABBY LOOKED AT THE UNOPENED BOXES STILL SITTING IN HER living room. She needed to finish unpacking. She needed to make the apartment a little less Tammy's and a little more her own.

A knock sounded at her door, and her spirits lifted. A visitor, a chance to put off the inevitable a little longer.

She walked over and looked through the peephole, saw Edge Logan standing in the corridor. She unlocked the door and pulled it open.

"Edge! What a nice surprise." Leaning over, she gave him a hug, then stepped back out of the way. "Come on in."

Edge walked into her messy living room. She hadn't considered how bad it must look to guests with all the unopened boxes. Of course, she hadn't really had many guests. It occurred to her she'd better do something before the dinner she was fixing for Clay.

"You want a Coke or a beer or something?"

"I'll take a Coke," Edge said. He looked incredibly good. In a darker, leaner, harder way, every bit as handsome as Gage.

Abby went into the kitchen and took a Coke out of the fridge, took a Diet Coke for herself. At least she'd unpacked in here.

Filling two glasses with ice, she poured the drinks and set them on the kitchen table, and both of them sat down.

"Has something happened?" she asked at the serious look on his face. Her heart skipped. "Is it something bad? Is Gage all right?"

Edge took a long swallow of his drink. "No, my brother is not all right. I just came from his place. Gage is in love with you, and he's miserable."

Abby's eyes stung. She glanced away. "He doesn't think it could ever work."

"I know you love him. It's in your face every time you look at him. Is that what you think too?"

She straightened in her chair. "I think your brother is an idiot. I think we're perfect for each other." Tears welled, and one slipped down her cheek. Abby brushed it away. "That's what I think."

Edge smiled and started nodding. "All right, then. I think he's an idiot too. Now all we have to do is convince him."

Abby shook her head. "First, there is no way in hell I am chasing after a man who doesn't want me. Second, you know your brother. His mind is made up, and there is nothing anyone can do to change it."

"Have you talked to him at all?"

"No. If he changes his mind, he knows where to find me."

"He won't change his mind unless you tell him how you feel. Explain things."

"Explain things," she repeated, her irritation growing.

"That's right. He's got this idea in his head. You know what happened to Cassandra, right? I figure someone's told you by now."

"I know they were involved. I know she died on one of Gage's expeditions, if that's what you mean."

"Talk to him about it. Maybe you can make him see it's no good to keep living in the past."

"No."

"Come on, Abby. You said you loved him."

She just shook her head.

"If you won't do it for you, do it for Gage. He needs you, Abby."

She started to say no—she wouldn't humiliate herself that way. She felt Edge's hand cover hers where it rested on the table.

"You're a risk-taker, Abby," he said. "You both are. Talk to him. Take the risk. Tell him what you think."

Abby wiped away another unwanted tear. "I'll give it some thought." It was the best she could do.

Edge downed his soda and set the glass back on the table. Abby walked him to the door.

Edge glanced around. "Your place looks as dismal as Gage's. With any luck, my hard-headed brother will figure things out before it's too late."

For hours after Edge left, Abby mulled over his words. Edge was right about one thing. She was a risk-taker, and so was Gage. It was one more thing they had in common.

By six o'clock, she had made a decision. Abby went in and showered, brushed out her hair, put on a pretty yellow dress and a pair of open-toed high heels. Khaki cargo pants and a T-shirt might have made her point better, but she was only willing to go so far.

Either Gage loved her enough to take a chance on them, or he didn't.

It was the end of May, and the temperature had reached the seventies. The sky was sunny, with just a few fluffy clouds. Abby drove her little Fiat over to Gage's apartment and pulled into a space near the rear alley entrance.

She almost turned around when it occurred to her he might not be alone. She thought of Gage's women friends and his sexual virility. How long would he go without a woman? Unease slid through her. She'd look like a fool if he was with another woman.

Maybe he isn't even home, she told herself, the notion giving her a moment's relief. She pushed the buzzer and waited.

"Who is it?" Gage snapped. Definitely not in a good mood.

"It's Abby. I was hoping I could talk to you for a minute. That is . . . if . . . if you aren't busy." Oh, God, did she sound pathetic? That was *not* part of her plan.

Gage hit the release, and the door unlocked. Abby walked into the leafy treed entry and climbed the iron stairs. Gage pulled open the door before she reached it.

For a second, he didn't move. His beautiful blue eyes slid over her from top to bottom. She recognized the heat before he quickly shuttered his expression.

"Can I come in?" she asked.

"Sure. Sorry. Come on in." He stepped back out of the way, and she walked past him into the living room. Through the doorway, she could see into the kitchen, which looked as bad as Edge had said.

And Gage . . . He was wearing a rumpled gray T-shirt that stretched over his powerful chest. A pair of faded jeans hugged his muscled thighs. He hadn't shaved in days, which only made him look sexier.

"I wasn't sure you'd be home," she said. *I wasn't sure you'd be alone*, she meant.

"Thanks to you and King, I can afford to take a little time off. You want something to drink? A soda or a glass of wine?"

"I'm not staying. I just . . . I had something I wanted to say, and I was hoping you'd give it some thought."

"I think I'll have that drink," he drawled.

She would rather have just said her piece and left. But she followed him over to the built-in bar. At least the living room still looked neat and clean.

Gage poured himself a scotch. Abby sat down on the sofa, and Gage carried his drink over and sat down in the chair across from her. The distance between them seemed to stretch even farther than that. She wished she hadn't come.

"Your brother stopped by to see me." Not what she'd meant to say at all. "He thought I should come over and talk to you."

"That's a surprise." He took a drink of scotch. "Edge usually minds his own business."

Abby took a deep breath, wishing she had accepted the glass of wine. Wishing she'd already drunk it. "He said . . . he said you loved me and that since I loved you, I should tell you all the reasons we should be together."

Gage's lips edged up at the corners, but his eyes looked sad. "You don't think I know all the reasons we should be together?"

Her pulse quickened. "I don't know. I didn't think so, or I wouldn't be here."

"To start with, you're beautiful, but that's obvious. When I look at you in that dress, it's all I can do to keep my hands off you. You're smart, and you're caring. You're tough when you need to be, and you never complain."

She felt the heat creeping into her cheeks. "Well, I did complain a few times, but—"

He grinned. "You're also stubborn, and you refuse to follow orders, even when they're for your own good."

"I know, but—"

"That's two more things I love about you."

"You do?"

"Yes." He took a sip of his drink, and the smile slid from his face. "It doesn't make any difference. If we were together, sooner or later something bad would happen. It almost happened in Mexico. When it did, it would be my fault, and I couldn't handle it."

He set the drink down and rose to his feet. "You need to go, Abby. You need to leave right now. If you don't, we'll end up in bed, and things will just get worse for both of us."

Her legs trembled as she rose from the sofa. "It's because of Cassandra, isn't it? It's always been because of her. Because you feel responsible for her death."

"I *was* responsible."

"It was an accident, Gage. She could have been driving down the freeway when a front tire blew and she was killed. Even if you'd sold her the tire, it wouldn't have been your fault. Bad things happen to people every day. The bridge was faulty. Cassandra fell and died. It wasn't your fault. It was an accident."

"It wasn't an accident! Cassandra died because of me! She didn't just fall into that gorge, Abby—Cassie killed herself!"

Silence fell. Abby's knees felt weak. She dropped like a stone back down on the sofa.

Gage ran his fingers through his hair. "I don't talk about it. I've never told anyone, but I guess you deserve to know the truth."

Abby said nothing. She just prayed he would finish the story, get it all out in the open at last.

"That day on the bridge . . . Cassie was halfway across when her feet slipped off the rope and she fell partway through." He pushed out a long, shaky breath. "She was scared, terrified. I told her to just hang on. I was coming to get her." He swallowed. "I was almost there, just a few feet away. I could have pulled her back up. I could have saved her. All she had to do was hang on."

Abby's eyes filled. She had never seen such anguish on anyone's face before. His eyes glistened. The bravest, strongest man she had ever known was on the verge of tears.

"I was almost there," he repeated, his voice thick and rusty. "She was looking up at me, looking right at me. I knew what she was going to do before she did it. I saw it in her eyes. 'I love you, Gage,' she said. And then she just let go."

Emotion clogged Abby's throat. Dear God. Rising once more from the sofa, she went to Gage, slid her arms around his neck, and just held on. A shudder went through his big body and he buried his face in her hair.

Abby didn't let go. What a terrible thing to do to someone, she thought.

Finally, Gage took hold of her shoulders and eased her away. "I don't want you to love me, Abby. I just can't deal with it."

Pity washed through her. She didn't want to make him suffer any more than he was already. But she had come this far. She might as well finish it.

"What happened that day on the bridge . . . Cassandra didn't love you, Gage. She hated you." He flinched. "That's right. Cassie hated you because you didn't love her in return. Because she couldn't be happy living the life you lived, and you couldn't be happy living any other way."

Gage just stared.

"She knew what killing herself would do to you. Don't you see? She did it to punish you. If she'd loved you, she never would have hurt you that way. It was a selfish, terrible thing to do."

Abby rested her palm against his cheek. "I would never hurt you like that, Gage. I love you too much to ever do anything that would cause you so much pain." She wiped a tear from her cheek. "Think about it, honey. Set yourself free."

The lump in her throat was so painful she could barely swallow. Turning, she walked out of the living room.

Gage didn't follow.

Abby hadn't thought he would.

She cried all the way back to her apartment. By the time she got there, her eyes were gritty but dry. She had given Gage everything she had to give. She would always love him, but in some strange way, she finally felt free of him.

Tomorrow night, she would talk to Clay Reynolds. With his help, maybe she could set a new course, find something in life to interest her besides the adventures she wanted to share with Gage.

Abby told herself that as she lay in bed that night.

But deep in her heart, she wished she had stayed, wished she'd had one more night with Gage.

CHAPTER FORTY-TWO

ABBY PUT ON A PAIR OF BEIGE SLACKS AND A LOOSE-FITTING GATH-ered print top in pale shades of blue. She didn't want to wear anything sexy. She wanted this to be a professional business meeting.

The supper she was making—baked chicken, baby yellow potatoes, and carrots, along with a crisp green salad—was healthy and not particularly impressive.

She wasn't trying to impress Clay as a woman. She wanted their conversation to revolve around the opportunities his influence with the museum might provide.

The doorbell rang. Abby wiped her hands on a dish towel, straightened the apron tied around her waist, went to the door and pulled it open.

Clay smiled as he walked in, leaned over, and kissed her cheek. He presented her with a bouquet of pretty pink roses. Not the best start to a business meeting, but the flowers were lovely.

"Thank you, Clay, that's very thoughtful. I'll put them in water." She walked back into the kitchen, and Clay followed. He looked handsome tonight, in a navy blue sport coat and a pair of gray slacks, his shiny blond hair freshly trimmed.

Abby walked behind the kitchen counter. It was a simple galley-style design, with a sink on one side, a breakfast bar on the other. The dining table in the living room had been set with blue place mats and her everyday white dishes.

Abby found a vase beneath the sink and bent down to pick it

up. When she rose, she felt Clay right behind her. She turned and managed to smile. "I need a little room if I'm going to arrange these flowers."

Clay took the bouquet from her hand and set it in the sink. "You can do that later." He lowered his head and began kissing the side of her neck. Abby squeezed out from beneath his arm and walked a few feet away.

"Clay, I invited you here to talk about doing something with the museum, finding some kind of work that might interest me." He caught up with her, turned her back into his arms.

"We'll get around to that. First things first." Clay caught her jaw and tried to kiss her, but Abby pulled away. She set her palms on his chest to keep him at arm's length.

"I really appreciate your friendship, Clay, but that's all I feel for you. Friendship. I'm not interested in anything more than that."

Clay's warm smile faded. "You want that job, don't you? There's always a price to pay for favors, Abby."

Surprise jolted through her. She started shaking her head. "I don't want the job that badly."

His expression changed from pleasant to grim. "I can't believe after all this time you've just been leading me on."

"I wasn't leading you on. I didn't realize you believed there was something going on between us. Friendship's all I've ever felt for you, Clay. That's all I want."

Clay moved closer. "I don't care what you want anymore. It's time to face reality." He smiled thinly. "I had high hopes for us, Abby. After you came back from Mexico, I thought we could finally make things work."

Abby kept moving backward. "I don't know what you're talking about. We've hardly even dated."

Clay stalked after her. "Your grandfather hoped for more. We talked about you whenever he was in the city." Clay's smile returned, but it looked forced. "He hoped we'd get together."

"I don't . . . don't have those kinds of feelings for you, Clay. I think I've made that clear."

Her back came up against the wall and Clay pressed himself against her. She could feel his arousal, and her stomach churned.

"I want you, Abby," he said. "I want your mind as well as your body. Let me give you pleasure. You'll see how good we can be."

Clay caught her wrists, dragged her over to the sofa, and pushed her down, used his body to pin her beneath him. Abby struggled, but Clay was sixty pounds heavier, and he was in prime physical condition. His grip on her wrists was like steel as he dragged her hands over her head. Trapping her with his weight, he cupped her breast and squeezed, bent his head, and tried to kiss her.

"Let me go!" When she turned her head away, he pressed his mouth against the side of her neck.

"Give us a chance, Abby. Let me show you how good it could be."

Abby struggled to get up. "Clay, if you don't stop right now, I'm going to scream."

One hand covered her mouth while the other slid down her body, into the front of her slacks. Abby sank her teeth into Clay's palm and bit down hard. Clay was the one who screamed.

"You bitch!" Blood trailed across his palm and dripped through his fingers. "I've had enough of your games!" Clay backhanded her so hard her ears rang. He ripped open the front of her blouse and Abby cried out. Her head was spinning, Clay's heavy weight pressing the air out of her lungs, making her even more light-headed.

A pounding started on the door. "Abby! Are you all right?"

"Gage . . . !" She tried to throw Clay off, but he slapped her again, knocking her head into the arm of the sofa.

"You said the two of you were over!" Clay shouted. "I should have had them finish you off in Mexico City!"

"What?"

The door crashed open, and Gage roared into the room. He took one look at her blouse and the red mark on her cheek and went after Clay like the lion he was.

Gage jerked Clay off Abby and sent him crashing into the wall. He grabbed the front of Clay's shirt, hauled him up, and punched him in the face, sending him flying backward again.

"Get away from me!" Clay shouted as Gage strode over, hauled him to his feet, and hit him again.

Abby shot up from the sofa. "Gage, stop! You'll kill him!"

Gage ignored her. "You hit her, you son of a bitch." A fierce blow knocked Clay against the end table, sending the lamp crashing to the floor. When Gage drew back for another blow, Abby grabbed his bicep and held on as hard as she could.

"That's enough, honey. Please stop, please!"

He looked at her over his shoulder, took a deep breath, and slowly released it. When he finally let go, Clay slid down the wall and didn't get up.

Gage turned to Abby, his blue eyes scorching. "What the hell is he doing here? You said last night that you—"

"I do love you. It's not what you think." Abby took a shaky breath. "We were supposed to talk about a job offer at the museum. I thought I'd be able to keep things more professional if I cooked dinner for him here instead of going over to his place."

Gage must have realized the implications of her decision, that if she'd gone to Clay's house, Gage wouldn't have shown up at the door and Clay could have raped her.

The anger in his face changed to concern, and he pulled her into his arms. "Jesus, baby."

Abby clung to him. It felt so good to be back in his arms. How could she have ever believed she could be free of him? She loved him more than ever.

Gage let her go, and both of them looked down at Clay. Blood dripped from his nose and ran from the corner of his mouth. One of his eyes was turning black and was swollen nearly shut.

Abby ignored him. "Clay said something about Mexico City. I think he may have hired the men who tried to kidnap me in the hotel."

"What?" Gage's fury returned. He walked over and hauled Clay up, dragged him across the room, and shoved him down on the sofa. "Did you hire those men who went after Abby in Mexico City?"

When Clay didn't answer, Gage drew back his fist. "It would be my pleasure to beat the living fuck out of you. Did you hire those two men?"

Clay nodded glumly.

"You told Abby that King mentioned Mexico. How did you know we were in Mexico City?"

"I figured you'd have to start by dealing with the government. You'd have to talk to people in the Anthropological Institute. I've worked with them for years. They knew you were staying at the Gran Hotel."

Gage flicked an assessing glance at Abby, then looked back at Clay. "What about the three guys in Denver who tried to abduct her?"

Clay wiped blood off his mouth. "I just wanted the map."

"You sonofabitch. You're going to jail—you know that, right?"

"You've got the gold. Isn't that enough?"

"Beating you senseless wouldn't be enough. Call the cops, Abby."

She walked over to Clay. "What you tried to do to me tonight . . . I don't understand what you thought you could accomplish."

His bloody lip curled. "You're worth at least twenty million bucks, sweetheart. I figured there was a chance you'd see things my way once I had you in bed."

Gage hauled him up and hit him again.

CHAPTER FORTY-THREE

TWO POLICE OFFICERS SHOWED UP AT THE DOOR. THEY TOOK ONE look at Abby's battered face, clamped a pair of handcuffs around Clay Reynolds's wrists, and hauled him away.

Since there was no proof he was behind the kidnapping attempt in Denver or the attack at the hotel in Mexico City, Gage figured the guy would cut some kind of a deal to lessen the assault charges and get off with a minimum sentence.

If he was smart, he wouldn't show his face in Denver again. As long as he stayed away from Abby, Gage didn't care.

Abby closed the door behind the officer who had remained to take their statements, walked over, and dropped down on the sofa. Gage sat down beside her. He wanted to pull her into his arms and just hold her, make sure she was okay. He wanted to kiss her, make love to her, but he no longer had that right.

"You okay?" he finally asked.

Big golden eyes gazed up at him, seemed to look straight into his heart. "I wouldn't be if you hadn't shown up when you did." She frowned as if a thought had just occurred. "Why *did* you show up? Why'd you come over?"

"There were some things I needed to say." He reached out and ran a finger gently over the bruise on her cheek, and his jaw tightened. He wanted to punch Clay Reynolds all over again. "I got sidetracked when I saw that bastard on top of you."

Abby gingerly touched her face. "Like I said, bad things happen every day."

"So I guess you were right."

"I was?"

"Yeah. I think maybe you were right about a lot of things."

Some of the color returned to her cheeks. "Which . . . umm . . . things do you mean?"

"After you left, I had plenty of time to think about everything you said. I thought of what happened in Mexico. All the things that could have gone wrong, all the things that did. I reminded myself you could have been killed. Nothing I told myself made any difference."

Abby just looked at him, but there was something different in her eyes. It was hope, he realized. The same feeling swelled in his chest.

He reached down and took hold of her hand. "I'm crazy in love with you, Abby. I tried to convince myself it wasn't true. Then I tried to convince myself it didn't matter. Nothing worked."

Her eyes welled. "Gage . . ."

He brought her hand up and kissed the back. "When I get home from a trip, I'm always ready to head off again on some new quest, but not this time. I can't stand the thought of going without you. No matter where I went, I'd always be wishing you were there to share the adventure with me."

A tear rolled down her cheek. "You . . . you want me to go with you? You want us to be partners again?"

Gage shook his head. The hope in Abby's eyes dimmed, and she glanced away. Gage caught her chin and turned her to face him. "I want us to be more than partners. I want us to be a couple. A married couple. The Logans. We'll do things that will make them remember our names. Will you marry me, baby?"

She swallowed. "What . . . what if something bad happened to me, Gage? It could, you know."

"I know it's a risk. But I figure being with you is worth the risk."

She gave him a teary smile. "That's what I think too. Even if something bad happened to you, I'd never regret one second of our time together."

Gage slid his fingers into her fiery hair, tipped her head back, and took her mouth in a gentle kiss. He'd meant to be brief, just sealing the pact he hoped to make between them, but Abby's lips softened under his and parted to invite him in. His heart filled an instant before lust slammed into him. The kiss deepened, turned hot and fierce.

It was all he could do to pull away.

"All right, then," he said gruffly. "From now on, whatever we do, we do it together, husband and wife."

Abby grinned. "Partners."

"Right." He smiled. "Except my word is final."

"Sure," she said, with the sparkle in her eyes that told him no way was that happening. "Your word is final. That goes without saying."

Gage laughed, loud and long.

Abby grinned. "So let's get married," she said, sliding her arms around his neck.

And so they did.

EPILOGUE

Four months later

ABBY STOOD NEXT TO GAGE ON A STEEP SANDSTONE HILL IN THE desert above a dry wash sixty-five kilometers from Sweimeh, Jordan. Maggie had done her usual competent job of arranging their first few nights in a luxurious suite at the Ishtar Hotel, a resort overlooking the beautiful turquoise waters of the Dead Sea.

Today they went to work.

Gage had been approached by a private collector who had come across reliable information that a cave in the hills above the sea held a cache of ancient leather scrolls dating back two thousand years.

Like the hoard of Dead Sea Scrolls found in 1947, these would be an amazing discovery. It was rumored they included the Book of Esther, missing from the original find, the story of the Jewish Queen of Persia.

The collector, a man named Thomas Dillard who was financing the trip, wanted credit for making such a remarkable discovery—and of course, the celebrity associated with donating such an import piece of history to the Antiquities Authority in Israel.

The problem was, the ancient Jewish scrolls were somewhere across the border in Jordan.

An even bigger problem was the group of terrorists that were rumored to be lurking in one of the sandstone caves in the area.

Abby glanced over at Gage. With any luck, the bad guys would stay in whatever dark hole they occupied.

The good news was, Mateo had arrived in Sweimeh several weeks ago and had been making arrangements ever since. They were ready for whatever lay ahead.

Abby grinned. Treasure hunting was never dull.

In the last four months, a lot had happened. She and Gage were married now, living in Gage's apartment when they were in Denver. Zuma and Carlos were settled in a nice quiet neighborhood in the suburbs, Carlos at the top of his class in the private school where Gage had enrolled him.

Jack Foxx was away, searching for a sunken ship off the coast of Florida.

In other news, Clay Reynolds was sitting in a cell in the Buena Vista Correctional Facility, a prison two hours outside of Denver. Abby hoped his three-year sentence would be enough to give him a badly needed change of attitude.

In Mexico, neither of the Velásquez brothers faced criminal charges, but the Mexican authorities wanted them badly, particularly Ramón, for his cartel activities.

Victor Alamán's fiasco at the airport had landed him in a Mexico City jail.

Abby's gaze returned to Gage. A light wind ruffled his thick brown hair, and a faint smile touched his lips. He was thinking, working out whatever problems they might face in their search for the scrolls.

Abby was thinking about what she and Gage had done in bed last night. Her husband was still the most virile, sexiest man she had ever known. And though they were now in the middle of the desert instead of a luxury hotel room, she wasn't worried. Gage could be very creative.

He reached down, took hold of her hand, and brought it to his lips. Love for him welled in her heart.

"See those wind caves over there?" He pointed and her gaze followed his to a row of openings in the wall of sandstone across the ravine.

"Those aren't mentioned in Dillard's notes."

"No, they aren't, and that's what makes them interesting."

"Shall we take a look?"

"Let's drive the Jeep around and come up from the back."

"Might be better to just go in the front."

"Maybe. We'll try it the easy way first." Gage kept hold of Abby's hand as he led her back down the hill toward the Jeep.

Abby thought about the last four months. As far as she was concerned, they'd been perfect. She loved living a life of adventure, and Gage loved having her with him. Yes, there was a certain amount of risk, but Gage was one of the world's most renowned experts on finding lost objects.

He always proceeded through legal channels—well, mostly—did everything he could to minimize the danger, and almost always delivered whatever he went after.

In this case, Abby was sure they would be bringing back the ancient scrolls.

When they reached the Jeep, Gage stopped and turned. "You know this wouldn't be nearly as much fun if you weren't with me."

Abby looked up at him and smiled. "That goes both ways."

"We're in this together, just like we said."

"That's right, we're partners."

His lips twitched. "Except if we disagree, my word is final."

"Absolutely." Abby bit back a grin.

Gage laughed. "I love you, honey. So damned much. Thank God I was smart enough to marry you." Gage pulled her into his arms and kissed her. Abby kissed him back.

Smiling, they climbed into the Jeep and continued their adventure.